To Viv all my love

Light of the Wicked

Fred

A Novel

By
Fred Hurr

Eloquent Books

Eloquent Books
An imprint of Strategic Book Group
P.O. Box 333
Durham CT 06422
www.StrategicBookGroup.com

ISBN: 978-1-60911-813-6

Light of the Wicked

A Novel

For my lovely wife Linda, who never gave up on me, and was always my source of encouragement, telling me I was a writer even when I did not believe it to be so.

Acknowledgements

Firstly, to my step-daughter Sarah Cooper, for diligently checking my draft chapters and knocking them into shape, and for telling me the book was great. Secondly, to Alison at First Editing, for going beyond the bounds of her professional commitment to let me know that she really enjoyed "reading" the book, and was looking forward to purchasing a dozen or so copies for her friends and family. This was praise indeed, and it touched me deeply. My thanks to all the staff at Eloquent Books for making it happen when I thought it was just a dream.

My sincere gratitude goes to Pastor Steve Houghton and the i61 Church in Conwy, who re-ignited the flame of faith and belief that gave me the inspiration to start the book and complete it in record time. I cannot fully express my thanks enough to my wife Linda, who never gave up believing that her husband was indeed a writer. She was always there to lift me up when I was down, to berate me when I said I couldn't do it, and to encourage me to have faith in myself.

Finally, I want to thank God for not giving up on me, for waiting patiently at the gate for the prodigal son to return and to bestow upon me unwarranted blessings. He is the Author, and I am the scribe.

Foreword

"There is evil in the world"
President Barack Obama—Nobel Peace Prize
Acceptance Speech—December 2009

In this, our new twenty-first century, when science and technology have increased and improved at an exponential rate even over the last one hundred years, there are still some profound gaps in our understanding of the way the universe works. Scientists can examine the tiniest of molecules, can trace the passage of invisible neutrinos through matter, can send unmanned rocket ships to the outer reaches of the solar system with pinpoint accuracy—and in time, we are told, when the mystery of the Higgs boson particle is solved, we shall know the answer to the ultimate question as to how and when was matter itself formed in the very first instant.

We can therefore be proud of the achievements of humankind. However, we are still so limited to the confines of our Earth's time and space. H. G. Wells shone a light on the hopes of mankind to one day transcend our confinement. However, the danger is that by doing so we may become enfeebled, not empowered, as dreams would have us believe. We have the Hadron Collider, but cannot measure the soul or the spirit of man. We do not have the means to see as cats and owls see, do not hear as dogs and bats hear, and in a real sense we could argue that they live in a different world to us, a world that we are blind and deaf towards.

In rare moments some individuals catch glimpses of other worlds, parallel worlds perhaps, and of non-human inhabitants of our world. Some wise man once declared, "Demons exist whether we believe in them or not." Perhaps it would be wiser to say, "God, angels and demons exist whether we believe in them or not."

In an odd scary way we want and desire the super-natural to exist. We want ghosts, hobgoblins, were-wolves, vampires, and forest fairies, but what we ab-solutely do not want is to encounter the paranormal in its raw evil form, which may cause us harm. De-spite circumstantial evidence and folklore, the above creatures probably do not exist. But God, angels, and demons, well, that is a different matter altogether.

If we had eyes to see and an articulate suite of new senses, we might observe the spirit comings and goings all around the planet. Homing in to the city, the town, to the main street of your community, you would be fully cognisant of angels resting, helping, and guarding all of the people and places that God in his wisdom holds dear. You would have a glimpse of another world intimately integrated with ours that is more holy than you could ever imagine. Of course, where there are angels there are their fallen brothers, demons we call them now, not wishing to bestow to any of them any fragment of their once angelic na-ture. They stick as close to us as we will allow. We are now their reason for existence; they mean to do us harm, and thereby hurt God.

The Psalmist asks, "What is man, that God is so mindful of him?" Man is created a little lower than the angels, but we carry within our genes, in our molecular structure, the wonderful gift of love. Love is the greatest gift of all, but it came at a price, such a high price. In bestowing love and free will, we were given the awesome ability to choose to love or not to love. Sadly, the absence of love can be evil in its most brutal forms. The Bible tells us that we should treat strangers with respect, with love even, for we may be entertaining angels in our midst. However, the good book also says to be watchful and beware, to be discerning, because we just might be inviting a demon into our lives.

"Yea, the light of the wicked shall be put out and the flame of his fire shall not burn."

Bible: Job—chapter 18 verse 5.

Part One

Chapter 1

A Thief in the Church

The sunlight shone brightly through the stained glass windows, creating multi-colored replicas of the saints on the grey flagstone floor. Motes of dust hung in the air, accentuating the silence of the nave. The great bell in the stone tower had just struck three in the afternoon. It was Tuesday—market day in Penrhos Bay—and the church was empty. The voices that had filled the choir on Sunday in worship of God were now just residual echoes, lost in times past.

High above the nave, at the zenith of the gothic arches, medieval sculptures depicting gruesome images of demons and devils looked directly down on the pews where the small congregation sat on Sunday. Evil eyes set deep into black drilled sockets remained untouched by the church's holy light. The distorted faces and mocking grins of the crude effigies served to remind those who sat below that Hell cordially reserved a place for the unrighteous.

The velvet hush that pervaded the sacred building was disturbed by the creak of the rusty, iron hinges as the great west door swung slowly open. The nefarious visitor Jonas Silth grasped the cumbersome iron latch in his rough hands and closed it firmly shut behind him. Leaning back against the door, the hooded man scanned the church to see whether anyone else was about. He padded silently forward on grubby

3

trainers, moving quickly across the wide entrance and slipping out of sight behind a huge stone column. He remained there awhile, holding his breath, and listening intently for any sound that might betray the presence of another in the hallowed church. Finally, Jonas decided that he was alone in the building, and it was safe to go about his criminal business.

He slipped off the hood, revealing a thin wasted face, one that had gone unshaven for days. The intruder retraced his steps to the west end of the nave. Around him on either side there were tables of Christian books and pamphlets that had been neatly set out for maximum publicity. In the center of one table was a large black book, prominently displayed for all to see. Beside it was a pen, with which well-meaning visitors to the church could leave their mark. He opened the visitors' book and read the most recent entries. Boring and banal statements littered the pages. The word "lovely" was used a lot. Lovely this and lovely that. All, no doubt, written by tourists who had come inside the church simply to get out of the rain, or to sit in a pew and eat their homemade sandwiches in peace and quiet. He flipped the page, and for a moment he had the urge to add his own words. He tried hard to think of something clever and witty to write, but nothing came to him.

At the end of this small chapel of books, cards and leaflets, he spied something much more interesting. Attached securely to one of the stone columns was a wooden box, with a notice above it that stated, "*Donations—give generously.*"

Excitedly, Silth grabbed the box with both hands and tried to wrench it from the wall. It remained secure. From a soiled canvas knapsack, he withdrew a bunch of tools and chose a well-used jemmy, perfectly designed to lever things open, like this box. The box had a small clasp and lock at the front that kept the contents safe, under normal ecclesiastical circumstances, that is.

Jonas looked furtively over his shoulder before swiftly inserting the steel tool under the lid and heaving upwards with all his might. The top of the wooden lid splintered noisily into pieces. The metal lock was still attached, but one half of the box could now be prised open to reveal the contents. He covered his hand with the sleeve of his jacket to avoid getting a splinter, and then lifted the shattered lid. He let out a low whistle. "Hello, hello! What have we here?"

The box was by no means full, but a casual glance told him that the collection of notes and coins probably amounted to twenty pounds. Reaching into the box, he quickly grasped the wad of money, leaving only a few copper pennies behind for charity's sake. He stuffed the jemmy back into the knapsack and put the money into his pocket. Patting his pocket, he whispered to himself, "Tonight we'll drink to God's wonderful bounty, amen! Just like taking sweets from a baby!"

Looking upwards to heaven, he raised his right thumb to his forehead in a sign of thanks to the Almighty and made a comic bow. Time to leave, he thought.

He inched the large oak door open a crack, so that he could see whether anyone was lurking about outside. "Don't want to get nabbed now, do we?"

There wasn't a soul in sight. He swung the door open wide, clearing the way to make a run for it, but then the strangest thing happened. As he lurched forward to cross the threshold, he was thrown violently back. Stumbling, he tripped over his own feet and fell awkwardly onto his back.

"What on Earth?" He pulled himself up onto his elbows and looked at the open door in utter consternation. Dusting himself down, he ran at the arched doorway, determined to make a fast exit. This time, his head encountered an invisible barrier as strong as a wall of solid bricks. Again, he careered backwards onto his heels, this time holding his head in his hands. "Ow! Bloody Hell!" he cursed.

He felt as though he had been coshed, a feeling he knew only too well. The poor man could not comprehend what had happened to him. He massaged his sore head and wondered what to do next.

"Perhaps it's one of those electric gadgets, a force field that's stopping me from going through, because . . ." His mind was reeling so fast he couldn't keep up with his own thoughts. Then, "Eureka!" He had a bright idea.

"There's got to be another way outta here!"

He ran down the nave, looking to the right and left. Tripping on the first step of the altar, he stumbled and knocked over a lectern with a Bible on it. The crash of the heavy brass lectern hitting the stone floor reverberated around the building like a loud clanging bell.

"Mary, Mother of Jesus, for Christ's sake, help me!"

Hurriedly picking himself up from the floor, he kicked the Bible out of his path. He had noticed a small door to the left of the sanctuary. Not wasting a second, he ran over to it, and grabbing the handle of the door, pulled hard. It held fast. Using his body as a ram, he barged against the door with all his might. It resisted, and did not budge an inch. All he got for his efforts was a sore arm.

Turning around, he ran back to the crossing of the nave and transepts. He placed both hands upon his balding head in a gesture of dismay. Confused and shaken, he was beginning to lose his nerve. He dragged a heavy oak table up to the side wall, clambered up, and tried to release one of the stained glass windows; they had not been opened for centuries. No luck. He gave up on that idea of escape.

He spent the next ten minutes frantically searching for another way out, but his attempts were all in vain. It began to dawn on him that he was trapped. There was evidently nowhere for him to flee. With frustration rising inside of him, he stood in the center of the church and screamed. "Yaghhhhh!" It sounded like the desperate cry uttered by a broken and wounded animal. Taking in deep breaths of air, he tried to calm himself down. Squinting his eyes, he studied the main west door, which was still standing ajar, just as he had left it only moments before. This time he was determined to get through.

He walked slowly and meaningfully with measured steps toward the open door. Instead of rushing headlong at the problem he moved forward cautiously, stopping a few inches from the threshold. He scanned the edges of the door jamb and the masonry of the arch overhead, but could glimpse no evidence of any security equipment. No wires, no cables or beams of light, nothing. He was puzzled. He could see right out into the churchyard, where rows of old headstones stood to the right and left of the gravel path that led into the church. He could even hear the

hum of traffic beyond the church walls. He was beginning to crack.

"This is madness! Just walk out, damn you!"

He was just about to do what his brain was instructing him, when his courage deserted him. He felt his
head again. There was now a large lump on his forehead where he had hit the impenetrable force.

"Hit what, though?" he said to himself.

He resolutely curled his right hand into a clenched
fist. "Right then! I've had enough of this. Here goes!"
he muttered.

Just as if he was aiming at someone's chin, he
threw his best punch. He put all his strength into the
swing—a knock-out blow if ever there was one. His
knuckles rebounded immediately and very painfully
off the invisible space. He jumped back in horror.

He was beginning to think that this was a bit unnatural. His left hand rubbed the bump on his head
as he shook his right hand to and fro in the air, trying
to shake off the hurt and pain. The pocket at his side
suddenly felt heavier.

An idea slowly began to take shape in his mind.
He dismissed it as nonsense. "Ugh? No! No, never!
It couldn't be. It just couldn't be . . . surely?"

The thought would not go away. Without further
ado, he walked over to the shattered donations box.
He lifted the broken lid, and scooping the wad of
notes and cash out of his pocket, he threw them back
into the box from whence they came. He was just
about to leave when another thought pricked his conscience. He put his hand deep into his jacket pocket
to make sure that he had indeed returned *all* of the
money to the box. His fingers found a hole in the

lining of his pocket. He ripped the hole wider, and found a single penny within the recess.

"I think I get it. Look, I'm taking it out and putting it back where it belongs, okay?" He held the small coin aloft between his finger and thumb, showed it to each of the four corners of the church, then ceremoniously waved the coin at Jesus, hanging on the crucifix. Dropping the single coin into the box, he closed the lid, and backed away slowly towards the west door.

At the exit, he made the sign of the cross on his chest, and then cautiously extended his fingers, as if to gently caress the unseen. To his utter amazement and delight his outstretched fingertips felt . . . nothing. His arm followed his hand as he stepped forward. This time he encountered no resistance. No force barred his way out. He passed through unharmed. Freedom at last! Once outside, he hesitated for the briefest of moments to glance back at the doorway. His countenance registered a look of utter consternation, but his fear had turned to wonder. Then he was gone, as swiftly as his legs could carry him.

Chapter 2

Witnesses

"What was that all about, may I ask?" There was a note of playful sarcasm in the captain's question.

"Well I, er, was just, um . . ." The youthful watcher shifted nervously before continuing. "I was protecting the church's property. I mean, people give generously and should we just stand by and see it stolen by some lowlife thief?" His confidence returning, he stood up on the crest of the roof.

"Sit down, Samuel." It was an order, not a request.

The two angels were perched upon the church, quite invisible to the humans below. Seated side by side, they surveyed the streets. It was late afternoon, and the sun was just setting behind the cliffs that walled in the seaside town. The taller and more muscular of the two was Bezalel, an angelic warrior, Captain of the Lord's Guard, bloodied by many skirmishes with the hosts of Hell.

"Let me ask you a question. You see all those people down there going to and fro—can you tell which one of them is a lowlife, just by looking at them?"

The youthful angel looked at his companion quizzically. "Is this a trick question, sir? I mean, is it part of my probation test?"

"No Samuel, it's just a question, okay?" The captain revealed a note of exasperation in his voice.

"Well in this case, sir, I guess not. From this viewpoint I can't see into their souls, can I?"

Sighing deeply, the captain said, "Well then, how could you tell that the thief in the church was part of the town's lowlife?" He waited a moment for the truth to sink in. "He could have been a desperately hungry man. Or perhaps he needed that cash for his children who are starving, or to buy some flowers for his dying mother in hospital. If you haven't been given the means to comprehend the nature of their souls, are you telling me that you, a mere watcher, have somehow acquired some deep spiritual discernment in the first month of your field training that has bestowed on you miraculous powers?"

The captain waited patiently.

"No, I guess not, sir." There was a note of submission in the voice.

"Now that we are agreed on something, let's follow the logic through."

Samuel, now feeling quite penitent, turned to face the captain.

"So do you think that you could determine the thief's heart and soul?"

"No, captain," replied Samuel, quietly.

"No, captain." He repeated Samuel's words more loudly, and with more emphasis. "Have you already forgotten that one of our most important rules of engagement is not to intervene in human affairs, unless it's absolutely necessary?"

The captain put his arm around the shoulders of Samuel. "Only in the direst of circumstances . . ." The captain's manner was gentle, but the voice was stern, "even if it's life or death for some poor individual, we do not act, understood?"

"Yes sir, perfectly understood." Samuel bowed his head.

"And certainly not for our own amusement, eh?" The captain stood up to his full height and towered over the new recruit. "Although in the case of this thief I have a feeling the Lord will use it to his benefit. For the record Samuel, this piece of lowlife is actually close to the Kingdom of God."

"Praise God sir!" Samuel rose up and stood beside his mentor.

"Yes indeed, praise God. Let us descend into the church. There are some other matters I need to acquaint you with."

Inside the building, the two angels stood together mid-way along the nave. The captain spoke: "Your little escapade was witnessed by the enemy. The strange behavior of our little friend trying unsuccessfully to exit the church aroused the curiosity of a passing demon."

"But sir, I had been there all afternoon, watching as instructed, and I can assure you that no other— certainly not one of them!—entered the church. I would have seen, surely I would have noticed . . ." his words trailed off into silence.

The captain was shaking his head. "Listen, I had the same problem when I was a new, raw recruit. Loads to learn, full of enthusiasm, you even know you're on the winning side! So what could go wrong? You did exactly what I did all those aeons of years ago—you underestimated the stealth and cunning of the enemy."

Samuel was now paying full attention.

"There was someone here, alright. He could see you. Watching the watcher, you could say. But he made certain that you couldn't see him."

"But where was he?"

The captain pointed to the carving at the highest point of the main arch. Samuel looked up. "Inside that gargoyle, a fitting place for an enemy spy, don't you think?"

Samuel shivered involuntarily.

"It was a good thing for you that whilst he was so intent on spying on you, he did not register my presence. He was so sure of himself that he made the same error as you. Your good fortune was that if he had decided to strike, I was on hand to save you." The captain paused before adding, "This time!"

Samuel's inner light glowed a little less. "Oh Lord, yes sir, please forgive me. I will be more careful next time."

"I know you will Samuel. We learn from our mistakes even when they are well meant. Remember this always: we are like spies in the land of the enemy. Our Lord does not reign here. His adversary does! So be vigilant at all times."

The captain motioned to Samuel and pointed to the stone demon above.

"Go smell that ugly face up there and tell me what your senses detect."

Samuel rose swiftly, and putting his countenance close to the evil features of the carving, took a deep draught through his nostrils. At once, he surged backwards away from the arch.

"Whoa! What is that? It's foul!"

The captain, smiling, said, "It's the residual odor left by the demon who was observing your antics."

"That's quite disagreeable, sir! Like a whiff from Hades."

The captain laughed. "What did you expect, frankincense?"

Samuel hovered, his fingers pinching his nostrils tightly shut.

"Sir, may I please come down now?"

The captain nodded. Now, sitting in a pew seat, he looked at Samuel and said, "What troubles me is that I think I know who that unpleasant odor belongs to. As soon as I got a whiff of it I knew whose it was. It belongs to Gathan, a very powerful and artful creature, a high servant of Rim . . ." he was about to utter the name, then checked himself, ". . . well we won't mention his name in this sacred place. But what bothers me most is why he is in this neighborhood."

Rising straight up and through the timbers of the roof, the captain shouted, "Come on, we have some urgent work to do!"

The two angels, now above the rooftops of the town, turned heavenward and simultaneously vanished in a flash of light.

* * *

In the ancient storehouse in the Kingdom of Heaven, the captain spoke to one of the curators. The angelic curator led them to a chamber that was bathed in a soft, golden light. Delicate sounds hung upon the air. It was like the echo of a great angelic choir humming exquisite musical chords and notes. Wavelets of pure harmony strummed their ears with infinite pleasure. The feeling of utter joy was so strong in Samuel that he quite forgot why he was there.

"Samuel! Samuel, get yourself over here!"

"Apologies sir, I was enraptured."

The curator smiled at the captain.

"Well, bring yourself back here and take a handful of these."

The curator carefully placed several small, golden implements that were fashioned like hanging flutes into Samuel's outstretched arms.

"What are these, sir?" Samuel asked.

"They now serve as warning chimes. Once, a long time ago, the metals you see were the finest of musical instruments, which played the music of praise to our Lord. The sounds from those pure golden and silver instruments rose directly to the ears of the Ancient of Days. These chimes were crafted by the Lord's own goldsmiths from the precious metals wrought from the wonderful instruments of the Fallen One, once our own dear brother Lucifer, now named Satan, Prince of Darkness."

Samuel dropped the chimes in terror and fright. The curator stooped low to pick up the chimes and handed them back to Samuel. "They can't harm or corrupt you. They serve only holy purposes now."

The captain also held several of the chimes in his grasp. Addressing Samuel, he commanded, "Come on, we must return to the church. We haven't a second to lose. And Samuel . . ."

"Sir?"

"No more of your tomfoolery."

* * *

Back at the church, the captain explained the significance of the chimes to Samuel. "Whenever a demon approaches, the chimes begin to resonate, emitting a sound which can only be heard by us. The wavelength is so pure and holy that it is utterly outside the hearing of the fallen ones. The greater the evil of the one detected, the higher the pitch—something no doubt you will learn in good time."

Samuel nodded, wisely preferring not to say anything about his own special talents.

"We place the chimes strategically around the structure of the church, both inside and out, so as to completely cover the surrounding atmosphere."

Samuel studied the chimes closely. "Won't the demons be able to see them?" he asked.

"No. Just as they can't hear them, so also they cannot see them. The light waves that the chimes emit are also pure and holy."

After they had positioned all the chimes, they resumed their surveillance of the neighborhood around St. David's Church. There was nothing going on, so they relaxed and began to converse.

The captain inquired, "So, how did you come to be transferred to my unit anyway? Forgive my bluntness Samuel, but you are definitely not the sort of material I usually get in my platoon."

Samuel's face dropped. "Well sir, until recently I was in the third rank of the Heavenly Choir in the celestial outer courts, and . . ."

The captain interjected. "That's an unusual honor for someone of your immaturity isn't it?"

"It certainly is," said Samuel. As he spoke, he began to visibly change before the captain's eyes. He seemed to glow with an inner light. Suddenly, it dimmed. "But I failed my probation there."

"Why?"

"Well, I got into the choir because of my voice. It has a very beautiful timbre, and my range is so wide that I can sing as no others have sung before." He said this with obvious pride.

The captain waited patiently for the rest of the story. Samuel sighed, and continued with his explanation. "But with such a gift I simply could not contain myself. I just wanted to praise Him at every opportunity and to the best of my ability . . . and that's where the problems began."

The captain listened intently.

"When the choir, in perfect unison, were singing sotto voce, I would be unable to resist the urge to soar above them. Like a climbing eagle, I would allow my chords to ascend to the highest notes—all, I might say, in harmony to the melody of the worship song being sung. But to their softer musical sounds I was strident and loud, and I would get louder every second until all the choir had to stop their ears for fear of broken eardrums."

"I begin to understand the problem. All talent and no discipline, eh?" said the captain.

"Yes. So the Choir Master, although very appreciative of my God-given talent, pointed out to me in an extremely kind way that perhaps I could do with some training of another kind, namely, as you have so keenly observed, in discipline. He did say, however, that my place in the choir would remain open until I returned . . . in a few centuries or so."

The captain laughed.

"Well, if discipline is what's needed, you are in the best place! And I am happy to have you!" The captain looked at Samuel thoughtfully. "And perhaps you will be able to interpret the chimes more quickly than I thought."

Chapter 3

Ora Pro Nobis

Maynard Jones was the stipendiary curate at St. David's, though he had not been seen at the church for several days. He had missed morning prayers, evening prayers, and all of his other daily duties that fell in between those holy tasks.

He rolled over in bed and half opened his eyes. It was still dark outside. A blast of icy wind rattled the old window-frame of the cottage perched on the side of the hill. The bedchamber was littered with unwashed clothes, and dirty cups sat on the bedside cabinet and on the chest of drawers. On the floor beside the bed was a small bottle of scotch. It was empty. The chamber spoke of disorder, chaos, and neglect. Jones was a shadow of his former self. Once, not long ago, he had been a person everyone liked to be around: tall, blue-eyed, and blond. Now he was a pitiable and pathetic creature.

Wearily, he pulled himself up and struggled out of bed. He didn't bother to switch on the light. Staggering blindly across the landing to the bathroom, he stood in front of the washstand. He dropped his underpants and urinated into the basin. His head ached with pain. In the medicine cabinet he found some tablets that his doctor had prescribed. Tipping the toothbrush and paste out of the mug into the porcelain bowl, he filled it with water from the tap and then swallowed four of the pills.

Stumbling and slipping precariously on the stairs, he managed to catch the rail to stop from falling headlong into the hall. In the kitchen he boiled the kettle, sat wearily on a stool, and waited. He made himself a mug of tea, and then made his way back upstairs. Sitting on the bed, he pushed aside the empty cups and set down the tea. His body was failing fast, and he knew it.

Spying the bottle of scotch at his feet, he picked it up and dangled it over his open mouth. A bead of golden liquid slowly dripped onto his lips, but nothing else. It was the last drop. He cursed and threw the bottle across the chamber. Switching on the bedside lamp, he winced as the light penetrated his eyes. He pulled open the drawer of the bedside cabinet and searched among the contents for more drugs. Discarded pills and empty boxes lay scattered. He picked out a plastic strip of antiretroviral pills. His CD4 cell count had been under two hundred for a long time.

Pressing out two of the tablets, he put them on his tongue, and taking a large swig of tea, swallowed hard. He coughed violently. Switching off the lamp, he fell back onto the bed, exhausted. He closed his eyes, but there was no peace in this world for him. Just a terrible aching pain that pulsed interminably through his body, and always the throbbing, tortuous hurt in his head.

He tried to pray, but in the gloom it felt like he was fumbling in the dark for a long-lost jewel and never finding it. His faith could not overcome the anguish. The sickness was the enemy of his soul and it was winning the war of attrition. If only he could just glimpse the light! Unfortunately, the dark enveloped him every time he tried to reach out to God. The persistent pain debilitated him and left him defenseless. Desperately longing for sleep, he remembered the sleeping pills. Turning the light back on, he grasped a handful of Termazepam that he had dropped from the bottle the night before. For a moment, with the capsules tightly held in his hand, he thought of swallowing them all. Peaceful oblivion could be his in minutes. He smiled at the idea ruefully. Dragging the mug of cold tea to his lips, he shoved a few of the pills into his mouth. He dropped the remaining tabs onto the carpet. He closed his eyes, hoping that sleep would come quickly and release him from torment, but knowing all the while it would take hours for the drugs to work. He knew their effectiveness diminished each time he took them, but still he carried on—sometimes, like tonight, taking them twice in the same evening.

Later, in that twilight halfway between dull consciousness and the deep comatose he so longed for, he began to see visions. Suddenly, the chamber became ice cold. He dragged the covers over his head. Strange haunting sounds enveloped the chamber. Muffled sobs and cries reached his ears. Drawing up his knees, he hid beneath the covers. These manifestations were coming every night now, and they terrified his soul.

The sounds faded, and he saw himself standing alone on a hill. It was dark. Before him a trio of rough crosses stood with crucified and dying men hung upon the timbers. He was at Golgotha. However, he was not facing the men—he was behind the crucifixion and could not see who they were. He heard their pitiful screams. The awful sound of souls being tortured rang out. They cried desperately for death to release them from their anguish. His body suddenly doubled up in pain. He could feel what they felt.

On the other side of the hill, crowds of people laughed and jeered. They threw stones at the wretched men hanging there. They shouted curses and blasphemies and taunted the central figure saying, "If you are the Son of God, come down from the cross and save yourself."

Then he heard the voice, devoid of power, shout, "Eloi Eloi Lama, Sabacthani!"

In his state of delirium, Jones saw a demon ripping pages out of a holy book. The torn pages were flying off into the wind. The demon, laughing, threw the book at him, striking him on the head and knocking him down. He picked up the book and tried to read the words but the pages were covered in fresh blood. He brushed it away with his hands. His fingers dripped with red blood. The written words in the book detached themselves from the pages and floated before his eyes. He mouthed the words aloud: *"Eternal Death . . . Everlasting Life . . . Sin . . . Atonement."*

Suddenly, he was on his knees and naked, with his hands bound tightly behind his back. He struggled, but could not free himself. He was in the doorway to St. David's Church. Ahead of him, in the nave, he could see several men dressed in white robes standing beside a burning altar. The smoke from the fire billowed into the roof timbers. His head was violently pulled back by his hair, forcefully gripped by someone who straddled his body. He looked up and was terrified to see his superior, the Reverend Stannard, menacingly holding a gleaming knife over him. He was dressed in the full regalia of a High Priest of Israel after the order of Aaron. Upon his head sat the golden crown inscribed with the words, "Holy unto YHWH." Above the priest's robe he wore the Ephod, and on his chest the Hoshen, the breastplate which held the Ummin and the Thummin.

"I have the sacrificial man, holy and blameless without spot! Perfect atonement for the sins of the world," intoned Stannard.

The men in the church all shouted, "Then let atonement be done, slaughter the sin offering."

Jones felt the blade touch his neck. Then he heard Jesus cry out, "Father, into your hands I deliver my spirit."

Next, there was a suffocating dark oblivion, a falling through emptiness, and then horrifying scenes of war and destruction surrounded him. He stood naked amidst the carnage. The brutalized bodies of women and children lay abandoned by the roadside. Columns of thousands of leprous people trudged slowly along the highway. The stench was terrible. On either side of the road were the relics of buildings, ravaged and ruined, demolished by bombs and exploding shells. Overhead, flying beasts screeched, demons with eyes of evil, swooping low to harry the pilgrims with whips and rods of iron, beating all the more those who stumbled and fell. Behind them in the distance, the city from whence they had fled was burning.

Some of the people cried out and wailed in distress, "O woe is Jerusalem, Jerusalem is no more!" Jones felt a stabbing pain in his chest as a passing devil pushed the tip of a spear into his ribs. Holding up his hands, he saw blood flowing from two holes in his palms, from which protruded iron nails. He tried to walk, to get away from this nightmare, but fell down, as his feet were crippled, bloodied, and crushed by two iron spikes.

The scene slowly dissolved into blackness and an overwhelming silence filled his brain. All pain passes. All will be well. Miraculously, all his pain was gone. Before him he saw a beautiful landscape—a lake of silver with numerous fountains and statues. Broad willow trees lined the banks of the lake. Their long, sinewy branches danced in the breeze. The light of the sun filtered through the leaves. Swifts and swallows darted across the cool waters of the lake. He wondered if he was in Eden.

He saw a young man in a white robe standing beside the water's edge. At first, he could not believe it. He recognized him. His heart began to fill with joy. It was Roger, his school friend, his soul mate, his one and only lover. He ran forward wildly and tried to cry out, but no sound came from his mouth. He stumbled and fell in the grass. Rising, he ran on, worried that the apparition might suddenly disappear. At last, he reached forward and clasped the shoulders of the lone figure.

He cried out earnestly, "Roger, Roger it's me, Maynard!"

The figure turned around slowly and smiled.

Jones cried out, "*No, no!*"

It was not Roger . . . but the risen Christ. Jones covered his face with his hands, fearing to gaze upon those eyes.

Absurdly, in his dream, in the trees, a telephone started to ring.

Jones began to rouse himself from a deep slumber. The ringing in his head persisted as his eyes tried to focus on something nearby. The lamp above the bed appeared hazy and blurred, swinging to and fro. *Ringgg . . . ringgg!* The phone was still sounding. He fumbled on the floor around his bed. His fingers found what he was searching for. He pressed the mobile to his ear.

"Yes . . . who, who is it?" His voice sounded empty and weak.

"Who is it!" the voice blasted down the phone. "It's me, for God's sake. Where are you?" Without waiting for a reply, the voice shouted, "You are supposed to be here. Helping me, remember? It's Sunday. Where the hell are you?"

"I'm sick . . . so very ill. I can't, can't be . . ."

"What's wrong with you? Jones, you are a malingerer, I should never have agreed to take you on."

"Stannard, listen to me, I beg you for mercy's sake," his voice pleaded desperately, "I am ill, I need a doctor, urgently. Please, please, help me . . . pray for me!"

His plea was cut short as the phone went dead.

Jones dropped the mobile onto the floor. Cradling his head between his knees he groaned and writhed in agony. Suddenly, his body went into violent spasm. He coughed and vomited, throwing up the remains of his last meal all over the carpet and onto his bare feet. Feeling nauseous and sick, he fell back heavily onto the mattress, wiped his mouth with the sheet, and passed out.

Chapter 4

In Another Place

In a dank and dark mine cavern at the bottom of a deep shaft, under the Great Ulm and not far from the church, a gathering was taking place. In the cramped underground chamber conditions were fetid and claustrophobic, but to those congregating there, the atmosphere was anodyne. The fouler the air, the better it was. About twenty or more gruesome beings stood silent, shuffling to and fro with impatience. No human, if they had unwittingly stumbled into this evil lair, could have hoped to survive the awful experience of an encounter with such undiluted iniquity. The faces and shapes of these beings were hideous caricatures of angels and humanity. Their eyes burned with malevolence, and from their mouths dripped venomous saliva that seeped slowly through their blackened and sharp-set teeth.

None dared speak as they waited for something wicked to come. An unnatural and powerful beast—an entity far more unpleasant than these demons could ever be. A loathsome being, who in an age long past was once pure, without sin in thought and deed, and gloriously counted as part of God's chosen host, was now totally degenerate, ungodly in every way, and an enemy of Jehovah for all eternity.

This company of demons, subordinates of Hell, had inhabited their present form for thousands of years, and like their Master, once were angelic, but now were crippled and misshapen in body, with twisted minds that sought only to serve their Master's evil plans. Yet, for all their deformities, they possessed a strength which was a far greater power than that of any ordinary mortal.

At the end of the chamber, there was a dais upon which there was an ornate chair—no ordinary piece. This seat was a throne fashioned from ebony and ivory. Dark jewels studded the arms and legs— strange rubies, sapphires, and emeralds that shone with an ethereal light which glowed from within the precious gems. The finely sculptured details of the throne depicted evil forms performing all kinds of cruelty and bestiality. The devils confined in this place knew that to even touch this throne was to suffer extinction at the hands of the Master.

Suddenly, the fiendish group turned to face the throne as one. They had spied in the center of the throne a greenish light, which steadily began to grow in power and energy. At the heart of this manifestation a form slowly began to take shape. The servants of the dark Lord murmured to each other and trembled in fearful expectation. This was no ordinary visitation. The demons shuddered as they began to comprehend just who was appearing before them.

The figure, changing by the second from phantom to solid aspect, was now seated on the throne. Its body, arms, legs, hands, and head had metamorphosed into a palpable form of infernal majestic stature. He was now neither angel nor man, not animal nor beast, but a monster of iniquity—a demon of incarnate evil. A pungent sulfurous smoke issued from the base of the chair and swirled around the figure.

The eyes of the seated one searched the gathering, focusing on each one in turn. None could hold his head high when confronted with those terrible, barbarous eyes. As their gaze met his, their very essence shook with fear and they wished in their dark hearts that this inquisition would not last long. With heads bowed low in obeisance, they knelt and waited to be addressed by their Master, Prince Rimmon, Lord of Lightning and Storm on Earth. When Rimmon spoke, the words were not like those any human could utter. The damned voice sounded like a tolling bell marking out a slow funeral rhythm, which held the listener by an occult power that they could not easily pull away from. The sounds that issued from the mouth of this creature were like dark waters tumbling over a hellish waterfall. Every syllable commanded attention, and each phrase resonated deep into the black hearts of his servants.

"Rise up, my trusted Lieutenants. I see you hang upon my lips for news, but first I bring tidings that will not please your ears."

The demons became restless, disturbed by Rimmon's remark.

Prince Rimmon raised his hand to quell their muttering voices.

"Be still! Let us get to the point, my friends. It is this, that there is too much goodness in this town of late, and that has drawn the attention of our great Lord in his palace in Hades."

The very mention of Satan made them even more fearful. Rimmon changed his tone to one of sympathy.

"I know that some of you have been too long away from home. You have not seen Hell for many years.

And yes, I know that I have promised you leave from this odious place, but my Master, my gracious Lord of darkness, knows what sacrifices you make. He is cognizant of the privations and pains you suffer in His service . . ."

He paused.

". . . but He is aware that each of you has more to give. You are not weaklings, not mere wimps like those doltish harp playing angels in Heaven. You are warriors of Lucifer, the invincible God of Earth. No soldier of the enemy can match you in battle, and every mortal on this planet trembles in abject fear at your feet! I told our great Lord that you will all gladly go beyond the duties of mere ordinary demons, to carry out great deeds so that your names will be inscribed in the black book of Hell for all eternity!"

The demons raised their fists and shouted praises in honor of their Lord Rimmon and his majesty Satan.

Rimmon stepped off the throne and faced them in a pose of authority and magnanimity.

"Great deeds will achieve great rewards. These will be given to those of you who succeed in the glorious name of Satan!"

The demons congratulated each other with a grisly glee.

"But . . ." Rimmon roared, "for all those that fail, a terrible torment awaits you at the hands of the Master himself."

The mood in the chamber turned black.

"I need not elaborate what will befall you . . ." The sentence was left unfinished.

The cohort of devils shrank back, frozen into a shocked silence at the thought of such diabolic tortures.

Rimmon allowed them to imagine such a fate for just a few seconds more, and then said, "Never fear my friends, I know you shall not let me down . . ."

"No, Master. No! We will never fail you!" The demons shouted in unison.

At this moment, the Master's form and countenance began to change. The loathsome figure began to undergo a strange metamorphosis. He now resembled a human youth in his prime—a thing of infinite beauty and strength, like a naked David confronting Goliath. His muscles were lean and strong, the lithe body perfect in form, and the head noble and true. Yet, the transition did not ultimately and completely materialize, but instead wavered back and forth, from dark to light, from beauty to corruption. Rimmon's powers of sorcery could not overcome the curse of evil that he carried in his heart. The appearance of beauty was flawed. It was skin deep only, for below the pale translucent flesh evil was exposed, and the true nature of Rimmon's awful persona was revealed.

The demons cheered at this display of occult transformation. The magic captivated their wicked eyes.

The beautiful figure towered over them, no longer benign in appearance, but taking on a new form of malevolence. The gaping mouth of the fiend took a deep intake of breath, sucking through its parted lips strange sinuous strands of sulfurous smoke. As the grey black smoke swirled around the figure, Rimmon's form changed into a scaly creature whose arms and legs ended in sharp gnarled talons. His head was disfigured with suppurating boils, and in his mouth were sharp fangs that could easily tear the flesh from mortal man. The demons in the front rank instinctively shrank back.

The beast sat upon the throne. A long, spiked tail curled around the base of the dais. The whole body was a malformation of natural animal life, a creation borne out of some evil mind, a creature that had never lived or ever existed among the fauna of Earth. The countenance was evil incarnate. In its lustful eyes there flashed a dark brilliance—an evil intelligence determined to entice, deceive, and subjugate every foe. The subdued demons were held in awe of their Master's powers. They all knew that what they had witnessed had been not only a demonstration of Rimmon's power, but a spectacle designed to illuminate their minds, a parable whose meaning was understood by all—use your own devilish powers to deceive and destroy the human race.

They began to chant, everyone praising Rimmon, the sycophantic ones genuflecting in the dirt.

The beast welcomed their praise and reveled in their subservience to him.

Now Rimmon began to alter, resuming his own special form.

"My subjects, let us return to the business at hand. I am fully aware that there is a phenomenal amount of sin in this place and I congratulate you all. I mention with great enjoyment and satisfaction that murder, greed, idolatry, debauchery, adultery, ignorance, and cruelty abound in this cesspool of a town. There are some fools, I am told, that worship our Master in unspeakable vice and lies, spreading iniquity without any help from us!"

The hosts cheered.

"I suggest that you add kidnapping to the list of your good work. That should stir things even more! And although I compliment you that there is much indifference to our adversary, nonetheless, there has been an increase of holiness around St. David's Church in recent times. This is most surprising, as I thought that this putrid edifice, this lackluster jewel of Christianity, was firmly in our grasp. Is it not?"

The question went out from his mouth like an arrow searching for a target.

Not one demon volunteered an answer.

"Where is Jusach? Is he among us?"

"I am here, Lord." A diabolical exsanguine entity stepped forward from the front line and knelt with his head bowed low.

"Ah, it is good to see you, old friend. Rise and tell me—what of the churchman, is he still our property?"

"Yes, my Lord, without a doubt he is. But his behavior of late, in his closet behind locked doors, gives me concern."

"Why so?"

"I think he has discovered a new religion, and I am not sure whether . . ." he paused at this point, ". . . whether he has been enlightened from—forgive me Master, for even daring to speak of the enemy—from on high."

The crowd of devils behind Jusach shifted nervously like a pack of frightened animals.

"I forgive you. Proceed."

"I can only describe what I saw, for I did not comprehend the actions of the man. He was seated at his desk and had several books open before him, and in his hand was a large magnifying glass, through which he studied strange hieroglyphs on the pages of a great book open at the center of his desk. I inched closer and peered over his shoulder, and saw that he was studying small bits of colored papers on the surface of the pages of the book, re-arranging them into a kind of pattern. Every now and then, he would open a wooden box and retrieve more of these tiny parcels of paper and stick them into the great book. I could only think he was creating a sort of . . ." he hesitated, "forgive me again, Sire . . . new gospel, in some strange new language or code which was entirely unknown to me. I could not, though I tried hard for Your Eminence, decipher the texts before me. And there was another great tome on his right called *The Philatelist's Bible*."

Suddenly the seated figure rose to full height, and throwing his arms wide, burst into uproarious laughter.

"You idiot and doltish demon! You are an imbecile!"

At this exclamation, Jusach prostrated himself on the slimy floor, his face pressed hard against the earth, expecting any moment to be dealt a mighty blow.

"Philately!"

The Master shook with guffaws of laughter.

"Get up, I say . . . this is no new religion, though might just as well be, for some of these crass humans revere this hobby of theirs like a religion. They worship these bits of paper, stamps they are called, as if they were depictions of the gods. Ha! This is good news. Whilst this man of God should be about his Father's business he has locked himself away to pore over silly scraps that mean absolutely nothing! You have brought me great news. It will be easy to control this man and we shall give him some rare delights to keep him away from all ecclesiastical matters."

A moment of silence followed. The host of demons began to fidget like frightened children facing a tyrannical father, ignorant of Rimmon's words. "Now tell me about the unfortunate curate, Mr. Jones. Is there anything in his life that is attracting goodness? No? Good! I hear that he is suffering, the poor soul, and will not long be of this world. My first thought was that we should continue his soul's angst in Hell . . . but then I had a more delicious second thought. Why not let the 'old man' upstairs have this miserable wretch. Let's face it, from reports received, Heaven is rapidly becoming a nursing care facility for the virtually insane. All the best people—or do I mean worst people?—come to us and most of them by their own volition. As one of our most loyal mortals said, 'The ignorant masses will more easily fall victim to a big lie than a small one,' and the greatest falsehood ever is that we don't exist!"

The demons chuckled. The Master had made a joke.

"So tell me, my trustworthy Jusach, can I assume that you torment this man daily?"

"Most certainly I do, Master. I work on him daily and indeed nightly, '24/7' as the humans like to say."

The demons laughed at this. Jusach continued.

"The man is in such turmoil and anguish that he has become his own enemy. At times I can simply sit and watch. These humans are, after all, such weak creatures."

"And our esteemed ally and friend the most Reverend Stannard," Rimmon sneered as he mouthed the words, "is he at all inclined to help the younger man?"

"On the contrary Lord, he has washed his hands of him, and is content to mind his own business."

The Master rose from his throne, took a step forward and put his claw-like hand upon Jusach's shoulder. "You have done well. I am pleased with you."

Jusach fell back into the ranks.

"Now where is Aggra? Step forward."

From the rear, another demon barged his way through the assembly. He was very different to Jusach, noticeably younger looking, physically leaner, and obviously capable of great agility.

Aggra knelt before his Master.

"I have a special mission for you. Go immediately to Lord Salus in the east, and make enquiries regarding rumors of a replacement for our ailing curate. Find out all you can and report back to me swiftly. And give Salus my sincerest greetings of affection."

Aggra bowed low again and vanished.

The Master sat back upon his throne and addressed his band of devils.

"You have all done well, but it is vitally important that you do your utmost to ferret out what is going on. Meanwhile, I want you to re-double your efforts. Continue with your venomous deeds. Generate slander and cruelty wherever you can. Keep a watchful eye for any individual who is about to choose benevolence over balefulness. Wherever there is kindness sow envy, increase malicious gossip, foster ferocity, and make them choose violence over virtue, especially amongst the drunken youth at night. Be merciless when it comes to persecution and intolerance and hatred, in particular where there are different races. You know the drill, now get out and see it is done! And remember, a great night approaches—Halloween."

They all clamored and cheered at the mere mention of All Hallows' Eve. Slowly, the figures began to fade away like ghosts and apparitions through the rock walls and the vaulted roof of the cavern.

"Gathan! Stay behind—I must have words with you." A solitary figure turned back toward the throne, knelt with his head bowed low, and waited to be addressed. Soon, the chamber was empty, and only the Master and servant remained. Gathan was a demon of high intelligence, a rare breed in the damned.

"About this unholy holy business—it is His Wickedness's view that something is brewing in this insignificant town. He senses that there are strange emanations of light going to and fro. Yet, I sense nothing at all. What about you?"

"Lord, your most eminent foulness, I am in agreement. There appear to be only the most common activities, small sparks of spiritual awareness in the humans that can easily be extinguished by timely injections of doubt or incredulity."

"So there is nothing unusual happening? No new clergymen or visitors to the town?"

"I believe the reigning bishop has not long to live, so there will be a new bishop. But bishops come and go without bothering us. If there were others of significance I would know immediately. My spies are everywhere."

"What about the enemy?"

"Again, I say nothing out of the ordinary. Just a few angels passing through on their way to more important places like Birmingham and London. There have been riots recently in the Capital as you know, but all we have here in this backwater are minor angels, apprentices mainly. They have been sent here to this innocuous place merely to learn the tricks of their trade. I myself saw the inept antics of one of them today at the church where the Reverend Stannard rules. It was comical to see this fool trying to protect the church offerings . . ."

The Master rudely interrupted.

"And did he see you?" The Master's tone turned ugly.

"Nay, nay Lord, he did not. I hid myself inside a gargoyle and was completely invisible to him."

The Master spoke. "We know that the enemy spies on us and we spy on them, but I do not want them becoming aware of your presence or that of any of the other demons on surveillance. That would alert them. We rule here in peace because the fools on Earth reject Him. I do not want to fight a battle for this tawdry degenerate place. We have larger issues on our mind at present."

Gathan said nothing.

"What of the global reports that are filtering in of revivals in major cities across the planet?"

"I cannot say, my Lord, but our network of demons would know in advance of any major disturbances."

"Be vigilant Gathan, be extra careful. Do not be complacent, I want no mistakes. I am sent here on a special mission because the Great One believes something horribly good is soon to occur."

"Here, Lord? In this backwater?" said Gathan incredulously.

Rimmon looked straight at his understudy.

"Bethlehem was an insignificant, god-forsaken place until . . ." Rimmon mused.

"Sire, surely not? An event of that significance would indeed be a catastrophe!"

The Master looked at Gathan thoughtfully. "Yes, well, that was a long time ago . . . it has been quiet for two millennia, apart from a few insignificant and puny revivals here and there. Who had ever heard of Moriah Loughor? Yet within months, through the intervention of the Holy Spirit . . ." Rimmon shuddered at the mention of that name, "we lost thousands of souls and the effects reverberated around the globe. The only satisfaction we got from that troublesome episode was that we were able to spiritually emasculate Evan Roberts so that he couldn't do any more harm to our cause." Rimmon leaned forward. "I hope you were not part of our defeated forces? Did you have a hand in that debacle, Gathan?"

"No, Sire, I believe that in 1904 I was in Austria fermenting discontent in the Baltic States."

"I am glad to hear it. I would not like to think that one of my trusted lieutenants was involved in that great failure!"

Rimmon stood up and paced around the gloomy cavern. Gathan straightened up to attention and watched his Master, listening intently.

"As you know, ordinarily I adore catastrophes, but not the kind that originates from kingdoms above. So if something is festering here in this town, we must find out what it is and strike quickly to destroy it—early enough so that it can't grow. Now go and search every road, street, alleyway, and dwelling in this ridiculous town, and report back to me tomorrow. Satan speed you, go!"

Chapter 5

Absent Angel

The lone figure lay on the altar steps, fully prostrated under the life-sized figure of Christ on the cross. Maynard Jones's body convulsed with sobs and desperate cries of anguish. Muffled utterances came from his mouth, which was pressed hard against the rough crimson carpet. Disparate sentences, confused words, bits of scripture, and jumbled verses issued forth like so much flotsam floating on an oily sea.

The church was in semi-darkness. A soft ethereal light filtered through the windows from the street lamps outside. There was a sense of desolation in the air. The sharp sounds of the angelic chimes set around the church repeatedly rang out a warning that a demon was near, but there was no sentinel to hear the call. A few feet away from Jones, but unseen by him, sat the loathsome demon Gathan, watching in an amused way the miserable demise of this once godly man. Gathan grinned and slid forward like a serpent. He came closer and hissed and whispered into Jones's ear. Gathan was a profoundly evil devil whose only desire was to assassinate and murder unfortunate souls. However, he knew that God's own were protected against such violence, so he would have to be especially devious to end this petty clergyman's life.

The curate struggled to get up. Slowly rising onto his knees, and with trembling hands, he wiped the tears from his face. Lifting his head, he fixed his attention on the crucifix. Raising his outstretched hands he gestured to the Man God in a pathetic homage to the cold, lifeless statue and exclaimed in a plaintive voice, "Forgive me Lord, I am the worst of sinners. I cannot go on anymore. My soul is in turmoil. My sin is too great to bear. I know your holy word condemns me to hell."

Standing, he backed away from the altar and made his way slowly to the front of the church. Gathan gamboled ahead of Jones, beckoning him. Jones obediently followed, as if pulled by an invisible wire. He brushed aside the heavy velvet curtain that hid the door to the tower, opened it, and began to climb the steep winding staircase. Out of breath, he stumbled up the last few steps and stepped out onto the roof of the high tower. Gathan was already there to welcome him. "Yes, yes, this way my friend!" he called.

Jones staggered over to the edge of the stone parapet and looked down at the ground far below. The lights of the town shone bright and clear, and the stars in the heavens shimmered brilliantly against a cloudless sky. Jones began to feel nauseous and dizzy from vertigo. His eyes tried to focus on the street lamps, but all was just a pulsating blur of illumination. His head pounded and ached. He shivered in the cold night air. Gripping the cold stone of one of the pinnacles, he heaved himself up with his last ounce of strength and stood precariously on the edge of the stone parapet. His legs felt weak, and for a moment he thought he might topple over the edge.

He went to step back down onto the roof, but Gathan, guessing his intention, used his hands to push him back up. Jones's head began to clear a little. What was he doing here? Fear began to grip his insides, and at that moment the evil Gathan stepped up beside Jones and, whispering with his accursed tongue, uttered evil words into the curate's ear. "Nearer to God are ye, my friend, heaven is just at hand."

There was sorcery in the demon's words that captivated the curate's soul. Jones steadied himself and stood upright, perfectly balanced between life and death. Gathan maneuvered himself away from the tower and was suspended in the air a few feet away. The demon allowed himself to dematerialize in part, and Jones, misguidedly sensing the presence, thought it to be angelic. He suddenly called out, "O Lord, take me into your arms! Save me!"

He inched dangerously near to the edge of the tower. Beyond him, Gathan had transformed himself into an apparition of someone that Jones desperately longed to be with in his hour of direst need. Before him now was the figure of a smiling, handsome young man, holding out his hands to Jones in a gesture of warm embrace. Jones's prayers had been answered! Roger was here to escort him home to paradise.

He heard his voice clear and sweet. "Come Maynard, come into my loving arms. I am here just for you."

The figure drifted slowly towards Jones. Without any hesitation or fear Jones stepped forward, eager to grasp the hands held out to him. At the very moment that his hands met Roger's, the appearance of the figure changed. What now held Jones in an awful embrace was such a malevolent creature, so terrible in appearance, that it made his heart grow cold with fear and loathing. It still resembled Roger, but it was as if he had risen from the grave. The eyes of the creature glowed red with fire and a thick black blood oozed from its mouth and nostrils. The very flesh of the thing seemed to tear off and blow away on the wind, gradually revealing the white of the bones beneath. There was a foul stench, too, that began to choke Jones's throat until he wanted to vomit.

The entity drew him closer and a cadaverous hand reached out tenderly to caress his head. Then the awful bleeding mouth spoke, "Come near to me Maynard, am I not your lover? Find eternal peace in me." The curate struggled to get free and recoiled in dread of the thing that held him captive. Looking back to the tower, he tried desperately to gain a foothold. "No, my friend, come, there is peace in my arms, I promise you peace. I am Roger."

Jones strained to release himself, but Gathan held him with all the powers of Hell. The demon's tongue caressed Jones's ear and all the while whispered evil endearments. The words began to have a hypnotic effect upon his mind and his ears only heard repeatedly "Come, come to me."

Gathan's arms encircled the doomed curate's body, and suddenly Jones's spirit gave in, his will to live now drained. At last there was no resistance left in his pitiable soul. Gathan felt the victory and screamed aloud, "Satan is Lord!"

At that instant, Gathan was struck by Samuel with terrific force. He lurched violently sideways, but like a hawk with a precious kill he kept a tight hold on his prey. Twisting around, he saw the angel Samuel trying frantically to free Jones.

Gathan spat venom at Samuel and laughed derisively. "Do you think you can subdue me? I am Gathan the Great, destroyer of men's souls!"

Without letting go of the curate's limp body, Gathan released his right hand and took hold of Samuel's neck. With terrible power the huge demon jerked the angel away, hurtling him far off into the dark night. Samuel turned in the air and flew back to Gathan faster than light. This time he managed to catch the demon from behind, and wrenching his face backwards, he dug his fingers into Gathan's eye sockets. The demon faltered and released his captive. Jones fell though the air, but in one swift movement Samuel caught him. He was about to fly away to safety with Jones in his arms when Gathan grabbed his feet in an icy grip. Samuel kicked with all his might, but the demon held him fast. With superhuman strength, the demon slowly pulled Samuel down until they were face to face with each other. The stench of Hell exuding from Gathan almost overpowered Samuel, but his resolve, although shaken, remained true. He managed with great difficulty to ward off the demon's clutches. Gathan's power sent them spiraling up into the night sky. Jones lay lifeless in the angel's arms, and was totally unaware of the battle raging for his life.

"I can crush you, Samuel, like a worm under my foot!" Gathan had grabbed Samuel's left arm and was turning him over and over. All the while, Samuel hung desperately onto the curate.

There was nothing Samuel could do to turn the balance of the conflict. He knew that he could not win. His only hope was to summon help from other angels.

Samuel used all the power of his voice to call.

"Brothers . . . angels of God, come to my aid . . . help me!"

At the sound, even Gathan shuddered and placed his free hand over his ear.

Samuel looked into the darkness above but no one came in answer to his call.

"It seems you are alone with me, pathetic one!"

All of a sudden, Gathan seemed to grow in stature and power. He grasped Samuel's head, and twisting him around with terrible force, made the angel cry out in pain so that he let go of his charge. The demon took his prize, stared straight into Samuel's eyes, and simply let Jones slip out of his fingers, falling to his death on the pavement below. Samuel struggled to free himself but it was in vain. His strength was no match for this demon. All he could do was shout, "No!" The sound reverberated through the heavens.

He saw the man hit the stone flags of the pathway with a resounding thud. His skull hit the ground with such force that it splintered into dozens of pieces. His spread-eagled body lay still now, crumpled, broken. The cracks in the stones started filling with his lifeless blood. The evil deed was done. Gathan released Samuel and began to rise into the night sky. "And you believe your God is greater than my Lord, hah!"

Samuel, bruised and battered, knelt beside the now lifeless body of Jones. He cradled him in his arms and looked up at Gathan.

"Curse you, Gathan, curse you, damn you!"

Gathan hovered over them and grinned back at Samuel. "Too late, my friend. I am already cursed and damned by one much greater than you."

* * *

All was quiet now. No people were about, no vehicles moved along High Street beyond the church wall. A light drizzle of rain fell upon the silent figure, lying still on the wet, shiny paving stones. Dark clouds moved slowly across the night sky.

Samuel and the captain stood beside the dead man. Samuel, shoulders dropped and head hung low, looked forlorn, sorrowful, and altogether crestfallen.

"Come on, soldier, you couldn't have done anymore than you did."

"I shouldn't have left my post," Samuel's voice betrayed his woeful spirit, "I didn't hear the chimes sound out a warning. I was too far off."

"You are right, you shouldn't have left your post, but I don't think the outcome would have been any different from what we are looking at right now."

The captain put his arm around his companion's shoulders.

"You could not defeat Gathan. He is too clever and too strong for you. The Lord knows even I might have been defeated by him."

Samuel looked up disbelievingly.

"He knows deeper truths than you, my friend, and that alone can give him victory over lesser beings."

In his despair, Samuel wasn't really listening to the captain's wise words of comfort.

"I could have got help . . . I should have got you!" He cried out pitifully.

Samuel pulled away from the taller angel.

"Samuel, listen to me. Even if I had gotten your message, I was too far away to help. Even if I had gotten back in time . . . I might have chosen to restrain you, rather than assist."

Samuel was shocked by the captain's words, and looked up in dismay. The rain fell heavier now and puddles began to form around the body.

"Why didn't He send help?" Samuel sounded so abject. "He sees all and knows all!"

The captain sighed. "Yes, He does. But this world belongs to Satan, and his demons rule here. Humans have to choose their own destiny. Jones chose his own fate."

"But did he, sir? I saw him being deceived by that pestilence! And you said . . ." Samuel pointed his finger at the captain, "you said we ought not to intervene, but I . . . in matters of life and death . . ." He broke off, unable to hold back his sobs.

"I know I did. But that is only when He wills it. We don't make those decisions, Samuel." He spoke tenderly, trying to console his partner who was so keenly feeling defeat. The captain put his arm around Samuel once more and drew him away from the body.

"Samuel, let me tell you something that is truly awesome, for it reveals the amazing heart of the God we serve. Mark this, when our Lord Jesus was praying to His Father, the night before the Crucifixion, the Scriptures tell us that he begged for mercy. Jesus was in agony, and drops of blood came from his brow. He petitioned the Father that if there was another way to atone for the sins of the human race, that he might be able to go that way, rather than face the terrible horrors of the impending cross, which he knew he could not avoid. The Father's heart must have been moved to compassion for Jesus. The Father and the Son did not have to go through this terrible encounter with evil. Yet, for the power of Salvation to work, it had

to be done. There was no other way. Without Jesus'
dreadful sacrifice upon the cross, all humanity would
be doomed to a holocaust of corruption and final an-
nihilation. Even we, the angelic host, the first created
beings in the universe, cannot begin to comprehend
just how eminently courageous and undaunted our
Lord was in that moment. He acquiesced, saying 'Father let your will be done, not mine.'"

The captain went on with the story. "We all know
of Jesus' own agony and the trials of the cross, but
have we ever stopped to think what the Father was
going through? What anguish He felt, what despair,
what utter desolation and loneliness in commanding His only Son to endure crucifixion? This was the
Son of God, and as a man he chose to be bruised,
beaten, humiliated and broken on the journey to Golgotha, for mankind's sake. Do you think that because
He is the almighty God that He was somehow immune from all the hurt? I am certain that Satan and
all of Hell rejoiced when they knew that the Father
was abandoning His Son to a final death, to seeming
oblivion.'"

"When finally nailed to the timbers of the cross
Jesus, in utter despair, cried out 'My God, My God,
why have you forsaken Me!' At the ninth hour of
the day, a supernatural darkness covered the land.
In that moment, the Father could look upon His Son
no more. He had to turn away, severing the intimate
spiritual bond that Jesus had always shared with the
Father. Jesus had taken upon himself all the sins of
the world, and the Father spurned Jesus utterly, so irrevocably at that moment, so that sin might die once
and for all in the perfect Savior, a man who was the
Son of God. Can you imagine how deeply that must

have affected the Father's heart? It must have broken. I think we do not have words to describe it. The most profound event ever to take place in all of time happened on that hill long ago outside Jerusalem. Samuel, I know all these truths, because along with thousands of angels chosen by God to be witnesses, I was there."

Samuel gazed at the captain's face and he saw joy. "God's love was given so that all might live. It was at a terrible cost to the Holy Trinity, but the greater truth triumphed over evil. The glory of the resurrection was yet to come. Jesus' sacrifice was finished. I would like to have seen Satan's face when some unfortunate demon brought the news that Jesus lives! Like the Father, we too must sometimes witness evil things, feel hurt and pain, and experience the paradox and profundity of love, but we must never forget nor lose sight of the truth that our Lord now reigns in the Heavens, and that we will, one day, see the ultimate destruction of Satan and all his demon angels, including Gathan!"

"No need for your curses Samuel, never utter a curse again—even to demons—for its evil will come back to you. Curses will not add to Lucifer's misfortune or to that of his demons for they are all, as Gathan did himself confess, eternally damned."

Chapter 6

A Riddle Wrapped in a Mystery

Taking a short cut to High Street, the man came across the church grounds, holding on to his umbrella with both hands as he battled against the wind and pouring rain. With the rim of the umbrella low and not looking ahead, he almost stumbled over the body of the curate. Stepping back in horror, he instinctively averted his eyes from the gruesome scene. Turning back, but not really looking at the corpse, he struggled out of his raincoat and threw it over the curate's mangled head.

In the lee of the church tower wall, his shaking hands fumbled in his pocket for his mobile phone. The police arrived, followed by a single ambulance. A uniformed policeman opened the double iron gates at the side of the church so that the ambulance could drive onto the grounds to get close to the body. A few onlookers on their way to work had paused by the boundary wall, trying to figure out what had happened. The pedestrian's coat had been removed by now, and a police photographer was taking pictures. The paramedics waited patiently for the go ahead from the police detective in charge to bag up the body and remove it to the van. After about an hour, but not before all the necessary procedures were complete, the body was taken by stretcher off to the ambulance. Within minutes, the ambulance was driving off down

High Street on its grim business. No siren was used to carry the poor man to the town morgue.

It had stopped raining, and the skies were clearing. One of the policemen said to another, "It looks like it might be a nice day after all, and I'm going fishing. Great, eh?" The church caretaker was busy with a broom and water hose, trying to eradicate the stubborn bloodstains from the pathway. In the shelter of the main entrance, Detective Paul Stewart was talking to the man who had found the unfortunate curate. The detective made notes in his small black book as the man answered his questions.

"So you are sure you saw no one else in the vicinity of the body when you arrived?"

"No . . . but I wasn't really looking. It was quite a shock and I was really shaken by what I saw, but I don't think there was anyone else about."

"And, for the record only you understand, you didn't move the body?"

"What! Are you mad, Inspector? I was horrified by the whole thing. I've never seen a dead body before, let alone one in that state . . . No, all I did was throw my coat over the man and then I backed away over there," he indicated the church wall where he had stood to call the police, "and believe me I didn't want to go back to it. In fact, I don't think I looked, either."

"Well, thank you, sir. Can you give your details to the sergeant over there, in case we need to contact you again?"

"Is that likely?" There was a note of apprehension in the man's voice.

"We have your statement and that may be enough, but it all depends on the coroner, you see."

"Oh, yes of course. I understand."

The plainclothes detective shook the man's hand and watched him as he walked away.

Inspector Stewart put the little notebook back into his pocket and walked over to the place where the body had lain. Something about this case bothered him. It didn't add up. He had been a copper for nearly thirty years, and he'd come to trust his instincts, right from the word go. It was as if he had a sixth sense that told him whether a case was going to be straightforward or not. At this moment, as he surveyed the crime scene, all his senses, not just his reliable sixth, were loudly exclaiming that this one was strangely wrong.

Stewart relished a challenge in his job; however, they were few and far between these days. He had started his career in the Metropolitan Police and God knows that in London, like in many other great cities, there was never a day or night when he wasn't tackling serious crime. As the years went by, he was repeatedly passed over for promotion. He had thought it was because his face didn't fit, so he had moved on to other forces. Leaving London, he went to Birmingham, and after a few years drifted on to Liverpool, always enduring the same problems, facing the same issues. He was a good, honest cop, conscientious, always loyal to his boss, and willing to take on the dirty jobs that his colleagues avoided. Life, he thought, was against him—that's all. His marriage had broken up when his wife found someone else who was a bit "luckier" than him. He'd ended up here, in this little backwater, working out the dull days of his final couple of years before early retirement. Beyond that? He had no idea really, other than a vague notion of traveling somewhere abroad to see the sights.

He looked again at the black pathway where only residual stains of blood remained. Then, he gazed up at the top of the tower.

"Llewellyn, come over here a minute, will you."

The detective sergeant dutifully obeyed his superior.

"Yes sir?"

"Does anything strike you as odd about this business?"

"Odd? In what way, sir?"

"In a bloody obvious way! This is where the body was found." He indicated with his hand to the top of the tower. The sergeant looked up to where he was pointing.

"Do you think that the curate, even with a running jump from the top of the church, could land here where we are standing?"

The sergeant seemed to be doing some sort of calculation in his head, and then said, "Er, no. I see what you mean."

"How far are we from the base of the tower?"

The sergeant ran over to the church wall and very methodically paced out the distance in long strides. His last step brought him to the point where the inspector stood.

"About twenty feet, sir."

"Sergeant, you any good at the long jump?"

"Sir, well at school I was pretty good, but running was my best sport."

"Get yourself up the tower and take a running leap and see if you can land anywhere near this spot."

The sergeant looked alarmed. "Sir, are you serious?"

The detective's expression was one of amazement.

"Well . . . what do you think?"

"No, I guess not." There was a pause, "But I do think, sir," he continued with all seriousness, "that this is a riddle wrapped up in a mystery."

"A bit like you, son," mumbled the inspector under his breath.

"Have you been around to the other side of the church?" Stewart asked.

"No sir, but the forensics people have, I think."

"Do me a favor, lad. Sprint around the building and tell me if you see any sign of building works, ladders, scaffolding, mobile cranes, and the like."

The sergeant sprinted off as he had been commanded, and within minutes he was back before the inspector, puffing and holding his sides.

"Well?"

"Nothing at all sir, not a 'mewp' in sight."

"Not a 'what' in sight?" the inspector queried.

Llewellyn stood upright, pleased that he knew something that the inspector did not.

"MEWP is an abbreviation. Stands for 'mobile elevated working platform.'" He had a smile on his face. "My brother-in-law Mick operates one . . . it's his job, in the building business."

The inspector gazed studiously at Llewellyn, but said nothing. After a couple of minutes of silence the sergeant asked, "Why did you want me to check?"

"Because if the curate did fall from a great height, but not from the tower, then what did he fall from?" He had a grin on his face and said, "And I wanted to eliminate . . . MEWPs from the enquiry."

Llewellyn had a puzzled expression on his face. "Oh, I see, yes sir, very clever, sir."

Stewart had started to walk back to the car when he heard the sergeant shout, "Sir, he could've fallen out of an aircraft!"

The inspector kept on walking.

* * *

Later in the forensics lab, Stewart was inquiring of the pathologist exactly what was the cause of death. The pathologist, taken aback, looked at Stewart somewhat surprised.

"Well," she said, and by the tone of her voice Stewart knew she was laboring the point, "the body struck a hard immovable object, in this case the ground, after being propelled by a force, in this case gravity, which resulted in multiple fractures to the bones of the face, skull, neck, spine and chest area, which in turn resulted in a massive trauma to the body's life systems, in this case mainly the brain, heart and lungs, thus causing immediate fatality—that is, the death of the said holy curate."

The inspector thanked the pathologist for her description.

"I accept all that you say, and I daresay you are right, but . . ."

"But? You daresay I am right. With all respect, Inspector—"

Stewart cut her off mid-sentence, "Please, humor me Miss Padelski, just a minute."

She folded her arms over her blood-stained white coat and leaned back onto the edge of the long metal table.

"Actually, it's Dr. Padelski."

"What I need to be absolutely clear about is this." He held up his hand in a gesture of "just hang in there, please." "Could this man have met his end by some other means? For example, could his injuries have been caused by some other person beating him to a pulp with a blunt instrument . . . I mean is it possible?"

He looked into her eyes, hopefully expecting a yes.

She sighed. "In my professional opinion the simple answer is emphatically," her voice rose a pitch, "NO! I could show you dozens of photographs of people beaten up with all kinds of weapons, blunt and otherwise, but none of their injuries would resemble those of Curate Jones." She cocked her head to the side and raised her eyebrows as if to say QED. "And, to convince you entirely, I can also show you photographs of people who have fallen, been pushed, or thrown themselves from high places onto concrete, tarmac, or stone, whose injuries would resemble those of Mr. Jones."

The inspector shrugged.

"Now, if you will excuse me, I have to clean up. I have a date and I don't want to turn up wearing blood as makeup."

Chapter 7

Say Nothing but Good about the Dead

The doorbell rang at the rectory. Mary, Reverend Stannard's elderly housekeeper, opened the door and was surprised to see two serious faced gentlemen at the door.

"Good morning Ma'am, I am Detective Inspector Stewart, and this is Detective Sergeant Llewellyn."

He showed her his ID. She squinted at the plastic card and nodded her head, but didn't actually read what was written on the card as she wasn't wearing her reading glasses.

"Is it possible that I could have a word with Reverend Stannard?" and he added as an afterthought, ". . . and please tell the vicar that I apologize for the early call, but it is important."

It had just turned eight in the morning. The Reverend Stannard had not even risen from his bed.

Mary was about to shut the door when the sergeant put his foot on the doorstep so that she could not close it. She looked at his foot, and then said, "Well I suppose you had better come inside."

In the hall, she continued to say, "He hasn't come down yet for breakfast, but if you care to wait, I'll let him know you're here."

At the top of the wide oak stairs, Mary tapped lightly on the vicar's bedroom door.

"Reverend, hello sir, vicar, sir!" she called in a loud whisper, her mouth close to the door panel.

The door opened a few inches wide, and a bleary eyed Stannard looked out.

"What on Earth is it, Mary?" There was more than a note of irritation in his voice.

"Pardon me, sir, but there are two police officers downstairs in the hall—an inspector, wanting to see you right away. They say it's important."

Stannard opened the door wider so that he could see down into the hall where the two cops stood waiting.

"Very well, tell them I'll be down as soon as I can."

The vicar pulled on his dressing gown and tied it securely at the waist. Sliding into his bedroom slippers, he smoothed his hair flat with a brush from the bedside table before going downstairs.

Stewart stepped forward to greet the vicar as he appeared at the foot of the stairs. The vicar was a full head taller than the inspector.

"Good morning, sir." He held out his hand, but Stannard placed his own hands into the pockets of his gown.

"Now, what's this all about? I hope it is something very important for you to intrude upon me at this hour of the morning!"

Mary stepped back into the kitchen, but did not close the door behind her. She was out of sight, but listening intently to the conversation of the men in the hall.

"Well, sir. Please prepare yourself for a shock. I believe a Mr. Jones, Mr. Maynard Jones, is your man at St. David's Church."

"Yes, that's correct."

"Well I am sorry to inform you that his body has been found at the foot of the church tower. The first indication is that he fell or perhaps jumped to his death sometime during the night."

There was a cry at the back of the hall.

Only Llewellyn turned towards the back of the hall. The vicar showed no emotion at all. Stewart thought this very odd.

Stannard spoke in a cold dispassionate tone, "And what . . . what exactly . . ." he seemed to be searching for the right words, "what exactly do you want me to do, Inspector?"

Both policemen were surprised by his disinterested response to the sad news.

Stewart had decided by now that he wasn't going to be browbeaten by this unfeeling clergyman. "I must ask you a few questions. Perhaps if we could sit down, I'll go through them as quickly as I can and let you get on."

For a moment, it looked as if Stannard was going to refuse the request. Then, the expression on his face changed from annoyance to mere compliance, and he simply said, "We can go in here." He motioned them to follow him into his study.

"Perhaps your housekeeper could offer us a cup of tea or coffee, sir. We have been standing outside since the early hours this morning."

Stannard simply ignored the request and closed the door. He sat behind his desk and waited for the inspector to begin his questions.

Inspector Stewart got out a small notebook and a pen.

Stannard's desk was littered and laid out with books and albums full of postage stamps, both rare and old.

Stewart noticed the collection. "I see that you are a stamp collector, vicar. I myself had a good collection when I was a boy. I had many hours of pleasure poring over . . ."

Llewellyn was fidgeting by his side, as if he was also about to utter something.

Neither of them got the chance. Stannard's next words were like a guillotine.

"Yes, I am sure of it Inspector. But I am not a stamp collector; I am a Philatelist, and a very prominent one at that."

All Stewart could do was nod.

"Yes, well . . . the church caretaker, a Mr. Wilson, identified the deceased as Mr. Jones—your curate—however, we will need to contact the next of kin to make a formal identification. Can you help us with that enquiry?" Stewart had given up saying "sir."

"I believe both his parents are dead. I am not aware of any brothers or sisters. In fact, I think the man had no close relatives. He had a . . ." Stannard hesitated before carrying on, "a friend in London, but I have no idea where." He said "friend" in such a way that it made Stewart think that Stannard was not trying at all to hide his contempt, but why? What would he have had against the curate's choice of friends?

"I see. Well in that case—"

The vicar cut in. "In that case, Inspector, I shall make myself available to verify the body as Mr. Jones, my late curate."

"I ought to say he is in a pretty bad shape, but I guess the undertakers will, er . . . tidy things up."

"Inspector, I saw action in the Army in various hot spots, the dead and dying are not shocking to me. Can we move on?"

"Why yes, of course." By this time, both Stewart and Llewellyn were beginning to have their fill of this uncaring man. Stewart couldn't quite reconcile in his mind the vicar's attitude with his being a man of the cloth.

"I will contact you, then, about viewing the corpse."

"Is there anything else?" Stannard was half rising out of his chair.

"Yes, there are a few other preliminary details. It would be helpful to know a few things."

Stannard sat down again.

"Was the curate, Mr. Jones, here long?"

"He joined my team about two years ago. He came, or rather he was sent, by his former bishop in a deal with my own diocesan bishop. Calling in a favor, as they say."

"A favor?" Stewart looked puzzled.

"I don't have to spell it out, Inspector; ecclesiastical confidences! And anyway, 'de mortuis nil nisi bonum!'" Stannard looked at them scornfully. "Latin a bit rusty, Inspector? Roughly translated it means: say nothing but good about the dead."

"Didn't someone once say the dead deserve the truth?" said Stewart, much to his sergeant's amazement.

"You are quoting Voltaire Inspector, the despised French polemicist, not someone I would have thought you'd have much interest in?" said Stannard sarcastically.

"You are quite right sir; it was a question in a pub quiz. Anyway you were explaining about the curate . . .?" The vicar continued.

"He was sent down from London because of some ecclesiastical misdemeanor. At first, I was not in the slightest bit interested in the man's shortcomings, or his sins at that, just as long as they did not interfere with his duties at St. David's, and left me free to pursue mine."

"And did they?" asked Stewart.

"Did they what?"

"His misdemeanors . . . did they interfere with his duties?"

The vicar looked pained. "Not exactly, but his health over the past six months has failed him, his duties too, I might add."

"You surely can't blame the man for being ill, can you?"

Stewart did not expect a reply, but he got one.

"In this particular case, Inspector, I can hold the man to account, for it was his lifestyle choices that resulted in his infirmities, which in turn rendered him unfit to serve the church."

Stewart glanced down at his notes. "And his sins? What are we talking about here, exactly?"

"Nothing for you to be concerned about, Inspector. No felonies of the criminal sort; however, there was a time," he mused, "when such things were considered most properly to be within the compass of the law."

"I see . . . well, no, I don't really. Can you be more specific as to the nature of these, um, issues?"

Stannard raised his hand to let them know he was done. Standing upright, he ushered them to the door. Stewart, open mouthed, still held the pen and notebook in his hands.

"I have religious duties to attend to. Perhaps you would be so kind as to put down on paper any other questions you have and I will endeavor to answer them. Let me know when you want me to identify the body. Oh, and very remiss of me under the circumstances, let me know when you can release the body. I'll arrange a suitable funeral."

Stannard called over his shoulder, "Mary, show these two gentlemen out."

With this last remark, he turned and went back into his study.

Mary shut the front door slowly. The click of the metal latch had a sort of finality to it.

She stepped through the open study door. Stannard had a magnifying glass in his hand and was closely examining some stamps in a book on his desk. With fresh tears welling up in her eyes, she dabbed at her face with the bottom of her floral decorated apron.

"Oh, sir, what a terrible thing to happen."

Looking up from the book, he gazed at her with pure disdain.

"Yes, yes . . . have my breakfast ready by nine o'clock, will you. I have to go out, and for God's sake woman, don't burn my toast again."

Outside, Stewart asked Llewellyn, "Well, what did you make of him, Sergeant? Think he was a model minister of a caring church?"

"Well sir, in my humble opinion, I thought he had more of the undertaker about him than the church."

Stewart could not stop himself from laughing out loud.

"You're dead right there!"

"Dead right! A good pun, sir" said Llewellyn, admiringly.

* * *

Early one morning, a few days after his first visit to the rectory, Stewart sat in his car, waiting for the vicar to leave the house. He knew that with the curate gone, the minister was taking morning prayers at the church. Stewart watched the tall figure in black disappear from sight at the top of the road. Giving him a few more minutes, just in case he'd forgotten something and was doubling back, the inspector got out of the vehicle and lit up a cigarette, tossing the spent match into the gutter. Stubbing the butt out on the pavement after only a few puffs, he walked across to the rectory and rang the bell. He heard it ringing at the back of the house. The housekeeper came to the door, drying her hands on a checkered tea towel.

"Oh, hullo Inspector . . . I am afraid you just missed the Reverend. He's gone over to the church."

"Well okay, when will he be back?" he enquired.

"In about an hour, I should think."

"Perhaps I'll try again later then," he half turned as if to go, "Actually it wasn't anything really serious. I just wanted to have a look at the curate's lodgings. I assume he lived in the town. It would help me finish the paperwork, tick boxes—you know a copper's work isn't done until the paperwork . . ." he let his voice trail off. "Perhaps I don't need to trouble the vicar, he's a busy man, I know. Can you point me in the right direction, Mary?" He smiled at her.

"Well if it's just routine, I guess it won't do any harm. I'll just get you the spare key to the cottage."

As she turned back along the hall, Stewart grinned and congratulated himself.

"Here you are, Inspector. It's just up the hill from the Grand Hotel, a little white painted cottage, last one on the row."

"Thanks, Mary, I'll have it back within the hour," he lied. "You have a good day now."

He found the cottage alright. It was the last one of a terrace of six dwellings, probably built in the mid-nineteenth century for the slate quarry workers. Whitewashed stone walls, grey slate roofs, and small wooden windows. Stewart knew before he went inside that they were "two up, two down" residences with no garden, but a small paved yard where the outside privy would once have stood. He guessed that there would also be a small bathroom added in later times to bring the place up to modern standards.

Opening the door to the hall, the first thing that hit him was the smell. It was a very unpleasant odor. It reeked of rotting meat and was foul. He instinctively placed his hand over his nose and mouth.

"God, what is that?" He stepped into the kitchen, drew back the curtains, and threw open the windows as wide as they would go. The atmosphere in the house was stale and airless. Retreating to the hall, he closed the front door, but went in search of windows he could open to let fresh air blow through.

Seated at the bottom of the stairs was Jusach, posted to report back to his Master when the new holy man arrived. He watched with amusement as Stewart continued to locate windows and doors to unfasten, trying to dispel the fetid air. Jusach thought the cottage just right for his tastes, but he was glad of the interruption as he was getting quite bored of house-sitting.

The inspector returned to the hall, and looking up the stairs, walked right through Jusach, who had not bothered to move.

On the upper landing, there were three doors leading off to bedrooms. The room to the left of the bathroom was being used as a storeroom. It was filled with several unopened tea chests and cardboard boxes, probably left over from when Jones had moved in. The inspector slit the tape that held the boxes and peered inside. Nothing unusual at all, but then what was Stewart expecting to find?

Some cartons contained clothes, all neatly folded. Others housed books, a few old Bibles. The tea chests contained bric-a-brac, personal items, and breakable ornaments packed in paper and straw. All pretty normal stuff. The inspector sat down on a tea chest that was sturdy enough to take his 200 pounds of weight. He withdrew from his jacket pocket a pack of cigarettes, and without thinking, put one between his lips. Striking a match, he hesitated before lighting the end of the cigarette, considering what exactly he was looking for. The match burnt perilously close to his finger. Jusach, sitting beside him on another box, snuffed out the flame with his fingers and was surprised to obtain no reaction from the man. The inspector placed the burned-out match back into the box and withdrew another. It flamed when struck, and just as he was going to ignite the cigarette, Jusach blew it out.

"I think someone here is trying to tell me I must give up smoking." Placing the cigarette back into the pack, he got up and walked into the bathroom. He thought about taking a leak, but changed his mind when he saw the state of the toilet and wash bowl. The once white porcelain bowl was encrusted with the remains of Jones's last supper, and the toilet was equally malodorous, caked with dry excrement. Several huge bluebottles buzzed around the lavatory. The mirror on the wall was cracked, and he couldn't see his face because of the coating of heavy dust on its silver surface. On the floor of the bathroom lay discarded objects: a bar of soap, a flannel, and numerous tablets of differing sizes and colors. Stewart bent down to examine them closely, thinking they might be illegal drugs. He poked at a few with the sharp end of his pen. They all appeared to have inscriptions. All were prescription tablets—legally obtained.

Stewart began to think that there was nothing suspicious about this man. No evidence of crime or serious wrongdoing. As Stannard had confirmed, the man was sick. Perhaps all that met the eye here was just as it should be. He was just another pathetic individual choosing to take his own life. The nagging thought returned, and he spoke it out loud to give it credence.

"How did the curate's body get so far from the tower? There has to be an answer."

Jusach sat on the toilet and laughed and cried out, "Oh, yes, there is a remarkable answer, but you will never wise up to it you stupid cretin of a mortal!" Jusach studied the inspector. "This man is not a holy one, I am sure, which means," he said with a deep sigh, "that I have to remain here."

Leaning against the door jamb, Stewart felt a wave of tiredness suddenly overwhelm him. He didn't like this place. It depressed him. He sensed that there was something not right, but he didn't know what it was . . . and that awful stink! It seemed to follow him around. He decided to leave. He was now dying for a smoke. He remembered that there was a good pub at the bottom of the hill, "The Tram's Halt." His face brightened as he recalled that opposite the public house there was a Fish and Chips restaurant where he could get his lunch after a pint. He glanced into the main bedroom without stepping in, surveyed the mess, and thought to himself that there was nothing significant to discover here.

He shut the windows and locked the door on his way out. Not looking back, he put the matter out of his mind. He was already anticipating a pint of beer or two, a cigarette, and then fish and chips to round off a bad morning. In the upstairs window of the cottage was the malevolent grinning face of the demon Jusach.

Chapter 8

The Philatelist

The curate's body had been released for burial. However, Stannard had other plans in mind. He made certain that there was no publicity about the death. There was no ceremony. He simply had the undertakers take the body to the local crematorium for incineration. A member of the staff unceremoniously scattered the ashes amongst the leaves and cigarette butts where staff and mourners stole a quick smoke during cremations. The vicar had even suppressed the local newspaper from reporting anything suspicious about the incident. The published article that appeared at the bottom of page six simply read, "local curate falls from church tower whilst carrying out maintenance." During the Sunday service following the disposal of the remains of the poor curate, the vicar gave a short obituary, telling the small congregation that Maynard Jones would be sadly missed, before going on to sing hymn 501.

Monday morning started just the same as any other day. The Reverend Sydney Stannard sat down to breakfast in the dining room of the rectory. Mary brought in a tray with a selection of lightly boiled eggs, buttered slices of white bread, toast in a silver rack, a porcelain jar of the best marmalade, and a pat of warm salted butter. She returned with a cafetière of freshly brewed hot coffee. Reverend Stannard placed one egg in a wooden egg cup, sliced off the top, tipped a little salt from the ornate shaker onto the steaming softness of the yoke, and then dripped a tiny drop of butter from his spoon to complete the ritual. Dipping his bread slices into the egg, he mused over the headlines in The Times.

The news was always the same, he thought. He was sure that if he scanned the headlines of The Times for the past forty years, the essence would be the same. Wars, famine, societal violence, the rich getting richer and the poor getting . . . well, more unpalatable. He smiled as he took another bite of the delicious egg and bread.

Folding the newspaper and placing it carefully beyond the marmalade, he picked up the latest copy of "The Stamp Collector" and studied the front page, which had a photograph of a very rare stamp found quite by accident in a nineteenth century ladies magazine. The lucky recipient, leafing through the magazine, had recognized immediately the worth of the stamp. It may have been used as a bookmark of sorts.

The person had purchased the magazine without declaring the contents. It was a second-hand bookshop—the magazine was for sale for just a couple of pounds, and the person had purchased it quite legally. Everything was aboveboard.

The Reverend Stannard was now onto his second egg, a little disappointed that it was not as soft as the first. He must have a word with Mary about it. Surely she could stagger the cooking schedule to get it right. He raised his eyebrows and sighed.

His thoughts returned to the rare stamp displayed on the cover.

"Yes, I would have done the same. There is no felony in doing such a thing. Why, the stamp could have easily been worthless! Would one have to declare the existence of a worthless stamp inside a magazine? Why, I think not, so logically it would follow that the deed and the acquisition of the valuable stamp is blameless."

He smiled at the cleverness of his logic, and then began to remember the good old days as a student at Oxford in the mid-sixties.

The Reverend Stannard picked up a little silver bell off the white tablecloth and gave it a shake. After just a few moments, Mary entered the dining room.

"Sir, is everything alright, with your breakfast, I mean? I done it just as you always want it."

He winced at her grammar and thought of the second boiled egg.

"Well, yes, it's fine. What I was going to say was this. I know that we do not have a curate at present to cover my day off . . ."

Mary looked down at the carpet, a little embarrassed, recalling the unfortunate death of the late curate.

". . . However, I do intend to take my day off today as usual. I don't think there is anything pressing in my diary today, and I have an important meeting to attend in Chester. If anyone telephones, please take a message and I'll return their call tomorrow. Will you do that?" It was a statement rather than a request. "If you will be so kind."

"Yes, of course sir." Mary then added, "And will you be home for dinner?"

"I shall be back around 7 p.m. That is, of course, as long as the trains are not delayed."

"Will that be all, Reverend sir?"

Mary did an awkward curtsy and left the dining room, closing the door behind her as she went. Pouring himself a cup of coffee with two lumps of brown sugar, Reverend Stannard raised the cup to his lips and took a sip. Leafing through the philately magazine, he searched for the advertisement at the back of the periodical. He checked the times of the event, and withdrawing his half hunter watch from his waistcoat pocket, noted the time. It was almost 8.30 a.m. He had plenty of time to catch the 09:20 to Chester.

* * *

The train pulled into Chester Station on time. It was just a short walk to the town center, and just a few streets beyond the busy shopping area to a quieter street where the Masonic Rooms were situated.

Inside, the main hall was filled with dozens of stalls manned by private stamp sellers, the Royal Philatelic Society and local organizations, the major auction houses, and the renowned purveyors of rare postage stamps. Chrysalis and Larmondy and Allen were represented by stands that were a cut above the rest, and behind these tables stood solemn dark pin-striped-suited men ever ready to politely hand over rare stamps in exchange for large amounts of cash or bankers checks.

There was a buzz of enthusiastic conversation emanating from all four corners of the hall. Here and there, earnest negotiations were enacted by individuals and groups hoping desperately to get hold of their most desired stamps. There was no laughter in the room. This was serious business, and all the transactions were carried out with polite servility and with lightly fingered handshakes to close the deal. Briefcases were clutched tight—even here, thieves were milling in and out of the crowd hoping for an easy take.

Reverend Stannard cruised slowly around the hall. Taking his time to survey the offerings on show, he disregarded the stalls bent on removing hard-earned cash from enthusiastic amateurs and used his expertise to hone in on the stands where the real merchandise was displayed under glass covers. There were small gatherings of punters fixated on particular stalls, heads bowed low, their magnifying glasses and monocles held close to the stamps, the expert eyes of the initiated fully appreciating and studying the wares. Stannard hovered at the rear of these little groupings, listening and eavesdropping on conversations, weighing the possibilities before he made up his own mind which stands to focus attention upon.

Walking slowly away from one such stand, he noticed another clergyman in his dog collar, clutching his briefcase close to his chest, and anxiously looking this way and that about him.

He watched as the man went quickly up the wide staircase to the balcony area where seats and tables had been set out for coffee and tea. Stannard followed the man upstairs, and seeing him settle at a nearby table, decided to join him.

Standing over the man before sitting down, Reverend Stannard introduced himself.

"May I join you? I see you are a man of the cloth. I am also, but as you can see, in civvies . . . it's my day off."

He held out his hand to the seated man.

The man in the dog-collar got up, and still clutching his case to his chest, held out his own hand. They shook hands and sat down at the table.

"Yes, pleased to make your acquaintance. Reverend Alexander Martin." As he spoke his eyes darted left and right in an agitated fashion.

"Please forgive me for asking, but you seemed troubled. Can I help at all?" Stannard chuckled, "We ought to be of help to each other I suppose, being men of God."

The man seated opposite shuddered involuntarily.

"Yes, yes, I suppose so . . . help, yes, well I don't know. I am in a bit of predicament. I traveled up from Norwich last night planning to spend the day here at the sales, hoping to sell some of my own collection. There is a need in the parish, and I thought by selling I could help to meet some of the need. But I am at my wit's end to know what I am going to do now, for I have just had a message from the bishop's office to return straight away on urgent business. I have not had the chance to even try to sell my collection to anyone."

"As you can guess, I am myself a serious collector. I have brought a fair amount of money with me today, intending to purchase some interesting exhibits, though not too highly priced."

The clergyman looked straight at Stannard, and smiled a very weak smile.

"Do you think this meeting, between us I mean, could be the Lord's doing?"

Reverend Stannard shifted uneasily in his chair and blustered out, "I, I, I suppose it could be." Thinking of what might be in the priest's briefcase his mouth began to water and salivate. "Well, I am inclined to agree with you. The Lord does work in mysterious ways."

Suddenly the seated man got up and thrust the briefcase into Stannard's hands.

"Look, I've got to telephone my office to let them know I am returning on the earliest train. Please take a look at the collection and let me know how much you are willing to pay me. I'll be back shortly. Please take care of the stamps—I have had them since I was a boy."

With that remark he turned, went down the wide staircase, and arriving at the foot of the stairs, disappeared into the crowd.

Stannard wiped his mouth on a white handkerchief. He placed his own case safely between his legs and started to open the straps on the brown leather case. He laid it flat upon the surface of the table and clicked open the catch. Opening the flap, he saw a battered old stamp album, the sort that was sold on almost every high street in the 40's and 50's. Before taking the album out of the case, he looked to see if anyone was watching him. Everyone else was engrossed in their affairs. He took the album out and laid it on the table before him. He wiped his mouth again, this time with the back of his hand. For no good reason, he began to tremble a little. The perfectly ordinary child's stamp album held his fascination, and the level of anticipation made beads of sweat break out on his forehead. Carefully, he opened the first few pages, and although his expectations inexplicably rose higher and higher, all he saw were the most common of stamps that were usually bought in packets from mail order advertisements. These packets, cheaply sold for a few pennies, contained hundreds of colorful stamps from all over the world, and many a boy and girl had spent numerous pleasant hours sticking them into their prized albums.

Stannard shut the album. He wasn't going to look at all the stamps in the book. It was obvious it was a cheap and nasty little collection. He thought of what he was going to say to the clergyman when he returned. Perhaps I should just put it back in the case and leave it here, he thought to himself. It's worthless, after all.

Tapping his fingers on the album, he wondered what to do. He flicked through the pages, only half noticing the common collection of stamps on every page. Suddenly his eye caught sight of something different, an old, faded brown envelope. He withdrew the envelope from the pages. There was no address or name on the front or back. He opened the envelope and drew out the contents slowly. What lay before him now was a collection of 1d intense black and grey Victorian stamps in mint condition. His heart began to race. He placed the palm of his hand quickly over the small packet of rare stamps. He guessed that there must be a dozen or so. If he was buying such a set here today, he would need at least twenty thousand pounds.

At that moment the clergyman returned, looking flushed and red-faced. He looked down at the album on the table under Stannard's hands.

"I see you have looked at the stamps. I know most of them are not valuable, but I just thought that some expert here would take a look and hopefully find something of interest, something of value."

"I quickly looked over your collection," he paused before continuing, "there isn't much there, I am afraid. But having said that, there are a few items that would certainly grace my own collection."

The clergyman sat down, a weary look on his face. "To be truthful, I haven't much time. What I was expecting to get was about four hundred or even five hundred . . ." His voice trailed off as if he had uttered something absurd.

Stannard took his hand off the album to show that he was not desperate to buy. He placed his hands in his lap. He knew he had about six hundred pounds with him, and had been prepared to spend it all.

"I tell you what. I could go as high as three hundred and fifty pounds, and that would go towards meeting your need, would it not?"

"I wish it were that simple. The money is needed rather urgently, for a friend, you know." His eyes seemed to beg Stannard to offer more.

Stannard did not want to think about the true value of the Victorian stamps in the album. Then again, he deliberated, they might be forgeries. This clergyman might not be what he seemed to be. Suppose he was a con man, and he were the one to be fooled. He couldn't take them downstairs to be verified, as that would raise the man's suspicions.

"Would you accept four hundred pounds? In cash, of course. You'd be lucky indeed to get three hundred from dealers down there in the pit."

"You have it with you?"

"Yes, I came expecting to make some purchases, I have been saving up funds for quite some time."

The clergyman stepped closer to Stannard.

"Let us shake on it, then. And I thank you for your generosity! I am sure the Good Lord will repay you."

Stannard handed over the notes. The clergyman shook his hand again and hurried off.

Stannard seated himself at the table and gestured to the waitress, "A regular coffee and brown sugar, if you please."

Stannard slipped the album into his case, and patting the side, smiled and muttered to himself, "God forgive me."

Chapter 9

Fear and Fun on Halloween

It was long past midnight, and it was a night for ghosts and ghouls. Grey clouds scudded swiftly across the dark sky and the bright yellow half-moon. The wind howled and moaned in the rafters of the old church, and the air inside the building was icy cold. The beautiful stained glass windows stood tall and proudly depicted the lives of the saints. The colorful scenes illustrated stories from the Bible. The visual parables informed the righteous and the unrighteous of how they should live in order to glorify God. In one window, a traveler was bent low over an unconscious man, left for dead on a desert road, whilst another man in priestly garb hurried by on the other side of the road. In another, a young shepherd boy faced a giant warrior with just a sling and a handful of pebbles. At the far end was a magnificent arched window, decorated with a scene from Jesus' ministry, the feeding of the five thousand. Every picture told the story: trust in Almighty God for everything, even when facing a mighty foe.

This was a favorite place for gatherings, especially after the sun had set. During the daylight hours, many visitors from near and far crossed the threshold to find peace, wisdom, and the meaning of life, but the last time that any searching soul had offered a prayer of thanksgiving to the living God was long gone. The old church was now a new age center, where all kinds of necromantic devices and objects were sold, from the old magic of the druids, to Wicca and witchcraft, the occult, and the dark arts. All visitors, whether naïve or learned, were encouraged to become disciples in these unholy societies. Séances, tarot readings, spiritualism—you could get any sort of divination as long as it wasn't godly in origin. The main sponsor of this enterprise, though hidden of course, was Lucifer.

At this hour, when all good people were soundly asleep in their tidy beds, a very elite circle of demonic confederates were plotting evil. Rimmon, Ganymede, and Gathan sat in conference together and planned some nasty surprises for the upcoming evening of All Hallows' Eve.

"I think it is highly appropriate that we have chosen to meet here," said Rimmon. "There is a wonderful atmosphere of defeat, don't you think my friends?" He gazed up at the holy images that were now barren of meaning to all the souls that passed through this establishment. "There is a delicious irony that we three are the only ones in this godforsaken place who truly comprehend the importance of these images of myth."

Ganymede burst into a profane laughter.

"Rimmon, you are so clever, and your wisdom is truly great!"

Rimmon smiled at the compliment. Gathan looked perplexed and remained silent.

"So, with Halloween nearly upon us, I desire to give our demons free reign to do as they please! They can dream up their mischief and create havoc in the town. So let me have your best suggestions. I am in a mood to grant wishes."

It was now Gathan's turn to grin and utter a chuckle of glee. Rimmon was talking his kind of language.

"Master, I have heard that in the olden days some of our followers on this night put pins and razor blades in caramel-covered apples, substituted poison concoctions for fizzy drinks, and put deadly ingredients into sweets for the little ones." Gathan looked rather pleased with himself for coming up with this menu of delights.

"Well done Gathan, you surpass yourself. I can see being on Earth is doing you good. You have my blessing." Rimmon held out his hand, and Gathan in obeisance dutifully kissed the Master's jewelled ring.

Ganymede watched the fawning demon genuflect in front of Rimmon. Frowning, he looked away in disgust.

"That all sounds a bit crude. I mean, razors in apples? Where can you obtain razors in this day and age?"

"We could use broken glass instead," declared Gathan.

Ganymede ignored the remark. "Let us decide upon something a little more sophisticated. Something that we will be proud of, and more to the point, some activities both devious and iniquitous that will reach the ears of our Father below. What I mean is this: do we squander such a special opportunity like this, when we could gain much favor with our Lord and Master? We certainly won't be mentioned in dispatches by carrying out childish japes and games."

Rimmon stared at Ganymede thoughtfully. "Yes, I see what you mean."

Ganymede, seizing the moment, reinforced his argument. He stood up between Rimmon and Gathan, completely blocking the demon from Rimmon's line of sight.

Bending low towards Rimmon he spoke in a whisper, "You have two options, Lord. Get vilified for instructing base-minded demons and devils to have free-for-all, which may end in disaster, or . . ." Here he paused.

Rimmon leant eagerly towards Ganymede, "Yes?"

"Or we devise a plan that will not only create chaos for the poor souls of this town, but will also plague the Christians and send their heavenly helpers into turmoil! We can marshal our best forces in strong phalanxes, but keep them hidden in the caves above the town, whilst our inferior brothers, creating pandemonium, will certainly cause the enemy to attack. Then, when they are confident of victory, we shall sweep down upon them from our hiding places and vanquish them with ease! Then we shall send our good tidings to our Lord, and wait with expectation of our just rewards."

"Ganymede, you are precious to me. When I am congratulated and rewarded by Satan for my plans for Halloween, I will make sure you are suitably commended."

Rimmon sat back with an expression of pure joy on his countenance, his eyes closed. He was already basking in the Master's light.

Ganymede settled back and wondered whether he should keep his mouth firmly shut in the future.

Rimmon opened his eyes, and with a broad smile commanded Ganymede, "Your ideas are perfect, but lack detail. We shall all meet here again tomorrow night and you shall share your inestimable thoughts with us. I am so excited!"

Gathan was all the more bewildered, as he had not been party to the whisperings.

"Ah yes, Gathan, you can hold fire on my blessing. Let us wait until we hear what wicked entertainment we shall have on All Hallows' Eve."

* * *

At the appointed hour, the three demons of darkness met again to draw up their devilish plans for Halloween. They were not alone this night. In the lower part of the building, a roundtable had been set, and several ladies were congregated eagerly. They all looked at the leader of their group, who sat in an ornate carved wooden chair. Madame Jezebel James wore an extravagant rich robe of the deepest black velvet with red, green, and blue astrological signs, and gold and silver stars and moons stitched into the material. Upon her head, she wore a strange contraption that was neither hat nor headpiece, but was in fact a pointed piece of metal that spiraled up from her head, glowing and changing hue every few seconds. She was in her late forties, but had a voluptuous body, which still retained some of its former beauty. Upon the tabletop were signs and symbols—the language of her dark art. It was obvious from the careful preparations that a séance was about to begin. The lady in the robe clapped her hands above her head ceremoniously, and all the lights in the chamber dimmed. The other women gasped at this trick.

"Ladies, let me warn you from the outset that we may be in touch with the powerful and playful spirits of the dead tonight. Please, PLEASE! Do not break the circle at any time during the proceedings. You do so on pain of death. If any of you wish to depart, then I advise you do so now."

She scanned each one in turn, letting her flaming eyes rest upon each one. No one moved, and none chose to leave.

"Then let us begin by joining hands."

Reaching to the center of the table, she lit an incense stick that protruded from the mouth of a dragon statuette.

"Close your eyes to protect yourself from sights no mortal should see."

Her voice boomed theatrically with sensuous resonance, and the ladies, breathing in the potent incense, began to feel intoxicated with a mixture of excitement and fear.

"I shall call upon my faithful spirit guide, but before I do, I shall warn each one of you that he is, or was in Earthly life, a great barbarian warrior who ravaged and pillaged across the steppes of Mongolia many hundreds of years ago. He is my rough diamond, but beware, he is a man of men, a warrior of warriors, and he had many wives and hundreds of children. His life was hard and short. He was slain by a band of fifty renegades, shot through with arrows that pierced every vital organ of his body. Yet, still he stood to face his foes with sword erect until death triumphantly took him into the depths of Hades."

The ladies trembled with fright at the thought of encountering such a creature.

"You will find his manliness irresistible, his powerful presence terrifying! His voice is like a hundred waterfalls and you will drown in its torrents if he addresses you!"

Rimmon and Ganymede were entranced by this woman's skills. Gathan looked on expectantly, fidgeting to and fro, jumping wildly from one foot to the other.

"Shall I summon Gathan the Great?" Her voice bellowed out and reverberated around the room.

The ladies in unison all cried out, "Yes, yes . . . yes."

Ganymede turned to Gathan and said, "I think that's your cue. 'Gathan the Great,' do your bit for the ladies!"

Madame Jezebel cried out, "Gathan, come forth!"

Gathan leapt twenty feet through the air and landed on the center of the table, which shook and rattled as he arrived in the center of their midst.

All the ladies screamed and trembled in terror. The woman in the robe merely smiled, and bowing her head, said, "Welcome, my Lord!"

The smoke from the incense tantalizingly outlined parts of the muscled and hairy body which he inhabited during these séances. Some of the ladies opened an eye to glimpse the form and trembled at what they saw. They could also smell his earthy, musty sweat. Mixed with the aroma of incense, it became for them all a strong, intoxicating odor. Madame Jezebel was busy chanting the words of ancient incantations that she thought held Gathan in her power. Meanwhile, Gathan the Great was amusing himself by blow-ing onto the frightened faces of the women. They all screamed with fear and delight as they felt his warm breath upon their skin. Leaping from the table and carousing behind them he went from one lady to the next, sinking his teeth into their necks and at the same time fondling their erotic parts. The women were beside themselves, and a few were on the point of fainting with desire.

The other two demons watched, hardly able to contain their laughter.

Rimmon at last turned to Ganymede and exclaimed, "Well that should keep him entertained for a few hours at least . . . shall we continue with our urgent business? Come, the night wanes too fast for my liking."

Ganymede was happy to oblige. "My Lord, I have concocted a marvelous menu of amusements for Halloween. You will be delighted and amazed at my ingenuity, I promise you. I have even given it a name! 'Night of Fear and Fun.' Fear for the mortals and fun for us. The night will be filled with the most atrocious, indecent and frightful acts—our henchmen will be fully occupied. I have written it all down so that you may read it at your pleasure." Ganymede unrolled a scroll of parchment and handed it to Rimmon.

Rimmon held it in both hands and quickly scanned the list of evil activities that his confederate had so cunningly devised.

"And Lord, as you will discover in my script for the night of Halloween, there is a wonderful high point, a devious plan involving our dear friends below."

They both turned to where Gathan was continuing with his "blessing" of the ladies.

"This little escapade will overshadow our enemy in the town and put the occult arts in high places. We shall rule this place with ease and our . . ." he paused to spit upon the floor, "Christian friends will be deliciously discredited forever."

"Well done Ganymede!" said Rimmon with admiration, clapping his hands together. "I knew you would not let me down."

Chapter 10

A Policeman's Lot is not a Happy One

Detective Inspector Stewart's flat overlooked the sea at West Shore. It was a one-bedroom cheap utility apartment, no garden, and had no frills or fancy decorations. It suited his lifestyle. Now divorced for over six years, he was set in his ways. He didn't want a live-in partner either, and to be honest, he had learned to do without sex. Every time he thought about it, he shuddered. He told himself he was past all that stuff.

It had been Stewart's day off, but as every cop knows, a policeman never stops working. If he is off duty and walking the street, shopping, going to the cinema, or at a football game, his eyes and his brain are always focused on the crowds, the people, and the suspicious-looking individuals, wondering what they are up to. Where is the crime and where is the criminal? Stewart was no exception to this rule. He just couldn't switch it off. After going to bed, he would often lay awake for hours, turning over in his mind all the annoying details of an unsolved case. Sometimes the breakthrough came suddenly—a eureka moment! Usually it wasn't a great big leap in imagination or a cataclysmic revelation, but rather just a little tweak of something, a seemingly unimportant scrap of data that shed light on the darkness. Or, it might simply be a connection between the unlikeliest of partners that proved to be significant.

The curate's case was something else. It stubbornly refused to untangle, and no revelations seemed to present themselves. He had been thinking about it all day. It was now around six o'clock, and it was dark outside. He sat in the kitchen nursing a mug of tea, unshaven, and still in the briefs and vest that he had slept in. He watched the smoke from his cigarette in the ashtray spiral upwards to the ceiling. From the living room came the sounds of the TV, which he had switched on earlier before being distracted by his thoughts and drifting into the kitchen. Unwashed pans, cutlery, and dishes were piled up in the sink, left over from this morning's breakfast. Lunch had been coffee, several biscuits, and three cigarettes. Dinner was sitting on the kitchen counter waiting to be heated up, a tin of beans. To that, he would add a couple of fried eggs and two slices of bread, washed down by a can of beer.

Sitting at the table, he doodled with a biro on a ruled pad of writing paper, trying hard to make sense of the facts surrounding Jones's death. He was hoping to see some correlation between the words that abbreviated the main points of the case, some link that might spark and give him a lead to follow. All the clues so far had led him down dark cul-de-sacs. The cigarette finally burned down to a stub. He pulled another from the packet, lit it, and took a deep drag. The smoke disappeared deep inside his body, re-emerging seconds later from his nostrils. He studied the paper, drawing imaginary lines between words, joining up in his mind words and ideas that were diametrically opposite. A rough sketch of the church tower adorned the center of the page, and beside it, circled several times in black biro, was the sergeant's measurement of "twenty feet." He tapped at the figures, and then threw the pen down angrily on the pad and cursed aloud.

"Damn it! If it wasn't for that one fact this would be an open and shut case of suicide!"

Picking up the pen, he began to methodically cross out all the notes he had made. One by one, he eliminated them from the equation. He looked in dismay at what was left: "twenty feet."

He sighed and took another puff on the cigarette. Leaving it between his lips, he once again made rings around the measurement.

Speaking aloud to himself, he reasoned it out.

"First point: is there a murderer lurking somewhere? Probably not. I have to reluctantly admit that there is no killer in the midst! There is simply no proof that another person or persons was connected with the incident. The forensics people have confirmed that there's no evidence of violence or signs of struggle either in the church, at the top of the tower, or on the ground where the body was found."

"Second point: his GP reported to the Coroner that he was suffering from AIDS and that it was incurable. In fact, if Jones hadn't killed himself, he would have died from the ravages of the illness in a relatively short time. He obviously knew that he was deteriorating rapidly, and that he would soon be hospitalized and become just a cabbage in a bed. There was no wonder treatment on offer, other than palliative care, which the doctor had said at the inquest that Jones had refused. He would only accept painkillers and sleeping pills. Ipso facto, the man killed himself."

The coroner had recorded death by suicide. The matter of the position of the body had to be discounted, as there were no corroborating facts to explain this unusual occurrence.

"Maybe a big bloody wind carried him twenty feet" suggested Stewart to himself.

He took the cigarette out of his mouth and took a sip of cold tea.

"And what about the vicar, what about him, eh?" his ruminations continued.

Stewart disliked the Reverend Stannard immensely, but honestly couldn't imagine, even in his wildest dreams, that he was in some way directly responsible for the curate's death. He guessed that there was certainly a fair amount of animosity between the two men, but not enough to be a motive for murder. The vicar might an offensive oaf but not a homicidal maniac. After all, he was a clergyman, for God's sake! Stewart thought about these men. They were supposed to be holy men. Weren't they supposed to be humanity's best, serving God and man? Wasn't that how it worked?

Stewart's own experience of church was limited to being in the Scouts as a boy, when he sometimes attended church on a Sunday morning with the troop. However, that was more spit and polish and uniforms than anything to do with God and Jesus. For all of his life until now he just didn't give credence to such matters. His parents hadn't bothered with all that. They were too poor, they had no time for such luxuries, like taking time off from earning a living and making ends meet to go to church. It had no meaning for him. Church was just another building on High Street. As the saying goes, church is just for christenings, weddings, and funerals. It was surplus to requirements, as far as he was concerned. Yes, he'd met Christians, well-meaning individuals, but not the kind of people with whom he would want to associate.

As a cop, he had seen enough tragedy and strife, and for that matter, meaningless and pointless death. Where was God Almighty in those situations? Maybe he was taking a day off. Even if he gave religion a second thought, he would probably agree with millions of others, that in this world the very idea, let alone the existence of a loving God, was just a story, a fiction created by people who couldn't face grim reality alone. As for these two so-called holy churchmen, Jones and Stannard, well, who would want to go to Stannard's church? The man was a walking contradiction of Christianity. Stewart thought he'd rather attend an atheist church, if there was such a thing. You'd probably get more tea and sympathy there than at St. David's. As for Jones, he didn't know the man, but surely it can't be right that a bloody homo should be a priest.

He shrugged. His thoughts came back to the case. As far as everyone else was concerned, the case was now closed. Stewart had officially archived the file on his PC, and yesterday he had dropped the case folder of papers into the out-tray on his desk. Inside the cover he had stuck a small yellow "post-it." It bore a large question mark in red ink and was underlined "not solved!"

It was a suspicious death. However, no crime was committed, and there were no culprits to arrest. There was no evidence to connect anyone with the death, and there were good reasons for suicide. All perfectly reasonable . . . except for the location of the body. A riddle wrapped up in a mystery.

He stubbed out the cigarette into the bottom of the glass ash tray. He finally pushed the whole sorry episode to the back of his brain, trying to let it go. However, still something nagged and gnawed at him. His sixth sense, although obscured at this time, told him that one day he would have the answer.

He walked back into the living room, slumped on the sofa, picked up the TV remote, and started flipping channels. In the end, he settled on an old film, one that he had seen before many times.

He was woken up by the sound of his mobile phone. The TV was still on, but showing something quite different now. He glanced at his watch on the coffee table. Nearly 2.30 in the morning. The ringing persisted. He picked it up, pressed the green key, and listened. It was the Superintendent at the station. "Stewart . . . you there? Sorry to wake you, I know it's your weekend off, but duty calls. Got a serious job for you. There's a body on the beach opposite the War Memorial. Dr. Padelski from forensics is already there. Get down there as quick as you can."

"Will do, sir." He cursed as he put the phone down. He struggled off the sofa and made his way to the bedroom to get dressed. Closing the front door of the flat behind him, he shivered in the cold air and went out into the street.

Chapter 11

Body on the Beach

Detective Inspector Stewart stood on the promenade, looking down towards the edge of the beach where the wind blew angry waves upon the shore. There was a lot of activity. Several people were clustered around a body that was now illuminated with mobile floodlights. The electric cables passed by Stewart's feet and were connected to a petrol generator that chugged loudly behind him. A bright, vertical shaft of lightning lit up the sky for a split second before darkness returned. Stepping off the concrete, he made his way down to the pool of yellow light.

Arriving at the scene, he saw Dr. Rosina Padelski, the woman from forensics, on her knees, bent low over what was left of a human body. She had a scalpel in her hand and was delicately teasing out a tiny object from the mutilated bone and flesh.

"Hello, Rosina. How are you?"

"You always ask the funniest of questions. Does it look like I'm alright? It's half past two, it's bloody freezing cold, as you English say, and I am picking my way through a cadaver."

Stewart was beginning to appreciate her wit. It was a very attractive trait in her.

"Well, I'm just about done here. There's nothing much for me to do. It's like searching for a needle in a hay house!"

"Haystack," he corrected.

She hadn't looked up in all this time, but standing, she said, "What?"

"It's haystack, not hay house."

"Oh, thank you. I like to be admonished with my English."

He replied by saying "you are welcome" in Polish: "Wy jestescie pozadani."

"Inspector, do you speak Polish?"

"No, not really. I had a Polish girlfriend when I was younger, and she taught me some words and phrases."

"Very good. Although your pronunciation is bad. Was she pretty? All Polish girls are pretty," she said with passion.

"As it happens, she was—far too beautiful for me. It didn't last long. She met a French man. I never saw her again."

"I'm sorry. Bloody French, eh?"

She turned to her assistants, gave them instructions about bagging up the remains, and stepped out of the circle of light to cross over to where Stewart stood. She held out her hand. It was warm to his very cold hand. He couldn't suppress a thought about where that hand had been just moments ago.

"You are cold, Inspector. Come, I have coffee in my car. I can tell you all about the corpse on the beach, or at least what I know."

They walked up the beach together, the sand granules crunching under their feet. At the entrance to the promenade, a couple of uniformed officers were talking to an old white-haired man who looked very frightened and disheveled. By the look of his clothes, he was a vagrant or a wino. Somebody had kindly put a thick blanket around his shoulders, and he was sipping a plastic cup of tea or coffee that he held tightly in both hands.

Stewart indicated the group to Padelski.

"You can interrogate him later. Come have some coffee. I have heard his testimony already from your colleagues. It's very interesting. But the man is very frightened by what he saw."

She raised the door of the hatchback, pulled off her white disposable suit, and placed it carefully, along with her over shoes and gloves, into a black bag. She tied it up before throwing it into the well of the trunk. She shook her head to free her hair, and taking out a thick lined coat, pulled it on and zipped it up tight to protect her against the cold night air.

Stewart looked at her intently, thinking that she was a very attractive woman and wishing he was thirty years younger. She was about five nine, he guessed, with rich, brown curly hair that fell onto her shoulders. She looked fit and enormously healthy. She made him feel old.

"Sit here Inspector, beside me." She patted the metal at the back of the car. She deftly unscrewed the aluminum flask and handed him a cup of steaming coffee.

"No milk, no sugar, I'm afraid."

He accepted the cup with a smile. She poured one for herself.

"Now tell me, Inspector, all about your Polish girl-friend."

He laughed before answering. "Shall we talk about the body on the beach first?"

"Okay, business before pleasure! But I'm not letting you go until you tell me, yes?"

"It's a deal."

"Okay, where to begin? I got a call to come, and when I arrived, there were several police and an old man, that one there . . ." she pointed along the prom to the man in the blanket. "He was having a fit and very scared of something, trembling and shouting, swearing—awful, bad words. He said that his mate was down on the beach, eaten by dragons."

"Dragons?"

"Yes, he clearly said dragons, I understood him well." She paused a moment and said, with a broad grin on her face, "Welsh dragons, yes!"

Stewart looked at her in amazement, but said nothing.

"Inspector, you didn't find my joke funny? I thought you English men like joke, no?"

Stewart looked at her with affection. He was beginning to like this girl.

"Very good, Dr. Padelski."

"Please, call me Rosina. What is your forename?"

"It's Paul."

She took a sip of the black coffee.

"So, I went to see the body. It was lying half in the sea, so with the police we had to pull him farther up, which meant all the evidence was washed away earlier. Bad luck. On the body there was not much to see. A gruesome death. I hope he died from fright, because if he didn't he would have suffered a slow death from a thousand bites."

"Bites? You mean he was eaten by an animal, or if he was in the sea, by a fish? It seems too incredible to be true."

"Yes, I agree. And what animals do you have here that could do such harm?"

"Well, none. We don't have sharks in the sea hereabouts."

"I can rule out sharks. A shark would have bitten right through his bones and they are all intact."

The inspector pulled a pack of cigarettes from his pocket and offered her one, immediately regretting it.

Standing up, she said, "Paul, those are bad for your body. You'll end up like him on the beach, all chewed up. If you are going to smoke let's walk." She locked up the car and they strolled back towards the policemen who were still with the old man. Stewart purposely stood downwind of Rosina so that the smoke from his cigarette didn't blow into her face. He said, "There's nothing I know of that could have caused such terrible injuries. There is a zoo a bit farther up the coast, but we'd have heard if any dangerous animals had escaped."

"The old man described dragons attacking his friend, pulling him down and biting him ferociously. All the time, he listened to his friend's screams and cries for help, too afraid to intervene. Then there was silence, except for the sound of the surf on the sands."

They had arrived at the little group. Stewart recognized some of the officers, who stepped aside so that he could address the man who was now holding an empty cup.

"Owen, can you rustle up another cup of tea?"

The old man stared at Stewart with eyes that displayed shock and horror. He was shivering, despite the thick woolen blanket covering his frail body. The smell of cheap alcohol was on the man's breath and Stewart instinctively drew away.

"You okay now? You're safe with us, and we'll get you fixed up in a nice warm bed for the night. You can look forward to a good English breakfast in the morning. How's that sound old timer?" Stewart tried to sound chummy, but not patronizing. The old man simply looked at him as if he was talking gibberish. Then he spoke.

"He only went down into the dark for a slash. Didn't want anyone to see him do it. He's a gentleman, our Dan. I could hear him singing, then he disappeared into the darkness at the bottom of the beach. Christ! Then all I 'eard was 'im screaming and crying out for help. Of course, I thought he was having a lark, bit of a joker, our Danny. So I shouted out . . . pull the other leg Danny Boy! But he didn't stop. Then I started down the beach. I got halfway down but I couldn't see anything. It was black, but I could tell where he was because of his screaming." He wiped his lips with the back of his hand. The blanket slipped off his shoulder. Stewart reached forward and put it back.

"Then, there was this almighty lightning bolt. It lit up the whole beach and I saw . . . it was horrible . . . they were eating him, four or five bloody dragons tearing at his flesh! He was still alive, then one of those things looked straight at me. I tell you, I froze on the spot. Its eyes burned bright red and in its teeth and mouth I could see bits of Danny. I was terrified. I turned and ran, but all I could hear was him screaming. Then it suddenly stopped, and all I could do was pray, dear God, Mary mother of mercy, let him be dead." The old man broke down and sobbed. His whole body convulsed and shook. Stewart put his arm around the man and called to one of the policemen.

"Take him back to the station and see he's sorted out . . . properly mind."

The young policeman led him away. Down on the beach, a police photographer was at work. The flashes went every few seconds, lighting up the gloom.

Rosina looked at Stewart sympathetically. She had witnessed a side of the inspector that wasn't normally on display.

"Well, Paul, what do you make of that?" she said, referring to the old man's fantastic tale.

"I don't know what to make of it. It's Halloween—could be some sort of sick, twisted joke. The fright sobered him up, but the old guy was drunk when it all happened. Maybe he suffers from the DTs!"

"DT?" asked Rosina.

"Sorry . . . delirium tremens: too much drink and you begin to see pink elephants, or . . ."

She was one thought ahead, "Dragons."

"Yep." He sighed.

"You know, in my village, good people don't go out on this night for fear of demons that walk the streets after midnight. All the doors are bolted and window shutters are locked until daylight the next morning. As children, we were allowed to sleep in our parents' room because we were so scared."

"Really? But that stuff is all myth and superstition, isn't it?"

"No, Paul. It's true. Our priest would stay in the church all night praying for the village and the people."

Stewart looked at her, trying to understand. "You religious, then?"

"No, not religious. I have a belief in God . . . don't you?"

Stewart was silent for a moment. "No. I guess I don't."

Rosina was surprised. She wagged her finger at him. "You don't believe in God, you smoke, and you don't have a woman to love! You're in very bad shape."

For a moment he felt sorry that his credibility in her eyes had dropped. She smiled at him, and taking his arm, said in a mocking tone, "I can see I am going to have to look after you and teach you a few things."

Stewart liked the sound of that.

Chapter 12

Halloween

The evening started innocently enough. This was the only night of the year when fools celebrated the dead, not thinking that their own deaths were soon to come. The Grim Reaper had sharpened his scythe and would be abroad tonight, searching for his victims. Witches and warlocks inscribed pentacles in secret places to carry out dark ceremonies of the occult, to invoke the souls of the deceased to return and roam the Earth once more for a single night, to take their revenge upon the living. Ghosts, ghouls, devils, demons, vampires, and pagan deities all transport themselves during the hours of darkness, their one black desire to cause mischief and mayhem. When faced with a demon on the street on "All Hallows' Eve," who can say whether it is a costume and a mask or the real thing? On this night, even the fauna were spooked. Black cats, hissing, obstructed the way. Owls, bats, and crows swooped out of the darkness to peck at your eyes.

Gangs of loud teenagers swarmed around the town center dressed in all sorts of outrageous costumes. Harry Potter with a red "z" painted on his forehead was swigging back vodka straight from the bottle. His mates wore horror masks, skeleton suits, and zombie and Frankenstein's monster costumes. Nearby, a group of intoxicated teenage girls, dressed as witches, waltzed arm in arm along the pavement and sang unintelligible words to a popular song. It was all good-natured stuff, and the policemen standing by the corner of the bank only smiled as the laughing throng passed by.

The cold weather had continued all week, temperatures still hitting zero by midnight. It was a night of gloom and dread, with grey clouds scudding across the sky. Every now and then, a bolt of lightning lit up the dark vault of the night, followed by loud cracks of thunder, but no rain fell. There was tension in the air. Along the rooftops, on spires, masts, and chimneys, sporadic bursts of luminous green electrical light burned bright for a few fiery seconds before moving on, as if searching for a place to rest.

Small bunches of younger children were safely herded by their mothers, going from house to house knocking on doors, calling "trick or treat" in shrill, excited voices, and collecting sweets and gifts in their little bags and wicker baskets. Each kid was in a costume and mask purchased from the local supermarket. Some wore pointed hats, dressed like witches in flowing black plastic capes. Some even sported miniature broomsticks. Others in red devil outfits with pointed tails and little pitchforks teased their friends. Horror masks of monsters glowed eerily in the dark.

Everyone was having fun to a time-honored ritual whose origins went far back into the dark ages of human history. Apple bobbing in water barrels, trying to bite an apple suspended on a string with your arms tied behind you, placing candles inside a pumpkin— these were all pagan rites of divination. It was always the apple that was used. It was all about Eve and the fall of man. The meanings of these games were long forgotten and people today, if reminded of these truths, would simply scoff and declare "stuff and nonsense," laughing off any objections, but on this night there were onlookers that believed. Angels and demons alike knew the intrinsic nature of these malevolent games. The angels shuddered at the sights of Halloween, whereas the demon servants of Lord Satan guffawed and cackled and encouraged the human fools all the more.

When all shades of past meaning are lost in the mists of time, does it signify that such practices are now devoid of the original elemental powers? The gamesters and the recipients might be totally ignorant of the hidden baleful actions, but the grievous effects are being meted out, measure for measure. The unseen referees and guardians are at work on this night. All "harmless fun," but there will be casualties, to be sure.

The congregations who had sat in myriad local churches the previous Sunday were unaware that the sermons that they were listening to were being repeated elsewhere.

Across the town, from Catholic churches to chapels of the Church of Wales, from the Assemblies of God to the Methodists, from Congregational churches to Baptist churches and to all the independents, the priests and vicars and pastors had torn up their well-studied sermon notes and preached a message that the Spirit had implanted in their souls. The Spirit of God was moving across the town, conceiving a spiritual unity amongst believers. The speakers told the faithful that Halloween was a celebration of Satan. It glorified all the icons in ancient culture that were evil. All the pagan religions that had existed in these isles before Christianity came were fostered and sustained by Lucifer.

The many and varied preachers denounced the frivolities and party atmosphere of the revelers on the streets. They spoke about the dangers of becoming involved in such devilish activities, no matter how innocuous they may appear. Yes, you will be ridiculed for taking up such a stance. Others will laugh at you for denouncing these activities. They warned the faithful that if they wanted trouble, invite the Devil in by donning a mask or wearing a satanic costume. No matter how comic and harmless it may appear, it pays homage to the Lord of Hell, and those who do so open the door to Lucifer and invite his demons in, exposing not only themselves, but also their children to the bestial influence of Hades.

Such sermons had not been heard in churches for decades, not since the last great Welsh Revival. The Word was delivered in power and in truth. Those that heard it were convinced in their heart and soul to obey. The advice was simple; lock up your homes and put a sign on your door, akin to the Israelites who smeared blood on the doorposts and lintels of their dwellings to protect them from the Angel of Death. The call had gone out on this night for prayer warriors to gather in homes and in the churches to pray against evil principalities and powers.

The angels had their commands. Stand and watch and repel any demon that tried to invade any holy or sacred place—that included the homes of believers and places of governance, hospitals, fire services, and police—but under no account take the initiative and engage the enemy. Remember that those humans who have chosen to be involved in these evil deeds of Halloween are under the influence of the God of this age.

Their orders were clear: watch, protect, and serve the true Lord. Build an impenetrable wall of spirit power, a fortress against the evil ones. Do not let them pass. It was going to be a night of anguish for the forces of good. Angel commanders reminded their cohorts of faithful warriors that the crucifixion of Christ was such a night, when thousands of angels were prevented from helping Jesus, the Son of God, in his most tragic hour of need. They saw him beaten and abused, suffering an ignominious death upon a crudely-fashioned cross, with iron spikes hammered into his body. They heard his cries and they saw his agony. They experienced his utter despair and they felt his isolation and the desolation when his own spirit was severed from the Father. Yet they could do nothing to aid their dying Lord.

However, God brought good out of the worst evil at Calvary. The captain asked Samuel to meditate on these other incidents recorded in the Bible. Why did God allow Joseph to be imprisoned? Or not prevent Daniel from being thrown into the Lion's den? St. Paul was shipwrecked three times. God allowed these events to occur for a reason. Let us not be quick to judge our God tonight, for He knows all: the alpha and omega, the beginning and the end.

On this night, emergency facilities were all on high alert. Accident and emergency staff at the local hospitals expected a high intake of bruised bodies, broken bones, and as the night wore on, drunks and those injured in street melees and fights. The cells would be filled with miscreants and petty criminals who would be out taking full advantage of Halloween to make a quick buck.

A group of nurses smoking cigarettes outside the main entrance to the Emergency Department noticed the first signs that something was wrong. The parking lot soon filled with vehicles and ambulances bringing dozens of very young children. Mothers carrying precious bundles in their arms hurried into the hospital needing medical help desperately. All the children displayed the same symptoms: repeated vomiting followed by acute diarrhea. Their faces were pale, and their limbs lifeless in their mothers' arms. The waiting room of the local hospital was full of crying children and angry parents who sought immediate help from beleaguered nurses and doctors. The GPs and locums were called in from surrounding districts to offer much needed assistance to the hospital staff. Outside of the hospital building, a band of angels stood guard, their faces grimly reflecting their inner feelings. Nearby, hordes of demons laughed derisively and jeered at the angels, who were bound by oath not to intervene.

As the early hours of the evening waned and the night wore on, the streets, the pubs, and the bars were steadily filling up, not with Halloween devotees, but with those people who only needed a trivial excuse to let rip. Fights broke out among youths who'd had too much cheap booze. The police moved in with vans and truncheons to maintain order, but even they knew that tonight was out of the ordinary. In the years gone by they had easily kept public order without drafting in extra forces. Tonight they had their hands full.

Violence was breaking out all over the town. Shop windows were broken and goods were stolen right on High Street. Rampaging youths hell-bent on vandalism smashed car windows and cursed every normal person they encountered. It was as if the town had suddenly gone mad, infected with some strange rabid virus. Serious crimes also occurred. In a back alley a tramp trying to hide in the doorway of a derelict factory was kicked to death by a group of marauding men, who screamed and laughed as the vagrant was tossed to and fro like a rag doll. Their last act before speeding off was to set the body alight. A group of grinning devils stood close to the burning man, warming their hands on the flames.

Angels in the vicinity surveyed the night's evil events. They simply stared in horror at what was unfolding before their eyes on the streets below. Their souls filled with righteous anger and deep regret that they could not muster their own gathered forces to counteract the chaos abroad that night. All they could do was hope and pray that it would all end soon. From below them in the church they could hear the prayers of the faithful calling out to their God to bring an end to evil.

* * *

Melanie O'Reilly was a Scouser with an Irish family background. A single parent with a daughter aged four, Melanie wanted to do right for her daughter. She wanted to bring her up good and proper, different from the childhood she had experienced. Melanie had been beaten by her alcoholic father, neglected by her mother, and at the age of fifteen, she had received her first conviction for drugs. Not many weeks after being listed on police files, she became pregnant. She didn't know who the father was. It could have been any boy of three or four that she had sex with at an all-nighter. She didn't care; she had no time for blokes. Those she had known were all losers.

After the baby was born while she was living in a hostel, she had been offered the chance of a flat in Golwyn Sands, a nice seaside town a few miles up the coast from Penrhos Bay. The flat was in a council-owned block full of girls like her, but it wasn't as bad as the hostel. At the end of the day, she could shut the door and have her own private space. The flat came with a condition, that she attend a drug rehabilitation clinic, which was run by a Christian charity in the same town. She was getting real help. She was off the hard drugs and now only smoked ten cigarettes a day—and the odd spliff now and again. Alcohol wasn't her choice of poison. She had seen firsthand what it had done to her mother. Life was good, in fact. Money was scarce, but she intended to get a job at the local superstore when her kid started school in just a few months.

She had promised her daughter Emily that they would go out on Halloween. It would be the first time for Emily. They had already been to the supermarket to get a witch's costume and broom, and now it was here.

Melanie had done up her face with red and black makeup, and the final result was really scary. She had intended to go out earlier than this, but she had been held up waiting for her box of groceries to arrive from Food Share, the local charity that helped people who were down on their luck. She had expected the two ladies to compliment her daughter on her Halloween costume, but oddly, they said nothing.

They did not live far from the center of town, so they could walk there in just a few minutes. It was nine by the time they started knocking on doors. In a short time, Emily had more sweets than she'd ever had in her short life. Melanie had to stop her from eating all of them at once. It was getting late, and there didn't seem to be any other children on the streets. Melanie was getting a bit worried because there were loads of older kids about, screaming and shouting and acting stupid. It seemed that every ten minutes, an ambulance rushed past on its way to the hospital, sirens blaring and blue lights flashing. Emily said she was feeling a bit sick. Melanie picked her up to comfort and chide her, saying that she had eaten too many sweets too quickly.

It was dark and getting cold. Taking a shortcut back to the flat, she headed across some open parkland. Halfway across, Emily held up her head and said, "Mommy, do you hear music?"

Melanie stopped. She could hear it too. It was instantly recognizable. It was a merry-go-round. Now they could see the multi-colored lights filter through the trees on the other side of the copse.

"Mommy, can we go see it, pleeease?" Emily begged.

Putting Emily down on the grass, Melanie clasped her small hand and ran to where the amusement ride was situated.

When they arrived, the carousel was going full tilt. The horses went up and down in time to the beautiful music. There were only a few children on the ride, but they were all laughing and enjoying themselves immensely.

Emily cried out, trying to shout over the noise of the music, "Mom, can I go on? I really love the horses, please can I? Say yes!" She was so excited.

Emily was dazzled by all the noise and lights. She laughed and giggled every time the horses went by in a blur of light and color.

"Mommy, mommy I like that one!" She shouted above the noise again, "I like the white and gold horse, I want that one."

The ride came to a halt. Melanie helped her daughter up onto the white horse's saddle. For a moment, before she let go, she had second thoughts. Would Emily be safe?

A man came over and took the money for the ride.

"Will my daughter . . . I mean . . . she's safe, isn't she?" Melanie questioned the man.

"Yeah, I'll slow it down this time, okay? And don't worry mom, I'll keep an eye on her."

When she asked how much, he waved her money away, and patting Emily on the head, said, "Have this one on me, it's Halloween, after all."

Melanie stepped back off the ride. She was still worried about Emily's safety, and watched with anxious eyes as the carousel got going again. Emily disappeared from view for a few seconds, and then, as the machine turned full circle, she came into view. Melanie called out to her, but Emily was already lost in a magical world of princesses and horses. She relaxed and got her mobile out to take a photo of Emily when she came around again. After a few rotations, she could see that everything was fine.

Above her in the night sky, lightning flashed, and moments later, thunder rumbled. She looked up and was worried now that it was going to rain and they would get wet, but hey, she thought, it's only water. The ride continued, and it was then that she noticed that Emily was the only child left on the ride. At first she thought that perhaps they had caught the last ride of the evening. She glanced at her watch. It was almost ten o'clock. Every time Emily passed her she waved, trying to catch her eye. At last, the ride began to lose speed. Emily waved to her mother as she went by, wearing a big frown on her face, sorry that it was all coming to an end. The carousel finally halted, but it stopped with Emily and the white and gold steed on the opposite side. She waited a few moments, expecting to see Emily come running around the side. The music stopped.

Melanie started to walk around the merry-go-round, calling out Emily's name. She thought maybe her daughter needed help to get down. "So much for the guy in charge," she muttered. Arriving at the other side, she immediately saw that the white and gold horse was empty, and Emily was nowhere to be seen. She ran on, hoping to see Emily back on the side where they had started. She completed a full circle of the machine, but Emily was nowhere. Melanie began to get anxious. What had happened to her daughter? Her precious, lovely daughter.

"Emily, Emily!" she cried out again.

She didn't know what to do. Where was the man who operated the ride? A terrible idea began to form in her mind. She tried hard not to think it, but it just grew inside of her. With tears welling in her eyes she said, "No, no! Please God, not my baby!"

She looked all about her, hoping to catch a glimpse of the man with Emily. She ran to the edge of the trees. Wildly brushing them aside, she scanned the dense dark undergrowth.

"Emily! Emily!"

Finally, she could not cry and shout anymore. She slumped to her knees. As she sobbed, her body convulsed and shook uncontrollably with pain and anguish.

* * *

It was some time before the doctor and policewoman could calm Melanie and get her to explain what was wrong. Minutes ago, when she had rushed into the police station, she was screaming and shouting. No one could understand what she was trying to say. At first they thought she was suffering from an overdose of bad drugs, her actions were so mad. She was distraught, quite beside herself, clothes unkempt and torn from the bushes. There was mud on her shoes and jeans. She looked a pitiable sight to the few people gathered around her.

The female cop whispered to the medic that perhaps she'd been raped. The doctor shrugged. Just as he was reaching into his bag to get something to quiet her down, she suddenly stopped screaming. Falling silent and collapsing onto the floor in a squatting position, she simply sobbed and whimpered. The policewoman knelt before her. Putting her hands upon Melanie's shoulders she said gently, "We need to know what has happened to you, can't you tell us? Then we can help you."

Melanie wiped the tears off her face with her hands. Without looking up, she said in a hoarse voice, "My daughter Emily . . . she's been taken by a man . . . she's only four!"

The female cop turned her head to look at the doctor and said in a hushed voice, "Oh my God."

Chapter 13

The Child Sleeps

Gathan retained his human form as he arrived at the rear of the old church that was now Jezebel's shop, meeting place, and home. He stepped into the building through an open door, where Jezebel was waiting as arranged. She stared at Gathan in almost disbelief. It was one thing to experience her spiritual mentor through the ether of a séance, but it was quite another thing to actually meet him in the flesh. With head bowed low, she trembled as Gathan stood before her with the child Emily in his arms.

"Where shall I take her?" he asked brusquely.

"This way, my Lord."

Gathan followed her as she wound her way up some stairs to the suite of rooms that was her private residence. Gathan deposited the child on the sofa of a lavishly furnished lounge that bore all the soft and subtle ornaments of a witch of high standing.

"What shall . . ." Jezebel's voice shook with fear as Gathan, still in human guise, stood before her, staring with the evil eyes of a demon.

"Do what I instructed, woman. Keep the child hidden. In time, you will miraculously discover her whereabouts by supernatural means. Your face will be on the front page of every newspaper in the land. This is how I reward you for your faithful service."

Jezebel wondered if she should kneel in gratitude.

"Sire, and what do I do with her? What if she tries to get away? I can't watch her every hour of the day and night."

"Foolish woman! I have put the child into a coma, a harmless sleep. She will come to no harm. Now avert your eyes!" The command came so strongly and suddenly that Jezebel instinctively hastened to cover her eyes with both her hands. After a few seconds, she opened her eyes and he was gone, back to the netherworld.

She gazed down at Emily and smiled. Reaching down, she brushed back the fair little locks that had fallen across her face. Jezebel had an uneasy feeling in the pit of her stomach, and was beginning to wonder if what she was doing with Gathan was really worth it. What she didn't know about Gathan's plan for delivering the child back to her mother was that the child would be dead.

* * *

Detective Inspector Stewart stood with Melanie in the park. It was still dark, but the area was lit up like day from the headlights of several police cars and four-wheel drives.

Melanie was crying again, and through her tears she was arguing with Stewart, trying desperately to make him and the other uniformed officers who stood disconsolately around her believe that what she was describing was true.

"Are you sure that this was the exact spot where the fairground ride was?" He was trying very hard not to sound patronizing.

She broke away, as if to emphasize her words, and touching the grass with her hands said, "I am not lying! It was right here. Why don't you believe me?"

Her face was full of anguish and stained with tears.

The group of police all stared at her. Some turned away, pretending to be busy at some task. Stewart stepped forward. He spoke in measured tones.

"We do believe you Melanie, but look—there are no vehicle track marks at all here, nothing at all. A heavy piece of equipment like a carousel would put down steel legs to ground itself, but there's no evidence of that. No indents in the grass."

Melanie put her hands to the sides of her face and shook her head.

Stewart stepped closer to her and tried to make contact, but it was clumsily done. She pulled away from him.

"Find my daughter . . . please," she begged.

Her eyes met his, and he saw there a grief so deep that he was shocked by the raw emotion.

"We will, don't worry." As soon as he'd said "don't worry," he knew it had been a stupid thing to say. Melanie remained silent and looking imploringly into his eyes. The tears started to flow once more.

Stewart had thought about asking Rosina to look over the site, but had decided against it. He knew she was exhausted after last night's awful business, but he made up his mind to call on her tomorrow. He needed to talk to someone who could decipher his state of mind. First the curate, then the body on the beach, and now this. All these incidents had aspects that he just couldn't wrap his head around. He'd been a cop for a very long time, but this was the first time that he had been totally perplexed. He just didn't know where to begin to unravel these awful crimes. Feeling inadequate and depressed, he took Melanie's arm and walked back towards the waiting police cars.

Chapter 14

Bewildered

Stewart rang the bell of flat number three. He could hear it ringing inside, along with the excited voice of a child. The door opened, and an old woman peered out at Stewart. A small girl of about eight or nine years clung to the lady's legs and shyly peeped to see who was at the door.

"Oh, I'm sorry, I think I have the wrong flat," said Stewart.

The old woman just looked at him without saying a word.

"I was looking for Rosina?"

At the end of the hall, he heard Rosina call out.

"Who is it, Mama?"

"Rosina, it's me, Paul!" He shouted past the old woman who had now opened the door wide.

"Paul? What are you doing here?"

"I wanted to speak to you . . . but sorry, I thought you lived alone."

Rosina came forward.

"It's alright Mama, he's a friend from work. Paul, come in please."

Paul walked into the flat. It was small, but nicely furnished. The old woman disappeared into the kitchen and the little girl stood beside Rosina, holding her hand tight.

Stewart felt awkward. He'd had this visit to Rosina all worked out in his head, but there were some things he didn't know about Rosina's personal life.

"Paul, this is my daughter, Sasha. Say hello to the nice man, Sasha." The child eased herself shyly behind her mother.

Rosina looked quizzically at Stewart and asked, "Is something wrong? A problem at work?"

"No, no. Nothing wrong." Stewart felt his face redden. "I just wanted to talk, that's all."

Rosina smiled. "Can you come back later, this afternoon?"

"Yes, of course. I didn't mean to intrude," he said apologetically.

Rosina put her hand on his arm.

"You aren't. It's just that we are about to go to church."

"Oh, I see." He stupidly hadn't thought that on a Sunday morning people still went to church.

"You can come with us if you want to."

Stewart blushed again. "Thanks, but no, I, er . . . have some things to do," he lied.

Rosina smiled again and said, "Then come back about four o'clock and we'll have some afternoon tea, just like the English do."

Walking back to his place Stewart felt down, but didn't really know why. He had really enjoyed his job, but lately it all seemed to be a chore. It irked him too that he couldn't seem to make any progress or breakthrough with these recent crimes, if indeed they were crimes. He always prided himself on his uncanny ability to see below the surface, to figure out what was really going on, even if all the clues pointed elsewhere. However, now he felt that he was missing something and that he was up against something he didn't understand. It annoyed him to think that maybe he was just getting old and that his faculties of detection were growing dull. He feared he was losing his appetite for the job.

He pulled out a cigarette. Concentrating on the smoke, he tried hard not to think anymore, but it was impossible. His head filled up with a conglomeration of vivid images: the mutilated corpse on the beach, the dead curate sprawled out on the stone pathway, his red blood still oozing out of his lifeless body, the sound of Melanie screaming. He was in his own waking nightmare.

* * *

He arrived back at the flat at four and Rosina let him in. Seated on the empty sofa, he asked where her mother and child were.

"They are sleeping. They are both at that age where they need an afternoon nap!"

Then she added quickly, "But we have an hour yet to talk undisturbed."

Rosina hadn't sat down yet. "Do you want a coffee?"

"Yeah, thanks. Strong and three sugars."

"Three sugars! You are crazy. Are you a diabetic?" she asked.

"No, I don't think so. Why?"

"Well believe me, you soon will be!"

He laughed. She went off to the kitchen to make coffee and returned a few minutes later with two mugs in her hand. The one she gave to Stewart had a bright logo on the side with a red heart. He read it. "I love Poland."

"Do you miss Poland?" he said, making small talk.

She shrugged. "Yes, of course, but I love it here, too. I make a good future for my daughter. For my mama too, although she needs nothing at her age."

"You still have family in Poland?"

"Not really, cousins and some other distant relatives. My father is dead. He was a policeman like you. He was killed in a shootout with some drug smugglers in Krakow."

She stood up and walked over to a shelf on the wall. Moving over to Stewart, she handed him a framed photograph of a man in uniform.

"Is this your Dad?"

"Yes, on a special day. He was awarded a bravery medal for rescuing a young boy from the river. The boy would have drowned. It's funny, but many children in Poland don't know how to swim."

"I guess you miss him?" Stewart seemed now to have got stuck in the groove of asking questions.

"Yes and no. If he had lived I would not be here in Great Britain, and many good things have happened to me since coming here. But I am sad that my daughter didn't really know her grandfather. He was a good man, a kind man."

As they sipped their coffee there was silence between them for awhile.

"So Paul, what is on your mind?"

He shifted his body on the sofa to try to give impetus to his words.

"I guess I . . ." he faltered, "I'm not sure. I used to be so certain of things, like working out a crime.

Catching the criminals wasn't difficult. Most of the time they're idiots, leaving clues to their whereabouts or identity all over the crime scene." He smiled, "Why am I telling you this? You know what I mean, yeah?"

"Yes, of course."

"It's just that these latest incidents—I can't read them, can't work them out. They have black spots that I can't see through. Sometimes just thinking about them I go crazy." He gave out a big sigh and continued, "Like the dead clergyman: where his body lay, it just doesn't add up. And now this poor kid whose child has been taken. I would swear blind that she's telling the truth, but there's no sign of any fairground ride. None of it makes sense."

Rosina gazed at him with concern.

"Rosina, you said something the other night. That poor guy on the beach . . . you mentioned the supernatural. You aren't really asking me to believe that the man was killed by something other than another human being?" He looked at her pleadingly.

She moved over to the sofa and sat beside him.

"I don't know how that man died. But what I do know is that no human could have inflicted those horrible wounds, and recall please what his companion said to us about dragons."

"But that's all nonsense," he blurted out.

She put her finger to her lips to remind him to talk quietly for fear of waking her mother and child.

She went on, "I know that in Poland many strange things happen. Bad things happen to people and no one can explain why or how they happen. My father understood and believed that if there is a God from which goodness comes, then there must be a Devil from which badness comes."

Stewart listened intently to what she was saying, even though it was incredible to his ears.

"My father used to say—sometimes the Devil makes us do a bad thing, but when he wants a job done quickly he does it himself."

Stewart heaved another deep sigh.

"Do you believe . . . in the Devil?"

"Yes, I do," she said, seriously and with meaning.

"Right, well, how the hell does a cop do his job when the culprit is the Devil? I can't go out and arrest him now can I?" he said mockingly.

"Don't be silly! But you can learn to pray," she said earnestly.

"I've never prayed for anything, I wouldn't know how," he said quietly.

"Are you an atheist, Paul?"

Her blue eyes looked straight into his, trying to measure the man.

He shrugged. "An atheist? No, I suppose not. On the other hand, I have never given God much thought," he admitted.

"Then perhaps it is time you did." She got up and went to her bedroom. She came back holding a book.

Sitting down next to him she held it out to him, not letting it go.

"It is my daughter's. A child's Bible, but I think it will be good for you until you have made up your mind. Then if you like you can get an adult one, yes?"

He felt his face redden. He had come to Rosina to get some answers, but here she was giving him a kid's Bible.

"Well, won't your daughter need it?" He didn't want to say no outright for fear of offending his new friend.

"Take it! You can return it." Rosina still held the book.

Stewart took hold of the book. She did not let go.

"You promise me to read it today?" she said, smiling.

He couldn't resist. "Yes, I promise. But where do I start?"

She finally let go of the Bible and said, "Begin at the Gospels in the New Testament. Then we shall talk later next week, yes?"

"I'd like that," he said sincerely.

Detective Inspector Stewart, tough cop, badly needed a friend right now.

"And I shall pray for you every day!" she promised him.

"That'll be a first, Rosina."

* * *

Sitting at his kitchen table with a coffee and a cigarette, he did what he promised her he would. He was reading the Bible. To find the gospels, he had to search the index. Flipping through the pages, he found the New Testament title page. It had a note under the title which said "Words of Christ in red." He wasn't sure what that meant. He turned the page to "The Gospel According to Matthew." Stewart had checked his small pocket dictionary for the meaning of "Gospel." Tidings that Jesus preached: good news. He thought to himself, "I sure could do with some good news." He wondered if he would get it from this book.

He read slowly, but soon got bogged down in the genealogy, all the "begots" and "begats."

He skipped chapter one and went on to chapter two. This part was making sense, especially the description of King Herod. Plenty of murderous villains around in those times, including a King up to no good. "Nothing much changes, does it?" he mused. In the following pages, he found out what "Words of Christ in red" meant, as there were several pages with red text, always telling what Jesus actually said. He got to chapter four, and before proceeding, flipped the pages to see how many chapters there were in the gospel of Matthew. Twenty-eight! Wow, quite a bit to read yet. On some of the pages there were simple drawings of Jesus. The sketches were very good, and he thought they would appeal to a young child, but he pondered how much a kid would really understand. It was simply written with no difficult words, but the subject matter wasn't exactly what you'd find in Enid Blyton—King Herod massacring the innocent children and all.

He pulled out another cigarette, put it between his lips and lit it with a match, and then decided to read on to the end of Matthew.

Part Two

Chapter 15

The Mission Field

Richard Benton spent the first few months after graduating from Oxford University as an assistant to the Bishop of Helmsbridge at the diocesan headquarters in Essex. His time was filled with such great and meaningful tasks as getting the bishop's morning tea, acting as the messenger boy by taking letters to other clerical departments and tidying up the bishop's office and desk every morning before His Grace arrived. The high point of the week was when the bishop entrusted him to proofread some of the weekly missives before they were posted to the outlying parishes.

Before going to the university, Richard knew he was called to the Ministry of God. Even as a teenager, he knew without a doubt what his purpose in life was. He had diligently studied the Bible and had listened carefully to all of the Sunday sermons that exhorted young men like him to enter the mission field. He had fostered great ambitions in his heart. He wanted to emulate the famous Christian heroes and the latter-day saints who had taken the gospel to the far corners of the heathen world, many doing so at huge personal risk and even facing death. He'd enjoyed all the enthralling stories of the "Lives of the Saints," of how their faith in Christ had never wavered, despite enduring terrible tribulations. How brave they had been when suffering persecution, torture, and all manner of privations. St. Stephen, for instance, when faced with imminent death, refused to recant his beliefs and chose to praise God even as he was being stoned.

He himself harbored hopes of going to China, like Hudson Taylor, or even going native in the wilds of Africa in order to bring Christ to unbelievers. He had kept these dreams and passions alive throughout college, even though he had discovered, from reading accurate and historical accounts, that there was a certain amount of exaggeration and hyperbole in all of these stories. Nevertheless, they were to him the stock and trade of his vision to serve God.

He remembered Sunday school tales of intrepid Christian missionaries who had crossed hundreds of miles of wide deserts on foot to reach distant tribes. Of those who had fought through the dense jungles of Africa and South America in the unrelenting sun of the equator. Though subject to disease and hostile natives, on they soldiered. They had braved the dangers of wild beasts and tribes of cannibals and head-hunting savages in order to deliver the gospel—the Word of God—to those remote regions where no spiritual light had ever shone before. These stories, no matter how fantastic, had lived in his heart and stirred him to do the same, whatever the personal cost. Sadly, he knew that as a result of the work that these missionaries had done in centuries past, there were probably more Christians in Africa than inside the borders of his home continent of Europe. The mission field was ready for harvest and the laborers still numbered lamentably few. Could it be that the mission ground for him was not to be in far-flung places, but in these isles of Great Britain? Perhaps for Richard there would be no jungles or deserts; maybe he would have to be content with the mundane streets and houses of London, Birmingham, and Manchester, for in this century it was a truism that the world and its peoples from all the wild and wonderful lands of the globe had migrated to the United Kingdom.

At Oxford, Richard had studied and worked hard, knowing that a first-class degree would be his passport to success as a clergyman in the life of the Church. He possessed no ambition to become a bishop, or even a charismatic leader in the Church; he felt his calling was to minister to the poor and to the sick, and to bring to them the truth that could set them free from poverty and ignorance. Doing well academically was simply a means to an end, but he was sure that attaining top results would enable him to command respect among his peers and future employers. He hoped also that it would allow him an amount of flexibility to choose his own career.

He had met his wife, Sarah, at a student party. Although both of them were shy, they soon found that they shared ideas about how modern Christianity really could make a difference in today's society. They had similar backgrounds, having been brought up in middle-class church-going families, in which God was acknowledged daily through the observation of "grace" at dinner, but was not consciously given credence between Monday and Saturday. Their parents' faith extended to attending church twice on Sundays and dropping some coins into the offertory. Richard and Sarah both instinctively knew that there was much more to be experienced in Christ than the mere convention of church.

They sat in a corner of the party, sipping white wine and exchanging views on the state of the world, swapping academic aspirations, sharing what they would do if their dreams were given a chance of actually coming true. After an hour or so, when the music was getting too loud for them to talk without shouting into each other's ear, and when some of their friends had begun to get visibly drunk and uninhibited behavior became the norm, they decided to leave together. They took a slow walk back to the college. It was one of those pleasant evenings in late autumn when the evening chill is not too cold to bear. The streets and pavements were covered in a carpet of yellowing leaves, fallen from the old oak trees that lined the avenues. The stars above the city shone bright in a black, cloudless night sky. Approaching the university lodgings, Richard surprised himself as he boldly slipped his hand into Sarah's own compliant hand. It seemed so natural, as if it was meant to be. Stopping under the stone arch of the gate that led into her college, she turned to say goodnight and smiled expectantly, waiting nervously for Richard to kiss her. He did, but it was so clumsily delivered that she knew immediately he had never kissed a girl before.

The next few months were times of joy. They found a mutually deep expression of affection and love growing swiftly in their hearts. They were in no doubt that God had meant for them to be together. In sharing thoughts from the heart, they were often amazed at how sympathetic and close they were in many ways.

At times, it all seemed too good to be true. They experienced no differences or disagreements, and never argued about anything. They decided early on that they were going to spend their lives together as man and wife. They knew deep inside that their future happiness was to be found in surrendering every part of their lives to God, including the much awaited sacrament of marriage. To their surprise, their respective parents gave full consent and they were married in Oxford early in the new year.

After the wedding, they moved to a cheap one-bedroom flat in the suburbs of Oxford, where they lived an idyllic life. The weekdays were spent happily attending lectures and tutorials, and the evenings studying side-by-side on the sofa, their hands often intertwined whilst flipping pages of textbooks, only letting go when a free hand was needed to jot down notes. On Sundays they attended a local Church of England church, entering into the fullness of worship and prayer. After church, they'd often laze around at home talking about what the future might hold and where the Lord might send them. Richard still dreamt of exotic places far away from England. Sarah was a good Christian wife; she listened with a calm, restrained enthusiasm as Richard waxed lyrical and described his passion to serve God. They would pore over maps of the world, tracing out South America, China, and the Far East with their fingertips, dreaming of the places where they believed the news of the gospel had not yet fully penetrated and needed to be preached. Sarah was always quick to add her support to these grand ideas. She declared that she would follow wherever her husband wanted to go, wherever he was sent, no matter where. To her mind, "meekness" was a spiritual strength, not a weakness. It was sealed in her heart: "The meek shall inherit the earth." She fully intended to obey her husband in all things, as she had promised to do in her wedding vows.

Richard got his first-class honors degree in Theology and Divinity as expected, and Sarah obtained a creditable 2:1 in English Literature. They discussed their options and decided that he should apply for a position in the Church of England, and not with the Methodists or other denominations with which, to be honest, they both had little or no contact. Sarah aspired to be a children's teacher, but it was agreed that she would put her own career on hold until her husband had obtained his preferred permanent position.

It wasn't long before Richard had been invited to attend several interviews for positions in the Church of England. The Church Times "jobs" page was full of vacancies. There may have been a recession in the land, but it would seem that there was an acute shortage of clerics. Richard knew he could apply and easily get a post as a curate or as an assistant team vicar in one of numerous parishes throughout England, but one morning, whilst scanning the situations listed as vacant, he noticed an advertisement for an assistant to the Bishop of Helmsbridge. It stated that a candidate with a first-class honors degree from a leading university would be preferred. As he read the notice again, the idea of being an assistant to a bishop delighted his ego. He felt a high degree of satisfaction that he had a first-class degree with honors, and not just from a leading university, but from Oxford, which everyone knew was the best university in the country, if not in the world. He glanced up with pride at the framed certificates which hung on the wall.

It didn't take much imagination to see himself strolling through the cathedral and diocesan office corridors carrying an armful of important papers and chatting with the bishop and his archdeacon about the great affairs of the ecclesiastical estate. He smiled at the thoughts filling his head. Yes, he could see himself working at the center of spiritual life, learning valuable lessons about life in the great Church of England. Sarah turned to look at him and said, "What are you smiling about?"

Richard returned from his reverie. "Nothing, really . . . there's a job here, that's all, as assistant to the Bishop of Helmsbridge. I was just imagining what it might be like. You know, rubbing shoulders with the high and mighty. Did you know that the cathedral in Helmsbridge was constructed in the thirteenth century?"

"Really? That old! But from the expression on your face I would guess you were already in the job. As for what it would be like, I think it would be very similar to being at Oxford: musty old buildings and stepping aside for crusty old men in funny gowns and hats."

Richard looked a trifle downcast at her observation, but rallied and said, "Well I don't agree. Transport yourself back to the early days of Christianity—it must have been fantastic to be at the heart of things!"

"Richard," she exclaimed incredulously, "that was then and now is . . . well, it isn't quite like that now, is it?"

Sarah questioned his reasoning. "I thought you wanted to get started right away and minister to the poor and the needy? Isn't that what you wanted, Richard?"

He fidgeted as he sat beside her on the sofa, and as he answered, averted his eyes from hers.

"Yes I know," he said, a little too forcefully, "but I have been thinking about that . . ."

She interrupted him. "And praying about it? This is the first time you've ever mentioned it to me, darling."

"Well, I haven't been exactly consciously praying, but I have been deliberating and talking to God, and I feel that a spell in the bishop's palace, at the hub of things, I might learn . . ." he paused, searching for the right words ". . . new and valuable skills and insights that would benefit us later when we do turn to more immediate forms of Christian work. Making friends with a bishop may be useful, too. Simply being a subordinate member of a vicar's team wouldn't give me those chances."

Sarah looked at her husband. She wasn't sure that his argument was a valid one, but she considered that perhaps it couldn't do any harm to delay their original goal, and anyway, she mused, it might be part of God's plan. If it wasn't, they would soon find out.

"So when are the interviews taking place?" she asked brightly.

"Next Wednesday morning in Helmsbridge with Bishop Laidlaw himself. Let's go together. We can get an early train and have a look at the cathedral."

* * *

The interview with Bishop John Laidlaw went well. It seemed that Richard fitted perfectly. It turned out that the bishop had attended the same college at Oxford as Richard. The bishop had not been impressed with the other candidates for the job, who were mostly from inferior universities, he confided to Richard, and so had offered him the post right away. Richard told the bishop that he would like a few days to think and pray about it. The bishop had smiled as he rose from his desk, and offering his hand to Richard, said somewhat peevishly, "Well let's hope the Lord isn't too busy to come back to you with a swift reply. Call me by the end of the week with your answer."

Returning home later that day, Richard and Sarah got on their knees to pray and seek the Lord's guidance. Richard had to be sure that it was the right thing to do, but in truth he had made up his mind on the train back to Oxford. At the end of their supplications, they interpreted the Lord's silence on the matter as an indication that no obstacles were in their way, and that the door was open. Richard called the bishop's office the very next morning to accept the job and to say that he could start right away. On Sunday evening they celebrated their good fortune with a bottle of cheap sparkling wine from the local supermarket.

The next few weeks were filled with all the ordinary tasks of settling into the job and into their new home. They borrowed some money from their parents to tide them over for the first few months. They paid a deposit on a spacious flat in a large Victorian house on a leafy avenue on the west side of the city, barely a fifteen minute walk from the bishop's offices, and near to the municipal swimming pool and the bustling center of Helmsbridge. Sarah spent her time wisely visiting second-hand furniture shops to buy inexpensive items of furniture and household appliances that had not been supplied by the landlord. Now and again, over a cup of coffee, she scanned the "jobs vacant" section of the local newspaper to see if there were any jobs she might be suited to do. She wasn't idle during this period. In association with a local Christian charity, she spent one day every week preparing food at a homeless shelter, handing out soup, sandwiches and smiles to the homeless of this wealthy county town. When she returned home on these evenings, it wasn't hard for Richard to notice that she was in good spirits. It was clear that it was Sarah's vocation to help others less fortunate than her.

The months went by and Richard's duties became ever more mundane. He was given no real responsibility. Yes, he attended several administrative courses on church management, fiscal and parochial, and he did learn many things about the day-to-day running of a cathedral and diocesan office, but he began to feel that there was something missing in the daily ordinances. He began to wonder if he had indeed made the right choice in taking this job. Whenever he tried to bring up the subject of his career with the bishop, of his desire to grow spiritually and to find his true place in the ecclesia, Laidlaw was always too busy to give his attention to what Richard was trying to say. It also was a disappointment to him that of the many other clergymen he worked with, he had not managed to make any friends or to find a suitable spiritual mentor and confidante.

The atmosphere of the diocesan office was like that of a place of commerce—a bank, or even a private company, with endless rounds of meetings, deadlines, targets to meet, programs to devise, and schedules and minutes to be typed and distributed. He had begun to find the regime tiring, and felt he was drowning in a sea of tedious duties. He felt he wasn't in control of his life anymore. It was very different than being a graduate at Oxford, where he had been highly respected. He was just a little cog in the great machine that was the Church of England, and all in the name of God. However, this wasn't the Lord he wanted to serve. This was no Christ-centered church; it was a corporation, where profit and loss values were prioritized over spiritual pursuits, where financial spreadsheets were more important than the Bible, and where stocks and shares took precedence over charity and alms.

He had tried to offset the gloom of his position by snatching moments of personal prayer in the shadowy corners of the cathedral, but even these sessions, brief though they were, dwindled under the pressure of work. For that matter, he never saw anyone else take time out to pray. Yes, there were prayers in the mornings and evenings as church convention dictated, and sometimes before important meetings, but the latter were perfunctory and never lasted more than a few minutes. The rituals of high office were observed every day. The never-ending work of "religion" was carried out to the letter of the law, but where was the spirit? After six months of this, Richard was becoming sorely disheartened. He was rapidly descending into depression. There was no one from his past or present that he felt he could turn to, not even his beloved wife and soulmate Sarah. To unburden himself to her would seem like failure, so he kept his feelings to himself and kept up the pretense that everything was alright in his house of God. It wasn't long before he had to lie to her to maintain the charade. Guilt followed, growing more burdensome by the day. It felt like a heavy weight pressing down upon him. He was very close to a nervous breakdown. Of course, he prayed to God more than ever, but it was a one-sided business. It was the prayer of a desperate man, full of inconsistency and self-pity. He cried out to God like so many troubled men before him, and felt at times as if he was no longer intimate with Christ.

The word of God, the Holy Scriptures, seemed dead in his hands. The words that had in times past leapt off the page to fill his heart and soul with joy were now silent and barren. Dark feelings and thoughts filled his aching mind. The Book of Job, which had once been for him the very fountain of wisdom and hope, now seemed to speak only of despair. Richard felt that he too was in the Devil's ash pit without a hope of rising. Here he was at the very heart of one of England's most influential dioceses, serving a much respected bishop, yet the very core of his belief was eroding. He felt that his faith in Jesus was slowly crumbling into dust under the sheer monotony of his work.

This was happening while he was ostensibly serving God in his chosen ministry. The bright dreams that had once filled his soul before he came to Helmsbridge had faded, and he was drowning in his own brand of spiritual ennui.

Richard had almost given up hope of his situation changing for the better. In moments of despair, he had thoughts of leaving the church, just giving up and joining the secular world. However, one day he received a message from the bishop to come and see him without delay. Richard tapped nervously on the door of the bishop's office. The bishop's commanding voice shouted, "Enter!"

Richard went in and closed the door behind him. Without looking up from his papers, the bishop spoke. "Sit down Richard, I have some news for you."

Richard settled uneasily into the straight-backed leather chair that faced the bishop's large desk. Bishop Laidlaw continued for some moments to shuffle papers around his desk before picking up a pen and tapping it against a letter he was holding.

"Yes. Yes, I have some news that I hope you will consider good tidings. I have received a communiqué from an old college friend who is now the vicar of St. David's Church in Penrhos Bay. It seems he has an urgent need for a curate—lost the previous incumbent due to illness. Young fellow unfortunately passed away rather suddenly." He put the pen down, and with his elbows on the desk, clasped his hands together as if in prayer. He stared at Richard, a studious expression on his face.

"It's a stipendiary appointment, and the position comes with a little cottage I believe, apparently rent-free, a gift to the church from a deceased benefactor."

Richard began to understand the significance of the bishop's words, but all he could stammer out was "I . . . I . . . I see."

The bishop continued, "The vicar, Reverend Stannard . . . he's a good man. Perhaps not bishop material, but solid and even-tempered. He'll probably let you get on with the job without interference, if I know old Stanners."

Richard was just about to ask a question, when the bishop cut him short. "So Richard, I know you have been happy with us at Helmsbridge, and would be content to stay for many years yet, but sometimes the Lord moves us on. What I want is for you to take this job. It would help me repay an old debt, if you catch my drift?"

He paused only for a second or two before carrying on, "Well good, that's settled then. Good man Richard, I knew I could count on you, and take my word for it, these opportunities are rare."

He then added thoughtfully, ". . . and if it doesn't work out, you can always return here after a couple of years, and I would be glad to have you back. You have proved to be an extremely valued member of my team."

The bishop rose from his chair and held out his hand. Richard got up and had to lean over the desk to reach the bishop's outstretched hand.

"Speak to the administration department. They have all the details and your transfer papers are already drawn up."

The interview ended abruptly, and Richard was left standing and looking at the top of the bishop's head, which signaled that the session was over.

Richard closed the door behind him, trying not to slam it in his growing excitement. In the outer office, Richard felt like leaping and shouting for joy. Instead he simply looked up at the ceiling, put his hands together and silently formed the words on his lips: "Thank you, God!"

Chapter 16

Newcomers

Samuel was standing guard at the curate's cottage, just as the captain had instructed him.

Jusach, arriving late for his shift, had seen the angel from afar and quickly withdrew to a nearby vantage place on the hill where he could watch without being observed himself. The captain had told Samuel that a new curate was arriving that day with his wife. They were a young couple, and given the awful activities of the past weeks, it was prudent to keep a close eye on them in case of more demon interference. Samuel had not quite gotten over the death of Maynard Jones and the bitter part he had played in the whole affair. The pain was still raw, but the wise words of comfort that Bezalel had spoken to him were having a healing effect.

It was an unusually beautiful day for that time of year. The sun shone brightly in the blue sky and a fresh breeze came off the hills. Samuel loved the sea and was content to sit for hours simply watching the waves roll in at the distant beach beyond the promenade—it was music to his ears. There weren't many people out now, as the summer season had drawn to a close and most visitors to the town came only at weekends. Several of the smaller hotels and guest houses were closed until the spring. The cleaners had been into the cottage in the last few days and had removed a great deal of the personal belongings of the late curate. Books, clothes, and boxes of ornaments were disposed of into a garbage truck without care or ceremony. It saddened Samuel to see all that was left of a man's life being so carelessly discarded and disposed of, but he was reminded that humans come into the world with nothing and leave the same way, so perhaps he was just being sentimental because of the recent tragedies.

Samuel shifted his viewpoint from the garden wall to the roof, from where he could better see a white steamboat that was moving so slowly it seemed stuck on the horizon. He felt a light breeze tickle the back of his neck and raised his hand to scratch the spot. It happened a second time, and without thinking he did the same, thinking it might be a fly. When it happened the third time, Samuel spun around and was surprised to see another angel smiling at him.

"Hello brother, forgive my little trick, I'm in a playful mood."

Samuel stood up, and backing away, took a good look at his companion. His appearance was that of a handsome youth, tall and lean, yet with obvious vitality in his limbs. His hair was long and hung about his shoulders and shone with a golden sheen. His eyes were a sparkling blue and his full, sensuous lips were curved into a welcoming smile. Samuel was troubled by this stranger; despite his angelic appearance there was something odd about this manifestation.

"Friend," said the stranger, "why do you retreat from me? I give you no cause." Samuel was bemused by the conduct of the being before him.

"Who are you? Where are you from? For I know you not," quizzed Samuel.

"That's better, and thank for your kind enquiry, without which we cannot proceed on a sociable level."

Samuel found his partner's mannerisms and patterns of speech strange and somehow ancient.

"My name is Ganymede, and where am I from? Why, I originated in heaven just as you did my friend, created by the Almighty One, the Ancient of Days."

"You may have been created by the Lord, but who do you serve now? I see a vanity in you which none of my brothers possess."

Ganymede laughed. His merriment sounded like tiny silver bells.

"Does not the preacher say in Ecclesiastes, 'Vanity of vanities and everything is vanity, so how can we escape?' Is it my fault that I was created so beautiful?"

Samuel found the angel alluring and even entrancing, but remained on his guard because he knew this attractive being was not one of God's anointed.

He wisely answered, "Beauty is in the soul, not on the surface of things, and those things which are mere verisimilitudes will perish in the end times."

"Ah, the 'end times,' about which much is spoken in the Book of Revelations. But who can predict the future, my friend? Did not the Lord make us to be creatures of free will, masters of our own futures? Can we not rather assume that anything might happen, even a future of our own design?"

"That is blasphemy! The end of the world and of your kind has been ordained by God Almighty. I can see your seducing ways, Ganymede, extend beyond your form. Your words seduce and cajole, but I will not have any of it, you are false." Samuel retreated again to the ground and stood in the entrance to the cottage to bar Ganymede's way should he try to enter. Ganymede watched him with some amusement, then followed and rested upon the ground, standing just a few feet away.

This time it was Samuel who spoke, "What are you doing here? What do you want?"

Ganymede looked at him with amusement.

"I want for nothing. I am complete and I am content, and as for being here? Well is it not a delightful spot?" He paused before speaking again, "But I came to visit you my friend. My odious colleague Gathan bragged that he had pulverized and battered you . . . he is a brutish fiend." With a deep sigh he added, "He is suited to his tasks, I suppose, but there are some of us who are more civilized, more sensitive. You must not judge us all by one mindless, obnoxious beast!"

Samuel was becoming confused, and was at a loss how to deal with this demon, for demon he was, despite the angelic disguise.

Stepping closer to Samuel, and placing a hand upon his shoulder, Ganymede asked, "Are you quite recovered? I have commanded that Gathan does not come near you. You need not fear him in future, I have seen to that for you."

Samuel snapped, "I don't need your protection, I have His!"

"Oh, don't be so churlish, I am only trying to help."

Samuel stared at Ganymede with anger.

"Samuel, don't look at me like that. It makes me feel unwelcome. Truly, I mean you no harm."

Samuel blurted out, "All demons are liars!"

Ganymede chuckled, "Only you can say that, but what if I say 'all demons are liars,' where does that argument take us? Into doubtful disputations, I should think. I cannot answer for my confederates, but speaking honestly is part of my nature."

"I don't believe a word you say." Samuel's voice revealed how agitated and anxious he was.

"Alas, even when such as I speak the truth you do not believe, how sad that is. You must be more discerning if you are to make a success of your assignment on Earth."

Samuel was exasperated, and wondered if he should simply attack Ganymede, but his recent clash with Gathan made him hesitate. Just at that moment, the captain appeared behind Ganymede. Samuel was greatly relieved to see his superior.

Without turning and still smiling at Samuel, Ganymede spoke, "Greetings Bezalel. We have not crossed paths for such a long while. How good it is for us to meet again."

The captain stepped threateningly between Samuel and the demon.

"Oh come now, I meant your friend no harm or injury. You know me better than that, Bezalel!"

The captain moved closer to Ganymede and Samuel saw, for an instant, the smile on Ganymede's face change into a frown, but it was not genuine, he was still playacting.

"Do you threaten me, Bezalel?" exclaimed Ganymede with amusement. "Have you forgotten we were once the dearest of companions and swore to be friends forever?"

The captain was silent, but remained resolute.

"I am sure you have not forgotten that I always bested you in our swordplay together."

"That was a long time ago, Ganymede, in another age when . . ." Bezalel stopped, unable to continue. He had an expression of great pity in his eyes.

Samuel looked from his captain to the other angel.

Ganymede finished the sentence, "When we both shared a faith in our mutual God."

"Yes, and before you chose to betray Him!" There was a note of sorrow in Bezalel's voice.

"I betrayed no one, my old friend. I simply saw what you all still fail to see, and what my Master had the courage to face and challenge: that Yahweh has corrupted creation by raising man to an exalted place in heaven and above us. We who were the Elect of God, the only created beings one with God, have been degraded to mere servants of these ridiculous humans."

The captain was about to draw his sword when Ganymede rose in the air.

"Put your sword away, I am unarmed. You disgrace yourself, Bezalel. Do you not see how your own passion has been spoilt by the absurd quest of your Messiah! Redeeming the human race! Why, the majority of these pathetic individuals want nothing to do with your Christ and your Holy God. You will see the truth one day, and then perhaps you will join my Lord and we can be friends once again."

"That will never be. I order you to depart, Ganymede. Do not return, for we have no need for conference with your kind. I warn you, Ganymede, next time I will strike, for you are my sworn enemy."

Ganymede seemed to ignore the captain's oath and gazed past him, speaking to Samuel. "I think you and I should be on the same side Samuel. Let these brutes like Gathan and Bezalel fight it out amongst themselves. Whichever Lord they serve they remain brutish and boorish. Goodbye my friend, until we meet again." Ganymede signaled to Jusach hidden against the hill.

"Come fellow, it seems we are not wanted here." In an instant, the demons vanished.

"Did you know of the other one?" asked the captain.

"No, sir. I fear that Ganymede had me hypnotized with his subtle power."

"That's Ganymede alright, you describe him well."

The captain turned to Samuel, who was visibly shaken by his encounter with Ganymede. He grabbed his shoulders with both hands. "Are you alright? Do not ever underestimate the foul Ganymede. His appearance is meant to deceive. There aren't many like him. He emulates his own master the Father of Lies. His evil is far worse than anything Gathan could throw at you! And that is not his real name, just an affectation. But he spoke the truth when he said we were friends. His name was Andreas, but now he has a despicable name given to him by Satan, and that name is known only to a small group of the dark host. There is nothing of Andreas left in that twisted body. Pray to God, Samuel, that he does not return."

Samuel looked at his captain and asked, "Does the arrival of Gathan and now Ganymede mean that something terrible is going to happen here?"

The captain frowned. "I don't know Samuel, but their presence probably means that Rimmon, one of the High Lords of Darkness, is also here. We must be vigilant at all times."

Chapter 17

A New Life

Richard and Sarah's move to Penrhos Bay went well, with no major mishaps. Their few personal belongings and items of second-hand furniture arrived on time in a small moving van. It took the men less than an hour to carry their things up the narrow path and into their new home. Sarah could not believe her eyes when she saw the little cottage for the first time. They had strolled up from the station in order to save the taxi fare and take in the sights of their new hometown. It was a beautiful, crisp winter's morning, and the sun, though low in the sky, felt warm on their bright faces. They were happy; this genuinely felt like the start of something new and good, especially after all of Richard's miseries at Helmsbridge.

The quaint cottage was literally built into a huge cleft cut out of the hard rock of the hillside. Made of stone and slate, and partly covered in ivy and flowering climbers, it blended into the steep face of the Great Ulm, which was the ancient name for the hill. The cottage looked down from its prominent position on the seaside town spread out far below. The wide sandy beaches would not have been out of place in the South of France. There was a wide promenade and an old iron post and girder pier that reached out into the deep waters of the Irish Sea. It truly was a beautiful place to live. Across the rooftops of nearby houses and the white painted hotels that lined the town front, large predatory seagulls swooped down on unsuspecting tourists, who were suddenly relieved of a bag of hot fries, a half-eaten sandwich, or an ice cream cone, snatched violently from a child's hands.

Beyond the rows of hotels, the swelling sea rolled and broke, wave on wave, onto the sandy shore. The pier was the main attraction with its café, small shops, and stalls selling all kinds of seaside bric-a-brac. It had been built in the heyday of the late Victorian period, when day trippers came by boat and train from the dirty suburbs and slums of Liverpool and Manchester. They came by the thousands every Saturday afternoon, in cheap summer suits and dresses, escaping from the miseries of their hovels and putting all memories of the working week behind them. When the summer weather was kind, the young lovers among them would sleep together on the beach all night. The trippers flooded onto the wide walkways and promenades, laughing with each other, listening to the brass band, and eagerly taking in everything the town had to offer. All enjoyed the gaiety and fun, even if only for a few hours, before traipsing back on Sunday evening to their grimy streets and another week of hard labor.

Those times were gone, but the promenade, pier, and hotels were still popular as ever, except that the majority visiting the town now were not day trippers, but retired middle-class ladies, aged and infirm, widowed, enjoying their sunset years without their much-loved husbands. In contrast to these genteel females, there was in recent times a new influx of visitors. Young men and women arrived daily, economic migrants from Eastern Europe, looking for jobs and a better way of life in the United Kingdom. Strange faces and foreign tongues were now seen and heard along the streets of Penrhos Bay and in the night-clubs, bars, and public houses.

Richard wanted to carry Sarah over the threshold, but she ran away laughing up the front path to the door. They pushed it open and peered into the dark shadows of the hallway.

"Oh Richard, I feel so happy! I am sure that this move is the best thing that could ever, ever happen to us."

Richard stepped in first, and Sarah, holding his hand, followed in silence, as if they were entering a sacred place for the first time. It seemed already that the cottage, this new home for them, was to be a haven of peace, a place where their own love could at last flourish.

Ascending the small staircase, they found an uncarpeted landing which led to two small bedrooms and a tiny bathroom. Both the bedrooms had the original black iron coal fireplaces. Sarah's mind was already running ahead to happy romantic times that they would spend here together, tenderly locked in each other's arms, watching the flames from the fire.

The cottage had been cleaned. The bedroom with the double bed was sparsely furnished, but would be comfortable enough for them. Sarah went to the small window and looked out.

"Which room shall be ours?" Richard asked, leaving it to his wife to choose.

"Oh Richard, this room please. How wonderful it is! It has a view of the sea and the far cliffs on the other side of the bay. It'll be lovely to wake up to that view every day!" she exclaimed.

"Even on dark and gloomy mid-winter days?" he teased.

"Every day is going to be wonderful here," she said, with obvious thrill in her voice.

Richard laughed and put his arms around her and hugged her, keeping her close to him. Then he swung her gently around and they collapsed on the bed.

Later, they unpacked some of the boxes that the moving men had left in the front room downstairs. Richard spent much of his time in the bedroom stuffing clothes into the wardrobe and the high chest of drawers, claiming the top drawers for himself. Sarah was busy in the tiny kitchen filling up the cupboards with crockery and tins of food.

She came to the foot of the stairs and shouted up, "Come down, I've made some tea and I have some nice cookies to eat."

"Be right down."

Sitting at the little kitchen table, they sipped their tea and smiled at each other. They were content and blissfully happy.

"Oh, what time is it?" Sarah suddenly said, "We mustn't be late for our first meeting with Reverend Stannard."

Richard looked at her with amusement. "We've plenty of time, and anyway it's not as if he's a bishop!"

* * *

Richard and Sarah shared a late afternoon tea with Reverend Stannard at the rectory. He had made them welcome and seemed to be a kind soul, if a bit aloof in his manner. In the course of conversation,

he told them that he had never married, but had consciously chosen to be "wedded" to the church, muttering something about St. Paul's admonitions in the
New Testament. He explained that Richard's duties
would not be too onerous, and that they would indeed be made lighter if Sarah would be prepared to
help out now and again. Sarah said she would only
be too happy to help, and was looking forward to that
side of their life at St. David's. Stannard elaborated
further, explaining that her assistance would be very
useful, as some of the problems he had been asked
to tackle in times past were, he thought, not suited to
a man. Stannard added that the previous incumbent,
also a bachelor, was not gifted in the delicate business of ministering to women. Richard, accepting a
proffered ginger cookie, tentatively asked about the
former curate. However, Reverend Stannard merely
expressed his regret and sorrow at the unfortunate
death of the young man, adding that the Lord's will
be done. He then indicated with a sweeping gesture
of his hand that this particular subject was closed,
and that he did not want to discuss the matter further.

After afternoon tea, Stannard gave them a tour of
the church. There was a small hall used by the Mothers' Union on Tuesdays, and on Wednesday evenings by a small Bible group made up mostly of old
women. This particular gathering had been disbanded
after the death of the late curate. Stannard said that
perhaps Richard could reconvene the group. The ladies did not expect deep teaching—simple spiritual
homilies would suffice. Their real motive for coming
along was for tea and cake and to catch up on local
gossip.

"Be advised, young man, all you have to do is stay around for one cup of tea after the lesson and then nip off. They won't even notice that you're gone and they will lock up the hall."

The well-equipped and neat kitchen was next on the tour. After this, they went out into the back hall, which was surprisingly cold. Stannard beckoned to them to follow him up a winding bare timber staircase to an upper room and toilets. Near the toilets, a grubby towel hung loose on a wooden roller. The upper room had no floor coverings; the varnished floorboards were dusty and in need of a thorough clean. The room was of a good size for meetings, or even games. It was evident that the room had not been used for a very long time. Richard ventured to ask what this room was used for. Stannard made a gesture of dismay, saying, "Oh, nothing really, health and safety regulations, and I believe the intricacies of local fire regulations, prohibit its use."

They followed Stannard back down the stairs to the cold hall and then through the big oak doors into the church itself. Standing in the nave, Sarah exclaimed with delight that it was indeed an impressive building. She inquired if it was very old. Stannard motioned them to the small table replete with leaflets. He picked up a leaflet and handed it to Richard, saying, "Here, read this. It gives you the entire history of the church, etcetera. I wrote it myself."

Richard handed it to Sarah.

Sarah noticed that the offering box on one of the stone columns was broken. Stannard watched her walk over to inspect it more closely. Before she asked, he said, "Yes, dreadful incident. It was broken into a couple of months ago. The thief made a real mess of the box, with a hammer and chisel, I should think. Inexplicably, the money was still in the box; must have been disturbed by someone or something before finishing the job. Mary, my housekeeper, whom you met earlier, noticed the state of the offertory later in the evening when she came to lock up the church." He then said rather gruffly, "If I had my way, I'd keep the building shut and open it only for services."

Richard exchanged a glance with Sarah.

They walked up the aisle together, and Stannard and Richard genuflected in front of the altar. Stannard indicated the main points, including the vestry and a small chapel off the south transept. Stepping through the "Devil's Doorway" situated at the side of the church building, they walked outside. The streetlights were just coming on as the sun began to set behind the gray hills. The exterior of the church had neatly cut lawns, and most surprisingly, a "pay and display" car park, which had several notices prominently displayed warning drivers that any vehicles left without permission or payment of the required fee would be booted, and a release fee of one hundred pounds would be charged.

Richard asked how it was that there was a public car park in the church grounds.

"A simple explanation will suffice. It's one of my money-making schemes. I charge for the privilege of letting the townspeople park their vehicles here. It's popular because it is right at the center of town and very close to the shops. I get a very good yield, which comes in handy for odd expenses here and there. Another of my schemes, which unfortunately is in abeyance until the bishop gets around to approving it, is to allow the telephone company Vodafone to erect a mast on top of the tower."

Another glance of surprise passed between husband and wife.

"Wouldn't the local planning department object to that?" asked Richard.

"As far as the town planners are concerned, the church is to all practical purposes exempt from planning law, which gives me free rein to do almost anything."

Walking on past the north corner of the church, they passed the exact spot where the curate had fallen violently, ending his all too brief life. Stannard hesitated at the place, looking down for an instant, then hurried on, quickly stepping over the accursed spot.

They had now arrived at the main gate to the church grounds. Stannard said that he hoped they had enjoyed the guided tour. He pointed towards High Street and beyond. "That's the best way back. I am sure you have many things to sort out at your new home and such. Take the weekend off, and come and see me in my office on Monday morning about 10am. That will suit me, and we will go over your duties." Richard and Sarah felt as if they were children being dismissed.

"Shall we not come to church on Sunday, I mean surely . . ." Richard's question was cut short.

"No, no. Please, there is no need. On Monday then, goodbye," and with that remark, the vicar walked briskly away in the direction of the rectory.

Nonplussed, Richard and Sarah looked at each other with consternation.

"What a strange man."

"Harmless enough though, I think," said Richard.

"Well, I think we should enjoy our weekend off to the fullest. How about a trek up the Ulm tomorrow morning? We can have our very own 'church' at the top of the hill with the sheep and goats as our first congregation."

Linking her arm in his, she drew a dazed and bewildered husband into the busy High Street and headed for home.

Chapter 18

The Box under the Bed

The first few months went by slowly, but Richard and Sarah enjoyed the time together. They had a lot of time on their hands, and just as Reverend Stannard had said, Richard's duties were light. The weekly schedule consisted of conducting morning and evening prayers, visitation to local hospitals and care homes, and chairing the odd assembly at local Church of England schools. A couple of evenings a week he led a Bible study for a small group of older ladies, and once in awhile was asked to preach when Stannard was out of town. His other duties included officiating at a few weddings and christenings and one funeral, in none of which Stannard showed the slightest interest. Even Christmas came and went without any fuss. Sarah thought Stannard was more Scrooge-like than Scrooge himself, as he said he'd rather not be disturbed over the festive season. Sarah said that Stannard was the epitome of humbug, and that he ought to be boiled in his own Christmas pudding. They both tried to brighten up the church and organized a carol service and a midnight mass, but only a few souls came. Richard and Sarah, to keep their own spirits up, attended a lovely carol service at the Methodist Church across the way.

Sarah headed up the Mothers and Toddlers group on Tuesday mornings, but it was poorly attended and on some occasions none came, especially if the weather was bad. Sarah had approached Stannard about securing some funds to buy some new play equipment for the children, but he had told her brusquely that there were no funds available, and anyway, any request of a financial nature should be submitted by her husband, as she had no official position in the church.

There was no outreach ministry of which to speak. No young people's meetings or clubs. Even the local Cub Scouts and Guides groups met elsewhere. In short, there was no spiritual investment in the local community at all. Richard had begun to think that this was by design, as if the vicar had reduced everything down to mere formality: weddings, christenings, funerals, and short Sunday services, in order to suit himself. Richard's initial enthusiasm was quickly dampened by Stannard. His suggestions for new programs were always met with prevarication and procrastination on Stannard's part, and no amount of requests and reminders by Richard had any effect upon the stubborn will of the vicar. If it was not for his wife, Richard would have become disillusioned by the untenable situation in which he once again found himself.

However, Sarah had wisdom—her price was far above rubies—and always reminded Richard that he should plan for the long term and not be too quickly discouraged. She was beginning to know when her husband was becoming depressed over something. Having come up against the vicar herself over church matters, she knew exactly how Richard must be feeling. In order to turn misfortune into good, she directed him to study more, especially when he seemed to be at a loose end. Take full advantage of the situation; after all, she joked, Stannard can't live forever.

"I am sure, Darling, that we shan't have this gift of free time forever, so let's use it wisely and prepare for the future. Go on now, take yourself up to the study and pray to the Lord for deliverance from this absurd situation. He knows you are frustrated. Seek His will. He has a plan for you, and it will prove to be wonderful. Be patient and redeem the time. Study the Scriptures. I'll call you when tea is ready."

She gave him a kiss on the cheek and then pushed him playfully to the stairs.

Richard sighed, "I love you. I really, really do."

"I know you do." She smiled. "Go on, get on with it!"

On days when the weather was fine, they would pack up a picnic and wander up the hill to the summit of the Great Ulm. Carrying on beyond the tram car sheds and tourist center, they would seek a quiet spot overlooking the Irish Sea and the sleeping isle of Anglesey. They spent many idyllic hours on the hill, young, free, and happy.

On one occasion Richard, with half a sandwich in his hands, gesticulated towards the wide expanse of water below them, "You know what, I've just had a brilliant idea! We should get a boat and go sailing together. Not a yacht, mind you, just a little dinghy. In fact, I saw one down on the beach for sale for only £250! Ready to sail, the sign said."

"Richard, you're a mad romantic fool . . . a boat?"

"I'm sure we could afford it, and . . ."

Sarah interrupted him with a grim expression on her face. "There's one big obstacle to overcome first, Richard." She said, seriously.

"Oh what, come on, don't dash my dream boat on the rocks! What is it?"

"I can't swim!" she confessed.

"You can't? I don't believe it. Why didn't you tell me? I mean, a husband ought to know if his wife can swim or not."

"I don't know. We've always been a long way from the sea, I suppose."

Richard's face was all glum. Then suddenly, he laughed out loud, and holding his sides, rolled over and over on the grass, unable to contain his amusement.

Sarah grabbed hold of him. "What is it? What's so funny? Tell me!"

Richard looked up at Sarah. "I've just remembered I can't swim either!"

"What? You can't?"

"I can't swim, not a yard! My parents never taught me."

They lay back on the grass holding hands and watching the clouds drift by. It was a time of marital bliss. All the problems of the past year or so seemed far away now, and although Richard was uncertain about his ministry and what God wanted him to do, he felt content enough and knew that no time is wasted in the service of the Lord, no matter how inactive. Sarah was always quick to remind him that "His ways" are, after all, not our ways.

During a normal week, Richard did not see much of Stannard. Their schedules always seemed to be drawn up so that they were apart. Perhaps another part of Stannard's peculiar scheme of things? Their weekly meeting on Fridays was perfunctory. Stannard wrote the agenda and acted as chairman, maintaining a ludicrous formality even though it was just the two of them. Even the Sunday service was a perfunctory, hasty affair. Stannard always arrived just in time and quickly departed as soon as duty had been done. Richard had reached the point at which he could not wait to get out of the Friday meetings, so he silently consented to all the vicar's actions, few that there were.

Whilst Richard was unhappy about his lack of spiritual duties, he acquiesced to the status quo because there was no way out of it that he could see. Who on Earth could he ask for advice? Stannard himself was supposed to be his mentor.

Once a month, Stannard attended the local diocesan meeting at the Bangor Cathedral office. On one occasion Richard asked, without any hope of getting a "yes," if he might attend. He was greatly surprised when the vicar agreed that he could accompany him to the next meeting. Perhaps Richard could make contact with someone at the monthly meeting that he could confide in, but who? It didn't take long for Richard to find out that most of the Clerics who attended, and this included the bishop, who was far advanced in years, were all copies and parodies of Stannard.

Meanwhile, at home alone, Sarah was enjoying "prettifying" the cottage. She had taken down the old dusty curtains, bought some material from the charity shop in the town, and made attractive new curtains. With windows cleaned inside and out, the paths swept, the rose bushes clipped, and the small lawn cut short with shears, the whole place was being transformed and was beginning to feel like home.

A thorough clean of the kitchen was needed. Even though the cottage had supposedly been cleaned before they moved in, there was grime upon grime in the oven, and she was certain that the previous tenant, the late curate, had not bothered to do any cleaning himself.

Late one afternoon, she was vacuuming in all the corners, cupboards, and under the beds, making a final attempt to get everything spotless, when the head of the vacuum cleaner banged against an object under the bed. She got down on her hands and knees to see what it was, and saw a box. Crawling into the recess under the bed, she could see it was a wooden box of some sort. Tugging at the heavy box, she at last managed to pull it out.

It was quite a large container. About two feet square and twelve inches high, it was made of sturdy varnished wood panels. It looked old and had obviously seen a lot of use, given the number of dents and chips in the surface of the wood. On the top were the initials MJ in black lettering. The box was secured with a small metal lock. It was then that she remembered that when she was cleaning out the kitchen drawers she had found a small brass key. She had left it in the drawer along with other odd bits and pieces, and not simply thrown it out, just in case. She went downstairs to get the key, and rather excitedly wondered what she might find within the mysterious box. She held the key at the lock, then hesitated. A prick of conscience interrupted her thoughts. What right had she to open the box? It should be returned to the owner un-tampered with. Her excitement waned and her curiosity quickly subsided as the disappointment set in. It would be wrong of her. She stood up, placed the key carefully on the dressing table, and went downstairs.

Chapter 19

The Journal

Later, when Richard had returned from the church, Sarah asked if he knew the previous curate's name. Richard replied that he thought it was Maynard Jones. "Why?"

"I've got something to show you. It's upstairs in our bedroom." Richard was intrigued and wondered what it could be. In the bedroom, Sarah explained how she had found the box, and that her thought was to open it straight away, before thinking the better of it. They sat on the bed together and looked at the box. Sarah turned the small key over in her hand. Richard spoke. "We should, by rights, hand it over to Stannard. He could forward it on to Jones' next of kin."

"He doesn't have any. Don't you remember the vicar saying as much?"

"Yes, I do recall that now, you're right," said Richard.

"Richard, what shall we do? I think giving it to Stannard would be a mistake. He'd probably dump it with the garbage."

They sat in silence until Richard suddenly stood up, and holding out his hand said, "Okay, give me the key. I'll open it. Whatever we find, we'll treat with the respect it deserves, and seeing what is inside, we can more easily decide what to do with it, agreed?"

Richard placed the box onto the bed and said, pointing at the engraved initials, "MJ—Maynard Jones, I presume." He inserted the key and removed the lock, then lifted the lid to reveal the contents. The box was filled to the top with all kinds of personal memorabilia, letters, papers, photographs, and small books. They removed the contents carefully and laid them out on the bed. They both felt rather sheepish and guilty that they were stealing a look into a stranger's private keepsakes. The chest contained several books, obviously old judging by their condition, but precious to the owner of the box. There was a small school hymn book. Dog-eared and ink stained, the fly leaf contained an inscription in neat lettering.

"Maynard Jones, Form 3B" and in brackets after this it simply stated, "[aged 12]"

There was a hardback copy of Richmal Crompton's "Still William." Inside the cover, there was a badly-drawn sketch of the main character "William," and underneath was written the words *"My Hero."* On the opposite page, in spidery disjointed letters, was written, *"This book belongs to M. Jones Esquire, Finchley, London, England, World, Universe."*

Other children's books and comics were also preserved here. Jones was obviously someone who was keen to hang on to his childhood, or at least remember it with affection. There were also some holiday postcards in the box, and holiday photos depicting different people, perhaps his parents and relatives? One small black-and-white photo featured a couple standing against the iron railings of a seaside pier. Sarah looked at it more closely and said excitedly, "Look! Richard, if I am not mistaken, that is Penrhos

Bay Pier. It is! You can see the Grand Hotel in the background!"

"So maybe he came here as a child on school vacations?"

Amongst the contents of the box there was a small plastic container with a medal inside. Richard removed it and showed it to Sarah. On the back, it was engraved with Jones' name and the date. It was awarded for winning a cup in a school competition for rugby.

"I wonder what position he played?" said Sarah, thoughtfully.

Sifting through the papers, Sarah found a photograph. It was of the rugby team in full uniform, shirts, boots, and all. The photo depicted all the members of the team. Flipping the photo over, Sarah saw that the young Jones had written in pencil the names of his fellow players, in order from top to bottom and left to right. The third person in the top row was identified as "me." The name of "Roger" was encircled. The front row crouched down on one knee, and the boy at the center held a large silver cup. A short stocky man, probably the sports coach, stood to one side, smiling, obviously proud of his boys' cup final achievement.

Sarah turned back to the photo and traced her finger along to a blond haired, tall boy with both arms crossed. It was Jones.

"Look Richard, this one here is Maynard Jones."

She held her finger against the picture pointing to Jones.

"And the boy beside him is Roger!" She explained the circled name.

"I guess they were probably close friends."

Richard gazed at the figure intently. "He seems to be a fit and healthy young man and tall for his age. Strange to imagine he died from an illness."

They carried on looking through the personal effects. There were various letters in bundles, which they both agreed not to read. Some more photographs of unknown friends and family, pictures of college groups, happy smiling students enjoying halcyon days. There was a city guide and a map of Barcelona and a ticket to the Sagrada Familia, the famously unfinished church by the Spanish Architect Antonio Gaudi.

At the bottom of the box was a black, leather-bound book. Richard lifted it out of the box and opened it to the first page. On it was written, *"This is the Journal of Maynard Jones, Curate of St. David's Church, Penrhos Bay."* It was dated two years earlier. The text was written in a neat script in black pen. Each page was headed by a date. Leafing through the pages, he saw that it was not compiled on every day, and often the gaps missed several days. Richard silently read the first few pages. As Sarah watched her husband's face, she saw it darken and grow sad. Richard carefully and slowly closed the book.

"Let's put his things back in the box."

Sarah picked up those items close to her and placed them back into the wooden box.

Richard did the same, but left the journal beside him on the bed.

"Sarah, after dinner I think I shall spend some time in prayer and then I aim to read the journal. I feel we are meant to know what it holds."

Sarah intuitively knew by Richard's manner and tone of voice that she should agree to her husband's request without question. She rose from the bed, bent low to kiss him on the top of his head, and quietly went downstairs.

The early pages of the journal were written in a remarkably neat writing style that enjoyed the use of flourishes and curlicues. Obviously, Maynard Jones took great care in forming the words on the page. The margins were littered with clever little drawings of various things that were mentioned in the script. The journal started at the time that Jones was made curate of St. David's, when he had moved to Penhros Bay from London.

Various entries described the little cottage on the hill and how delighted Jones had been in being billeted there. There were sketches of flowers and birds and one very good drawing of the head of a goat with large horns and devilish eyes. The accompanying notes detailed the walks taken on the Great Ulm or on the beach at West Shore. Everything was to be enjoyed. It was clear from the entries that he was a sensitive, thoughtful and kindly soul.

Later in the journal, he also recorded comments on passages that he had read in the Old and New Testaments. His considerations of the verses did not reveal deep revelations of spiritual truths, but certainly showed a thorough working knowledge of scripture and how it applied to modern man. Jones was fond of using abbreviations in the journal. Richard began to pick up some of the meanings of these abbreviated words. "STD" was obviously Reverend Stannard. "RG" was his friend Roger, still living in London. "SD" was St. David's Church, and "TO" was short for time off, which he always followed with an exclamation mark. The only entry Richard was puzzled by was "A." In the more recent sections of the diary, Jones made single statements, usually at the end of a day, of which the following was typical: "A not here today, thank God." Or "A here again, a most unwelcome visitor." "A visited me during the night—worse than a demon!" "Talked to STD about 'A' but got little sympathy from the white-walled sepulcher." Jones had written under this particular entry, "I am coming to believe that STD actually hates me!"

In the winter months, Jones had begun to write more and more about his growing feelings of despondency. Richard stopped reading for a moment and recalled his days in Helmsbridge and his own pain and disillusion.

The regular comments on daily Bible studies became scarce and were replaced by musings about his spiritual state. There were scraps about unanswered prayers and notes referring to "unfinished tasks" presumably set for him by Stannard. Little by little, Richard began to chart the demise of the man, not just spiritually, but mentally and physically.

On one page he had written a single entry in large separated capital letters, in total contrast to the first sentences which were scribed in orderly handwriting. Richard could almost feel the pressure of the pen on the page.

"Results confirmed—A is here to stay!"

The entry was underlined several times in an erratic way that spoke of high emotional conflict. Richard was still bemused by "A." Who was he, or she? It was Sarah who supplied the answer as they talked about the journal one evening. She just came out with it as they stopped to consider the meaning.

"Richard, I think the poor man had AIDS!"

Richard looked shocked. He scanned the other entries on the previous pages where "A" appeared.

"I think you may be right. If that's the case, it would explain so much I didn't understand."

"It surely does explain Jones' comments about Stannard," remarked Sarah.

'Then I guess he was a practising homosexual?" said Richard, sadly.

"And Roger I suppose was his life partner? Their friendship survived long after school days," Sarah conjectured. Richard had a strange, bemused expression on his face.

"But how did he get all the way through Bible College and being appointed curate in the first place? I just don't get it."

"Richard you are a trifle naïve. Didn't you meet any gay students in your time at Oxford?" she asked.

"What, in the college?"

Sarah raised her eyebrows as if to say 'yes'.

"No, I don't believe I did," said Richard, a bit peeved. "What about the church teaching . . . proscription on homosexuality!" Richard exclaimed.

"What about it indeed? Do you think the church's prohibitions stop anyone from loving Jesus, even gay people?" she said with some passion. "We are in the twenty-first century, after all, the church doesn't burn gays at the stake anymore."

Richard was pensive and silent.

"Richard what about that guy from Exeter, Paul-what's-his-name? He used to hang around with Giles. You remember Giles, surely?"

"Yes, I remember Giles. We did a workshop together on 'Needs in the Community.' Nice guy, very bright."

"Yes . . . Paul and Giles?"

"Come on, they were just good friends!" However, the more he pondered it, the more he saw that Sarah was right. He was being painted into a corner, as usual, by his clever wife.

"Wow, I am a bit naïve, aren't I?" confessed Richard.

"Just a bit darling, but it's an attractive trait in you!"

Sarah continued with her own reading. Richard put down the journal and started to think about the diary in a new light. After a few moments of silence he spoke to no one in particular.

"He could have helped the man in his desperate hour of need!"

Sarah looked up inquiringly.

"Stannard," said Richard.

"Yes, he should have . . . I am beginning to get very worried about our Reverend Mr. Stannard."

Over the next few days Richard read the journal with newly enlightened eyes and began to understand the sad life of Maynard Jones. A man who had loved God, who was devout in many ways, and yet was plagued and hounded by strong feelings of guilt. From the entries, Richard could see that a lot of Jones' problems originated in his early years, in particular during the time spent at boarding schools, away from his parents and family. Cruel regimes were the order of the day at these places, and all English boarding schools were founded upon the principle 'spare the rod and you spoil the child,' resulting in hard and unrelenting discipline and inflexible rules and regulations that had to be obeyed whatever the circumstances. One of Jones' entries, which reminisced about his friendship with Roger, read, "The lives of young boys at public schools are for the most part unholy and filled with cruelty. The whole sorry mess should be done away with." The final entries became caricatures of the earlier pages. Words often hastily scrawled became an unintelligible scribble so that Richard could not make sense of some of the passages. The meandering style was not focused anymore, but indicated his chaotic state of mind, and Richard began to think that it was also a sad reflection of his whole life. It was a great pity for it to end in such a melancholy way, with no one on hand to help. Richard began to feel a deep sympathy for Jones and was sorry not to have known him. Perhaps they could have been friends.

One of the final passages read, "Surprisingly lucid today, despite feeling wretched. Have read my Bible and prayed and have experienced a peace not felt for a long time. Have come to a conclusion regarding my spiritual state, and it now seems a lot clearer to me. Through no fault of my own, I was thrown into despicable situations, especially the one I found myself in at Chiltern's Boys School. Had it not been for Roger and his courageous love for me, I think I would have happily jumped off the rooftop. I can see now I was born with a certain proclivity, but whether over the formative years it was nature or nurture I guess doesn't matter. The die was cast for me. The absence of my mother for most of my life, attendance at male-dominated schools, even the graduation to university life and the clergy all "cemented" in me a particular bent, like a brick set into a wall. Roger and I enjoyed happy times living together in London, but I was becoming aware that adulthood could never compare with the pure sublime joy of childhood companionship. As a man, the fumbling in bed in the dark served only to gratify desire, and after satiation what remained was only the desire for more. The essence of true love and affection was lost in my manhood amidst the sordid trappings of sexual desire and lust. I began to believe it could never be regained or revisited. We can never turn the clock back. When I shared my thoughts with Roger, he became moody and offish, so I didn't talk about it anymore and we began to grow apart. That is why I came here, to get away and to find myself again. I can't remember which holy saint said truth can only come out of deep suffering and total surrender to God. I am beginning to understand this. I know now what true love is. The desires of the flesh can only inhibit and bar the way to true love. The human spirit must break free from these entrapments."

Richard was amazed at the clarity of thought and read on.

"I fully comprehend now what St. Paul meant when he said he would prefer that Disciples of Christ should not marry. I have read and re-read the Epistles over and over again to get to the heart of the truth. I know the pain will return, but I am not afraid anymore. I have bought the field and have the pearl in my hand. Thank God, I am out of the clouds of obscurity and can see my way forward. I know there is no cure for my unhealthy state; there will never be a return to normal life. This dreadful disease will eventually reduce me to a pitiable condition. In some ways, the suffering will cleanse me. But still, I don't want to experience the final hours of torment that I know will come. My flesh is afraid, but my spirit is strong, yet I pray and ask the Lord to take my soul and spare me from such an agonising death.

Jones continued this period of circumspection in his journal, and Richard felt close to the man. "The only way for me to truly live is to shed this body and return to Jesus as a spirit, where I shall be free of disease, free of all the petty vanities of love, and where one day Roger and I may share a peace and joy that passes all understanding. I know He understands me and that He will forgive this prodigal son, soon to return home."

Richard, placing the journal down, pictured in his mind the image of the Father waiting patiently at the gate for the prodigal son. Closing his eyes, he prayed that Maynard Jones was indeed at rest with Jesus in Heaven. He smiled as he thought to himself, recalling Jesus' words to the Sadducees when they sought to entrap him with a ridiculous question, "There are no marriages, no husbands and wives, no shades of relationship one way or another, no homosexuals in Heaven, only resurrected souls whose eternal purpose is to worship the living God."

Chapter 20

Things Done in the Dark

Sarah struggled up the hill with the shopping bags. Quite a few times, she had to rest to catch her breath before starting again. Samuel walked by her side. He had been given charge of keeping watch over both her and Richard. This was one occasion in which he wished that he was human and could give Sarah assistance with her load. The weather had improved of late and there were the first signs of spring appearing as buds began to show on the bushes and trees.

Richard had gone to Chester for a church conference and wouldn't be back until late, which gave Sarah plenty of time to prepare a special dinner. She had bought some candles, two pieces of steak and a bottle of expensive wine, not that they could afford these luxuries. However, they had been so happy as of late that she wanted to give him a good homecoming. Despite Stannard's odd ways of running a church and parish, she and Richard had much for which to thank God. She was looking forward to his return and to celebrating their good fortune.

As she approached the front gate of her cottage, the old woman who lived next door peered out through the curtains of her front room. Sarah put down the bags to find her house key. The old woman came out. "Hello Mrs. Williams, how are you today?" said Sarah.

"Well enough, my dear . . . I just came out to tell you that you had a visitor today."

"Oh? Probably someone for Richard I should imagine."

The old woman grinned and said, "No . . . he made a point of asking for you . . . except he said 'Sarah Finchley.'"

The use of her maiden name surprised Sarah.

"I told him that there was no Sarah Finchley in these whereabouts, and I told him that your name is Benton, Mrs. Sarah Benton, married to the local vicar."

"What did he want? Did he give a name at all, or a message?" she asked.

"No, I didn't like the look of him to be honest—we don't get many of his type around here."

"What do you mean, Mrs. Williams, 'his type?'"

"Oh, I don't mean to be offensive; it's just that colored people aren't so common in this town. Anyway, I told him that if he wanted to talk to Mr. Benton, the vicar, he should call at the church. I gave him directions."

Sarah had to grab the wall to steady herself as she felt a rush of blood go to her head. The nosey old woman saw the reaction in Sarah's face.

"Something wrong, my dear? Not bad news, I hope?" she enquired, trying to glean more information about the strange visitor.

"No, I am just out of breath from climbing the hill."

Mrs. Williams stood waiting for more information.

"Well, thank you for letting me know. I suppose he'll return if it was important."

"Is that your maiden name then . . . Finchley?" asked Mrs. Williams.

Sarah didn't answer, and turning the key in the door, pushed it open with her foot. Collecting the bags, she stepped quickly inside and shut the door behind her. She heard Mrs. Williams' door slam shut. Sarah began to tremble. Her head was spinning, and she thought she was going to faint. She knew full well who the visitor had been. It couldn't be anyone else. She felt as if her whole world was about to collapse. Tears began to form in her eyes, and it wasn't long before she was crying and sobbing uncontrollably. Samuel had witnessed this bewildering change in Sarah, from happiness to misery, and he did not understand what had happened to cause this sudden metamorphosis. He stood beside her and tried to comfort her by sending out waves of love, but it did not seem to help his unfortunate charge.

Samuel stayed close to Sarah but was at a loss as to how he could comfort the curate's wife. He could tell that she was still desperately upset about something very important. Sarah looked at her wristwatch. It was late. Richard ought to have been home by now. She thought of contacting him on his mobile. Looking at the phone, she could see that Richard had not called to explain why he would be late returning from Chester. She found his name on the phone and was about to hit the call button when she suddenly felt a wave of fear wash over her. She knew that if she spoke to him, her voice would betray that something was wrong. She put the phone down on the kitchen table. It was dark outside now. The shopping bags lay on the floor, unopened.

All sorts of hopes and fears went through her mind. It was all so long ago. She had been only sixteen when she had met Morgan. She had been infatuated with him. He was handsome and exciting. Older than her by five years, he seemed so sophisticated and she had loved his warm, friendly manner and his strange, charming accent. She had met him at the youth club in the village. He was a friend of Matt's, one of the youth club leaders. Sarah had just turned sixteen, and had been appointed as assistant leader to the group.

Up until then she had led a pretty sheltered life. She was an only child, and her parents had certainly cared for her with love, but it was always tempered by strict discipline. She had been a student at the local Girls High School, but where her schoolmates had been given more freedom as teenagers, she was given less. Her parents' overwhelming desire was to see her go to the university and get a good degree. Sarah appreciated their wishes, and she did not disobey them, but inside were growing desires of her own, and some of those were physical and emotional. She had never had a boyfriend, and at age sixteen, she felt a strong urge to find out what that was like, when Morgan had literally walked into her life.

She had been sitting in the kitchen with the other club leaders, sipping hot chocolate, when Matt had waltzed in, dragging Morgan with him, and introduced him to everyone as his best mate. Sarah had never had a conversation with a black man before, and she was embarrassed to find she couldn't take her eyes off him. Morgan had noticed her staring at him, and found he was immediately attracted to her.

She was the image of a fresh country English girl. Shoulder length blonde hair, freckles on her face, and no make-up to mar her milk-white complexion. Her blue eyes were bright and young. She was slim and just beginning to fill out in all the places that a woman should. He was captivated by her, and she him. By the end of the evening, they had spent the best part of two hours just talking, but more than words were being exchanged.

Sarah's father arrived to pick her up in his car as he did every week, not allowing her to walk home with her friends. She was reluctant to leave that night. Morgan made it very clear that he wanted to see her again, soon. By chance, they did meet again before the next club night. Sarah had been doing some study work in the Town Centre Library when she saw Morgan in one of the aisles, his head deep in an atlas. She crept up behind him and surprised him. It was plain he was overjoyed at seeing her again so soon. He told her he'd been checking out South America, which was where his next trip in the Navy was taking him. They talked and talked, about nothing really, but before long they were holding hands under the table.

At the next club meeting, Morgan came early to see Sarah. Her father dropped her off as usual outside the club. In the last few days, all Sarah's thoughts and dreams had been about Morgan, but she knew that if her parents found out they would stop her from coming to the youth club. Matt was aware of what was happening, so he gave Sarah freedom during the evening to spend time with his friend. After dark had set in they had walked down the lane to the edge of the woods and under the moonlight they had kissed.

It was Sarah's first. The feelings that it stirred within her surprised and excited her, and Morgan knew enough about girls to fan the flames of her ardor.

The following weekend Matt was out of town at youth leader's training, and his small flat, which Morgan was sharing whilst on leave, was free for Morgan to use as he wanted. When Morgan had suggested they stay over on Saturday night, Sarah had at first been shocked at the thought. It was dead against everything that she had been brought up to believe. It meant lying to her parents, and to sleep with Morgan meant having sex, which until now she had not seriously thought about. Although her mind warned her to say no, her heart and body screamed yes. It turned out to be a wonderful, magical night. They had sat on the floor drinking wine and eating titbits of food and laughing. As the candles grew shorter, Sarah became intoxicated with the wine and with Morgan. As he undressed her slowly, she felt waves of desire pulse through her, and when they actually made love, it was as though she had found heaven. The feelings that coursed through her young body were sweet and strong and were like nothing she had ever felt before. After, they lay in each other's arms whispering words of love and endearment.

In the days after that weekend they began to feel the pain of the impending separation. Morgan declared that he would rather resign and stay with her. They could talk to her parents, bring it out into the open, and plan for the future. He was like a kid with a new dream, but Sarah, now knowing a man's body and the fullness of his desire, had become a woman. She had the wisdom he lacked. She knew it wouldn't work out. In the end, they pledged to wait. She would finish her studies, and they would start again and pick up their love when he returned from the Navy. With many tears shared, he finally departed, and there followed many sad days for Sarah.

Her parents still knew nothing, but despite noticing the change in her moods, they could not elicit the truth from her. After a while, they had put it down to "just being a teenager."

Chapter 21

Dark Stranger

The tall stranger entered the church by the side door. Pinned to the wall outside there was a sign that read "Coffee Morning & Afternoon—All Welcome." He pushed the door open and heard voices coming from a room to the right. As he walked into the hall, those gathered at the tables stopped talking and stared straight at him. He was an odd sight to their rheumy eyes. The afternoon coffee assembly was normally attended by no one under sixty. To see a young man enter was a pleasant surprise. After the momentary silence, there erupted a collective muttering as the group of ladies wondered who the stranger was. A very large woman sat behind a single trestle table taking money for the refreshments.

He was obviously in the wrong place, and was about to make a smart exit without speaking to anyone. To cut him off, a pair of older ladies stepped forward to greet him.

"I expect you'll want a cup of tea, young man," said the first lady.

"Or coffee," said the second lady.

They took his arm and led him to an empty seat at their table. People were still staring and chattering.

"I expect you'd like some of our homemade Victorian Sponge, too." The two ladies returned with a mug of hot coffee and a generous slab of cake. "Now, you tuck in young man, don't mind us, we don't stand on ceremony here, do we, Ethel?"

"No of course not, Edith!" said her friend.

Putting the cup to his lips and smelling the aroma of fresh coffee, he suddenly became very hungry and thirsty, too. He drank the coffee down in a few long gulps, and ate the cake almost as quickly. He glanced up to see everyone watching him. "My apologies ladies, for my manners. I didn't know I was that hungry, and the cake is delicious." Edith looked at Ethel.

"Hungry young men need feeding, Ethel, get him another round of cake and another mug of coffee."

Before he could protest Ethel had disappeared into the kitchen, and in seconds had returned with more cake and another steaming mug of coffee.

"How much do I owe you for the refreshments?"

Edith looked shocked in a playful mocking way. "No charge. We are here to help the needy, and today you are one of our needy! Isn't that right Ethel?"

"Yes, that's right," said Ethel.

They both beamed at the young guest as he finished off his second helping.

Wiping the crumbs off his mouth he said, "You might be able to help me. I came here to find the vicar's wife, and Mr. Benton, of course. I was told I might find him here."

"You've got that wrong young man," replied Ethel. "Bless you, he's not the vicar, that would be Reverend Stannard. Richard is only the curate of St. David's."

"Oh, I see. So where would I find him, the curate, that is?"

Edith piped up.

"He's not here today. Gone to Chester for a conference, I think. He is normally here with us on these afternoons. Richard usually gives us a reading from the Scriptures, and then we all pray and have tea."

Ethel interjected, "You're not here to give the reading instead are you?"

"No, definitely not. Not my cup of tea, or coffee, you might say!" he laughed, holding up his mug.

Edith and Ethel chuckled, appreciating his little joke. Edith leaned forward to speak to the young man.

"But I dare say you'll find Reverend Stannard in the rectory just around the corner, you'll not miss it. It's a big old house. Too big for one man, we all say."

Ethel frowned as she gave him a piece of advice. "Please excuse me for being blunt and straight to the point young man, but don't expect a warm welcome. He's not fond of . . ." she paused, "of foreigners like yourself."

Edith looked shocked. "Ethel, really! How can you say such a thing? This young man might have been born in Bangor."

He stood up. "No offense taken ladies, Ethel is right. I was born in Ghana. Thanks for the advice, I appreciate it." The young man shook hands warmly with them both.

"We don't know your name?" they asked in perfect unison.

"It's Morgan. Morgan Enenoah at your service." He made a theatrical bow.

As the door to the hall closed, the voices inside rose to a deafening crescendo and several women rushed over to Edith and Ethel to hear all the news.

* * *

Edith was right—he had no trouble finding the rectory. Going straight up to the door, he rang the bell, and from somewhere deep inside the house he heard it ring.

Stannard was in his study poring over his collection of rare stamps and searching the Internet for the best price he could get for his new acquisitions. These were his pride and joy. He heard the front doorbell, but carried on examining the stamps. The bell rang again. Jusach, Stannard's personal demon, was reclining on the sofa taking a nap.

"Mary, Mary!" Stannard hollered out. "Answer the door . . . if you please."

The bell sounded once more. It was then that Stannard remembered it was Mary's afternoon off.

"Damn, who on Earth can it be?" He got up from his desk and made his way to the front door. He opened it and did not trouble to disguise his displeasure at being disturbed. He also made no attempt to hide his reaction at seeing a black face staring at him from the doorstep.

"Yes, what is it?" he said rudely.

"Good afternoon sir, I wonder if you could help me. I am trying to find a friend of mine, someone I haven't seen for a number of years."

Now thoroughly annoyed, Stannard was just about to shut the door in Morgan's face when he remembered that he still had his dog collar on.

"Well young man, it may surprise you to know that I am not here to assist in the recovery of displaced persons." He said with heavy sarcasm.

"No, I mean to say, well I think the person I'm looking for is the wife of your curate. Sarah Finchley. That was her maiden name."

For a moment, Stannard did consider closing the door, but a second thought entered his mind, sown there by Jusach, who was curious about this odd person.

"You are an old friend of Sarah's, not a relative, then?" he said, squinting his eyes at Morgan.

"No, not a relation, Sarah and I were friends once, several years ago."

Jusach, the stunted demon, was at the vicar's side. He whispered again into Stannard's ear, "Find out what this is all about . . . I smell something amiss here." Stannard opened the door wider and stood back. "Perhaps you had better come in. I may be able to help you in your quest."

Sitting in the vicar's study, Morgan surveyed the room. It was all alien to him. He'd spent most of his working life aboard ocean-going ships as an able-bodied seaman, sailing the world's seas and oceans. Stannard returned and sat at his desk. "Would you like some tea Mr . . .? I'm sorry, you didn't give me your name."

"My family name is Enenoah, Morgan Enenoah. As for the offer of tea, no thank you. I've just had coffee at your church hall."

"That's good. Now, how may I help you?"

"Well I was looking for Sarah Finchley, that used to be her name. I understand she is married to your assistant."

"Yes that is correct," said the vicar patiently.

"I was told I might find her at the church with her husband."

"Please forgive me for asking, but as vicar, and like a doctor, I need to abide by certain rules of confidentiality, you understand."

Morgan nodded.

"Were you close friends?" Stannard emphasized the word "close," insinuating an intimate relationship.

"Well, sir, yes I suppose we were for a short time, and then I had to leave on a ship to South America. I'm a seaman serving in the Navy. Then one thing led to another, and my job kept me away from the UK. I lost touch with Sarah, but I promised myself that upon my return to Great Britain I would look her up."

"So this is just a social visit, it is nothing untoward?" said Stannard, obviously disappointed.

Jusach poked the vicar in the side of his head to encourage him to pursue the subject. Stannard instinctively scratched at the place where the demon's long fingernails had pinched him.

"Untoward, sir? I'm sorry, I don't understand the word."

"Quite. You are not the bearer of bad tidings I hope? I may assume you have good intentions towards Richard and Sarah?"

"Oh, yes . . ." Morgan stammered, "I just wanted to see Sarah again, and I know she's married, but I . . ." There followed an awkward silence.

Stannard was clever enough to understand much from the silence.

"Do they have any children?" asked Morgan.

"Richard and Sarah? No they don't. As a young curate, my advice to Richard would be to leave that sort of thing until much later in his career," quipped the vicar.

Stannard was quite satisfied by the conversation with this young man. He felt that there was something here that he might use to his advantage at such a time when he might want to get Richard to do something discreet for him.

Jusach had a perplexed expression on his face. He had moved to where Morgan was sitting and was studying him intensely, trying very hard to read the young man's mind, but without success. Nevertheless, he was sure that there was more to this man than met the eye, even the eye of an old demon. Jusach wanted to abandon his watch on the vicar and follow the young man, but he hesitated to act, because if he was wrong and could not justify his actions, he would be charged with dereliction of duties and then would have to face the wrath of Rimmon.

Morgan held out his hand to Stannard, but the vicar ignored him and showed him to the door and said, "If you come back on Sunday to the morning church service you will certainly find both Richard and Sarah in attendance." Before Morgan had a chance to express his thanks, Stannard had closed the door.

Chapter 22

Confrontation

Instead of going straight home, Richard headed for the rectory. The whole business of Maynard Jones' demise and the awful truth about Stannard's lack of compassion had angered Richard to the point that he'd decided to confront the vicar. He banged several times on the front door impatiently with his clenched fist. He was enraged and was barely able to control himself. He waited, but no one came. He banged louder this time, and then heard Stannard shouting from inside, "Alright I'm coming!"

Without waiting to be invited in, Richard brushed past Stannard and went into the hall.

"I need to speak to you right now and it can't wait." Richard's whole body was shaking with righteous anger. Stannard was still holding the door open. Richard turned and shoved the door. It shut with a loud thud. Stannard looked at him as if he had gone mad.

"How dare you burst in on me like this? What on Earth do you think you are doing?"

Richard ignored the vicar's remark and held up Maynard Jones' journal.

"This is what I am doing. This journal belonged to your previous curate. Sarah found it in the cottage, hidden away from prying eyes. It tells of a man in desperate need of help . . ."

It was Stannard who now pushed past Richard, and disappearing into his study, took refuge behind his desk. Richard followed him. ". . . a desperate man in need of your help, Stannard. He was gravely ill, confused, and in spiritual torment and you could have given him aid, sympathy, and kindness."

Stannard slumped into his chair and fixed a pair of frightened eyes on Richard.

Richard faced him across the desk and scoffed at him, "But you gave him none. Even when he was dying, he cried out to you for help to get him a doctor, but you cut him off." Richard raised the journal, and pointing to it, said, "It's all in here. The poor man chronicled not only his own abject fears and trepidations, but he describes your cold-hearted attitude and behavior Stannard! The man was your curate. He was your responsibility. Doesn't it say somewhere in your oath as a Minister of God and Christ that you will do all you can for those in your spiritual family?" Richard was shouting now.

"Look at you!" Richard pointed to the books and albums of stamps spread out on the desk. "You are more interested in bloody stamps than the souls of men. You do not have the love of God in your heart! Why do you go on with this masquerade? Why don't you resign and be done with it!" Richard was beside himself with anger, but as he looked at the pathetic caricature of a man of God seated behind the desk, he began to feel pity. The silence that followed gave Stannard his chance to muster a defense, and Jusach, ever his close companion, was filling him with evil. Richard had bowed his head and was now feeling weary and crestfallen. He had thought that by confronting Stannard with the truth the man's hypocrisy would be exposed, and perhaps he would be shamed into a state of contrition. He was mistaken. Stannard stood up and with rage on his face shouted at Richard.

"How dare you lecture me on my oaths to God and my vocation? What do you know of life? You are still wet behind the ears. Jones deserved all he got for he brought it upon himself. The man was a blasted homosexual, a disgrace to the Church. He signed his own death warrant by doing things that are abominable to God. He had AIDS! And if that disease wasn't sent by God to rid this world of these people . . ." He began to splutter and shout, and waving his bony fingers at Richard, he cried, "Remember Sodom and Gomorrah. The Lord gave no quarter there. He erased their kind off the face of the Earth. When I saw Jones' mangled body in the mortuary I felt no sympathy for him. He can rot in hell. He can get his sympathy from the Devil for all I care, and there are many of my clerical brothers who would stand by me. Now get out! And don't think I shall not write to the bishop about this outrage. Get out I say, this instant!"

Richard looked at Stannard with real pity in his eyes. "You are far sicker than Jones ever was." Richard threw the journal down on the desk. "Read it if you dare! Read his journal and pray that God will forgive you."

Richard turned and walked briskly away. Flinging the front door open, he left the rectory. Stannard shouted at him as he went down the path. "You think you are so holy and righteous, Benton! Try asking your wife who visited her this afternoon!"

Richard turned back, only to see Stannard slam the front door shut. He stood alone and wondered what the vicar had meant.

Chapter 23

The Truth Comes Out

Sarah was beside herself. Feeling a sense of deep shame and guilt, she wished that she had told Richard all about Morgan long ago, or at least before they had married. She thought to herself, "The word of God is true when it says your sins will find you out one day, even if it is years later."

She was in abject fear of losing her husband because of a wrong she had done as a teenager. Surely she could not be held accountable—she was so young, barely into adolescence. She didn't love Morgan, it was pure infatuation and curiosity and a longing to know about the forbidden things of love and romance. She paced up and down the hall, looking anxiously at the door, expecting Richard at any moment.

What was she going to say to him? She had to tell him the truth. It was no good thinking she could hide this from him. Her head ached as she turned the matter over and over in her mind. What if she could head Morgan off? Maybe he wouldn't return, but what if he went to the church and told others, Stannard? Oh God no, please not him. The tears began to flow. Her face was blotchy from crying and her eyes red. Try as she might she could not stop herself from weeping.

At that moment the door opened and in strode Richard. It was obvious he was angry and she thought he must already know. She ran to him sobbing, "Oh Richard, please forgive me, I am so ashamed of myself, I ought to have told you, only don't leave me, please."

Richard, shocked at her behavior, used his hands to push her away from him, but still holding her said, "What on Earth is the matter? Why are you crying?"

She raised her eyes to his. "I, I . . . you don't know? Oh Richard, I am so sorry, so very sorry."

"Come on, you had better sit down and tell me what this is all about." He guided her into the living room and sat down beside her on the sofa. He hugged her gently, momentarily forgetting the incident with Stannard. Samuel stood in the corner of the room staring at them. His heart was troubled.

"Now why are you so upset? Why are you apologizing to me?"

She dried her face with a handkerchief, dabbing at her eyes as she spoke. "You came in so angry. I thought it was because of me. I became frightened."

"I was angry because I just had a blazing row with Stannard about his treatment of Jones. I thought it was about time someone told him what a cruel man he really is, and I purposefully didn't call you beforehand because I knew you'd try to dissuade me from going."

"Oh, I see, I didn't realize." She said in a subdued voice, trying hard not to sob.

Richard put his arm around her and looked at her tenderly. "Now, what is this all about? Sarah, I think you should confide in me. I am a clergyman, after all." He joked.

"Richard, it's not a joke, and I do have a confession. Something I should have spoken about when

we first met, when we first fell in love. But I thought
the past was over and done with." She took a deep
breath before continuing, "I apparently had a visitor
this afternoon. Mrs Williams next door spoke to him,
though I did not. But from her description, I know
who it was."

Richard was now looking worried.

"It was someone who I knew when I was sixteen, a
man." Sarah was speaking very slowly and her breath
was becoming labored. Biting her lip she went on. "I
don't know how to say it."

The worry on Richard's face was now one of deep
anxiety. He withdrew his arm from her shoulder.

"It was all stupid," she blurted out, "I was naïve
and young. I didn't really know what I was doing."

For the second time today Samuel looked upon
Sarah with deep compassion. He was aware now
that the source of her grief was her own wrongdoing, something that had stayed secret for many years,
but now had caught up with her and was causing her
much pain.

With tears falling onto her cheeks she related the
story of her affair, leaving the worst for last.

"After Morgan had gone back to sea I found out
I was pregnant with his child. We only made love
once."

Richard suddenly stood up and looked down at her.

"So what happened? Where is the child now?
My God, the child must be ten years old at least. So
where do you keep it! Was it a boy or a girl? And is
the child black or white?" Anger had crept into his
words.

Sarah began to sob again, her body heaving with
shame.

"There is no child. I miscarried at six months. The child was born dead."

Richard immediately felt ashamed at what he had said in anger.

"What happened then with the man? Did you continue your relationship?" he said accusingly.

"No, I swear I haven't seen Morgan since then. He went away and I never heard from him again."

"Until now, that is!" Richard turned his back on Sarah. "Is he expected back? Have you agreed to meet him?"

"No, Richard. I don't want to see him. I love you!" She rose from the sofa and tried to put her arms around him, but he pushed her away brusquely.

"Don't please, I need space to think this over. You have betrayed me, lied to me."

Horrified, she gazed at her husband, who now seemed so distant from her. Samuel instinctively moved beside her to let his warmth comfort her. He knew the whole story now, but he could see that she was full of regret and totally repentant. Her soul was clean. All that her husband had to do now was find it in his heart to forgive her, especially as all this had occurred before they had met. Grabbing his coat from the hall, Richard headed for the door.

"Richard, please don't leave me . . . don't go," she pleaded.

The door slammed behind him as he ran down the path, disappearing into the failing light.

Samuel had to make a decision. Should he stay with Sarah or follow Richard? The man needed help now more than her, but what could he do? Samuel made his choice, and in a split second was beside Richard as he ran towards the promenade.

Chapter 24

Reunion

Richard slowed, and out of breath walked towards the shore. Arriving at the wide promenade, he carried on walking, but in no particular direction. The sky was darkening with the last few rays of sunlight illuminating the lower edges of the clouds. His mind was filled with all kinds of questions that had no answers. He felt numbed by Sarah's confession. Her disclosure that she had been pregnant at sixteen had destroyed his faith in her. How could he now believe anything she said to him? If she had been unable to tell him about the most important episode in her life, what was he supposed to think of her now? She had hidden the truth from him all this time, and it was the same as lying. He'd never trust her again.

He thought with pain that her parents were culpable too in this deception. They knew about it and still did not think to let him know before the wedding. I suppose, he thought, they were glad to get rid of her. His conscience chided him, "No, no, that can't be true. They supported her to go to university. What am I thinking? She is my wife and I love her, but . . . why had she lied to me?"

Samuel could sense that Richard was struggling with his thoughts. His whole manner and body language was one of despair. Leaving the promenade, he struck out along the shoreline until he came to a place where the waves of the sea crashed against the bottom of the cliffs and he could go no further. He sat down on the sands and wept tears of anger, frustration, and disappointment. The same question kept repeating itself over and over again in his mind until the mantra had lost meaning, and becoming abstract, simply dissolved into pain. Why had she kept this terrible secret from him all these years? She had betrayed his love. The only thing he could feel was the immense loss of trust and the end of true love.

The turbulent sea crashed against the rocks, and with each surge the waves came nearer to his feet. The tide was coming in fast. He shivered as the cold night air invaded his bones. The skies began to darken; a storm was coming. Pulling himself up, he perfunctorily brushed the sand off his trousers and started to walk back towards the promenade. Samuel followed him a few yards behind. Every step that Richard took was like lead, as if he was a robot, a mindless automaton on a mechanical journey to nowhere. He slipped and tripped as his feet encountered the raised timber step of the old pier. It was late now, and no one else was about. Everyone had long ago gone home. The small shops, booths, and amusements were all boarded up. Everywhere along the pier were signs of the holidaymakers and day-trippers. Windblown litter gathered in corners, fish and chip bags, empty cans, and cigarette ends. Slowly, steadily, everything was blown into the waters below.

At the end of the pier, Richard halted and looked absentmindedly at the sea. The waves violently churned against the old rusted steel stanchions that held up the timber deck. In the distance he could see the lights of a ferry bound for Liverpool. Overhead gulls squawked loudly, diving fast and swooping low over the waves in search of morsels of floating food. The rain came in on the wind and lashed at Richard's unprotected face. He turned his face away.

It was a cold night. He drew the collar of his thin jacket up around his ears to ward off the shock of the night air and to escape the vile blasts. Seeing a shelter nearby he pushed himself into a corner on the lee side, and closing his eyes, wrapped his arms around himself in an effort to stay warm. His mind was numb and his body weary, and it was not long before the strain of the past few hours became too much. Exhaustion set in and he fell into a deep sleep.

Samuel stood on guard to make sure that no one came near to disturb the young man. The hours passed by. Then suddenly a bright light began to shine in front of him and illuminate everything around. Samuel knew instantly that it was the Shekkinah, the glory of God's presence. There was only one such emanation in the entire universe that was manifested in this way, the Spirit of God. The angel fell to his knees and bowed low his forehead, touching the planks of wood.

"Samuel, Samuel . . ." the Spirit's powerful voice shook the pier.

Samuel dared not raise his eyes to look upon the Spirit of God. The voice of Yahweh spoke. The words of God flowed through him as pure energy and strengthened and emboldened him. The light of glory felt warm to him, like liquid waves of pure love passing right through him, unceasingly.

"Speak, Lord, for your servant listens." The angel trembled, hearing the mighty voice of God.

"My good and loyal servant, I come to give you a command. The man that you protect this night is to be used mightily in my plans. I am about to do something in this place that will cause reverberations around the world. Your bravery in facing the evil one has come to my attention, and I am proud of you, my faithful warrior, my true and courageous servant. I endow and charge you this night with power so that you can stand against Satan and his dark angels. I provide you with a sword of truth which when plunged into the evil heart of any demon will banish him to the fiery pit until Judgment Day. Guard this weapon well, it is yours forever. We shall see a glorious victory over Lucifer and all his renegade angels. I, Yahweh Sabboeth, have commanded you this night."

The light vanished as quickly as it came. For Samuel, the supernatural experience of God instantly ceased. A profound silence returned. Samuel did not move nor open his eyes for a long time. He trembled still. He felt the residual power of the Lord of Lords coursing through him.

Finally, standing erect he raised his arms to the heavens and exclaimed with joy, "Praise the Almighty One, the Living God of Heaven and Earth! Hallelujah, He is Lord!"

Behind him, Richard stirred and appeared renewed. He felt strong and alive in a way he had never experienced before. The presence of God, unknown to him, had imbued him also with heavenly power. A new life and a new strength coursed through his veins.

He sprang forward and started to run along the pier heading straight for home. As he ran, he shouted at the top of his lungs, "Father, forgive me! I have been a fool. I am sorry for the pain I must have caused Sarah this day. Forgive me, Lord."

Samuel laughed as he ran beside Richard. They praised God, angel and man in unity as God intended it to be.

Sarah was waiting at the door as Richard arrived. She ran straight into his arms.

"Oh, darling I have been so worried about you. You've been gone hours and you didn't answer your phone . . . I wanted to say . . ."

Before she could utter another word, Richard placed his hand gently over her mouth to stop her.

"Never mind all that. It is me who should apologize. I have been such a fool."

They walked arm in arm into the cottage, and Richard shut the door with his foot.

Sarah looked into his eyes, and she could see that something had happened to her husband. His eyes sparkled and his face shone. Even his smile was somehow magnified.

He kissed her on her lips, pulled her close and told her he loved her deeply. She felt the ardor and the passion of his desire for her. With abandon she pulled him towards the stairs and up to the bedroom. It took only seconds for them to completely disrobe and fall onto the bed naked, wrapped in each other's arms. The night air was cold, but they were oblivious to it. They kissed and caressed and found a new closeness that night, an intimacy that they had never experienced before. It was as if all their inhibitions had been rolled away. Every time their bodies touched, there was a wonderful quiescence of mind and body and spirit.

Samuel hovered over them, delighted to see this reunion, but he was perplexed, never having witnessed this miracle of human love first hand. Suddenly, he felt drawn into them, and falling, became entwined in their joy. He felt the amazing tenderness and strength that pulsed between the compliant bodies. He experienced the full weight of their love and loving as they became one flesh. As an angel, he knew he would never know these feelings of utter pleasure, created so uniquely by God for man and woman. Then as they reached the ultimate moment, the point of intimate sensuality when truly the passion of one lover dissolves and merges into the beloved, he was honored to know and feel, if only for a moment, the quintessential act where man and woman experience life as God intended it to be. He felt the surge as Richard's orgasm became part of his wife's inner body. Their spirits became one. Two lovers, but one body and one flesh.

Samuel was wonderfully overwhelmed by this episode, and releasing himself, was thrown back across the room. He gazed at them now, the silent unmoving pair of lovers, as they descended into a quiet peace and holy contentment. Rising up through the roof, Samuel flew upwards into the brightly starred heavens, singing and praising until he could sing no more.

While laying beside each other in the bed, enveloped in the soft darkness, perfectly satisfied, content, and knowing love, Sarah turned her head to whisper in Richard's ear.

"Richard," she said softly, "do you believe in angels?"

"Well yes, I guess so, as they are mentioned several times in the Scriptures."

"I don't mean in the Bible, I mean here and now. Aren't they sent to protect us?"

"Mmm . . . I don't really know. Why?"

"It's just that over the last few days I have felt the presence of someone with us, and tonight in this room, I think I knew that an angel was here, sharing our moment of joy."

Chapter 25

Troubles Redeemed

Morgan walked up the path to the cottage to see the smiling faces of Richard and Sarah waiting for him at the door. Richard stepped forward, offering his hand. "Welcome, you must be Morgan, please come in."

Morgan, Richard, and Sarah stood for a moment awkwardly facing each in the small living room of the cottage.

"Can I get you a tea or coffee, Morgan?" Sarah asked brightly.

"Yes, thank you." Morgan had expected quite a different kind of welcome, and he had hoped to be free to talk to Sarah alone.

"Please sit, Morgan. I know this must be difficult for you, and please believe me when I say I think I understand your feelings. Sarah and I have talked and prayed about the time she spent with you when she was younger, and well . . ." Richard stopped mid-sentence, then spoke again, "I think it's best if you and Sarah talk it over alone. I know she has a lot to tell you, some of it pretty important stuff. She has gone through great distress these last few days and my only request, Morgan, is that you treat her with respect and understand what she suffered all those years ago."

Richard stood up and offered his hand again to his visitor. Morgan rose from the chair and shook Richard's hand warmly and said, "You can trust me. I'm not here to cause any trouble. I just wanted to put things straight. I heard so many rumors when I got back to Britain that I didn't know what to believe."

As Sarah passed Richard in the hallway he kissed her on the cheek. "I'll go for a ramble across the Ulm. Call me when you are ready. Don't rush it." Richard pulled on his coat, hat, and scarf and left them alone together.

Sarah handed the mug of coffee to Morgan.

"He seems like a good man, but I suppose being a curate, he ought to be, eh?"

"Being a clergyman is no guarantee of good character," she said, thinking of Stannard.

Morgan nodded. "I think I get your drift, I met your vicar yesterday."

Behind the cottage, Richard headed up the steep winding path that the sheep and goats used to wander all over the great rocky hill. By the time he reached the top, he was out of breath and sat down on a rock to recover. Samuel, his sword at his side, was already sitting on a rock, wondering just what might be going through Richard's mind. He was learning much observing Richard and his wife. He could see that their lives were difficult and that the pains they suffered were at times hard to bear. Yet, frail as they were, they always managed to find a way through the troubles and they came to depend and love God more, despite the situation.

Richard struck out again for the summit. He could see the funicular winding its way back and forward from the bottom to the top and vice versa, carrying hardy tourists who braved the wind and cold clime of the Great Ulm. He promised himself that as reward for his exertions he would buy a hot chocolate and an iced bun at the Summit Café before he set out on the downward trip. Before going into the café, Richard strode across the car park and jumped over the low stone wall that stopped cars from going over the edge. Carrying on a few yards more, he stood at the edge of a steep incline that descended all the way to the sea far below. To the west, he could see the Isle of Anglesey and the famous Puffin Island, and in between the bits of land he could just make out the tall striped lighthouse whose bell boomed at regular intervals every hour of every day and night to warn ships of the dangerous rocks. To the north it was just a great expanse of sea all the way to the Isle of Man and beyond.

He loved this place, and compared to other places he had lived this was Heaven on Earth. The sea and the rocks spoke of timelessness, and he always felt nearer to God here. He often came here to pray. He recalled when he and Sarah had come up after dark one night to watch the stars. It had been cold but dry, and as they lay upon the grass they'd spent hours of contentment close together, side-by-side, holding hands and talking about nothing in particular. It had all made sense in a very intimate sort of way. They had stared at brilliant stars that shimmered in the cloudless sky in awe of the beauty of the universe. Richard had recited from memory the lines from Psalm 8, one of his special favorites: "When I consider Your heavens, the work of Your fingers, the moon and the stars, which You have ordained, what is man that You are mindful of him?"

Sarah had turned towards him and kissed him, saying, "Darling I love you so very, very much." Then, in almost the next moment, she had exclaimed aloud, "But you know what infuriates me the most about you?"

Richard had been shocked and surprised, his mouth agape.

"Every time we do this—looking up at the night sky—you say, 'Wow, did you see that shooting star?' and by the time I turn my head to see it, it has already vanished."

To Sarah's surprise, Richard had jumped up, standing tall, and theatrically throwing his arms aloft cried out, "Okay, Lord. We want the most amazing shooting star that has ever been seen to cross the sky from here to there."

Richard pointed to a high point in the Western sky and described the arc he wanted the shooting star to take.

"And I want it within the next thirty seconds."

Sarah was now expectantly standing at his side. As soon as he had uttered his request he started to count aloud.

"One, two, three, four . . ." he got as far as fifteen when a great shooting star suddenly appeared, flaming white and hugely bright, traveling between the exact two points that Richard had picked in the sky. The star sped across the night sky and the sound was like the roar of a great wind, whoosh, curving beautifully until it reached its final mark, then faded from view.

Richard and Sarah had gazed at each other with their mouths open in wonder at what had just occurred. Richard clasped Sarah close to him and proclaimed, "Wow!" They stayed like this transfixed, for several minutes, the shooting star still passing through their minds again and again.

"Richard, that was amazing! The shooting star was awesome. God heard your prayer and answered it in style."

Remembering the awesome moment, Richard walked back across the car park to the café, enjoying the memory of that special night when God came close to both of them. He found an empty seat by the window, and sliding in, ordered a hot chocolate. He didn't bother with the iced bun, although they did look delicious. He had been there only for about ten minutes when his mobile phone rang.

"Richard you can come back home now, Morgan's gone."

"Gone happy?" he asked.

"Well, I don't know really, but he's left a lot wiser than he came. He's a good man."

Richard put the phone back in his pocket, and leaving the summit, made his way home with quite a jaunty step in his walk.

Samuel, smiling and laughing, aped Richard's gait, and they both made their way happily down the hill.

Part Three

Chapter 26

The New Bishop

The Electoral College had finally done its job. After three days of discussion and bitter negotiations in the cathedral, the evangelicals had won the day. Much political maneuvering and deal-making went on before the ultimate decision was made. Each faction had fought hard to get their man elected to this high post in the Church of England and Wales. The importance of the bishop's office could not be undervalued, for he is the venerated pastor of the clergy and shepherd of the flock in the image of Christ. He is the one who decides what form of ministry shall be carried out to fulfill the church's mission, God's great commission on Earth.

The conservative arm of the College wanted to maintain the status quo. The late Bishop John was an ultra-conservative and was opposed to any radical change occurring in the church, whether in the church government or at a provincial level. During his term of twenty-four years, congregations had quietly diminished. A death in the congregation meant another empty pew in the church. There was no effort made to replace and renew. The ever-waning vitality of the church in this region had been likened to an old man dozing off and waiting expectantly for the undertaker to call.

Bishop John's supporters knew it was going to be a tough battle to get another man like him chosen for the job, but then they had numerous contenders to choose from, and they were quietly confident that the brash and absurd tactics of the "new thinkers" would frighten the College members into making a sensible decision. On the other hand, their opponents, the evangelicals, did not depend upon the machinations of church government and secret deals. They believed that God himself would prevail and deliver the right candidate. The evangelical clergy and indeed senior laymen had received scriptural confirmations. At prayer meetings, the Holy Spirit had made known His desire for change. Their candidate, Canon Nigel Jeffries, was indeed a Spirit-filled man, and he already had a reputation for applying action where it was needed. At crucial times, that meant getting on his knees and praying all night. This discipline had been learned in the valleys of South Wales, Evan Roberts' country. Jeffries had accepted Christ as his savior as a young teenager and never looked back.

Accepted as an ordinand at the Church of England as a young man, he went to Cambridge University to study Theology. He did well, and early in his career as a man dedicated to God he was appointed as Chaplain at Wycliffe House School. His innovations and passion for his work earned him a good reputation, which finally reached the ears of the Archbishop, who wasted no time in poaching him for his staff.

Bishop Jeffries' special interest was the study of "Church History." Some might have imagined that he would retire to the dusty halls of church libraries. This was far from the truth. His devotional studies and deep searches of the Old Testament were, for him, a way to get closer to and be more intimate with his own very personal God. Many honors and top level jobs came over the next decade or so, seemingly without effort. Standing at six foot, and quite bald-headed, he was an imposing man, but never intimidating. People meeting him for the first time found his manner warm and friendly. He was articulate and more than willing to get involved. Now, at the age of forty-nine, happily married with five young children and with a whole host of responsibilities both personal and ecumenical, he felt ready to make his mark.

The old guard had lost the day. They had wanted all things to remain the same. In their eyes there was no reason to change the status quo. Didn't the scriptures confirm that God was the same yesterday, today and forever? How they would fare under the new bishop would soon be evident.

The new bishop's inauguration took place on the first weekend of January. It had been a grand affair, but Jeffries was anxious to get the ceremonies over with so that he could start the real business of reforming and revitalizing, of bringing clear thinking and biblically-based teaching back into a muddle-headed confused church.

After his inauguration, he had decided that his first priority would be to visit as many of the churches in the diocese as possible. One of the first on his list was St. David's, in Penrhos Bay.

Sitting in Stannard's office, the new bishop scrutinized the taciturn vicar. He scanned the room, taking in all the details that revealed what kind of man Stannard truly was. If you want to know in what a man truly believes, study his sanctum. Jeffries knew that a great deal could be learned by studying a man's habits, as manifested in the objects and books with which a person surrounded themselves. It was apparent that Stannard had not taken any trouble to hide his wants and desires. At Stannard's left shoulder stood Jusach.

"How old are you now, Stannard?" the bishop inquired.

"Approaching sixty-three, Your Grace," said Stannard.

"Oh, please call me Nigel, I don't feel comfortable with 'Your Grace.' I grew up in the South amongst the collieries; I can't imagine any of my dad's mates calling me 'Your Grace,' can you?"

Stannard winced at the use of the term "mates" and replied, "No, I suppose not."

"And what name do you go by? How do you like to be addressed?"

Stannard was caught in a trap. No one ever used his first name. It was "Vicar" or "Reverend"—that was the way he preferred it. He did not encourage intimacy of any kind from his parishioners or even his friends.

"My name is Sydney. Sydney Arthur Stannard, Your Grace," he answered nervously.

"Well, is it Syd? Or Art?" said the bishop playfully.

"I prefer Sydney, actually," said Stannard, rather peevishly. He was beginning to feel sick.

Jusach whispered into Stannard's ear, "Tell that oaf of a bishop to get lost."

Stannard shook his head suddenly as if to dislodge a flea in his ear.

"Now, Sydney, what's all this I hear about your late curate jumping off the church tower?"

The bishop was not one to waste words. He preferred to get straight to the point. Why give up a trait of a lifetime that had served him well in the past?

Jusach said louder this time, "Go on, tell him . . . tell him that Jones got he what he deserved."

Once again, Stannard shook his head irritably.

"Are you alright?" the bishop inquired.

Stannard instinctively put his hand to his left ear to scratch it. "Yes, I am perfectly fine, Your Grace."

The bishop placed the fingers of his hands together as if he was about to pray. He was looking straight at Stannard and waiting for an answer, then for a moment his attention was drawn to the right of Stannard. He looked directly at Jusach, who began to feel rather uncomfortable, although he could not believe that the bishop actually saw him.

"Well, as you are probably aware, it was a most unfortunate incident," began Stannard.

"Quite." The bishop maintained his searching stare at Jusach. Aware that the bishop was not looking at him directly, but at something else, Stannard was growing nervous.

He continued to explain, "He was ill just before his death and, if I may say so, I believed that . . . well, he was not exactly in his right mind."

"Really? Do you mean he was deranged, as a result of his illness?" probed the bishop.

"No, not mentally deranged, but momentarily unhinged and quite unable to control his faculties, and this may have been due to his medications, which I understand were unusually strong analgesics."

Jusach suddenly felt an enormous pressure against his body. He knew what it was immediately, and realized that he could do nothing to stop it. The prayer of a holy man can do much harm to a servant of Satan. As the bishop initiated silent prayer against this particular evil entity, Jusach was slowly but inexorably pressed back against the far wall. As he tried to cry out, he discovered that the force exerted on his body had rendered him mute. Try as he might, he could not utter a sound. He was pinned to the wall as if he had been nailed there. The bishop returned his gaze to Stannard, and smiling said, "Prior to his death, was he hospitalized?"

"I don't think so. He took some time off—several weeks in fact—and I of course covered all his duties."

The bishop smiled. "That was good of you Sydney. His care then? Was he looked after, by his GP and a visiting nurse?"

"I believe so, yes." Stannard was unsure of himself now.

"But you are not sure, it seems?"

"Well I had all of my duties and his to perform. It wasn't easy. I did telephone him to make sure he was not in need of anything," Stannard deliberately lied to his bishop.

"I see, and the police and the coroner were all satisfied that there was no foul play involved?"

"Oh absolutely, the verdict was death by misadventure," said Stannard, almost brightly, sensing the inquisition about Jones was nearing its end.

"I understand the local rag reported that it was an unfortunate accident, a fall whilst carrying out maintenance on the tower. Was that possible? Plausible, even? Surely our curates are not normally encouraged to do repairs to the building fabric, are they?"

Stannard began to fidget once more. He decided to brazen it out.

"To be honest, Nigel, the editor is a close friend, and I called in a favor. I thought it would do the church harm to have a sleazy headline in the newspaper dragging up all kinds of innuendoes about the man."

"You knew he was a homosexual, then."

Stannard sighed. "Not until after he had joined us here. By that time I could do nothing about his appointment."

"By that, you mean you wanted rid of him," said the bishop.

"Well I certainly did not agree with his lifestyle. It is anathema to me, Bishop . . . and yes, I would have moved Heaven and Earth to have him moved on," exclaimed Stannard boldly.

"Where was the unfortunate man buried? I hope you gave him a decent send-off?"

Stannard's heart was pounding in his chest. He chose to lie again.

"I discovered he had no living relatives, so I administered a simple ceremony and had the local undertakers scatter his remains in the Memorial Rose Garden. I believe he would have liked that, he was a keen naturalist. I will have a plaque made and erected there soon."

The bishop nodded but offered no further comment.

"And the new curate? Richard Benton, Oxford man. Not a homo, I suppose," he said with a laugh.

Stannard flinched. "No, as you say, not a . . . he is married and seems more suitable, but we did have a difference of opinion just the other day. I found his manner offensive . . . and I would welcome the chance to talk to you about it now, as I think you may need to discipline the young man and set him right."

Stannard's manner changed somewhat. He was growing in confidence now, as he believed he had a genuine grievance to share with the bishop and he assumed that the bishop would support his claim.

Saying nothing, the bishop rose from his chair and perused the shelves of books. Stannard shifted in his chair uneasily. The majority of the books on the shelves and in the bookcases were on the subject of philately. Interspersed with those tomes were also dozens of stamp catalogues ranging from the 1950s to the present day. However, there was one small open bookcase on the other side of the room, as far away from the desk as possible, that did contain some ecclesiastical works. There were a few Bibles, mainly the Authorized and King James versions, a copy of Strong's concordance together with Matthew Henry's commentary, and a small volume of Wesley's sermons. Judging by the dust that had collected on these shelves, it was clear to the bishop that this part of the room was not visited often. Stannard watched in horror as the bishop wiped the dust off one of the shelves with his index finger and examined it closely.

"Regarding your spat with Benton, put it in writing and email me your thoughts on this matter. Do it today, please, and I'll read it tonight. Well, I must be going Sydney. Thank you for the tour, most interesting and informative." He extended his hand towards Stannard, who by this time was standing. They shook hands. The bishop motioned Stannard back to his desk.

"Don't worry, I'll see myself out, and be sure to thank Mary for her delicious tea and Welsh cakes. Must go, things to do and people to see, other churches to visit before dusk. God bless you."

As the bishop left the room, Jusach, suddenly released, fell headlong to the floor. Finding his voice again, he cursed the bishop with numerous foul oaths.

Stannard stood dumbstruck. He felt he had been dismissed like a schoolboy. He was unable to utter anything, no benediction, not even a simple good-bye. He slumped back in his chair and said to himself scornfully, "The man's an utter fool. God save me from all proselytizing evangelicals!"

* * *

The bishop was addressing Richard. "I'm telling you now Richard, so that you know. I know this is going to sound crazy and you'll probably think me a madman but God has spoken to me. I have heard his command so clearly and I am going to obey Him. No pussyfooting around. I am the bishop now, and I can do as I please within reason and as long as God approves. There are going to be some radical changes in this place."

Richard could not quite comprehend what was happening to him as of late. First, he knew he had been touched by the Holy Spirit whilst asleep on the pier. His soul felt as if it was on fire, and when he read the Word of God it leapt out of the page with such power. Now, the new bishop was standing in his kitchen, a mug of tea in one hand and a biscuit in the other, telling Richard and Sarah about his amazing plans.

"Firstly, Stannard has to go. I will suspend him temporarily, but my mind is made up." The bishop's countenance was stern.

Sarah cast a glance to Richard. There was a half smile on her face.

"No need to bother you with the details at this juncture. He can stay in the rectory until after the Crusade." Casting his eyes around the kitchen, he said with a laugh, "I expect you're happy to remain here for awhile?"

Sarah grabbed Richard's arm, "We love it here!"

"Good. I shall confine him to quarters so that he will not be in the way during our work. Secondly, I am putting you in charge of the Crusade, Richard. We'll hold it in St. David's Church. I am told it can seat over four hundred, though of late I think it has held less than four, including Stannard."

The bishop took a large bite of the biscuit and continued to talk, crumbs falling from his mouth. "You'll be in charge, I'll be here to help and I'll co-opt some people from my office. It'll be good for them to actually get out into the real world." He paused for a moment as if trying to recollect something. "Ah, yes. I have fantastic news! We shall be joined by my good friends Simon James and his dear wife Serena. They are marvelous evangelists for Christ, and because of their rock and roll music background, they will draw in many."

Sarah began to sing the song made famous by Simon in the sixties, "Bi bi bobbi, bi bi bobbi . . ."

"Well done, Sarah. Who would ever have thought that such a silly song would be used so greatly by God, eh? It's amazing, or should I say, it's typical of God. Kids in small villages in the darkest parts of Africa sing it, even if they've never heard of Simon."

They all laughed together. Richard was about to ask a question, but the bishop put up his hand, still holding half the biscuit.

"Plenty of time for questions, Richard. Simon and Serena are arriving in ten days, so we should get cracking. I am staying over tonight. I'll deal with the awful Sydney in the morning, and then we'll meet in the church at ten o'clock. Cancel all your appointments for the next two weeks. We have the Lord's work to do!"

Chapter 27

The Blue Mercedes

The powder-blue Mercedes-Benz automobile sped along the highway on cruise control, the needle on the speedometer stuck on seventy. It was about two o'clock in the morning and there were few other vehicles on the road. The woman driving looked at her companion, who sat in the passenger seat. Simon and Serena had been husband and wife for over 36 years now, and they had shared almost all their time together, on stage and off. They were still as much in love as when they had first met at the auditions for "Jesus Christ Superstar" back in the sixties. When they had first seen each other across the boards of the Adelphi in London, she had recognized him immediately. After all, he was already a famous pop star with three number one hit records that had topped the British and American charts for weeks on end. He was handsome, tall, and slim and had a charisma that went beyond the usual celebrity star. She hadn't had the nerve to speak to him directly, but over the next few days she had found herself staring at him all the time, and embarrassingly he had noticed her attention.

Between rehearsals she had been grabbing a quick coffee when she turned around to see his smiling face only inches from hers. His hand was outstretched toward her. "You're Serena Handley, aren't you?" She was so surprised that he recognized her.

"And you are . . ." but before she could finish the sentence, he leaned forward and whispered, "You are right, but please don't tell anyone else!"

He grabbed a coffee with one hand and with the other steered her gently towards a couple of vacant seats.

"I saw you at the Empire in that wonderful musical by . . . by . . .?"

"Epstein," she said.

"You sang and acted the part beautifully. I was very impressed."

"Thank you. Though, if we are dishing out compliments, I love your music but have to confess that I haven't bought any of your records." She blushed and looked down.

"Hey, don't worry about it, everyone else has!" They laughed. The bell rang for the start of the afternoon rehearsal.

"Are you free on Saturday after the show? Maybe we could eat. I know a great little Greek place in Frith Street in Soho, Jimmy's, that stays open forever and . . . no one will recognize either of us, I promise."

The rest was history. Their love affair made all the newspapers and the front page of all the glossies. However, just when they thought their lives were perfect and could not get any better, they received a phone call one night as they were relaxing in their Chelsea flat in London.

"Hello Cliff, how's business? We must get together soon to chat about my future."

Serena had looked across at Simon. "Is that Cliff Richard?" she mouthed silently with her lips.

Simon put his hand over the speaker and shouted, "Yes, it's Cliff Richard, darling."

"Carry on old chap . . . what's up?"

Simon's smile died on his face as he listened to what was being said at the other end.

"Cliff, seriously, I really appreciate your kind offer, but I don't know, it's not really my thing. I know it works for you but . . . okay, okay, I'll talk it over with Serena . . . yes, and call you back. I promise."

Simon put the phone down and sat next to Serena on the sofa.

"You can guess what that was about, can't you. Some big American evangelist is in town on Saturday night at Wembley Stadium in London. Cliff is singing and he has invited us to come."

An awkward silence fell between them.

"Anyway, we can't go. We're performing!" Simon got up and looked down at Serena. "What a pity," he said with a wicked grin on his face.

"Simon, you know full well that this weekend is our weekend off. We could go . . . what's the harm?"

"Oh come on. What's the harm! I love Cliff, but I don't want to be him!"

"Sit down here with me, there's something I wanted to say and I've been holding it back for weeks."

"Oh God, you're not pregnant are you?"

"NO! You idiot." She hit him with a sofa pillow. "It's just that, well . . . we have this wonderful life, great careers, money, really great friends, and yet sometimes I feel rather . . . empty." She looked at his face to judge his response before continuing.

"Simon, I love you darling, and I'm deliriously happy with everything we have and all that brings me so much joy, but . . ."

Simon held her hand in his, "But what? What else is there?"

"I don't know really, I just feel empty, like a bit is missing."

"And you think God might be the missing bit?" He said it kindly, not with his usual sarcasm.

"Simon, who knows? But Cliff's call tonight just might mean something. Call him back for me, will you please, and tell him we are coming. I am not going without you, but I am going."

The stadium was packed. Cliff had sung beautifully, as if inspired. Luis Palau was the speaker that night. Simon and Serena had been given celebrity seats. Serena held Simon's hand tightly throughout the sermon. It was as if she was reluctant to let go. Luis spoke eloquently and gently about the love of God, explaining that God loves each and every one of us, rich or poor, black or white. He explained that Jesus had died on the cross for us, to cleanse us from all sin, and that God had prepared a way through the sacrifice of His son so that we all could be reunited with Him. Palau went on to say that we could experience the perfect life in Christ, restored to fellowship with God. All we had to do was repeat this prayer. Luis went through the prayer of forgiveness slowly, before saying, "If you said that prayer in your heart, believing that Jesus died for you and that you accept him as your Lord and Savior, then come down here and show everyone that you really meant it."

Suddenly, as if moved by a force she couldn't refuse, Serena let go of Simon's hand, and slowly but surely made her way down the steps to the podium, where others had already gathered. Simon watched her go for a few moments, then got up and followed her down. They both gave their lives willingly to Christ that day.

* * *

Simon was still dozing in the passenger seat.

"Honey, we're nearly there—it's just a few miles on, I think. Did you put the code in the Sat Nav?"

"Yeah I did. I'll sort it, you keep your eyes on the road."

Simon recalled the postcode on the satellite navigation system by tapping in the points with his fingertip.

The machine voice spoke. "Stay on the current road for five miles."

Simon looked up at the road ahead then suddenly screamed aloud, "Serena! Look out!"

Serena stiffened immediately and stared at the road ahead. Simon threw up his hands instinctively to protect his face from the impact. He shouted again, "Stop the car . . . pull over, pull over!"

The Mercedes shuddered violently, the tyres screeching and skidding as the vehicle came to a sudden halt. Before the car had finally come to a complete stop, Simon had opened the passenger door and was exiting the vehicle. Jumping out, he ran back along the highway. Serena was shaken by the suddenness of the incident and by Simon shouting at her so menacingly. She pulled up the handbrake lever, switched on the hazard lights, and got out of the car to see where Simon had gone. He was about

100 yards away, standing motionless in the center of the dual carriageway. Serena ran as fast as she could, and catching up with him, threw her arms around his shoulders. She twisted him about and was horrified at what she saw. Simon's countenance expressed utter confusion and shocked surprise.

She shook him. "Simon . . . Simon! What on Earth happened? Why did you shout for me to stop?"

Simon's haunted eyes turned to hers and away from the road. "Didn't you see him? Standing in the highway . . . I . . ." his words faltered, "I thought we were going to hit the guy head-on!"

"Who? Simon, who? There was no one. I saw nothing."

They both looked at the road behind. The roadside lamps illuminated an empty stretch of road. There was not a soul in sight.

"Come on Simon, let's go back to the car." Serena put her arm around his shoulders and tried to guide him back towards their parked Mercedes, but he resisted, still dazed, reluctant to leave the scene.

In the distance they heard the sound of a car. Soon the headlights of an oncoming vehicle, traveling fast, lit up the highway. Simon and Serena stepped against the hard shoulder to avoid the car, it came so close to them. As the car raced past, two teenagers leaned out of the windows shouting obscenities. "Stupid idiots, get out of the road!" A beer can, thrown from the car at the standing couple, clattered on the concrete road, tumbled and bounced, and then came to rest near their feet.

Another vehicle, blue lights flashing, came into view. Seeing the couple standing on the side of the road, the car came to a sudden screeching halt, and then reversed back along the highway, stopping just a few yards from Simon and Serena. Simon raised his hand to shield his eyes from the flashing lights. A young man got out of the driver's seat and approached them.

"Evening sir, madam, is there something wrong? Car broken down is it?" said the sergeant, showing them his police ID and badge.

Inspector Stewart, in plain clothes, stood beside his police vehicle slowly buttoning up his overcoat, pulling up the collar to ward off the cold night wind. He strolled over to where Simon and Serena and sergeant Llewellyn stood talking.

Not addressing the couple Stewart said, "Okay sergeant, what seems to be the trouble?" Stewart hated working at night, the graveyard shift. He knew that good people were tucked up in bed and all the rest creeping around at night were villains. He looked weary and sounded overtired.

"I was just asking these good people if they needed assistance, sir."

Simon was still dazed and shocked by the incident. Serena stepped forward and tried to explain to the weary detective.

"My husband thought he saw a man in the road, only I saw nothing. We stopped the car to make sure. Simon ran back along the highway, but found nothing."

"I tell you, I saw a man standing right in our path. I was dead sure we were going to hit him straight on, and before you ask, I am not drunk, nor having hallucinations!" insisted Simon.

The detective and the sergeant both stared at Simon, who was quite agitated.

"With all respect sir, that may be for us to decide. Who was driving?" asked Stewart.

"I was," volunteered Serena.

"And what speed do you think you were doing?" Sergeant Llewellyn was now writing in his notebook.

"I know what I was doing, because I saw the speed limit sign back there and slowed down to fifty miles an hour. I put it in cruise control to maintain the speed."

"And neither of you has been drinking this evening then?"

Simon turned to face Stewart. He was regaining his composure and his senses.

"We have driven up from Surrey. We are staying at the Alpha Hotel in town. We shall be here for a week. As you can appreciate, we are both extremely tired and really just want to continue to our destination. And to answer your question, we have not imbibed any alcohol today." Simon's speech was polite but firm and delivered in his best upper class accent.

Stewart looked at them both for a moment. "Suppose I should really ask the lady to take a breath test." Simon, exasperated, was about to say something more, but Serena squeezed his arm and smiled at the policeman before her.

"But as no one was hurt . . .and no damage done . . . I guess we can dispense with that formality."

Serena touched the detective's arm. "Thank you, that's very good of you."

Simon still looked a bit put out.

Sergeant Llewellyn, his notebook and pencil poised, said, "We have your hotel name, but not your own?"

Serena answered, "Mr. and Mrs. James, Simon and Serena James."

Stewart and the sergeant immediately exchanged knowing glances. Both Serena and Simon knew that look and what was coming next.

"Oh my God! Not . . . Bi Bi Bobbi Simon James?" Llewellyn said excitedly.

With a glum expression on his face Simon nodded, "Afraid so, banged to rights, you might say."

"Well I never," said Stewart. "Fancy meeting a famous pop star in the middle of the night on my watch, in Wales of all places!"

Serena smiled again and said, "So are we free to go now?"

"Yes, of course. I am sorry to have kept you both. Don't just stand there gawking, Llewellyn, escort Mr. and Mrs. James back to their car." Stewart actually gave Simon a little salute.

"Good night, sir, and you too, madam."

Llewellyn walked them back to their car, and Stewart could hear him jabbering away the whole time.

Back in the patrol car, Llewellyn could not stop talking and smiling.

"They're down here for a crusade or something at St. David's. Christians, both of them, like Cliff. Here at the invitation of the new bishop. Friends of his, they said."

"Maybe we should interview them again on some pretext or other, and you can ask for a signed photo, eh?"

"Really sir? That would be fantastic!"

* * *

Stewart did in fact decide to see them again, but not strictly on police business. He left his card at the hotel and Simon contacted him that evening.

"Is it about the incident on the highway, Inspector?"

"Yes and no. Sorry, that sounds a bit vague. I really want to hear again what you saw or what you thought you saw. It might just tie in with some other strange happenings that have occurred in the town lately."

"I see. Well if you can come to the hotel about eight thirty this evening we shall have eaten by then. Should Serena join us?" Simon asked.

"Oh yes, of course, no problem. Three heads are better than one, they say."

"Good. We'll meet in the bar. I am looking forward to seeing you again, Inspector." The line went dead.

Stewart got to the hotel at eight twenty, not wanting to be late. He had walked across town to get some exercise, of which he got precious little these days. He was overweight, but had no inclination to do anything about it. Beer, cigarettes, and food were his only comforts. He smoked on the way over, knowing that he'd be unable to in the hotel bar now that public smoking was banned everywhere.

He sat on a stool at the small bar counter and waited for them to arrive. The place was quiet, deathly quiet, with no other guests in sight. There wasn't even a bartender, so he sat drink-less and cigarette-less and desperately needing both. He heard them before he saw them. Simon was laughing as they came into the bar. He came straight over to shake Stewart's hand.

"Good evening, Inspector. I hope you are well?" Simon inquired politely.

He stood up and remained standing until Serena sat down at one of the nearby tables. "Yes, thanks, I'm fine."

"Drink, Inspector? What can I get you?" Simon had wandered around to the back of the bar.

"Darling, your usual?" he asked Serena.

"Yes please, but not a large one," she answered.

Simon poured out a gin and tonic and added ice and lemon.

"Inspector? Are you off-duty? A scotch, maybe?"

"I am, as it happens. Yes, a scotch with a drop of ginger and no ice, thanks."

Simon seemed to be the consummate professional bartender, and soon had all three drinks on a tray placed on the table. Stewart figured out that they were both over sixty, and yet they looked so much younger, full of vitality. She was still very attractive. She had long auburn hair, a slim build, and her face shone with an indefinable quality. He too looked no different from photographs taken over thirty years ago. Yes, his hair was graying at the sides, but it was still thick and wavy, and at six feet he was a handsome man. By contrast, although he was at least ten years younger, Stewart felt shabby and old.

"Your good health, Inspector." Simon held his glass aloft.

Stewart looked puzzled. "I hope you don't mind me asking, but it's not many establishments that allow guests to help to themselves to the booze . . ."

"Ever the policeman, Inspector, looking for crime everywhere. It's simply explained: Serena and I come here at least once a year to do a show at the local theatre. The original band comes with us and we bash out all the oldies, even, dare I say, Bi Bi Bobbi. It's fun, and the proprietors here treat us like family. In fact the hotel is closed for the season, re-opens next week, but the owners said we could bunk down for as long as we want to. But don't worry, I'll add the drinks to the bill, all above board Inspector."

"I didn't mean anything . . ." Stewart looked a trifle embarrassed and wished he'd kept his mouth shut.

Serena broke in, "So what's this all about, Inspector? Simon told me what you said on the phone, and I for one am intrigued."

Stewart took a deep breath and launched into his description. He told them about the curate's death and the strangeness of where the body was found. About the grisly murder of the vagrant on the beach and his mutilated body, and about Rosina's comments regarding the unusual nature of the injuries. Then he described the events of Halloween, culminating in the kidnapping of the child and the distraught mother's bizarre testimony regarding the carousel. Before continuing further he looked at them both. They had serious expressions on their faces now.

"I think I'm slowly going mad or something. None of this makes sense, well not to me anyway. And when you mentioned seeing a person in the road who turned out not to be there, I started to think that the trend was continuing . . . if you get my meaning. Does it make sense to you?"

Stewart's face registered confusion. He was beginning to wonder if coming here and involving these dear people had been a good idea.

Serena spoke first. "May I ask, Inspector, are you a Christian, a believer in God and His Kingdom?"

"That's the second time I've been asked that recently."

"And?" They looked at him quizzically.

"To be honest, I guess not, but a friend gave me a Bible, a kid's Bible, and I am reading it," he said, but without a lot of conviction.

"Well then, even if you haven't gotten very far with your reading, I am sure you have encountered an important theme in the Bible already, namely that there are two kingdoms in this world: the Kingdom of God and the Kingdom of the Devil, otherwise known as Satan." She stopped to let her words sink in.

"I was afraid you were going to say something like that. To actually entertain the idea that these events have been caused by supernatural means is outside my realm."

Simon leaned forward to emphasize what he was about to say, "You are not alone. We were once in that same place as you, full of doubt, skepticism and disbelief, but as some wise man once said, 'Demons exist whether we believe in them or not.'"

"And you think that these things are done by Satan?" There was more than a note of skepticism in his question.

"At this point, it is hard for us to say, but it is possible. When the Lord is about to do a mighty thing, the enemy will surely increase his attacks."

"Is the Lord, as you say, about to do a mighty thing?"

They both answered in unison, "Yes."

Simon continued, "We believe so. Our mission here is to preach the gospel and to bring people to Christ, but it is the Holy Spirit that does the real work in the hearts of men and women alike, and we have been invited here for a specific spiritual purpose."

Stewart settled back into his chair looking perplexed.

"Don't take our word for it, Inspector. Read for yourself what can actually happen when the Spirit of God moves to a specific locale. I suggest you ask at the local library or look on the Internet. Search for Evan Roberts and the 1904 revival in South Wales. Over one hundred thousand souls were "saved" in less than three months. It could happen here in this town if God wills it. And if God is preparing such a spiritual event again, then you can bet there will be opposition from supernatural quarters."

They sat in silence for a while, sipping their drinks. Stewart was dumbfounded by what he had just heard.

"But what can I do? I can't put demons in jail!"

Serena replied, "No you can't, but as a born-again Christian, you can fight back."

Born again? He had heard Rosina mention that, but he wasn't sure what it meant.

Simon leaned across to Stewart. "From what you have told us and from what we have shared with you, I think you are getting the picture. You need to ask yourself: If there is a God, do I want to know more about him?"

"Yes, I see what you mean." He sounded less confused, but needed to leave and think this through.

Serena asked, "Do you mind if we pray about all this?"

They bowed their heads and Stewart listened silently, his own head bowed. He was amazed at the power coming through their words of faith. Serena's prayers in particular struck him. Her passion came across so powerfully, speaking in Jesus' name and by the Holy Spirit, binding and uttering invocations against the Devil and all his works in this place.

Stewart was shaken by all this new knowledge. He was being introduced to a new language even, new words knocking at the door of his sparse vocabulary.

He felt he was on the edge of some great truth but did not yet know how to grasp it.

At the end of the prayer session he said, "If you need protection while you are in town just let me know, I might be able to furnish you with a couple of discreet minders."

Simon smiled and said, "Thank you Inspector, but we have our own protection, around us at all times; they are the angels of God."

They all laughed. Serena came over and hugged Stewart. He didn't expect that and responded a bit stiffly. She said, "Now, promise us you'll come to the event on Friday—seven o'clock at St. David's Church. I promise I'll save you a VIP seat, no, two VIP seats in the front row. Is it a deal?"

He felt he couldn't say no.

"I guess it is, and I think I know who to bring along, too."

They walked him to the door and Simon shook his hand warmly. Waving goodbye from the sidewalk, he headed home not knowing what to think about the things he had heard from Simon and Serena. Years ago, he would have scoffed at their words and dismissed it all as nonsense, yet something inside of him now was asking him to believe, no matter how fantastic it all seemed to be.

Chapter 28

Demons Gather

Rimmon sat upon his throne brooding, a clutch of parchments held tightly in his claw-like hand. The cavern was in semi-darkness. Lamps set in the walls emitted a pale yellow light. The roof of the huge cavern was covered in strange, sharply pointed stalactites that hung menacingly above the heads of the demons that stood before the throne. It was a cold, forbidding place.

Ganymede and Gathan and a few other high courtiers waited nearby for the outcome of their Master's deliberations. They had been in this position for over an hour, in quiet attendance. They dared not speak amongst themselves, for fear of disturbing him. The cavern in the mine was filled with all manner of demons, devils, hobgoblins and ghoulish imps.

There rose from this great mass of damned entities a low muttering, of which, fortunately for their sakes, Rimmon seemed unaware. The murmuring was starting to become perceptibly louder by the minute as they grew ever more weary and impatient. Gathan sensed their unease and tried to catch Ganymede's eye to urge him to interrupt Rimmon, but Ganymede was preoccupied with his own particular ruminations.

At last, Rimmon stirred, and glancing up, indicated that he wanted Ganymede's ear. The horde of demons fell silent and every eye was set upon the Lord seated on the throne. Ganymede took a few steps, bent low, and placed his ear close to Rimmon's open mouth.

Shaking the papers in his hand, Rimmon said, "What am I to make of these reports? Even my old ally Lord Salus makes fun of me for suspecting trouble in this pathetic place. He says I have been too long in the wilderness, that I am losing my wits. But I am convinced that something is afoot in this pestilential town. All my intuition tells me so. But here lies my predicament: our great Lord Satan is certain that I am wrong and has been on the verge of humiliating me for even raising the matter. If I dare speak again without hard evidence, I may spend the next thousand years looking after the frozen souls in Siberia. Gathan, tell me again what our spies are telling our majesty in Hell." Ganymede retreated.

Gathan stepped forward like a soldier, and saluting, prepared to give his report again.

The entire throng below the dais moved as one, surging forward en masse to inch nearer to the throne to try to catch what was being said. Gathan drew himself up to full height and spoke. "The reports coming back from all over the globe are that there are preparations under way for a major attack on our fortresses. Over the past few months, our agents have recorded the arrival of many important members of Heaven's household. They stay in secret places for a few days then leave, heading straight back to Heaven in haste, my Lord. After their departure, much activity is then observed with many, many angels going to and fro between churches and other holy sites. One of our most trustworthy spies managed to secret himself in the cathedral chapter in London and overheard the following conversation between high clergy. They said, 'So it comes to pass soon then. We must rally the people and begin to pray in earnest.'"

Rimmon silenced Gathan with a wave of his hand. Gathan backed away, bowing low as he went. "What of the new bishop and his new curate at St. David's?" he said peevishly.

Jusach stepped just one pace forward and said with false confidence, hoping to reassure his Lord and Master, "The bishop is a fool sire, he is more fitted to be a jester than a high priest, and as for the new curate, he is a stick insect with about as much power as a gnat in a hurricane."

"I can do without your amusing anecdotes! When I want humor I'll ask for it. Now get out of my sight."

Rimmon beckoned Ganymede with his finger and he drew near once more to Rimmon.

"I am in sore need of good advice . . . what can I do when all these reports appear to herald a concerted offensive against our forces worldwide? Satan, Lord Lucifer, is persuaded that soon, we shall all suffer an onslaught never seen before in this accursed universe. I know what is behind his fears—he is terrified that it is the second coming!"

Ganymede threw his head back and laughed uproariously. "Surely not! Does he still believe in those myths just because some madman wrote them down and they got included in their stupid so-called holy book? Why, it's been over two thousand years since those so-called revelations were written."

Rimmon wagged his finger at Ganymede. "Guard your tongue, Ganymede, there are too many ears in this hall who would report loose talk back to Lucifer."

Now it was Ganymede who leaned forward to whisper in Rimmon's ear.

"Sire, for sake of argument, let us take these reports seriously for a moment. Have there been any sightings of the . . ." and he paused, not wishing to say the name, "you know who, the third person of that ghastly group?"

"Good point, Ganymede. You are my savior at times. I think the answer to your question is definitely no. If he had been in attendance at any of these meetings, we surely would have known." Rimmon's face brightened as he began to formulate a new plan in his mind.

Ganymede, emboldened by praise, added, "And might I suggest, that where we do see evidence of him, then that is where the attack will come."

Rimmon sat back upon his throne with a look of complete satisfaction on his face.

"Maybe this little putrid, pestilential place will be our making. If the enemy strikes here, we shall be ready and we will crush them utterly. Satan shall be amazed at our skill and ingenuity in outwitting the forces of good."

Rimmon stood and faced the horde of minions who had been waiting for instructions. "My friends, I think you will now all applaud me, for I am a great demon indeed!"

There was a confused silence, until Gathan stepped forward and shrieked at the top of his voice, "Hail Rimmon, Lord and Master . . . Hail Rimmon!" Gathan made sure that the applause went on for several minutes, until Rimmon span around and vanished from view.

The clamor of praise immediately ceased and was followed by a collective sigh of relief.

Chapter 29

Headlines

The local newspaper was emblazoned with the headline *"Child still not found—Medium claims she can find Emily."* The front page article was continued on the center pages, with photographs of Jezebel sitting at a séance table, of a merry-go-round, the kind mentioned by the child's mother, and finally a photograph of Emily herself, taken on her fourth birthday. It depicted a beautiful, adorable little girl, smiling and happy.

The article didn't pull its punches. The main target for their vilification was the police, in particular the bumbling efforts of Detective Inspector Stewart, whom the paper said, *". . . couldn't find a 100 ton merry-go-round in a haystack, let alone locate the missing child."* Stewart was quoted as saying, *"We are continuing our investigations and are hopeful that we can solve this difficult crime."* What the words said and what was meant by them was understood by all the readers of the "Weekly Express," namely that there had been no progress whatsoever, and that the child was lost.

The photograph that took center stage was of Melanie holding a toy pony to her breast, seated with Madame Jezebel, whose hands hovered over a crystal ball. The words under the photograph spelled out, "Mother hopes that Madame Jezebel's amazing powers can discover Emily's whereabouts." The article went on to say that the Express's editor had set up the meeting between Melanie and the spiritualist medium in the hopes that where the police's natural methods had so lamentably failed, the "supernatural" might succeed. There followed a few heart-rending paragraphs describing in colorful, exaggerated language Melanie's sorry state of mind and sufferings. Readers were informed that she had lost fourteen pounds in weight since the disappearance of her daughter—that she was at her wit's end and could neither eat nor sleep.

Her tirades against God and the police were vitriolic. "Why had God allowed this to happen? I thought he was supposed to be a God of love!" She was sick of getting cards and letters from so-called Christians offering prayers. Melanie said she didn't want anyone's prayers. She just wanted someone—anyone—to find her darling Emily safe and sound. As for her comments regarding the police, she had nothing good to say about them. Her criticisms were listed. She claimed that she was treated like a madwoman, forcibly restrained by uncaring officers. She felt Detective Stewart should be made to quit. He had been so rude to her, making her feel like a criminal. She said he had not believed one word of her testimony regarding the events in the park on the night of Halloween. The newspaper editor took up this call, saying that if Detective Inspector Stewart was found to be incompetent, he ought to face discipline and dismissal from the force. The article went on to challenge the police to publish its case findings in the newspaper to demonstrate that something credible was being done.

Melanie wept as Madame Jezebel comforted her, unaware that her beloved daughter was no more than ten feet away, hidden in a room directly above her. Gathan was in attendance to ensure the proceedings went according his plans. The local paper's reporters were there with a photographer. There was even a female reporter from one of the national dailies.

Madame Jezebel had prepared the scene skillfully. The round table was polished like glass and the strange cabbalistic signs and symbols that decorated the top surface shone like jewels in the flickering candlelight. The room had been carefully lined with damask-rose drapes of velvet-red hues and with silken scarves of green and black. Here and there, silver and gold ornaments of astrological and occult significance had been expertly placed to maximize the flow of dark energies. To the unseen eye, it was a mere casual arrangement of objects, but in fact it inscribed all the points of the evil pentacles with satanic numerology at its heart. The lights were dimmed, and an altar of curious design at the end of the room was flanked by two great black candles whose flames flickered in the shadows.

The atmosphere was cold and unwelcoming to those initiates who did not understand the obscure ways of spirits and divination. Jezebel herself was dressed as a high priestess in a pure white robe trimmed with gold filigree and a loose hood draped over her black hair.

"Hey, lady, do you think we could have some more light in here for my camera?" the photographer said tersely.

Jezebel's eyes flashed angrily at him. "No, we cannot! The atmosphere must be perfectly attuned for my spirit guide to appear."

One man nudged his friend and whispered, "He got told, didn't he!"

His companion said in reply, "I'll be glad when this hocus-pocus is over, it gives me the creeps! You up for a pint of beer after?" The other man nodded.

Melanie was showing signs of stress and strain. Her face had all the features of weariness and lack of sleep.

"I need absolute silence and I warn you, do not approach me or come nearer to the table during the séance. It may prove dangerous."

The assembled reporters exchanged glances, winking at each other.

"We are here tonight to discover the whereabouts of this poor mother's child." She squeezed Melanie's arm to comfort her again.

"You all may see and hear things that will shock and frighten you, or you may simply be in a state of disbelief. It is no matter to me, for I know and I believe in the other world where spirits roam. After we have finished, you may check the room for hidden equipment or machinery. You will be wasting your time, for there is none. What you are about to experience is a reality that does exist in a world parallel to our own, and at such moments as this, the divisions between these worlds can be breached by the use of old magic."

There was a hush in the room now, and all started to fall under Jezebel's charms. She lit a candle at the center of the table. Beside it lay three small oil pots, which when lit, gave off a sweet intoxicating aroma. The smoke rose upwards, twisting and turning slowly like an immaterial snake. Melanie allowed herself to be mesmerized by the scene before her. It seemed to bring a blessed relief from the pain that had overwhelmed her.

"Son of Genghis, Gathan, come forth! We desire your presence, Lord."

Gathan smiled, for he loved being called Lord, even if only by this stupid old hag.

Jezebel took Melanie's hands in her own and began to chant in mysterious tongues, a language long extinct in the world at large and used only by a chosen few. Her head swayed from side to side. Her eyes were closed, yet she seemed to be gazing at something on the table. Then, the most extraordinary thing happened, and the surprise of the onlookers was audible.

"Come, O Gathan, Lord and Master, we have need of your wisdom this night." Jezebel opened her eyes suddenly. The flame from the candle appeared to dance in her eyes, and the smoke swirled around and around the perimeter of the table edge, becoming thicker by the second. It coalesced into a round mirage, at the center of which, quite unmistakable, was the face of a Mongol warrior, the features sharply defined, the nose flat, the eyes almond-shaped and the lips tight and thin, revealing jagged yellowing teeth.

The group of newspaper people stepped back into the shadows. One of the photographers raised his camera to shoot, but his hands trembled too much.

Melanie had an expression of sheer fright on her face and gripped onto Jezebel ever tighter.

"Welcome, my Lord. We are honored by your presence," said the medium, head bowed low.

"I am gratified to be here." The vision in the smoke turned to gaze at the persons shaking in the shadows and uttered imperiously, with menace, "Who are these cretins who seek my favor?"

One of the men gathered there broke away from his confederates and ran for the door, dropping his camera on the way and not stopping to retrieve it.

"Hah! Yes, run from my sight, fool! For I am Gathan the Destroyer." Those remaining clung onto each other in fear.

"Lord, Lord we know of your mighty powers, but we do not ask you this night to fight on our behalf. Instead we seek your wisdom on an important quest."

Jezebel faced the phantasm in the smoky mist, and Gathan played his part in the charade.

"What is it you seek?"

"The fair damsel who sits beside me has suffered a grievous loss. Her only child, a daughter of only four years, has been taken from her. She is distraught, as the soldiers here can do nothing to solve this evil abduction," Jezebel pleaded well.

"How can I assist the damsel in distress?" Gathan inquired.

"Lord, you know all, see all, and through your wisdom can put this poor mother's mind at ease by searching the Heavens and the Earth to find the child."

"But only if it is my pleasure to do, Jezebel."

"Yes, only if my Lord wishes it so," said Jezebel obediently.

"Then chant the ancient words to help guide me whilst I penetrate the dark, seeking the light."

Jezebel chanted low, sweet sounds, using her voice like an instrument, like a flute playing a haunting melody. Melanie's head was now resting against the bosom of the spiritualist like daughter and mother. The face in the smoke vanished and was replaced by swirling mists, bursts of light, and strange eerie sounds like birds shrieking in the wilderness. Some of the newsmen, recovering from the initial shock of their supernatural experience, were busy scribbling notes on pads, recording everything, lest they forget later what they had witnessed this night. The medium stopped chanting and said, "My Lord is returning." The face re-appeared in the smoke above the table.

"I have found the child."

Melanie started up and looked straight at the apparition, giving it all her attention.

"Do not grieve, the child is safe. She sleeps. I, Gathan, son of the Great Genghis Khan, have warned her abductors that they all will suffer a slow death at my hands if the child is not returned within seven days."

Melanie started to speak, all her fear gone from her, "My Lord, I am so happy. Thank you. Thank you . . ."

She thrust her hands towards the image. Jezebel swiftly pulled them back before speaking aloud, "Lord, you are mighty and gracious, you are all merciful. We are all in your debt. Farewell, O Gathan, farewell."

The demon was happy with himself. Pride swelled his heart. It was a compelling performance. As he rose through the ceiling, he looked back at the pathetic group now clustered around the table. "What is it that He sees in them, these cretins, that He is ever mindful of them and sends his angels to look over them? It is beyond my comprehension. If I had my way, I would annihilate the whole human race."

Chapter 30

A Very Present Help

The newspaper headlines and front pages carried the reports of the séance and the extraordinary visions seen by the reporters and photographers. Melanie was quoted as being "ecstatic" that her daughter would be returned to her safe and sound. Madame Jezebel, photographed outside her occult center, said that the church and the public were misinformed about white magic and the good influences it can bring to the community of Penrhos Bay. Included in the article was a short response from Nigel Jeffries, the newly-elected bishop, who said that the Bible clearly tells us that mediums, spiritists, and clairvoyants are serving Satan and that it is unfortunate that the mother of the missing child has been drawn into the web of deceit and evil.

The final comment in the main article was from the Superintendent of Police, who had stated, ". . . that the police would always follow up on any information brought forward, but in this case no new data had surfaced that would be of use to the police." The pages dealing with letters from readers expressing their views, often passionate, all concerned this case and the use of a medium. It would seem that the public was undecided about the merits of using such methods.

Alone in her home, Melanie read and re-read the articles from several newspapers that were spread on the floor in front of where she sat. There were also numerous photographs of Emily scattered about her, depicting the child from birth to the present. Outside, a noisy group of reporters and photographers waited impatiently for any news about the missing child. Melanie wiped the tears from her eyes. She used a pretty little handkerchief adorned with flowers that she had given to Emily on her fourth birthday. The home that she normally kept so clean and tidy was now in disarray. She was neglecting herself and hadn't even bothered to buy food.

Fortunately for Melanie, a social worker had visited her earlier that day and promised to arrange the delivery of a food parcel. "Food Share" was a church-based organization that collected and distributed food and other essentials to those in dire need and who had for whatever reason fallen into that void between being unable to help themselves and receiving emergency support from local agencies. Two ladies from the GF church, Michelle and Linda, had initiated the programme only a few months before. They had quickly begun to realise that there were many starving in this town, despite the affluence of most people's lives. Over seventy parcels had been delivered since the opening.

Rosina and Sadie rang the doorbell and waited on the step. Both held a large box crammed to the top with food that would last someone at least a week. Melanie rose wearily from the carpet and walked slowly to the front door. It couldn't be helped, but all the reporters and photographers immediately knew what was happening. The cameras burst into life and eager reporters shouted questions at the two women. When Melanie appeared at the door, they all surged forward, pressing against Sadie and Rosina, who almost dropped the boxes. To escape the melee, they pushed past Melanie into the hallway and slammed the door shut behind them.

"That's awful! Do you have to put up with that all the day and night?" said Sadie sympathetically.

"I don't really notice it," replied Melanie sadly.

"Shall we put this food away for you?" said Rosina, heading for the kitchen.

The kitchen was a mess. They both looked at Melanie and had the same thought. Sadie put her arm around Melanie and directed her to the living room.

"Look, you just sit down and we'll put the stuff away and make us all a nice hot drink and a sandwich. You look like you need it."

Melanie smiled weakly at Sadie. "Thank you."

In the kitchen, Rosina was already busy cleaning up the mess and tidying everything, whilst Sadie emptied the contents of the boxes into the cupboards and fridge. In a short while, all three women were sitting together in the living room sipping hot mugs of tea and munching on sandwiches and biscuits. Rosina was the first to break the silence.

"We both have young daughters and can imagine what you must be going through."

Melanie looked at them and couldn't stop another tear from falling onto her cheek. Sadie moved beside her and put her arms completely around Melanie to comfort her. She began to weep. All the anguish and the pain had been kept back behind a dam of emotions that was at the point of breaking.

"Let it out, Melanie. We'll stay with you as long as you want."

Melanie's body convulsed and she sobbed deeply, the tears now flowing freely.

Rosina prayed silently. After a few minutes, Melanie dried her face and said, "I'm so sorry. I just feel so helpless, and I miss my baby so much. At times I feel that I can't cope."

"Please don't be sorry. None of this is your fault," said Rosina.

"But sometimes I feel guilty. I think that we shouldn't have gone out that night. I should have said no to Emily when she wanted to go on the ride. If I had been a good mom, none of this would have happened, would it?" She looked imploringly at Sadie and Rosina.

Rosina bent down to pick up the newspapers that were scattered across the floor. She read the headlines and felt dismay in her heart.

Laying the papers neatly aside, she knelt before Melanie and asked, "The séance that you went to . . . all the papers said you were happy. But now you are sad again?" Rosina waited for Melanie to respond.

"I was at first, but days have gone by and I don't have Emily back, so I don't know what to believe."

Rosina took Melanie's hands in her own. "Can I share something with you that may be hard for you to take in right now?" Rosina looked straight into Melanie's reddened eyes. "Nothing good can come from people like the lady you went to see. You were desperate, and I can understand that you would go to anyone to get your daughter back, but only bad comes from bad. That medium is in touch with spirits, evil spirits, and no matter what you were told, it is all lies. I suspect that the whole thing was constructed simply to get this woman's name and picture into the paper."

Melanie had stopped crying and was gazing intently at Rosina.

"There is only one person you can turn to in these situations."

"Do you mean God?" said Melanie plaintively.

"Yes," said Rosina.

"I have prayed. I used to believe at one time. That was before I got into drugs and sex and drinking."

Sadie wrapped her arms around Melanie a little tighter to give reassurance.

"Can we pray with you now?" asked Rosina.

Melanie simply nodded.

"Abba, Father, we ask that you give strength to Melanie and bring her comfort during this terrible time. We pray, Father, that you bring Emily back to her mom, safe and unharmed."

Sadie added her own prayer, "Lord, you know how a mother feels when her child is lost. How much pain she feels and what she is going through, we are asking right now for a miracle in this situation so that Emily will be found soon safe and unharmed."

"I pray also, Father, that you bring peace to Melanie's heart, supernatural peace that comes only from you. We also bind the enemy, in the name of Jesus Christ, that Melanie and Emily will no longer be troubled by evil spirits."

When the prayers had been said, both Sadie and Rosina hugged Melanie.

Releasing Melanie, Rosina said, "If you like, we could come and visit you again?"

"I'd like that, thanks," said Melanie, a little brighter now.

"Then we'll pop in tomorrow, okay?" said Sadie.

Leaving the house, they passed through the gauntlet of newsmen but said nothing, even though they were pestered right up to the door of their car. Sadie drew away from the curbside and said to Rosina, "My heart just went out to her. I just kept thinking, what if I was in that awful situation with Lauren . . ." she couldn't finish the sentence.

Rosina was still praying for Melanie. "We should contact the pastor right away, Sadie, and get others to pray. I truly believe that God is going to help Melanie and bring her daughter back safe."

Chapter 31

A Blessing in Disguise

The Superintendent sat at his desk with several copies of the local papers, open to the offending pages. His hands were flat, as if he was trying to hold the reports down as he studied them closely. Stewart sat waiting for his boss to say something. He'd been called in just as soon as he had arrived at the station. The super's office was large and bare. There were no trophies on the wall. No photographs of the superintendent with famous people or those high up in government. He was a private sort of man with no ambitions to be one of the greats, which is why he was in charge of a small town police department. However, things had changed lately. It seemed that emails from London and telephone calls from the Commissioner of Police were now a daily occurrence. The recent events culminating in the disappearance of Emily O'Reilly were putting the spotlight onto his small, hitherto quiet world. He was a good man, and his subordinates liked him. He was fair and gave no favor to anyone for any reason. He was one of the old-school, a dying breed, a truly honest cop.

"I guess you've seen all these headlines and articles? They're not very complimentary about us, and it seems, I'm sorry to say, that you, Paul, are the main target for all the heavy flak." He didn't look up. Stewart simply nodded. Superintendent Carlton looked up when the Inspector didn't reply.

The Superintendent was shocked at Paul's appearance, "God, Paul, you're a wreck! You're not letting this case get under your skin, are you?"

"Not really, sir . . . it's just that I am not sleeping too well."

"Well, I'm not surprised. But you have to look after yourself, man. You know that's the first rule in our game," he said with some sympathy. "Look, this is going to sound harsh. I know the good work you've being doing since you came here, and I'm certain that you're burning the midnight oil trying to solve this bloody abduction case, but it's no longer just a local problem. The adverse press we are getting has been passed up to my bosses." He stood up, came around the desk, and sat on the front edge.

"You look sick, man. Seeing you like this has made up my mind."

Stewart looked at the Superintendent, guessing what was coming.

"I am being pressured to take you off the case. It has already been decided that another force is sending a team in. They're arriving tomorrow morning, and I've agreed that you don't need to do a handover. They will go over all the files and reports and contact you if and only if they need to."

Stewart looked depressed and sighed. He didn't try to hide his feelings.

"It goes against my better judgment, because I know what sort of man you are and I know you would prefer to see it through. But politics, the press, and the reputation of this station have all come into play. I hate it because it's got nothing to do with good police work. For most of my career I have managed to avoid all that stupid stuff." He began to walk around the office.

"Boss, I'm sorry . . ."

The Super cut him short, and pointing his finger straight at Stewart, he said resolutely, "No, don't you apologize. None of this is of your making. You haven't failed me, man—every force has unsolvable cases; their books are full of them. But let's pray this doesn't turn out to be one of them!" Stewart sat hunched in the chair.

"I'm putting you on paid leave with immediate effect; full pay, no questions about it. Some hot-headed idiots in London who jump when the press pass sentence on us wanted you summarily dismissed. I told them that won't happen on my watch. So if you go down, I'll come with you, understood?"

"Thanks," said Stewart, his voice subdued.

"I want you to use the time wisely, Paul. Take that trip you're always talking about. A change of air will do you good."

Stewart said, "Any other time in my career I would have resisted this decision, fought back against the buggers, but now . . ." he took a deep breath in, "Super, I agree. I need to find myself again and this case has me beat. My head really is so confused, nothing adds up. I don't know which way to go."

Paul Stewart got up from the chair and held his hand out to the Superintendent. "Thanks Boss, I really appreciate your support."

The Superintendent showed him to the door. "If there's anything else I can do, just call me, and if these jokers find anything new I'll be sure to let you know. I'm not casting you out into the darkness, Paul."

Paul Stewart walked silently through the outer offices, not turning to look at his colleagues, not wanting to say one word. At the top of the steps outside, he paused and took a deep breath of cold air. He instinctively went to his pocket for his cigarettes, but having second thoughts, changed his mind. As he walked home, all he could hear in his head was what the Super had said: "I'm not casting you out into the darkness." Why was it important? Then it dawned on him, it was something he had read in the Bible that Rosina had given him. He tried to remember the words, but only snatches of it came to him: ". . . that men loved darkness rather than light because their deeds were evil." He quickened his pace. Suddenly, he wanted to get home to read more.

Arriving back at the flat, and without waiting to remove his coat, he picked up the Bible and flicked through the pages, trying to find the verse about darkness and evil. After a few minutes he was going to give up, and then he remembered praying with Simon and Serena. He wondered if you could pray for something like this. He wasn't sure how to pray, what to say, whether to speak out loud or just say it silently in his head; however, it just seemed to come out naturally, "God, show me this verse," and then he added, "please." He picked up the Bible once again, and in the palm of his hand the book fell open to the Gospel of John, Chapter 3, verse 19, and there in front of him in red letters was the exact verse he sought. He sat down slowly on the sofa and didn't know what to think, but he read on and continued reading for the next few hours without stopping.

* * *

The next day, Stewart got up early and cooked a breakfast of ham, eggs, toast, and coffee, something that he hadn't done for ages. Instead of leaving the dishes in the sink, he washed them up, the frying pan too, and put them all away in the kitchen cabinets. He gazed around the kitchen, and thought that later he would tidy the whole place up. It badly needed it, and had been neglected too long.

After his shower he strolled over to the Male Box, his local barber. His turn came, and he sat down in the chair. "Hello Sadie, how's life with you?"

She swung the gown over his shoulders, buttoned it up and looked at him in the mirror, giving him a really great smile. "Life's very good, thanks, how about you?"

"Well, funny you should ask. You know I'm a cop, right?"

"Yeah," she replied, standing with the scissors and comb in her hands.

"It has been tough lately, but yesterday I did something that I have never done before." He whispered the next words, "I read the Bible! Well, not all of it, but I can't put it down."

"Wow!" Sadie smiled her broad, trademark smile.

"I know it's unbelievable. I don't know what's happening to me. But I know it can't be bad."

The rest of the salon was now tuning in on the conversation and listening intently.

"The same thing has happened to me. I met this lovely lady Linda and she invited me to church. It has been wonderful, I feel like I am a new me! Lauren and I go every Sunday, and during the week we go to home meetings. I'm really enjoying it, and some things have happened to me that have changed my life." Sadie was beaming.

Stewart looked at her and he could see that she was expressing real, undiluted joy.

The barber shop was still. Sadie and Stewart saw that everyone was looking at them, even those sitting in the other chairs. Stewart and Sadie looked at each and burst into laughter.

"I think you'd better cut my hair!"

During the next fifteen minutes or so, Stewart and Sadie talked about God, church, life—the list was endless, but it was all packed into a few short moments in a hairdressing salon. Sadie explained to Stewart how to get to the church, and he left, but not before promising he'd see her there on Sunday morning and leaving her a big tip. He strode out into the morning feeling unspeakably happy, and also thinking that he'd never really looked at Sadie before, but today he thought she looked great. Maybe, just maybe, he'd ask her out one day if he could find the courage.

Crossing High Street, he decided to continue with his re-make of his persona. In M&S, he chose a whole new wardrobe. He bought new shirts, trousers, socks, ties, a fashionable winter sweater, and a couple of new jackets. He was amazed when the lady at the till asked him for nearly three hundred pounds. He hadn't spent that much money on himself since, well, since he was still with his wife. In fact he used to enjoy going out with her to shop and browse. Unlike most men, he liked to see her buy new clothes and spend time trying them on. Happy times, but long ago now. He surprised himself by feeling quite light-hearted. No regrets anymore. The past is past and you can't change it, you can only change your-self if something needed changing. He sighed, then smiled to himself. Nothing was going to drag him down again. He made a promise to himself and he intended to honor it. Burdened with bags, he hailed a passing taxi to take him home.

The next day he got sucked into housekeeping, cleaning, and washing and tidying up his bedroom too, which normally was a pile of garbage. Be-fore getting ready to go to church, he found he had enough time to go to his local supermarket. His trips to the supermarket were always depressing—seeing families and couples in the aisles talking, laughing, and joking. He'd throw almost anything into the trol-ley as long as it fit some basic criteria. First, can it be opened, warmed up in the microwave oven, and consumed straight from the can or plastic container? Second, will it stay on the shelf or in the refrigerator for weeks and not go off so that he could eat it any-time of the day or night? Items that always suited that bill were baked beans in a can, baked beans and sau-sages in a can, spaghetti or macaroni in a can, soups and custard in a can . . . the list was endless.

But on this Sunday morning, he looked at the pro-duce with new eyes. He filled the trolley with fresh meat and fish, newly baked bread, cheese from the deli, and fresh fruit and vegetables from the green grocery. He was actually enjoying the whole expe-rience. He bought a cafetière and some Colombian coffee. Wheeling around the aisles, he caught him-self whistling a tune and more than once exchanged glances with other shoppers, bidding them good morning. He felt like Ebenezer Scrooge born again on Christmas morning.

When he arrived at church, he couldn't quite believe his eyes, and had to ask if he was in the right place. The person at the door greeted him with a big smile and handed him a leaflet. He stepped into the place and was at a loss for what to do. He was in a bar. The building was the bar and recreation center of a caravan park just a few miles outside the town and right next to the beach. The room had a long bar counter just like a public house. The tables, chairs, and sofas were assembled just as you might expect to see them in a large bar or pub. At the end of the room was a raised stage area with half a dozen musicians getting ready to play. There were guitars, a full drum set, an electric piano, and a tall bass. Several microphones were set up for the singers.

Stewart was dumbfounded. Was this a church? He had only been in churches at funerals and weddings, and those had been model examples of ecclesiastical architecture: cold, lofty, hard pews, and a pulpit at the business end. This was something else. It was a bar, plain and simple, and surely it couldn't masquerade or pretend to be a house of God. There were no wooden pews, Bibles, crosses, or crucifixes, and no vicar in a black dress. All these thoughts turbulently rushed through his mind. Suddenly he wondered what he was doing here. His confidence drained away. He glanced around at the few other people that had arrived early to see if anyone would notice his retreat. As he turned to go, Rosina and her young daughter walked in. She saw him immediately and came straight over to his side.

"Paul, what are you doing here?" she said with real warmth in her voice. Hugging him, she said, "This is wonderful! Sasha, say hello to Mr Stewart." The little girl was shy, and spying some friends arriving, asked if she could go and play.

"Paul, I am so surprised. Come and sit down here," she guided him to a sofa. "To be honest, I was going to invite you, but I thought I would wait a little after I heard the news at work about you being put on suspension." She placed her hand on his. "I am so sorry, Paul."

He shrugged. "Hey, please don't lose any sleep over the situation. I'm actually enjoying the time off."

She looked at him with disbelief.

"No, really, Rosina. I am really glad that I have some free time to think about my future."

"And?" she said.

"It's too early to say whether I stay in the force or take retirement and do something completely different, but what I do know is that I'm not going on as I did before. I'm beginning to get a new perspective on life. I'm not sure what's driving this transformation, but I want it, whatever it might be."

Rosina was about to say something, but held back and smiled. "You look different, too," she said admiringly.

"Yeah, I got a haircut and bought some new clothes." He stood up to show his new clothes off. "And speaking of haircuts, there's the lady responsible for my new coiffure, and by the way, for inviting me here today."

Sadie spied Paul immediately and came straight over with her own daughter, Lauren. Sadie and Rosina greeted each other with a long hug.

Paul said, "You two know each other?"

"She cuts my hair, too, you know, but not in the barber shop!" said Rosina with a laugh.

"And our daughters play together, we go to the same house group, and . . . have I left anything out Rosina?"

"Yes, we sometimes deliver food parcels and then have a drink together."

"So Paul, what do you think of our church? I should have warned you, sorry," apologized Sadie.

"Honestly? Well I was just about to run, and it's not like me to flee from a pub, when Rosina came in and rescued me from my fears."

They all laughed together.

"But I must say, it is a pretty odd place to congregate to worship God, isn't it?"

Rosina spoke up first, "Well Paul, I think you will soon come to know that God isn't in the building—he's in us—so it doesn't really matter when or where you worship God. The real truth about church is this: we can't build it. Jesus builds his church and he inhabits every stone and every brick, because his people are the building blocks, and I guess the cement that holds us all together is the loving relationships we share. The religious people who believe they have to actually go to a church, a fancy building, have got it all wrong. Christ's church is here—" Rosina pointed to her own heart, and then, to Paul's surprise, she tapped on his chest, "– and in there too."

Sadie looked at Rosina in awe. "Rosina, that was lovely, what you said."

Stewart still felt a tingling sensation in his breast where Rosina had touched him.

"I'll be back in a minute guys, I need to talk to a friend." Stewart watched Rosina weave through the crowd of churchgoers.

"Do you want a drink?" Sadie saw his surprised expression. "No, not that kind. A coffee, tea, or hot chocolate? There's a machine over there. Sit down and I'll get you one."

The church began to fill up quickly as it got closer to eleven. He picked up a beer mat off the coffee table. It had the usual sort of diagram motif that you would expect to find, except this one had a name written across the top, "God's Free Church," and in the center was the motto, "Down to Earth Spirituality." Sadie returned with the coffees and a juice drink for Lauren. The service started with something that sounded like a rock song, except the words were different. On the big TV screen, the lyrics of the song were displayed to a backdrop of beautiful scenes of mountains and forests and waterfalls. The words proclaimed Jesus as Lord and called him the Savior and King of Kings. Everyone was standing now, men, women, young people and kids, all singing loudly together. Some were dancing in the spaces between the tables, chairs and sofas. He'd never in his life seen anything like this.

Stewart decided he was going to jump straight in at the deep end. Sink or swim, he thought. He sang the unfamiliar words, and soon enough found he was actually enjoying the experience. After awhile, all the children ran out of the building to enjoy their own planned activities, and everyone else, sitting down, settled quietly to listen to the sermon. He could see that some people had Bibles and had spread them out on their laps to follow the scripture references given by the speaker. For those that didn't have Bibles, the verses referred to were displayed on the big screen.

The speaker, a tall gray-haired man in his fifties, casually dressed in an open-necked shirt, introduced himself as one of the pastors of the church. His style of delivery was dynamic and interesting, and Stewart was on the edge of his seat, carefully following every word. This was all so new to him, but he felt something inside clamoring for more. After the pastor had finished, there was a short prayer time, and then some more music and singing. At the end, everyone hung around talking and chatting. He even saw some people ordering real drinks from the bar that now appeared to be open.

Sadie and Rosina had sidled off somewhere to collect their kids and Stewart was left sitting alone, but not for long. First a couple came over and introduced themselves, asking whether this was his first visit to GFC. After they said goodbye, hoping that they'd see him next week, the speaker came over and shook his hand. At that moment Rosina and Sadie returned. They all sat down together and talked mainly about him, but he found he didn't mind. Upon leaving, he kissed Sadie on the cheek, and holding her hands in his, he warmly thanked her for inviting him. As he walked back to his car he chuckled to himself, "What a weird place! But I'm definitely coming again."

Chapter 32

Walking on Water

The offshore waters were disturbed only by a gentle breath of wind. The delicate breeze plucked at the surface of the sea here and there, creating little waves that were born in an instant and then vanished before the moment had time to speak.

Samuel, since his encounter with the Holy One, had seemed to grow in stature. No longer possessing the physique of a mere minstrel, he displayed the body of a lean warrior of God. His whole demeanor and light shone brighter. It had been a bravely earned gift from the Creator himself.

"It's so beautiful here," observed Samuel to the captain.

They walked together a mile from the landfall of Penrhos Bay.

"Yes it is. I thought you needed a respite after all your troubles lately and I know you love the sea."

Ignoring the captain's last remark, Samuel honed in on the earlier statement.

"Troubles?" Samuel stopped walking on the water and swung around to face the captain.

"My choice of words are in error. Not your troubles, but those in your charge."

"I am not troubled though, my Captain. Isn't our duty to care for and protect the saved?" There was a note of uncertainty and inquiry in Samuel's voice.

"Of course. Please do not stumble over my poor choice of words."

They continued to stroll on, parallel to the shore and moving forward in the general direction of the Great Ulm. It truly was a stunning vista. The ancient rocks and cliffs of the Great Ulm were untouched by thousands of years of ocean waves. It must have been a hard, forbidding, and unrelenting sort of place for the people who had lived here in pre-history. To the south of the Ulm was Penrhos Bay, a delightful sea-side town. If these two angels had been walking by only two centuries earlier, no such place would have existed. There would have been only the wide sweep of mud flats between the east and west shores. A wild habitation inundated daily by the cruel sea, where only sea creatures that scampered over the mud between the tides and the birds of the air could survive. Farther south the dark mountains of Snowdonia stood like great sentinels, capped with new falls of snow, ever watchful, and upon the valleys and slopes of the lower hills deep forests of green hid all kinds of animals, affording them food and shelter.

"I brought you out here to talk of things to come. This town will soon be under siege by the enemy and a great battle will ensue in the coming days. Our God has chosen this humble place to be the start of a mighty awakening among his people. We converse here so that the enemy cannot eavesdrop and come to suspect our Lord Christ's true purposes. We have been given only a glimpse of what he intends to do, but it will be great, and its effect will be felt across the globe in many hearts."

"I knew that something of the kind must be coming," Samuel's voice became more reverent, "after the Spirit of the Lord spoke to me and gave me the sword."

The sword was hung about his waist in a silver scabbard. As he spoke, his right hand instinctively clasped the hilt.

"You have a very important part to play in His plan, Samuel." The captain halted.

"You will fight alone. In that way, the enemy will not suspect at all that the person you guard so well is the key soul in this spiritual battle that will unleash the power of the Holy Spirit."

"The man Richard, the new curate. Is he the one?"

"Yes, it is he," said the captain. "What I am about to tell you has come straight from God's throne. He has placed much trust in you in this affair. Be assured the Spirit of God shall be at your side, but he will be undetected by Rimmon's evil servants, and you must engage the enemy using your own strength and wits. The Spirit will guide you, but not protect you. The battle will be yours alone."

Samuel became pensive, a question growing in his mind. "But sir, surely there are warriors among the hosts far more skilled and capable than I to carry out this crucial task?"

"You are right, there are," agreed the captain.

"Forgive me, but what about yourself? You are eminently fit for this purpose."

The captain smiled at Samuel. "I am glad you think so! But God does not agree with you."

Samuel lapsed into a deep silence.

"I have been appointed captain general over ten thousand handpicked officers and warriors of Christ and I shall be nearby, but hidden. However, I shall arise with my army at the right time and vanquish our foes."

Samuel's eyes grew bright.

"And you, my friend, will vanquish your own foe and perform a wonderful deed on the night of the crusade. Together we shall deal such a mighty blow to Satan's forces that they will be scattered throughout the Heavens."

"Praise God!" shouted Samuel. Quite spontaneously, he began to sing about the glory of God in the angels' own sweet tongue.

The captain put his arm around Samuel's shoulder and smiled. There was real love in the embrace. Little waves splashed over their feet. The wind was rising and bringing storm clouds. They rose, climbing together into the heights, the captain's arm lazily draped around his companion—the perfect picture of angelic affection, brotherly love, a rare quality seldom found on Earth. True love, agape—unconditional love inspired by God.

Chapter 33

Miracle of Sorts

For those that had eyes to see the spirit realm, it might have looked odd to see a large, tall, and fiercely imposing angel, armed with a shining scimitar, standing guard in front of a small seaside hotel. Certainly, those arriving and those already gathered inside were unaware of the angelic presence. The heavy rain blew in off the sea and lashed the front of the hotel. It was not a night for venturing out on any pretext, but it seemed that all had been curious about the couple's invitation and none had refused to come.

The lounge of the hotel was half-full with clergymen, and not just any clergymen, but the leaders and heads of local churches from all denominations. They had all been personally invited to the hotel this evening by Simon James. The grandfather clock in the hall struck seven o'clock. Simon looked at his watch and announced, "Before I welcome you all tonight, I think we shall wait for another ten minutes for any stragglers to arrive. They may be delayed by the atrocious weather."

"Is the weather always like this in North Wales at this time of year?" asked Serena genially, hoping to stimulate some conversation, as there had been precious little so far. Some of the guests offered answers, and for a moment everyone was quite happy to chat about the weather.

Simon was handing out drinks from the bar and Serena mingled amongst those gathered to while the minutes away. A few latecomers entered, arriving at the same moment. They were two elderly men and a large, middle-aged woman. The men were the minister from the Methodist Church and the pastor of the Evangelical Church at the edge of town. The woman was one of curates from the Holy Trinity team. Serena bade them welcome. Simon scanned the group and counted heads. There were, in fact, more than he expected, but he supposed that some had brought along a colleague or friend.

To put the assembled group at ease, Simon explained that everyone had not been invited to hear him and his wife sing, especially not the infamous song "Bi Bi Bobbi . . ."

Someone muttered, loud enough for all to hear, "Thank God for that."

Simon laughed. "Well yes, but I do thank God that sometimes on rare occasions He does ask me to sing."

Simon, taking stock of his assembled guests, registered quickly that the task ahead of him was not going to be easy. He could see by the way his guests had seated themselves, occupying chairs so that there was always a vacant seat between them and the next person, that they were not inclined towards meeting together, and Simon noticed by the lack of conversation that they were not on intimate terms. Before continuing, he said a silent prayer asking for God's leadership and wisdom.

"As I said to each one of you on the telephone, I invited you here to tell you all about this weekend's concert and crusade. Let me make it clear that I am not, as it were, 'singing my own praises,' but simply asking that you and your churches support us in this spiritual endeavour."

A few chairs moved as the occupants shifted uneasily.

"You are already aware that Bishop Nigel, the new Bishop of Conwy, whom some of you have already met I understand, has asked Serena and myself to lead this event. Please be assured that this is not the first time we have led such an event. Serena and I have been doing outreaches like this for over thirty years now, but I hasten to add this: We are here to serve you."

A man in a dog collar raised his hand to ask a question. "Simon, I am Richard Cowell of the URC in town. Might I ask, if you are leading it as you say, why it is being held in the Anglican Church of St. David's and not in one of our churches, which I might say have better facilities than does St. David's?" The minister waved his hand from side to side to illustrate his point.

"Richard, to answer your question, it is being held at St. David's because the idea for this event came from Bishop Nigel, who in choosing not to be here tonight is clearly saying that this is not an Anglican event, but rather, he hoped, a combined effort. He is simply providing the venue and not using it to proselytize. On a more practical point, to change the venue now would cause some difficulties, especially as that church has excellent sound systems that I can assure you my wife and I do need in order for the concerts to go well."

Richard seemed to be satisfied with the answer, so Simon continued. "Nigel has been telling me that there has been a spate of awful occurrences of late in the town, especially on Halloween. The bishop has told me that God has spoken to him and that what the Lord requires is for all of us, the Christian community in Penrhos Bay, to link arms and defend this place against the principalities and powers of this age."

A man suddenly stood up in an agitated state of mind and exclaimed in a strong Welsh accent, "If God has spoken, then why has he spoken only to the bishop and not to me and to the rest of us? Does God want us to be under the control of the Church of England? I say to you, young man, that my ancestors fought hard against English tyranny and many lost their lives fighting for that just and holy cause. What do you say to that?" He sat down, arms folded, and stared aggressively at Simon.

Simon glanced at his wife, sending her signals urging, "For God's sake, pray, pray before we have a riot on our hands!"

Without rising from her chair, the lady curate from Holy Trinity spoke up, "Jane Seymour, Trinity. Concerning Halloween, I read the reports in the local newspapers, and I'm sure that most of the troubles were just hi-jinks on the part of young people drinking too much alcohol."

"Weren't there also some serious crimes? Two murders and a child kidnapped?" retorted Simon politely.

"Yes, that too . . . but pick up any newspaper in the land and you'll read of similar tragedies."

Before Simon could comment further the curate went on to say, "I have been curate at Trinity for several years and the bishop is head of our diocese. But

his predecessor, who was bishop for over two decades, never once stated that God had commanded
him to do anything with all the other churches. I am
of the belief that it is ordained by God that there are
various denominations, because in that way God
reaches everyone in the community, whatever their
point of view on religion. But where does God say
we should put aside our differences and work as one
church? I think this whole business is a trifle naïve, the misguided actions of a bishop who seeks to
bring so called 'new ideas' into a community that has
weathered most storms in the past without help from
the outside."

Simon knew that her last point was directed at him
and Serena. It was pretty obvious that although he
had invited these ministers, they had all come with
their own agendas.

Another individual rose to speak—the minister
from the Presbyterian Church. He was a gray-haired,
balding man, dressed in a dark gray overcoat and
scarf, which he had not removed despite the warm
temperature inside the hotel. "I think I can speak for
most of us here, being the senior clergyman in the
town." There were a few grumblings at this remark.
"I think we all would have been disposed to support this so-called outreach," he emphasized this last
word disdainfully, "if we had been given more time
to put it before our committees and trustees and then,
of course, sought the Lord's guidance. I suggest that
a period of at least six months preparation would be
necessary. Is that something you can oblige us by ar-
ranging?"

"Well sir, I am only here until next Sunday," Simon
said rather curtly, becoming a little fed up with the

unbridled opposition and procrastination. He sighed, and was about to carry on when a young man stood, obviously wanting to speak. He asked Simon if he could speak. Although already feeling weary about the unexpected direction of the meeting, Simon sat down and gave the man the floor.

"I am a new Christian and I am just so surprised that you all talk this way. We all worship the same God, don't we, despite belonging to different denominations? Simon and his wife have given up their time to come to Penrhos Bay to help us and all we seem to want to do is put obstacles in the way. I don't understand." The young man looked genuinely confused.

"May I enquire what church you belong to?" said one of the ministers in an offhanded way.

"God's Free Church," said the young man proudly.

"I thought so. You are aware, I suppose, that your so-called pastor is not an ordained minister, and has no formal religious qualifications?"

"I didn't know that, no. But does that really matter if people are coming to Christ? People like me who would never have thought of stepping into an orthodox church?"

The minister scoffed. "You are very naïve, young man, even to ask such a question. It's not even a proper church—they meet in a café! Cappuccino Christians is what I call you. A cup of no substance and with fake froth on the top. Come in dear atheist, have a free cup of coffee, we'll have a chat about Jesus and hey, presto! Pack your suitcase, you're going to Heaven."

Simon had obviously had enough of the controversy, and was just about to abandon the meeting, when, quite suddenly, the bottles of hard liquor and wines lined up at the back of the bar began to shake and clink together. The lights flickered on and off and on again, and the glass chandelier hanging from the ceiling trembled. The tables in the room shook and the sound of a great wind enveloped them all. The Methodist minister shivered, turning up the collar of his overcoat, and cried out, "Could someone shut that door!" All turned to see if someone had indeed entered and left the door to the hall open, but there was no one and the door was closed tightly.

All were totally surprised and shaken by the incident. There was a prescience in the air, and all of them knew that something was about to happen; it was so palpable to all. To their utter astonishment, a small, bright flame, like that created by a large candle, appeared above Serena's head. Simon gazed at his wife in awe. At the moment the flame appeared, she began to speak in a language that was of no Earthly tongue, and yet, as they all listened intently, the tone was clear. The spoken words were strong and full of warning. Serena was merely the vehicle—the Spirit of God was among them and was speaking. Many of the ministers, recognizing the holiness of the moment, bowed their heads and felt afraid. The female curate had a strange expression on her face, a look of disbelief, and stood staring at Serena. The young man from GFC wore a great smile and could not remain still, he was so excited. Serena ceased speaking, and Simon drew closer to her, taking her hands in his, as the flame above her head extinguished.

Then quite unexpectedly the Welshman rose from his chair. The flame had transferred to him, and the anointing of the Spirit was upon him. He spoke in a gentle and tender way, "You are all my beloved children. Yet I have this against you: that you fight among yourselves like vultures over carrion. Are you not my sons and my daughters? All equal in my family of love? If I were to choose favorites from among you, who would stand? Are you not brothers and sisters of one flesh? Behold, I am going to do a mighty thing in this place, with or without you. There are people in this town who need you to heal them, need you to comfort them, need you to bind up their wounded hearts, need you to bring them the gospel of peace of my son Jesus Christ, so that they may know my joy eternal. How will you accomplish my will if you are divided? Hark, hear my words. Let those that have ears to hear understand what I am saying. Pray now and consider your ways. We can do this together, or you are free to choose desolation, a wilderness of your own making. The Lord your God has spoken."

The Welsh minister sat down heavily on his seat. He was visibly shaken by the experience of being filled with the Holy Spirit.

Silence followed, and it seemed that none dared speak. Then there was a quiet sob and a low cry of anguish from another, until the entire assembly of clergy began to weep. The female curate was the first to break down, crying out pitifully, her voice tremulous with emotion, "Oh Lord forgive me. I see so clearly now that my thoughts are not your thoughts. I know that I have erred against your ways. I freely confess, Lord, that I have harbored thoughts of enmity against my brothers in Christ." She paused and looked at each person in the room, her eyes wet with sadness, "Brothers, I ask, no I beg, your forgiveness," she said with great humility.

The Presbyterian minister got up and strode across the room, pushing chairs roughly aside, to where the Welshman sat. Grasping him by the arms, he lifted him to his feet saying, "Ian, you and I were good friends many years ago, and now look at us, we haven't spoken in a civil way to each other for nigh on twenty years. God allow us to repent this night for our folly." Ian Jones put his arms around the tall, thin man and hugged him, tears falling from his eyes.

"Andrew, it is I who should seek your forgiveness." He searched deeply into his friend's eyes. "Will you forgive my stupid ways?"

"Yes, yes! My friend, yes!" cried Andrew deliriously.

Simon and Serena had become mere bystanders. Simon's meeting, with all its human intentions and endeavor, had been hijacked by the sovereign Spirit of God. Serena squeezed her husband's hand and kissed him on the cheek. The young man from GFC just could not stop grinning as he looked from one to the other. Then the curate from Trinity came over to him.

"I am sorry for what I said to you about your church. Perhaps I could come to your church one Sunday?"

"And have a cup of frothy coffee with me," said the young man, smiling.

"Actually, I hate coffee, but tea will do!" They both laughed together.

Everyone in the room was touched by the Holy Spirit. God had searched their hearts and found them wanting. His grace and mercy had shone a light into their darkness. There is no condemnation for those that are truly in Christ.

Everyone was reluctant to go, and so they sat and talked and prayed together into the early hours of the morning. Before leaving, they all made generous offers of help to Simon and Serena, promising to do their utmost to assist in making the crusade a success. More importantly, they all agreed to pray day and night to bind the works of the Devil and for the many lost souls who might come to know Christ as their savior and redeemer.

The effect of the anointing did not fade, either. It went on mending relationships, restoring lost friendships abandoned long ago, and caused a wonderful lasting unity not just between the clergy, but also their congregations.

The time ended with all gathered in a circle on their knees, praying, worshipping, and praising God. Thanking him for his timely intervention. These clergy were not evil men, but were simply misguided souls, like sheep that had gone astray, but had now come home when they heard the call of the shepherd's voice.

What had happened was not a miracle, but rather a commonplace act of God. He may be feared by many as God Almighty, all powerful, capable of destroying or creating worlds at the touch of his fingers, but on this Earth, he is better known as a humble Lord, servant of all, who limits himself and works miracles in the hearts of ordinary humanity.

Simon and Serena climbed the stairs to their bedroom later that night full of wonder at how good God is, full of expectation and excitement, wondering what He was going to do next.

The angel on guard outside the Alpha Hotel remained vigilant. The demons, who had witnessed the night's events from the outside, knew that something extraordinary had taken place. They had sensed the presence of God within and had cowered back in fright, retreating to a safe place in the distant darkness. Seeing the faces and the behavior of the departing clergymen, talking animatedly, arm in arm, enlivened and invigorated by their experiences inside the Hotel, made them wonder just what actually had occurred. They knew that something dreadful had happened, something holy. It troubled them deeply. In haste, they flew back to Rimmon's lair in the deep caverns below the Great Ulm to acquaint their Master with these portentous and bad tidings.

* * *

Richard and Sarah, who had not been able to attend the meeting at the Alpha Hotel because of a prior engagement with the bishop, were astonished as Simon described yesterday evening's encounter with the Holy Spirit and how deeply it had affected all the clergyman.

"You should have seen it Richard, it was like a game of two halves. During the first half, I don't mind saying, I was growing thoroughly discouraged and had almost decided to abandon the evening. I have never come across such animosity between church leaders. It was plain that God was grieved. When the Holy Spirit came, one old chap pulled his collar up around his ears and asked someone to close the door for fear of the draught."

"Oh, I wish we had been there!" said Sarah.

"Don't fret about that. It was pretty obvious that those who needed to be there were, and boy did the Lord deal with them efficiently . . ." said Serena.

Simon interrupted, "You know I have been pondering on how fast it all happened. Of course we know the Holy Spirit can perform in seconds what would take us years, but these ministers . . . although they appeared hostile I honestly believe that deep down in their hearts they were still God's leaders. All that the Holy Spirit had to do was clear away the garbage and the baggage that had accumulated over the years in order to expose and revive their good souls."

"So what you are really saying, Simon, is that the Spirit of God is in fact a mere garbage collector!"

Both couples laughed.

Richard spoke. "Well, all we've got to do between now and Friday is get this show on the road."

Sarah looked at her husband and said kindly, "Richard, I think God has already done that, don't you?"

Chapter 34

Preparing for War

The captain general Bezalel held a war council in the nearby medieval castle at Conwy, which had temporarily become his divisional headquarters. All of the high battlements and towers housed guards watching for any signs of demon activity.

The main hall was filled with fifty angelic warriors of the holy army's first order. These valiant battle-scarred officers had fought Lucifer's dark soldiers many times. They had commanded the brigades and battalions of the Lord's impressive armed forces to combat the echelons of Rimmon's evil band of devils. Every single warrior gathered within the confines of this ancient stone castle was spoiling for the fight. They were ebullient and ready to engage the enemy. Their moment would arrive soon, but each angel knew that for victory to be certain, they would have to obey their officers down to the smallest detail. The enemy was a ferocious, evil foe and they knew from past campaigns that he should not be underestimated.

The captain general explained to his assembled officers that the enemy was aware that the Holy Spirit had visited the town. He said, "Rimmon will even now be preparing his onslaught on the town and its people. The dark maneuvers perpetrated by Rimmon's foul devils on Halloween night will seem like a picnic, I am sure, compared to his plans for this coming weekend."

The officers murmured and whispered among themselves. Bezalel raise his hand for silence.

"Even now, our brother angels are sowing seeds of confusion among the demon forces throughout the land. To their ears and spying eyes, it will seem that the Spirit of God is working only with the human leaders of this town, and that no great defensive force of angels will be employed. Rimmon must not become aware of our presence here. All manner of diversionary tactics will be exercised to make him think he has the upper hand. Even though he has knowledge that his adversary intends to carry out a work of the Spirit, he will believe that God has blundered by underestimating Rimmon's hold on this town. We know that he has requested extra legions of demons and that he will instigate chaos to test and undermine the faith of Christians hereabouts. He will try his worst to upset the balance of power in his favor and he will have his supporters among high officers in ruling places. It is with regret that we have to fight against not just our spirit foes, but also against evil men. There are many mortals in this town that would benefit much if Rimmon took complete control."

The captain general continued, "Based upon reliable intelligence, I have carefully calculated that on Friday evening there will be various attacks by the enemy, not just in this town. It is known to us that several of the surrounding towns and cities will suffer violent assaults from squads of demons working in a concerted fashion. It has been decided that our response will be an appropriately measured defense, doing just enough to stem the tide but not to overwhelm their forces. We will save that for Saturday evening, when all Rimmon's scattered forces will descend upon this town with total victory on their minds."

"Rimmon will expect us to retaliate to his first attacks, and we shall give ground in some of the skirmishes. He is a vain Lord, and he will not be able to resist the chance to summon all his demons in one great, concerted assault upon the heart of the crusade, St. David's Church. It is there that we shall spring our surprise attack—we shall hit them hard and send them all to the pit of judgment. Our forces shall come at them from three sides, from both flanks and from above to cut off their escape. At the same time, another force will splinter off to attack Rimmon's hideout under the hill, to utterly annihilate their headquarters, once and for all."

There was a great cheer from the assembled officers.

"I want all the section leaders of troops of one thousand to stay. The rest of you officers go and make your angels ready for the battle. Until then, be alert, be vigilant."

The dismissed officers went without delay to convey the battle commands to their own officers and fighters.

Bezalel invited ten senior officers to gather around him to discuss the final strategies and tactics to ensure that victory was swift and certain. They planned every move of their forces to the last minute detail. Their full frontal attack on Rimmon's army would be one of total surprise, and they would strike just at the moment when Rimmon and his henchmen were confident of their own military success. His soldiers would fall and flee in the face of the holy warriors, only to be cut down by the secondary ranks of angels with flaming swords. Bezalel confided to his officers that if all went to plan, the fight would end in the complete disarray of the demon forces. They would scatter across the Heavens and be cast into the fiery abyss. The news of such a resounding victory would echo straight to the halls of Hell and shake the throne of Lucifer himself.

* * *

In a private room off the main cavern, Rimmon's emissary to Satan had been on his knees in front of his Master for over an hour. Ganymede, Gathan, and other close acolytes stood by, also waiting. Rimmon tore up the parchment for the twentieth time and threw it at the emissary's head.

"If I ask for too much, I shall be declined, and if I ask for too little, it will seem a trifle in my Master's eyes and he will decline my request," he bellowed.

Ganymede shrugged his shoulders as Rimmon glared at him. Gathan contorted his features in an odd way as if to convey, "Yes, we understand your predicament, but . . ."

"Ganymede, you are often wiser than I, why can't you tell me what to write?"

Ganymede wondered if this was a compliment or an accusation and could not decide, so he chose the tactic of being obsequious. "I, my Lord? Nay, I could never be wiser than you and as for advising you, I merely pick at the edges. It is your own wisdom that cuts to the quick." He bowed low.

"Yes, alright, you may be inferior in all matters to me, but I command you to be wise, to conjure up some cleverness for this moment. Then you can go back to your silly vanities."

Seizing their opportunity, the others around Rimmon backed slowly away, leaving Ganymede to face Rimmon alone. Even the emissary relieved his pain by prostrating himself, thus ending the agony in his knees and neck.

Ganymede was on the verge of panic, but seeing that he could not deflect the question on to others, tried desperately to think of something that would please his Lord. The more he reasoned the more his mind was blank. Becoming flustered, he tried to articulate a sentence that he hoped would make sense. Rimmon leaned forward, pen poised, ready to record the words of wisdom.

"I, I . . . think . . . that under these special circumstances, and given the balance of power and the inadequacies of our adversary, notwithstanding the untimely visit of the unmentionable third person of the three . . . erm . . . thoroughly distasteful trio of . . ."

Rimmon stood and bellowed, "What are you gibbering on about, you imbecile?! Gathan, pull his arms off!"

"Lord have mercy! It wasn't gibberish, it's the way my mind works. Of course you don't normally hear such machinations because I speak only when I have arrived at the . . . answer."

Rimmon studied Ganymede's face to see if he was lying. Gathan's muscled arms stood at the ready to carry out Rimmon's command.

"Then I give you five minutes to think silently. Make your next utterance be the answer that I need or else it will be your last spoken words."

The look of shock and horror on Ganymede's face was final. He had never found himself in this place before. He had always been able to handle Rimmon's temper by some artifice or another. It was plain that Rimmon feared for his own safety because of this wretched town. His thoughts wandered to the times when he had been posted to Paris in the eighteenth century. A time of superlative riches, high fashion, tyrants with absolute power on the throne of France, drunkenness and debauchery, fine wines, and lace handkerchiefs. He sighed at the memory.

"Well, you seem deep in thought, my friend. By my reckoning, you have sixty seconds to formulate my answer."

Ganymede caught sight of the evil grins that spanned the faces of nearby demons. They were already becoming excited at the prospect of seeing his arms flung across the room.

Ganymede's mouth was as dry as a desert at high noon. The palms of his hands sweated and he thought he was going to faint. Then suddenly he laughed out loud, as a brilliant, simple thought was born in the wilderness of his empty mind. It was a little green shoot that immediately grew leaves and sprung up. Numerous petals of every hue sprang forth, and what he now saw was a glorious and beautiful flower. It had saved his arms.

"I pray you have something to laugh about?" said Rimmon very seriously.

Composing himself, Ganymede stepped in close and whispered, "May I, Lord? These nuggets of wisdom are for your ears only."

"Yes, of course."

Rimmon dismissed all but one from the room. The emissary was commanded to remain and make ready to take the message to Hell.

"My Lord, the answer to a complicated task is often the simplest," explained Ganymede.

"Yes, get on with it. My patience is running out."

"Well, if you do not know what to write, then do not write anything!"

Rimmon's face darkened.

"Anything, that is, that will incriminate you or place you in an adverse position."

Rimmon's face lightened a little as he tried to comprehend where this was heading.

"So here is the beautiful answer, the elegance of which I am sure you will appreciate. Instead of asking for some fixed number of reinforcements and possibly angering Lucifer, curse his wonderful name, simply lay out the problem as you see it and then ask Him to allocate the required number of demons to win the day or night as he sees fit."

Rimmon had gotten lost somewhere along the way and was now looking puzzled.

"So, Ganymede, what you are saying is," he paused, "that I should . . ." he paused again, but seemed unable to carry on. Ganymede coached his Master gently, nodding his head all the while he was speaking.

"That you should ask His Highness to come up with the answer."

"That I should ask . . . yes, I see it now. Very crafty of you, Ganymede." Looking smug and satisfied, Rimmon spoke, "Now tell me exactly what I am to write on this parchment and then this poor fellow can be on his way."

Chapter 35

Speaking in Tongues

Richard and Sarah had their hands full. They had been thrown into the deep end by the bishop and it was a case of sink or swim. After listening to Simon describe the events at the Alpha Hotel, where several clergymen had experienced a supernatural encounter with the Spirit of God, Richard, in particular, had wondered if he was capable of carrying out the massive task of organizing the Crusade in such a short period of time. He had shared his misgivings with Sarah one night as they lay in the darkness. She had felt that something was wrong even before he had spoken.

"Richard, just because you weren't at the meeting, you have no reason to feel inadequate."

"I should have been there," he complained.

"The Lord knew exactly who was to be there and that is that. You can't second guess God!"

"You're not very sympathetic, Sarah."

"I am. I would love to have been there too, but we weren't. Doesn't that tell you something?"

"No, it doesn't," he said petulantly.

"Richard, you are behaving like a child. Have you forgotten already how you felt on the pier? You told me that you had been touched by God."

He turned over in the bed away from her.

She put her hand on his shoulder. "Listen to me, the bishop has great faith in you. He's going to give you St. David's after old Scrooge has left. He wouldn't have put you in charge of this whole thing if he didn't have confidence in your abilities. Think on this as well, the Holy Spirit has anointed local ministers who'll be your partners. Simon and Serena, world famous singers and evangelists, are leading, and the bishop himself will be at your side. Instead of seeing this as a trial, see it rather as a wonderful opportunity to serve God. Trust in Him and you'll bless Him. It's not always the other way around, you know, and I think sometimes we ask too much and don't give enough back."

As Richard lay still in the dark, he could feel Sarah's breath on his neck. He turned over to face her.

"What would I do without you? You are right as usual," he said tenderly.

"Without me at your side, you'd probably sink into oblivion."

"And which oblivion would that be?" he joked as he dug his fingers in her side to tickle her.

"Richard, don't, please . . . don't!" she cried.

The next day they were at the church very early. Before morning prayers, and with help from other church members, they had assembled the temporary staging needed for Simon and Serena to perform. Others were busy cleaning and tidying so that the whole church would be spick and span.

Later in the morning, Simon and Serena arrived to oversee the setting up of all of the public address systems, the microphones, and the speakers. It took hours to get it right, to the satisfaction of Simon, who wanted it to be perfect. Sarah had time to sit and have a coffee with Serena. It was a delight to hear about their lives and their conversions when they were both on the edge of showbiz stardom. Having set everything up to his satisfaction, Simon joined his wife and Sarah and suggested that Richard join them for a moment of prayer.

They sat in a corner of the church hall and Serena led them in prayer and very quickly launched into praying in tongues. Sarah could feel Richard stiffen and go quiet, retreating into his Anglican shell. This was something he wasn't used to. Sarah could feel the power and devotion of Serena's entreaties, even though she could not comprehend the meaning of the strange sounds. Simon closed the session by praying normally and asking God to bless every detail of the preparation for the event.

"Come on Simon, we still have a lot to do." Giving Sarah and Richard friendly hugs they hurried from the hall. Richard sat down again.

"I think I could do with a cup of coffee." He looked up at Sarah.

"I'll get you one. Just sit still and relax for a minute."

Returning with the coffee, she sat down beside her husband.

"It's the speaking in tongues, isn't it?" she said seriously. "Why does it bother you?"

"It doesn't sound real to me. Sounds like babble. In fact, the Greek word for it, 'glossolalia,' means just that—meaningless uttering in a non-existent language."

"But isn't it recorded in the Book of Acts that St. Peter and the disciples spoke in tongues?" argued Sarah.

"Yes it is, but it also says that those listening heard their own languages being spoken and understood clearly, which means that they weren't speaking gibberish."

"Alright, but do you think someone like Serena would speak gibberish whilst praying to God? Come on, we know the kind of people they are, honest and trustworthy. It doesn't fit to think of them engaging in some shabby trick to make them look good, does it?' Sarah looked at Richard and waited for his answer, which was slow in coming. She added, "Use your logic, Richard. What makes sense here? Do you trust Simon and Serena?"

"Yes, of course, but you are doing it again!" he complained.

Sarah raised her eyebrows as if to say, "Doing what?"

"You know, pushing me up against the ropes, then giving me the knock-out blow."

"You deserve it. So if you trust them implicitly, then it follows that in spiritual matters their gift of tongues must be real, for they would not deceive us, would they?"

She wasn't about to let her husband off the hook, either. "Doesn't St. Paul say in his epistles that it is right to desire the gifts of the spirit? And that includes the gift of tongues."

"I guess so," said Richard, admitting defeat.

"I know someone else who has the gift—someone quite close to you," she said mysteriously.

"Who is it? I want to know!" Richard burst out.

"Me! Silly."

"You! I don't believe it. You never told me, and I've never heard you pray that way."

"Firstly, I don't have to tell you everything. A woman has to have some secrets. Secondly, I use it when I am praying on my own for really important things, like when you rushed out the other day and left me."

"It works, then? I came back."

"It works and it feels so intimate, as if you are in the presence of the Holy Spirit."

"And do you know what you are actually saying?" he questioned.

"No, not in words, but in feeling, yes. It goes deeper than mere words. I believe it's my heart and soul speaking to God directly, without my mind interfering. It's difficult to explain, really."

Richard saw that her eyes shone brightly as she spoke about this.

"Do you trust me?" she said, grasping his hands.

"I love you, and of course I do," he said passionately.

"Then promise me this. Ask God every day over the next few days to give you the gift of speaking in tongues. Will you promise?"

He hesitated before answering, not wanting to agree unless he meant the promise undertaken.

"I promise."

"Then I think you will be amazed," she said affectionately. "Come on, there's lots of work we need to do to get this show on the road."

Chapter 36

The Grand Hotel

The uniformed commissionaire, standing at the door of the five-star Grand Hotel, situated on the promenade, looked up at the steel gray sky. Small icy drops of sleet came in on the wind and fell upon his face. He adjusted his peaked cap and drew up his collar to ward off the cold. Stepping a pace back into the lee of the main doorway, he pulled on his black leather gloves. John Maxwell had been forced to take early retirement from the London Metropolitan Police because of a serious injury sustained whilst carrying out his duties. Unfortunately for Maxwell, it had left him handicapped, with little capability in his right leg. He felt he was lucky to get the job with the Grand, given his disability, but the Hotel thought it was a good deal having an ex-officer on the door.

The Grand Hotel was far too ostentatious for this small seaside town, but it had been built at the same time that the new international golf course had been opened. Apart from St. Andrews in Scotland, Penrhos Bay was the only real links course in the north of the United Kingdom. At this time of year, when golfers were swinging their clubs in Spain or Florida, the Grand was quiet. There would be a small rush at Christmas time—mostly regulars who came back year after year—for the Grand put on a splendid holiday vacation for those who could afford the exorbitant price, complete with top entertainers performing at the New Year's ball. It was a time when, for a few days, the rich and luxurious atmosphere of past times could be experienced once again.

The commissionaire pulled back the sleeve of his overcoat to check his watch. It was nearly time for a much-needed break of hot coffee and toast and butter in the hotel kitchen. His assistant Gerald would cover for him and he could put his feet up for half an hour or so. The sleet was turning to snow, and the color of the clouds over the Great Ulm cliffs heralded a big storm on its way. He was just thinking to himself that he should bring up a broom and some salt bags to clear the steps of ice and snow when three limousines glided slowly to a stop outside the hotel entrance.

Grabbing the large umbrella, he scrambled down the steps, dragging his disabled leg behind him. He wasn't sure which car door to cover with the umbrella. All three cars were old but immaculate Rolls Royce pre-war models. The first and last were black, and the central vehicle a deep blood-red color. He couldn't see into the cars, as all of them had smoke screen windows. He waited for a door to open. He wondered who the hell this might be, as there had been no notice from the hotel manager about guests arriving this morning. The outside door of the middle Rolls opened and a uniformed driver in gray jodhpurs, jacket, and peaked cap ran around to the rear door and smartly opened it so that the occupant could alight from the vehicle. Maxwell quickly hopped over to the vehicle, umbrella held high. The first thing he saw was a pair of petite, shiny red high heels and two shapely legs in sheer black stockings that swung elegantly out onto the concrete pavement.

"Welcome, Madame, to the Grand Hotel."

The woman who stepped out of the blood-red car was so beautiful that Maxwell's jaw dropped open. Dressed in a pure white fur coat with red trim at the hood, sleeves and hem, with her long blonde curls falling over the open neck of the coat, she strode forward, not showing any cognizance of the commissionaire. As she went up the stairs, Maxwell could barely keep up, but she waited at the top for him to come and open the door for her. Inside the lobby, a great glass chandelier hung from the center of the ceiling and the thick pile carpet had the hotel's name embroidered in rich gold letters against a deep blue background. She went immediately to the desk and addressed the female receptionist, "Please get the hotel manager."

The receptionist looked her up and down and for a moment thought of saying, "Can't I help?" but one quick glance into the woman's cold green eyes convinced her otherwise, and she said rather meekly, "Right away, Madame."

The commissionaire stood in the lobby watching the woman, but kept one eye on the vehicles just in case another guest decided to enter. He could smell the woman's perfume. It was strangely alluring, heady yet sweet, but it also had some indefinable quality that made him feel uneasy.

The hotel manager, Mr. Aubrey Westbrook, was a product of the old school, an anachronism in this day and age, but he had the right manners for the type of guest that frequented the Grand. Middle-aged and tall, dressed in a dark pin-stripe suit with a carnation in his lapel, he was the perfect image of a high class servant.

At first he seemed peeved at being disturbed, but as soon as he saw the lady in the fur coat his whole demeanor changed.

"Madame, welcome to the Grand Hotel," he said with a broad smile upon his well-shaven face.

"I am the hotel's General Manager, Mr. Aubrey Westbrook." The accented voice spoke of Eton and Oxford, but it was certain that Westbrook had been to neither.

"If you would follow me, we can discuss your needs in my office."

Allowing the woman to enter his office he turned to the receptionist and said in a haughty tone, "Julia, be so kind as to get some tea, and use the best china."

The lady dropped her hood and unbuttoned her coat to reveal an exquisite and very expensive dress. Around her neck was a single string of pearls and she wore matching pearl earrings. Westbrook had no doubt that they were real, along with the large diamond rings on her fingers. She crossed her legs as the manager sat down behind his wide oak desk. He tried very hard not to stare at her legs, face, and voluptuous figure, which was now on display.

"So Madame, how can I help?" he asked, trying to keep his smile as natural as possible.

"My employer, Count Rimmon, would like to stay here for several days. Probably eight days, along with his entourage. My employer has some business to take care of."

Aubrey Westwood was pretty good at recognizing accents, but he was nonplussed by her manner

of speech. It seemed to contain several subtle quali-
ties that he thought might originate in England, or
maybe France, or Russia, or even the USA. The more
he listened, the more confused he became. Her mannerisms also were unusual and spoke of breeding and
elegance, but he was at a loss to place her in his men-
tal filing system of typical guests.

"He requires a suite for himself and at least six
other rooms all on the same floor, preferably the top
floor. Is that possible?"

Her green eyes shone like sparkling emeralds.

"Well, let me see." He turned to look at his com-
puter screen on the desk. "I think we shall be able to
accommodate your party."

"Are there any other guests staying on that floor,
or booked to stay?"

"None there at the moment, Miss—?" he waited
for her to reply.

"You don't need my name, Mr. Westbrook," she
said coldly.

"No, of course." He glanced back at the screen and
tapped the keyboard.

"There are some guests arriving in a few days
time, who I am sure will not be of any trouble to you.
There are a group of elderly . . ."

She cut him off abruptly, "Please, put them somewhere else."

"I, er . . . yes, I am sure I can rearrange it. Now
about the hotel tariff. I could give you a splendid discount, I am sure."

"Discount does not matter. We will pay you cash.
How much is the bill?"

"Well, there are in fact ten rooms on that floor, so
let me just calculate the costs. Will you be dining
with us?"

"You will have all food sent up as and when required. Just put a generous amount on the bill, especially for iced champagne."

The hotel manager scratched his head and tried to come up with a suitable amount. The figure that showed on his calculator seemed enormous, but nevertheless he added twenty percent.

"By my reckoning, the bill would come to nearly twenty thousand pounds."

The lady showed no emotion at all.

"Good. Round it up to twenty five thousand to cover any contingencies. I will speak to the Count right away."

Taking a mobile telephone from her handbag she spoke into it without dialing. Westwood was unable to identify the language. It was very strange and somehow seemed ancient.

As she stood up she said, "The Count is satisfied with your establishment. One of his men will bring you an attaché case with the money right away. You may keep the case if that is convenient for you. Do you have an underground car park where the vehicles can remain during our time here? Yes? Good, and my employer can access the hotel via the car park without publicity? He is a very private man. Do you understand?"

"Why yes . . . yes." Westbrook began to feel somewhat unnerved, as if he were being dictated to and his hotel being taken over.

"Are the rooms ready for occupation?"

"Yes, we are always ready for our guests," he said proudly.

"Good, then let us go."

* * *

Rimmon stood in the center of the room, sipping a glass of cold champagne. The richly furnished suite was perfect in all respects. He was staring at Ganymede.

"I'm not really sure if I like you as a human female."

"I am not sure I like it myself," replied Ganymede, standing up to admire himself in a full-length mirror.

"I think I could get used to most of this strange anatomy, except for these things!" he cupped his hands under his full breasts and jiggled them about.

"As appendages I can't imagine why mortal men drool over them, and as for the rest, well there are just too many fat molecules!" he said, patting his behind.

Gathan gazed at Ganymede with an expression of disgust, "Then why didn't you choose a manly form like we all did?"

"I thought it might be fun, Gathan, a concept that you simply do not comprehend."

"Now now, my friends, let's not bicker. We are on vacation, after all."

Gathan made himself busy. Ganymede sat down on a sofa and started to paint his long fingernails.

"Have you posted sentinels at all the entrances?" demanded Rimmon.

"I have Lord, just as you requested," said Gathan.

"Do we have any visitors watching us?"

"There are a few, not hidden—three or four most tame examples of Bezalel's troop."

"Good. Ganymede, have you done what I asked you to do?" said Rimmon sarcastically as he watched him applying red paint to his nails.

Ganymede looked up. "I have done exactly what you instructed. I have created a cloud of unknowing all around the hotel. The watchers will be able to see and hear, but what they see and hear will be quite different to what is actually happening. However . . ." he hesitated, "there is One who sees all and knows all."

"You are right. But he will not intervene. To do so would be to break his own covenant with Lucifer."

Rimmon strolled over to the French windows, and opening the doors, stepped out on to the balcony. The snow was falling heavier now, and large snowflakes began to blanket the balcony floor. Rimmon held out the palm of his hand and a snowflake landed upon it like a dying butterfly. He studied it closely.

"Ah, the wonder of creation, His compound fractals the work of genius, but lo, what happens if I step into the warm?" He turned around so that his hand was within the room and the snowflake disintegrated, leaving behind a tiny speck of water.

"One day we shall see all of His creation disintegrate, just like this flake in my grasp."

Ganymede clapped. Rimmon looked up and smiled, admiring his own wit. "Where is that pest Jusach?"

Gathan stuck his head out of the main door and shouted down the hall, "Jusach, get in here!"

The demon came hurrying in just as Rimmon sat down upon his throne.

"Ah, Jusach. Now what is this I hear about you allowing a mortal to get the better of you?" Rimmon said playfully.

"Master, I was taken by surprise. I was certain, as you might imagine, that the bishop could not see me, when all of a sudden I felt his eyes upon me and then he started to pray. I was pushed by some holy force against the wall."

"And you could not free yourself from this prison?"

"I could not, Lord. I struggled and tried my hardest, but I failed." Bowing low, he expected a tirade of abuse to come upon him.

"You may go," said Rimmon tersely.

Jusach backed out of the room as fast as he could, heaving a great sigh of relief as he went.

"It seems we must deal with this new bishop ourselves. He could be a great hindrance to us all." Rimmon looked across at Gathan. "Let's ask our friend the Reverend Stannard to come and pay us a visit. Organize it straight away. I will entertain the eminent vicar this afternoon, and we shall find out more about this troublesome bishop."

* * *

Stannard took the lift up to the top floor. He fingered a business card in his hand. It read "*Count Rimmon, Philatelist, Collector and Purveyor of Rare Stamps.*" No address and no telephone number or email. He had thought about bringing the penny Victorian stamps, but decided against it, choosing instead to play his cards, or rather his stamps, near to his chest. The lift doors slid open and Stannard was confronted by two large men, both over six foot tall and weighing two hundred and twenty pounds each. Dressed in dark blue suits, shirts, ties, and black shined shoes, the two guards made Stannard feel nervous. This, after all, was not his usual territory.

In a thick Russian accent one of the men said, "Follow me please."

Stannard heard the doors of the lift close behind him and began to feel even more nervous.

The guard knocked gently on the door of Rimmon's suite. Zurvan opened the door wide enough to see who was knocking.

"Lord Rimmon's guest is here."

Stannard heard the words clearly enough and thought to himself, "Lord?"

Zurvan opened the door wide. "Please come in sir, my Master is expecting you."

The scene that met Stannard seemed like a clip out of an old black and white gangster film. There was Rimmon, seated in an ornate, high-backed regency style chair, dressed in a cream colored bespoke double-breasted suit, striped shirt and silk cravat, pinned with a gold brooch studded with diamonds. White spats covered his brown patent leather shoes and a neat pink carnation was set into his jacket buttonhole. Ganymede, with her long legs crossed, sat idly on the sofa, preoccupied with painting her nails and looking like Marilyn Monroe. Every inch of Gathan epitomized the Godfather's bodyguard, standing respectfully to the rear of Lord Rimmon. Standing six foot six, weighing a solid two hundred and forty pounds, he appeared as a towering black man, wearing dark designer shades that made him look even more intimidating.

Stannard hesitated. Rimmon did not rise from his chair.

"Gathan, be so kind as to get a chair for our guest," he said, smiling at Stannard.

Gathan offered the chair, placing it just a few feet away from where Rimmon was seated. Stannard sat down.

"I understand you wanted to discuss some stamps, sir?" Stannard asked quizzically.

"Yes, yes—in good time, Reverend Stannard. Your reputation precedes you. I understand you have a keen eye for a bargain, especially for penny blacks!"

Stannard began to feel apprehensive. "I have dealt with the purchase of such stamps, but I believe I have always paid a fair price. In fact, only recently at the Chester exhibition I bought some excellent examples of the stamps you speak of."

"That is very interesting," said Rimmon, staring intently into Stannard's rheumy eyes, "but here I am being an inhospitable host. Would you care for some coffee or tea perhaps? I know you English clergymen adore tea!"

"Thank you, no." Stannard fidgeted in his chair. "Could we get down to business?"

"Why of course, if that is what you prefer?"

"Yes, that is precisely what I would prefer," said Stannard sharply.

"I also know that surprises are not always welcome, but this is necessary. I would like you to meet an old friend. Zurvan, ask our second guest to come and join us."

Zurvan left the room by a side door and left it ajar. Stannard had his eyes fixed upon the door and the person who came through it made him jump to his feet in fright.

"I think you two gentlemen have met before?" said Rimmon.

The man was dressed in a clergyman's outfit— black suit, shirt and dog collar—and he was carrying a smart black attaché case. Stepping into the room, he stood silently staring at Stannard. It was the Reverend Alexander Martin.

Stannard looked from Martin to Rimmon in a very agitated fashion. Ganymede momentarily ceased painting her fingernails to watch the drama unfold.

"Please Mr. Stannard, sit down. Mr Martin, put the case over here on the coffee table, unopened."

Stannard was in shock. Crazy questions were spinning around his brain. How could this man be here, and what was his business with these others?

Martin did as he was told and then took a pace back to stand beside Gathan.

Stannard sat down slowly and gazed at Martin, wondering what the hell was happening.

"Does it not say in your Bible, Stannard, that someday your sins will find you out? I am afraid for you this is that day."

"I don't understand what is happening. Why have you brought me here?" said Stannard with a perturbed expression on his face.

"All will be revealed, have patience, my friend. Let us examine the facts, shall we? At Chester I believe you bought a stamp album from this man and you paid him a paltry sum, which would have been very generous had not the album contained some very valuable items. Is that true or untrue?"

Stannard's face, now white and pasty, had drained of all natural color. Unable to speak, he nodded.

"The items in question are conservatively worth about twenty thousand pounds, I think."

Stannard nodded in agreement.

"Good, I am glad you do not disagree. I see that you can be an honest man when you want to be."

Rimmon leaned forward and opened the attaché case. He spun it around on the glass surface of the coffee table so that Stannard could see the contents.

Stannard stared at the case in horror and pushed himself back into the chair. Gathan stepped around to the back of the chair and placed his hands on the vicar's shoulders.

"Look, I'll make restitution and hand back the album and the stamps and Martin can keep the money." His voice betrayed that he was really scared. His hands began to tremble.

Rimmon turned to look at Martin. "Well, Reverend Martin, I think that the vicar's offer is a fair one, what do you think? Shall we accept his offer?"

Martin smiled, looked straight at Stannard and said, "No."

Stannard's demeanor visibly changed from one of fear to one of utter dread. He looked down at the attaché case. It was filled with batches of new fifty pound notes which must have amounted to several thousand pounds, but it wasn't the money that attracted his attention. It was the gun.

"Ah, my dear friend, do you recognize the pistol?" asked Rimmon.

Stannard stammered, "It's, it's . . . an army pistol."

"You are right, it is. It is a British army officer's service pistol from the sixties, if I am not mistaken." He paused. Stannard did not look up. "In fact, it is your pistol."

Stannard tried to get up, but Gathan's strong hands held him down.

"But it can't be, it's not possible, I threw it into the Thames when I was ordained as a priest."

"So you did. But as you might imagine, we have clever ways and means for dredging things up, please excuse my pun."

Stannard looked anxiously at Rimmon and then at Martin. "Do you mean to shoot me? Because of the stamps? I said I will repay you and I will do anything, but please don't kill me."

"Whatever gave you such an incredible idea? Do you think we are gangsters? That we'd gun you down in the Grand Hotel and chuck your body in the dumbwaiter?" Rimmon laughed out loud, which set all of them off laughing. Stannard began to wonder if he was in a madhouse, or if perhaps he was having a nightmare. He pinched his own leg to find out.

"Come, come dear fellow, don't jump to conclusions. I simply want to make you an offer. One I feel that you will not want to refuse."

"Martin, get the vicar a glass of water. No, on second thought, make it a whisky."

Rimmon waited while Stannard gulped the drink down in one.

"Now, listen carefully. The cash in the case—and by the way they are not forged notes, you have my word—amounts to exactly fifty thousand pounds. I am prepared to hand that over to you. You can keep the penny blacks if you agree to my proposal. All in all that amounts to more than seventy thousand pounds. Add that to your own nest egg, and I am sure you could live out the rest of your life quite comfortably."

Stannard looked utterly miserable now. "What is it that you want me to do?"

"I want you to kill the bishop."

Stannard's mouth dropped open and he exclaimed, "Good God, are you mad! Why on Earth would I do such a thing?"

"Because if you don't I shall let Gathan tear your limbs off one by one, and then he'll decapitate you with his claws."

"His claws?" Stannard now looked terrified. Gathan's hands pressed down upon him, and Stannard
uttered a cry of pain. He looked to the side to see
Gathan's long, black, bony claws digging into his
shoulders.

Stannard screamed aloud in sheer panic. Gathan
clamped one of his demon hands over the vicar's
mouth. Stannard began to tremble with fear and his
bulging eyes looked up to see not a well dressed
quartet, but instead the features and forms of gro-
tesque and gruesome demons. He was now so frightened that he urinated involuntarily, the liquid from
his body dripping through the fabric of the chair and
onto the carpet.

"I see we have influenced you quite enough, Reverend Stannard. Are you now prepared to listen to
my proposal?"

Stannard felt his blood turn to water and he passed
out, his mind unable to resist anymore fright.

"Get some water, Gathan, and throw it over him,"
ordered Rimmon testily.

Gathan picked up the champagne ice bucket and
emptied the contents over the vicar's head.

Stannard awoke immediately, gasping for breath
and spluttering.

Gathan grabbed Stannard's head and forced him to
look at Lord Rimmon.

"Now, my friend, I am only going to say this once,
so mark my words. You will take the attaché case
with the money and the pistol. On Saturday, we will
arrange for you to be able to walk up to the bishop
and shoot him dead. If the young curate is with him,
kill him also. When you have done this good deed for
me, I shall have you spirited away to any place in the

world of your own choosing. My companion Zurvan, alias the Reverend Alexander Martin, will be with you at all times, so do not think of betraying me. If you do, I shall make sure you keep an appointment with Gathan to suffer a horrible death that is beyond even your wildest imagination. Is this clear?"

Stannard managed to nod his head.

"Good, now we have an agreement. You may go. Zurvan, escort our precious friend to his home."

Zurvan immediately changed back into his human form. Stannard had to be assisted to rise from the chair. Zurvan picked up the attaché case, and taking Stannard's arm, steadied him and led him away.

Just as they reached the door Rimmon spoke. "I say, Stannard, I suggest you use some of that cash to buy another pair of trousers. I think you have soiled the ones you have on."

Everyone in the room broke into raucous laughter and Ganymede, unable to control himself, fell off the sofa.

Chapter 37

The Inspector Calls

Stewart arrived back home from the local supermarket to find he had an email from the boss. It read, "I know you're on leave Paul, but something has come up that I don't want these new boys getting their hands on. Seems an ex-copper is doing security at the Grand and would like to have a chat with us about a strange bunch of guests. Do me a favour—pop over there and have a word with the guy. John Maxwell is his name, late of the Met. It's probably nothing, so keep it low-key and informal. Thanks, keep me informed if it amounts to anything. PS. Missing you around the place."

Stewart checked his watch. It was nearly midday. He decided to rustle up some lunch then walk over to the Grand Hotel to meet Maxwell.

Yesterday's snow had turned to slush. The skies were still gray above Penrhos Bay; more snow was on the way and the forecast was for dropping temperatures, tonight falling below zero.

He saw the commissionaire sweeping the melted ice and snow from the top of the hotel steps.

"You Maxwell?" asked Stewart in a friendly way.

Maxwell looked down at Stewart. "Guess so. You from the local Nick?"

"Detective Inspector Paul Stewart, good to meet you." He held out his hand.

Maxwell hobbled down the steps and shook Stewart's hand firmly.

"Boss says you might have a problem at the hotel, that right?"

"Let me put the broom away and then we'll talk."

Maxwell hobbled up the steps, went inside with the broom and re-appeared seconds later without it. Momentarily taking Stewart's arm, Maxwell eased him away from the hotel entrance towards the rear.

"I've got something to show you first. Come and have a look at this."

"How did you get that?" Stewart asked, pointing to Maxwell's leg. "Not in the Met, I hope?"

"Afraid so. Got blasted by a young villain with a gun. Shattered my knee. Some years ago now, but it still damn well hurts even after seven years."

"And the villain?" asked Stewart.

"Yes, got him alright. He's doing time and will be inside for another ten years yet."

"Good, justice was done then."

"Perhaps, sure my knee wouldn't agree though," retorted Maxwell dryly.

At the back of the hotel, they both stopped on the concrete ramp that led down to the underground car park beneath the Hotel building. Maxwell pulled a gadget out of his pocket, aimed it at the doors, and pushed a button. Hidden machinery hummed into life and the roller shutter doors started to open slowly.

Inside Maxwell switched on the lights. There were only about half a dozen cars parked, but Stewart immediately saw what Maxwell had brought him down for. All lined up neatly in a row were three immaculate Rolls-Royce limousines. Two were black, the third a crimson red. They were beautiful. Stewart walked over to them and instinctively placed his hand upon the bonnet of one of the vehicles. He stroked it as though touching a rare and precious animal.

"These belong to my guest, Count Rimmon, apparently," said Maxwell.

"A Count! There's no such person anymore, is there?"

"Manager thinks he might be Russian."

"These are Silver Ghosts aren't they?" Stewart asked.

"No, they're later than the Ghost. Last Ghost was made in 1925 or thereabouts. These are about a decade later. They're all the same model—the Rolls Royce Phantom."

Stewart walked around the car nearest to him, admiring the lines and the paintwork. He gazed into the interior. "You can almost smell the luxury. What would they be worth do you think, in this condition?"

"At a guess, two hundred thousand apiece," said Maxwell.

"Phew! And they all belong to the man upstairs. Just one odd thing I notice—the number plates are indecipherable."

"I see what you mean. To be honest, I never gave it a thought, I just assumed they were registered in some foreign country."

They crouched down in front of one of the cars to examine the plates closely.

"It's not any kind of lettering I recognize." Running his finger over the script, Stewart said, "It's more like an ancient text, pre-Egyptian, I should think."

"You an expert on that kind of stuff?" asked Maxwell.

"No, just a hobby. Interested in ancient history. Gets your mind off the beat."

"Tell you what, I'll take a photo and email it to my stepdaughter Sarah Cooper. She's a senior lecturer in Linguistics and Philosophy at Warwick University, got her Doctorate last year, clever girl. She'll know what it is, or will know someone who does."

"Sounds good. Let me know the result. But you didn't bring me over here to admire the Count's automobiles . . ."

"No I didn't. Let's nip into my cubby hole and have a coffee together and I'll tell you what worries me about this rum bunch."

Maxwell led the way through a door in the car park to a sparsely furnished room with a table, two chairs, and a PC, the monitor showing multiple images from the hotel's CCTV. "Coffee fine?"

"Yeah, white and one sugar, thanks."

Waiting for the kettle to boil, Maxwell pointed to the screen and tapped the keyboard.

"Look at this. I can zoom in using the cameras to any part of the hotel, that was until the Count and his friends moved in. Now I can't access the top floor at all."

Stewart looked at the monitor. It showed various rooms, hallways and public areas in and around the building.

"When I tap in 'top floor' this is what happens." The screen images disappeared and were replaced with snow interference. "I had the maintenance man check it over, and he can't find a fault, but I still can't see what those buggers are up to."

"Anything else?" Stewart inquired.

"Since they arrived, no food has gone up, only ice buckets and champagne, and plenty of it. House-keeping staff are turned away, and even the manager was fobbed off when he went up. One of the Count's henchmen said he was indisposed. Told Westwood to come back later, but said it in such a way that he was in no doubt not to return."

"Private party then, eh?"

"Very, and that's not all. They paid in advance, in cash, twenty thousand pounds in fifty pound notes. The manager was afraid they were forgeries, so I took them over straight away to Barclays and had the manager there examine them."

"And?"

"All kosher: genuine British currency."

"That's a lot of money to have in one hit."

"Sure is. Their bank manager wondered about Russian money laundering, which is why I contacted you guys."

Maxwell poured hot water into the coffee mugs and handed Stewart the milk and sugar. "Oh yes, another thing. Yesterday the Count had a visitor during the afternoon. Stayed about an hour and left with one of the goons. He looked a bit worse for wear after meeting with the noble Count."

"Who was it? Anyone you know?"

"Only by sight, never had the chance to make his acquaintance, but from what I've seen of him I don't think I want to. It was the vicar from the church in the town. Stannard's his name, I think."

"Stannard! You're right about not wanting to be friends with him. I met him a couple of times while dealing with the suicide of the curate. He's a cold fish, and obnoxious as well."

"But what does Stannard have in common with these thugs?" said Maxwell.

"Perhaps they go to his church! That would make sense," said Stewart humorously.

They sipped their mugs of coffee in silence.

"Tell you what, John, why don't I go up to see this Count. Flash my copper's badge. They daren't refuse me entry. I'll tell them I'm checking on the large amount of cash, etc."

"You want me to come with you?" asked Maxwell, but with some reluctance in his voice.

"No, prefer to do it alone. I'll come and see you afterwards."

The lift doors opened at the top floor and two burly men barred Stewart's way, not allowing him step out of the elevator.

"Tell your boss the cops have arrived."

"Give me your ID," said one of the men coldly.

Stewart handed it over and the man walked down the hall. The other man stuck his foot in the door to stop it from closing.

In a few moments, the other man came back and beckoned to Stewart to follow him.

Stewart stepped into the Count's suite. Gathan and Zurvan were playing chess at a table near the French window. Ganymede was sitting on the sofa reading a book. Light piano music played in the background. Rimmon was seated at a desk writing a letter on hotel stationary. He rose from his chair as Stewart entered and greeted him warmly, shaking his hand and returning his ID card.

"Ah, Detective Inspector Stewart, how good of you to call. Have a seat and tell me how I can help you."

Stewart sat down and scanned the room. The others did not seem to take any interest in him and everything seemed cozy, but a policeman is always looking for crime. "It is merely routine, sir, sort of our way of welcoming strangers to our fair town, you might say. The hotel manager informed us that he paid a large sum of money into the bank yesterday, which he received from your staff in payment for your stay here. Is that correct?"

"Why yes. Have we done something wrong, Inspector? Mr Westwood seemed quite satisfied with the arrangement."

"No, I don't believe you have broken any laws. It is just that when such a large amount of cash is deposited into a British bank, the bank staff are obliged to ask about the origins of the money. Money laundering in this country by foreign nationals is big business I am afraid."

"Oh I see. Then I can give you a perfect explanation of the provenance of my money. The money, along with other large amounts, was withdrawn from my bank in London, Coutts, after being transferred electronically from my bank in Switzerland. I can, of course, provide copies of the transactions."

Stewart was fumbling in his overcoat pocket for his small notebook and pen. He withdrew his pocket New Testament Bible and laid it on the glass table. The flaming eyes of Ganymede, Zurvan and Gathan were suddenly on him.

"What are you so assiduously searching for, Inspector?" asked Rimmon politely.

"My notebook, sir, if you don't mind. I just wanted to make a few notes."

"And what is that on the table?"

"It's a New Testament. I've just become interested in the Bible," said Stewart distractedly, still looking in his pockets for the notebook, which he finally found inside his jacket.

"The Bible, really. A quaint little book of myths and stories suited more to children and the weak-minded than an intelligent man like you? Much overvalued, I believe, and a perfect anachronism in this modern world, wouldn't you agree?"

"Excuse me, I guess I should have brought a dictionary. 'Anakrowhat?'"

"Anachronism, Inspector: belonging to another time."

"No I don't agree really. I have found it very interesting," said Stewart with some conviction.

He pocketed the Bible back into his overcoat. "You are not a believer in God, then?"

"Oh, but I am! A passionate believer in God Almighty, but you should not take as truth everything you see in print. There are always two sides to a story, and in this case, I and my associates belong to the other side of the story," said Rimmon cryptically.

"Well I'm pretty new at this, so I am not sure what you mean. Perhaps I could continue with my questions?"

"Yes of course." Rimmon's attention was drawn to the other side of the room, where Gathan was making the gesture of drawing a knife across his own neck, intimating that if Rimmon gave the order he would sever Stewart's head from his body. Rimmon shook his head.

"I don't think we need to have copies of your bank papers sir, but thank you for offering. Can you explain why the hotel staff is not allowed to enter this floor to carry out their work?"

"Inspector! There you go again, suspecting felony where there is none. I am a very rich man. I am very powerful in my field of interest, and I am sure you will understand that a man in my situation has enemies, which is why these dear friends travel with me, to make sure I am kept perfectly safe. The reason for withholding entry to the hotel people is one of security alone. My own men keep the rooms clean, and I want for nothing."

"That's interesting, sir. Apparently you do not order any food from the kitchens?"

"Again a very simple explanation. I have a rare eating disorder, and my food is specially prepared for me."

"And your men? I assume they have normal appetites?" said Stewart, with just a touch of sarcasm.

"They prefer to eat outside of the hotel." Rimmon stood. "Now if you please, Inspector, this interview is beginning to become tiresome." Gathan rose from his chair and stood close to Stewart.

Stewart got up and put away his notebook. "One last question. The commissionaire saw the Reverend Stannard arrive yesterday, but said he looked poorly when leaving. Any reason for that?"

"I could ask that you speak to Reverend Stannard yourself, but I will oblige you. Stannard came here to discuss some business. He has some rare postage stamps to sell and I am interested in buying them. As for his health, he complained that he was suffering from the onset of influenza and, not wanting to catch anything myself, I terminated the meeting until another time."

Stewart shook Rimmon's hand. It felt icy cold. He looked into his eyes and saw animosity there, despite the polite manners.

On his way out, Stewart described his meeting to Maxwell. Stewart had to admit that everything seemed above board, and that there was nothing to report.

"And the CCTV cameras?"

"Don't know John, they've probably got some jamming device."

"My best hope then is that they leave soon, and good riddance to them all! They are a queer bunch," said Maxwell.

"I agree. As for Rimmon himself, I would go as far as to say that there is something evil about the man, but what that is exactly is beyond me."

"Take it easy, Paul. Call in for a coffee sometime, I could do with the company and I'll get that information for you about the number plates."

A few days later, Stewart got a telephone call from Maxwell.

"Don't know if this is going to help you or hinder you in your inquiries Paul, but my stepdaughter says that the script on the vehicle registration plate is most interesting. It is in fact an old Sumerian form apparently, and roughly translated means 'Hades or Hell.' So putting two and two together, our esteemed visitor is a nobleman from the underworld!" joked Maxwell. "Though which underworld, I wouldn't like to speculate."

Paul didn't say a word in reply. He felt as if someone had just walked over his grave.

"You still there?"

"Sorry John, I am just as confounded as you are."

"Well, to my way of thinking, this Count Rimmon is a rich eccentric individual who likes to play elaborate jokes on people."

"You are probably right. Anything to report over the last few days?"

"No. Not a thing. They are an odd bunch but they aren't breaking any laws and they've already paid their bill upfront, and with a generous tip, I'm told."

"Case closed then, I suppose," said Stewart.

"Guess so. See you around."

Chapter 38

The Old Railway

Samuel was sticking close to Richard, making sure no harm came to him. A great deal depended on him over the next few days. Richard and Sarah had labored day and night to organize the Crusade, which was only two days away. They had arranged all the logistics for the weekend, ensuring the church buildings were ready for Friday evening. They had attended several meetings with other church leaders who now pledged to help. They had led countless prayer sessions across the town every night, sometimes not getting to bed before the early hours of the morning, quite exhausted, only to get up early to start all over again. They had plenty of helpers, but even these people needed to be managed. All these people needed to know what to do and when to do it, and what was required if something went wrong, like if some key individual didn't turn up. The bishop was most insistent on these arrangements getting carried out to the letter. He was in the habit of saying, "If you get the little details right then the Holy Spirit will take care of the rest." On top of all of that, the bishop was expecting the enemy to do their worst to disrupt and interfere with all the arrangements—even with the mundane things like the electric lights.

"Have plenty of candles, matches, and flashlights, and make sure the batteries aren't dead, Richard, just in case!" was his most popular watchword of the hour. "We don't want to end up in darkness, do we? That would suit Lucifer very well," he insisted.

However, in truth the planning and preparation was going well. Richard was becoming the man of the hour. His reputation was growing by the day and he was well respected in the town and beyond, where news of his prayer meetings had been spoken of with excitement. Since his infilling by the Spirit, Richard had begun to fully understand the tenets of one of his heroes Evan Roberts; first, confess all known sin, second, deal with and get rid of anything of doubtful value in your life, third, be always in readiness to obey God, and fourth, confess Christ publicly. Some people were wondering if this was the beginning of another major revival in Wales. Richard himself was becoming acutely aware of what was being whispered and talked about in the churches across the region, and knowing that he had been irrevocably changed by the Holy Spirit, he was indeed ready for whatever God had in store for him. His dreams of missionary work of long ago were now becoming a reality, but he would never have guessed from what quarter they would have come to him.

Sarah had busied herself marshalling all the ladies of the churches, who were going to assist in various ways, from preparing refreshments in the hall to being available on the Crusade nights to provide counseling and help if it was needed. In the background, several teams were putting together the stage and sound systems, the lights, the car parking, security, and first aid, and those charged with welcoming guests were preparing themselves. The bishop had sent out personal invitations to many dignitaries and local politicians, and he was expecting them all to attend, such was his enthusiasm for the event.

Samuel was in awe of everyone involved, of the industry and sheer hard work that all had applied to accomplish their appointed tasks. He had never seen anything like it before. He was beginning to like his time on Earth and often wondered whether, when called, he would actually want to return to the Celestial Choir. Shadowing Richard these past few days had brought him the awareness that humans in the service of God, though made of clay, were so vitally important to God's plans to usher in the Kingdom. Samuel began to understand in a deep profound way that the union of God, angels, and men was a powerful force for good. He recalled Ganymede's words to him outside the cottage. Words so filled with deceit that they deceived even the great author of such lies. He suddenly felt an encompassing wave of pity flow over him for those angelic brothers who would never know the joy and wonder of the new Heaven and the Earth.

* * *

The shortest route from Penrhos Bay to Conwy was to follow the railway. The line departed from the center of town, traveling south for a mile or so, with the golf course on the left and the sea on the right. The track then curved gracefully, heading west before straightening up. It looked as if it was going directly into the castle itself, but those Victorian railway engineers knew what they were doing. The railway began to decline gradually, crossing over the river on a long steel girder bridge, and by the time it reached the grounds of the castle, the line disappeared into a wide tunnel cut right through the granite rock under the castle's foundations.

The castle was the brainchild of a master mason, James of St. George, who worked for Edward I, King of England. It had been standing since 1285 Anno Domini, and had never been captured by enemy forces. It was impregnable, a stone fortress with eight circular towers that overlooked the estuary, the river, and the land around. Connecting the towers were monumental stone walkways which soldiers could easily move along to meet attacks at any quarter of the castle. Edward had the castle and fortifications built after fighting in the Holy Lands, where he had seen Crusader castles and how ingeniously they had been constructed to resist attacks and sieges. He had applied this knowledge well.

The castle's layout meant that an entire army could be hidden there, a fact that captain general Bezalel used to his great advantage. Because all the recent demonic activity had been centered on Penrhos Bay and in the towns along the southern coast, he knew that Rimmon and his spies would not be searching in Conwy. As far as they were concerned, nothing good or bad came out of Conwy. The river had silted up years ago, the local fishing industry had died, and the only revenue the town achieved was from tourists coming to view the medieval castle and town walls. They came, took their photographs, and left, moving on to the next item on their itinerary. Some demons had diverted to Conwy to make a quick reconnoiter, but had seen nothing to report. Bezalel had taken great care that his forces were not seen.

The hour of the battle was fast approaching, and the captain general was putting the final touches to his strategy. Everything needed to be planned to the smallest detail—for want of a nail the battle could be lost. He and his officers were examining the old drawings and maps of the railway. It had already been decided that their route into the heart of the enemy's territory would be along the railway. Many years before, Victorians on vacation or on weekend trips would take the steamer trains into the very center of Penhros Bay. They would pour out of the station straight into the town's amusement palaces, hotels and guest houses, restaurants and cafés, and down to the edge of the sea to the beaches and the pier where all was sunshine, gaiety, and laughter.

The host of angels would drop into the dark railway tunnel under the castle and then move at lightning speed, following the iron rails until reaching their target destination. It was a foolproof plan. Rimmon would be wreaking havoc in the town and would be thinking that he was about to overpower the meager, weak force of angels guarding St. David's and the other churches, when suddenly he would be hit by a tidal wave of angelic warriors. Bezalel rolled up the maps and plans and announced to his faithful band of officers that all they had to do now was stand in readiness and wait for the call.

Chapter 39

The Crusade

Richard busied himself around the church, checking every last detail to make sure everything had been done as ordered and all was ready. He rushed over to Sarah, who was standing talking to Serena.

"Excuse me for interrupting. I just wanted to check if everything is in place, and Serena you and Simon are happy with the sound systems, etc.?"

Serena said that all was fine and he shouldn't worry.

"Good advice Richard. I know you are anxious, but now is the time to exercise faith that you have done all that is needed."

Serena made her apologies and went off to find Simon.

"Look, Richard, if you don't stop worrying you'll be the cause of something going wrong. Find a quiet place and spend a few moments in prayer . . . and ask God for a spirit of calm. Go on." She gave him a playful shove.

"Alright, I'll be upstairs. But come and get me if something happens."

"Richard!"

"Alright, alright! I'm going."

The bishop was talking to Simon on the stage. Serena came up and hugged them both. "I think something wonderful is going to happen tonight, I can feel it in my heart," she exclaimed.

"My dear, I would expect nothing less than wonder with both of you here. And given what happened at the hotel, I fully expect something more than wonderful!" The bishop had a look of excitement in his eyes.

Serena's expression changed to one of concern. "Are you sure Richard will be okay? He seems a bit anxious."

"Oh, he's a young man, and this I think is his first real stab at responsibility. But I knew the first time I laid eyes on him that he was right for the job, and I think the Lord is going to raise him up in a remarkable way. Just mark my words and watch this space."

"Well there's no time better than now! Let's pray for Richard and that everything goes according to God's plans tonight and tomorrow."

They formed a circle, arms around each other's shoulders, bowed their heads, and prayed. Their prayers were interrupted after only a few minutes, when one of the people assigned to the door came running up the nave. "I think you should all come and see this," he said, and then turned back along the nave. "Come on!" he shouted.

The bishop glanced at his companions as if to say, "What's this all about?"

As they arrived at the main door they could hear loud voices from outside the church. The steward threw back the doors and the bishop, Simon, and Serena were shocked. Serena put her hand over her mouth in an expression of pure glee and laughed. Simon and the bishop exchanged glances and stood on the threshold, both quite dumbfounded. Outside the door there were hundreds of people queuing and waiting to enter. The line of people went down the path and disappeared around the corner of the church.

"Hey, Bishop! Aren't you going to let us in?" someone shouted good-naturedly.

Sarah arrived, and seeing the crowds, gasped, "I think I should get Richard."

The bishop made a grand gesture with his hands, and bowing before the mass of people, cried out, "Welcome my friends, right this way!" He led a procession of people down the long nave of the church.

Richard was amazed when he saw the mass of visitors pushing up the nave and through the aisles, determined to get a good seat.

"But it's not time yet!" he said, looking at his watch.

Sarah smiled at him and joked, "Well I guess you'll just have to ask them to leave and come back in fifteen minutes."

Richard grabbed her by the elbow and pulled her aside from the crowds of people entering the church. "It happened, just now, when I was upstairs," he blurted out.

"Did it really?" She gave her husband a big hug.

"It just came! I was praying normally and then I felt, well the Spirit take hold of me and the next minute I was praising Him in this wonderful strange language, truly a language of love. I felt that my human soul was suddenly animated by the Spirit of God, a taste of things to come beyond death."

"Oh Richard I love you."

* * *

As well as the human visitors around the perimeter of the church, there were hundreds of angry demons, trying desperately to gain entry and hoping to disrupt the event. Second upon second they loosed fiery darts and arrows at the angels, but none found its target. The angels, wearing full battle armor, wielded great shields to protect themselves from the onslaught. The devils and demons cried out loathsome obscenities and blasphemies, hoping to goad the angels to leave their posts. Once in a while, some of the demons rushed headlong to engage the angels face to face, but were quickly dispatched to the pit of fire by the sharp two-edged swords of the defenders. Even more foolhardy were the devils who tried to breach the main door, where there stood two great cherubim. These angels were the same ones who had guarded the gates to the Garden of Eden after Adam and Eve had been expelled. These angels were the most powerful of all angelic beings. Their armor was impregnable, and the huge swords they held were perpetually alight with fire. Those hapless demons who tried to confront the cherubim were instantly destroyed in a flash of lightning.

The evil forces also tried to influence the men and women steadily entering the church. They whispered all kinds of arguments into the ears of the crowds, hoping to get them to change their minds or sow doubt about why they had come in the first place. They cajoled and threatened, but nothing worked, neither subtlety nor coarse means had any effect. It was as if there was an invisible force keeping all the people immune from such odious entreaties.

Trying another tack, the demons possessed a crowd of noisy drunken youths who were passing by. They jumped over the church wall and began to scream and shout at the lines of people. Picking up stones and cans, they threw anything they could get hold of at the waiting lines. Not content with this behavior, they tried to get even closer to punch and kick the people standing in the queue. Stewart had foreseen that this kind of thing might happen, and had requested that his boss send a squad of tough police officers. They were congregated at the back of the church keeping a low profile, that is until Stewart blew on a whistle, which was the signal to come running.

The police came around the corner of the church like a fierce band of marauding soldiers. Within minutes, those thugs who had not fled in fright had been overpowered, handcuffed, and bundled into police wagons. All the people witnessed these valiant efforts and cheered and clapped as the last youth was thrown into the police vehicle and secured.

Peace was restored. The demons were distraught, seeing that none of their evil machinations had proved effective.

Rimmon was watching all this from across the street, atop a high building, with Ganymede at his side.

"This is too painful to watch, Ganymede, it's a debacle, and I think your plans are failing miserably!" he said irritably.

Ganymede thought, "My plans, indeed! Why is it that this fool is never ready to take the blame?"

"All we have to rely on now is Gathan; at least he can be trusted to deliver. He should be here with the body of the child very soon and that will put an end to this holy spectacle." Rimmon looked keenly along High Street to where Jezebel's occult center was situated at the far end of town.

Chapter 40

Samuel's Clarion Call

Jezebel sat on the bed next to the child. She was nervous and tired. She checked her watch for the tenth time. It was late. Gathan had told her he would be at her place to pick up the child an hour ago. He was going to take the child and place her at the back of the town supermarket in a safe place. Then Jezebel was to go to the police station and say that she had seen the whereabouts of the little girl in a trance and would direct the police to the location only a few streets away. Jezebel would then be front page news and everything would end well. Except things weren't going according to plan.

Jezebel looked at her watch again and then down at Emily sleeping. The child was pale and looking thin. Jezebel wondered how the child's mother must be coping. Jezebel had never had children of her own, but she could imagine the pain Melanie must be going through. She was cheered by the fact that in a short while it would all be over and the mother and child would be happily reunited.

The atmosphere in the apartment began to grow icy cold, and suddenly Gathan stood before her in his demon form. Jezebel recoiled in horror at the thing she saw before her. It was a monster, gruesome in appearance and frightful to behold.

"Stand aside woman. I am here for the child!" Gathan shouted at her.

Jezebel, full of fear, trembled at his words, but something deep inside told her to stand her ground. "What are you going to do with her, Lord?" she asked, her voice breaking.

"Lord? I am not your Lord. I am Gathan the Destroyer. Fool of a hag, I have amused myself by deceiving you. You ignoramus, did you really think I was doing this for you? Ha!"

His hot breath blasted her face. She withdrew onto the bed, trying to distance herself from this hideous creature.

"You are vulgarity itself, mere scum. You think you have power? You have been duped, used. You are my slave, and if you were younger, prettier, and not so ugly and fat I might spare you from death, but I have no further use for you."

"Stay back, Gathan. You'll not take this child. I know now that you mean her harm. You are evil! Get back to hell where you belong."

Gathan laughed uproariously. "Now I can add 'ridiculous' to my description of you, Sorceress. I am going to crush your skull in my claws and feed your body to the rats. Then I shall take pleasure in extinguishing the life out of this little doll and discarding her remains outside the church tonight."

Jezebel laid her body over the child to protect her. Gathan mocked her and laughed derisively. He reached forward and was just about to pull Jezebel off the child when a great crash behind him made him turn around. There standing before him was Samuel, his armor shining brighter than the sun and the sword of truth hidden on his back.

Gathan simply gazed at Samuel and cried, "What is this? A youth in toy armor. Come for another beating, have you? Is this all your God can muster, a puny choir boy?"

Samuel, standing firm, looked straight into Gathan's malevolent red eyes.

"I am here for the child, Gathan. Step aside or meet your doom."

"Ha! You jest with me!" Gathan roared at Samuel. He towered over him by at least three feet, his body as solid as iron, his muscles black as ebony, and his fanged teeth now drooling with saliva as the battle heat overtook him. He leapt forward, but Samuel darted to the side, sending Gathan sprawling over tables and furniture. Jezebel bundled the child into her arms and ran for the lavatory, locking the door once inside.

Gathan about faced and turned his hateful eyes upon Samuel. "I am going tear you apart, angel! You will cry out for your God, but he will not come to your aid." Again, he sprang forward with all his might, this time knocking Samuel to the floor. Gathan's momentum had carried him forward, and he crashed against the toilet door. A pitiful scream came from inside.

"Quiet woman, I shall deal with you later, after I have amused myself with this pathetic excuse for a warrior."

Gathan stepped slowly towards Samuel, exercising caution this time. He circled his prey, looking for an opportunity to catch hold of Samuel. But one advantage of being small is that you can move more quickly. Samuel dodged and outsmarted Gathan every time he made a lunge for him.

"Trying to make a fool of me, are you?"

Samuel watched his adversary carefully, searching for that moment to trick the great beast into making a wrong move and catch him off balance.

"I am getting bored with this, angel. Come to me so that I can rip your head off."

Samuel said nothing. He crouched like a panther and stared fearlessly into Gathan's eyes.

"Now you die!" Gathan, instead of surging forward, bent low and pulled the carpet upon which Samuel stood. Caught completely by surprise, Samuel tripped backwards and was unable to check his fall. He landed on his back, now vulnerable to Gathan's attack. In a split-second Gathan was on top of him, his loathsome spittle dripping onto his face, his teeth bared ready to tear the flesh from Samuel's face like a wild hungry animal. "Now, my good little friend, beg for mercy!"

But the smile on Gathan's hideous face suddenly changed, and a loud cry of pain issued from his gaping mouth as his head was thrust back in agony. Samuel had drawn the sword of truth from the scabbard hung on his back, and thrust it with all his might into Gathan's heart.

Gathan staggered to his feet, his features contorted with rage and pain. He had a look of complete disbelief upon his face. His eyes looked deep into Samuel's own, searching, searching for an answer to Samuel's triumph. Samuel put his foot roughly against Gathan's chest and with a mighty pull, withdrew the sword.

"This world will be a better place without you, Gathan. You are on your way to the fiery pit to await the coming of the Lord."

In the briefest of moments, Gathan ceased to be. As he vanished from sight, his howling cries echoed through the room then slowly died away.

Placing the sword back into the scabbard, he knelt to thank God for his victory. Rising high above the building, he sang out a victory cheer that resonated across the town and beyond. Demons nearby heard the angel's cry of triumph and trembled at the sound.

Lowering himself into Jezebel's apartment, he opened the door of the lavatory where he found Jezebel crouched upon the floor in the corner trembling, but still shielding the child.

Chapter 41

The Call is Answered

Bezalel was waiting patiently with his captains and lieutenants on the highest tower of the castle when they heard Samuel's call. It came as clear as a ringing bell resonating through the night air. The captain general addressed his valiant band in a loud voice that echoed around the castle walls. "Angels, here this night, let God be proud of you. Do your duty and flinch not in the face of the enemy. They have chosen a dark path with Lucifer, but he shall not prevail—not on this night, nor any other! I desire nothing more than to see this town rid of his evil pestilence. Show no mercy, stand tall, and cry 'When God is with us, none can defeat us!'"

There was a great cheer from the angelic host.

Turning to his officers, he cried, "Give the order to advance! Let's go to war!"

The commanders flew to their stations and within seconds the vanguard of the angelic army surged forward into the railway tunnel, heading swiftly towards Penrhos Bay. Hundreds and then thousands of battle-hardened warriors of Christ were now hurtling along the track, keeping low to the ground, so that the enemy would not have any warning of the deadly force that was now fast approaching them. By the time the front line of soldiers had turned the bend by the river's edge, Bezalel had caught up with them and was leading the charge. If only humans had the eyes to see the Kingdom of God in action, they would have witnessed something so extraordinary that night.

The snaking line of angels, shoulder to shoulder and head to toe, raced through the night, but no sound was heard upon the air. A great silent army, sweeping along the railway track as if it were a great iron and steel express locomotive hurtling forward. The resplendent, supernatural incandescent light emanating from the charged hearts of the warriors was a sight to behold. There was power in the light that came from their ethereal bodies, an illumination and force that originated from the primary light that blasted miraculously into the dark-filled void at the beginning of creation itself.

Bezalel and his vanguard arrived at the railway station arch, passed through, and scattered in all directions to catch the enemy unawares. Behind the vanguard came the rest of the angelic force, and following up in the rear were the splendid cherubim astride pure white stallions that flew high into the night sky, ready to fall upon their unsuspecting prey like hawks swooping down for a kill. Everything profane on this night would know the full weight and power of God's holy army.

It was Ganymede who first raised the alarm. "Master!" he screeched aloud, "We must flee!"

Rimmon looked to the skies and saw two terrifying beasts bearing down upon them. "Satan save us!" he cried in abject fear.

Rimmon and Ganymede wasted not a second and vanished into the deepest dark.

The two horsemen reared up, and pulling on the reins, turned their steeds around to seek other prey, too late to catch the arch-demons.

Bezalel and his forces were fighting skirmishes all across the town. On the rooftops, in the alleyways, and on the by-roads the angels vanquished their foes. The demons fled in terror when they saw the angels coming at them with swords drawn. Thousands of demons had already been dispatched back to Hell and to the pit of judgment, but the angel horde would show no mercy, and sought to seek and destroy every devil alive that night.

Bezalel cried out to the passing cherubim who sat astride their gleaming stallions. "Benjamin, Aster, any sight of Rimmon or Ganymede?"

The angels reined their horses in and shouted back to Bezalel, "Yes, we almost had them, but we were not swift enough and they have flown."

"Pity. I was hoping to meet them face to face."

The angels rode on, having spied a group of retreating devils. They harried them across the sea and on into the dark night. Bezalel rose high above the town to see how the battle fared. Three of his guards kept pace with him, not wanting to see their commander caught unawares. All across the town demons were fleeing, chased by warrior angels in close pursuit. The army of Satan was to be given no quarter, and the angels would see that none would survive the battle.

Bezalel, searching the main thoroughfare, saw Samuel in human form walking towards St. David's Church with a woman at his side; he was bearing a small child in his arms.

As Samuel approached the church he could hear singing and praises being sung to God. He smiled. He drew the child close. He held out his free hand to Jezebel. As she took it, her heart began to sing, and she was glad to be walking with an angel.

Chapter 42

The Child is Found

Every available square inch of space in the church was taken up. People sat in the nave and in the aisles, content to squat and sit cross-legged on the floor when all the seats had been filled.

Simon and Serena had done a magnificent job in entertaining the crowds of visitors. Simon, of course, told his own story of how at the point in his life where the song "Bi Bi Bobbi . . ." had reached number one in the UK and American charts, he had become an overnight star. Even young kids in Africa, not having heard of Simon James, could sing the words of the song. Leading the congregation, he got them all to perform a rendition of the famous song. Over six hundred people sang their hearts out, including the bishop, who seemed to have no clerical inhibitions. Simon and Serena sang some beautiful Christian songs they had composed, and the audience was enraptured with their performance.

True to their promise, several seats in the front row had little stickers attached to the chairs saying "Reserved." Sitting in the front seats were Paul Stewart and Sadie, and Rosina and Melanie. Rosina had managed to persuade Melanie to come, although the mother was understandably still very emotional and sorely depressed at the loss of her precious daughter. But she needed comfort in these hours of anguish.

Paul Stewart listened intently to Simon and Serena as they described the height of their stardom, when they were recognized on the streets and had so much money in the bank that they didn't know how to spend it. The glitz and the glamour and the celebrity status, Simon explained, had left them both feeling surprisingly unfulfilled and lost. It was then that their friend Cliff had invited them to a Christian rally at Wembley Stadium, where he was singing that night. They both attended and that evening committed themselves to Christ. Paul recognized elements in the tale that corresponded with his own feelings and thoughts over the past few weeks, and he began to understand what he wanted to do next. Just at that moment, as if she knew what he was thinking, Sadie clasped his hand, turned her head and smiled.

Simon and Serena came to the end of their session and told everyone that there would be a thirty minute comfort and refreshment break, but added jokingly that tonight they needed a miracle: "It's more like Jesus feeding the multitude!"

The bishop grabbed hold of Richard and Sarah. "I think we should give a hand and help out the caterers, don't you? I'm not sure they'll be able to cope."

Meanwhile Paul and Sadie headed for the door. They had decided to get some air. Rosina had her arm around Melanie, who was trying hard to keep back the tears again.

Samuel and Jezebel were just coming up to the church lychgate. To Samuel's utter surprise, the path that led up to the church entrance was lined on either side by hundreds of angels. There were angels on the roof of the church and on the tall tower, on nearby buildings, hanging out of trees, and standing all along the perimeter wall. The illuminations from this beautiful host radiated out into the night, dispelling the dark so effectively that it seemed like day.

Samuel hesitated by the gate and gazed in wonder at his angelic companions. He turned to Jezebel with tears in his eyes. "Oh lady, I wish you could see with my eyes!"

"Maybe she can, just this one time." Bezalel stood beside them both. He placed both his hands upon her shoulders and sent a silent request to the Spirit of God. Immediately, she saw the host of angels. Her face shone with wonder and she gasped.

"Samuel, this is awesome and so magnificent . . ." she was almost lost for words, ". . . so magical!"

"No Jezebel, not magical. Just godly," he corrected her.

The angels began to cheer, and went on cheering as Samuel carried the child, who was beginning to stir from her long slumber, to the entrance of the church.

Paul and Sadie emerged from the church to see Samuel and the child and Jezebel just a few yards away. They thought nothing of the trio until Samuel stopped and spoke to Paul.

"Inspector Stewart, this is the missing child Emily O'Reilly. I would like you to take her to her mother."

Samuel gently passed the child into Paul's hands. Paul was dumbstruck, and Sadie turned and ran back into the church to tell Melanie.

Jezebel gazed into Samuel's eyes. "Thank you Samuel, for saving Emily. I have seen more good this night than in the whole of my sorry life."

Samuel hugged her tenderly. "You were very brave lady, in the face of much evil. Don't forget to tell the mother that her daughter was not harmed and will have no memory of this episode in her life."

Bezalel then spoke kindly to Jezebel. "You had better go inside. I think you will have to try to explain to Inspector Stewart how the child came to be reunited with her mother. How much you tell him of your own involvement I will leave to you. They will probably think you mad anyway. But stay here tonight with these good people and you will be blessed." As he turned to go he hesitated and said to Jezebel, "Is that your real name—Jezebel?"

"No, it's one I made up to go with the . . . well you know. But I think it's time to start using my own name, which is Grace."

"That's much better!" laughed Samuel.

Grace took one last look at the gathering of angels, trying to imprint the scene and every detail onto her memory. Slowly, the image began to fade until her world took precedence once more.

Melanie heard Sadie crying out and thought she heard Emily's name. She stood on her chair to get a better view, and spied Stewart with her daughter, who was now fully awake and shouting happily for her mommy. Sadie grabbed hold of Melanie, propelling her down the nave towards Emily. Stewart stopped, and without saying a word handed the little girl into her mother's waiting arms. Melanie was crying tears of joy, and Emily was hugging her mom. Rosina dropped to her knees and started to cry, which set

Sadie off, until all three women were bawling their eyes out. Then suddenly, Emily raised her head and said, "Mommy, where's the merry-go-round? I want another turn."

The news of Emily's return spread through the church like a wildfire in a dry forest. Within minutes it reached the ears of the bishop, who was helping to serve tea in the side hall. Richard and Sarah looked amazed.

"I didn't know her mother was here tonight," said Richard.

"She's sitting in the front row. Bishop, this is a miracle!" said Sarah.

"I think we'd better go see for ourselves, don't you?" said the bishop.

They found Melanie and Emily in the center of a great crowd of smiling people who made a path for the bishop when he arrived at the edge of the throng. Upon reaching the mother and child, he knelt down beside them and said to Melanie, "You must be the happiest mom alive!"

Melanie looked at the bishop, and then back at her daughter, who was now happily eating some cake. "I feared the worst, but now she's found!" The expression on her face said volumes more than words could ever say.

Standing up, the bishop turned to the crowd of onlookers. "Okay, let's all return to our seats and give this lady some breathing space. Then we'll start the second half of tonight's program."

The people dispersed but couldn't resist looking back at Melanie and Emily. It was a miracle alright.

Stewart managed to pull Grace aside. "You know that you and I need to have a little talk. You have a lot of explaining to do concerning the mysterious return of Emily. But I guess it will wait until the end of to-night."

"You are right on the money, Inspector. Mysteri-ous is what it is, and I don't know if you are going to believe any of it," said Grace.

"Oh no, not another one!" said Stewart in despair.

Chapter 43

Murder Most Foul

Saturday night was the night for the dignitaries to attend the crusade. Bishop Nigel had personally invited all the leading churchmen from the region, regardless of faith or denomination. He had sent invitations to the Mayor of Penrhos Bay, to the town and county council members, members of the British and Welsh parliaments, heads of big businesses, and the personalities of stage and sports. It remained to be seen who would actually accept the invitation.

Angels patrolled the town in large numbers, but there was no sign of any demon or devil in the vicinity. The battle had not just been won, it had been a complete rout of the enemy, and captain general Bezalel had got his wish that the town be rid of Rimmon's evil influences. He was also very proud of Samuel's part in the whole affair. He had proved himself a valiant warrior. Bezalel was very glad that Gathan was gone and that they would not meet again until judgment day. As Samuel had said, the world could do without his evil influence. The cherubim with their flaming swords had returned to heaven, their work done.

Samuel was standing atop the church tower, thinking deeply about the events of the past few weeks. Just a short time ago, he had been dismissed from the heavenly choir in disgrace, and now he was being treated by his warrior companions as a hero. God had honored him with the sword of truth when he could so easily have chosen a stronger angel with more battle honors than a novice like himself.

He knew by instinct that God often chose the weak to overcome the strong and powerful. The stories in the Old Testament were full of amazing examples of this, such as the boy David killing the giant Goliath with one small pebble and a sling. He had been victorious over Gathan. True he had been fearful of confronting the demon face to face, but an inner strength had given him a sure hope of victory. He wondered if God or Bezalel would call upon him again to face fear and danger.

The news about the recovery of the child Emily was all over town. Now that the demons had been banished from Penrhos Bay, there was an air of freedom and joy about the place. People passed each other on the street and shared smiles, wishing their counterparts a "good day" and a "God be with you my friend."

Initial reports on the first night of the Crusade said that after the furor surrounding Melanie and Emily had died down, and after the bishop had preached a sermon of repentance and forgiveness, more than five hundred men and women came forward to accept Christ as their Lord and Savior. There were so many souls seeking Christ that the bishop was quite overwhelmed, and had to lead them in a prayer of salvation and then bless them en masse. Richard had stood by his side to help in the prayers all night. Reports poured in until the early hours of the morning. Across the town, the Holy Spirit was busy saving souls. Crowds of people were knocking on the locked doors of churches, desperately seeking spiritual guidance. Several churches mustered together and answered the call. After midnight, they found their pews full of people wanting to know about God. In one extraordinary instance, a crowd of about forty people, including many young people, had congregated outside the town police station. When the Sergeant on duty came out to find out what the ruckus was about, he was promptly told by the people on the steps to go back in and bring out a Christian policeman to minister to them. He returned with Police Sergeant David Jones, who was led by the spirit and preached about Christ right there under the blue lamp, in uniform and all. Not one of those who were gathered in front of the station refused the call, and to his utter amazement they all knelt and worshipped God. The bishop, Richard, Sarah, Simon, and Serena listened to these stories and could only express wonder at the power of God.

"What shall we expect tonight?" said Simon, looking around the small group.

"More miracles I should think," said Sarah.

"Let's pray, shall we?" urged the bishop.

The dignitaries arrived in big black limousines and smart cars and were escorted into the church to their VIP seats by stewards. The Lord Mayor was wearing his golden chain of office. The bishop greeted each arrival personally, thanking them profusely for coming and supporting the Crusade, even though many saw it as a social function and not a spiritual event. The inevitable photograph opportunities were taken. The dignitaries stood alongside Simon and Serena, or with their arms around their shoulders, trying to make it look as if they'd been friends for years.

Richard opened the evening with a short prayer before Simon and Serena took the stage. This night they sang a few more secular songs: hits from the sixties right through to the eighties. By the time the interval came around, everyone was thoroughly enthralled and entertained by this charismatic duo.

The bishop motioned to Richard to follow him. "Richard my boy, won't you take a look at the stars! How brightly they shine. It's as if the heavens have been cleared of Lucifer's pollution." The bishop put his arm around Richard. "I wanted to tell you how much I appreciate your hard work and effort in making this event an outstanding success." Richard was about to say something, but the bishop held up his hand. "I know you are probably thinking that you haven't done much, but believe me, your dedication has made the work of the Holy Spirit easier—that is if the work of the Holy Spirit is ever easy with us ignorant and stubborn mortals!"

Richard was going to protest.

"Credit where it's due, Richard, you've earned it. You and your lovely wife Sarah are just what this parish needs, and I have decided to appoint you vicar. I hope you will accept the invitation?" The bishop looked at Richard, not wanting to presume that his answer would be yes.

"I don't what to say, Bishop. I never expected a reward, and I never had that in mind at all."

"I know that, and that's why I have so much confidence in you. Will Sarah agree to the appointment?"

Richard smiled, "Oh I think she'll be ecstatic!"

"Then let's shake on it. Reverend Richard Benton, welcome to your church."

At that moment, a lonely figure turned into the church grounds. It was Jonas Silth, the petty thief. Richard and the bishop watched him approach and noticed that there was something quite odd about his manner.

Above them in the tower, Samuel and several angels watched him as he approached the two men. Silth came straight to them, and spitting in their faces shouted, "Ah, I see you! I know who you both are! Gloating over your victories! Destroyer of the fallen! Where is the mercy of the Lord when he judges and condemns the sons of Lucifer?"

The bishop stepped in front of Richard to confront the man as he continued uttering profanities. Richard was unsure what to do. Silth pushed his face right into the bishop's, and calling him obscene names, grabbed the bishop by his arms and tried to wrestle him to the ground. The bishop was a strong man and resisted the attack.

"Be quiet! I command you!" shouted the bishop at Silth.

Silth laughed derisively. "Who are you to command us? Do you think you can control us?"

"Richard, I thought so. The man is possessed, take hold of him now!" the bishop screamed.

Grabbing an arm each, they tried hard to put him into an arm-lock to secure him, but Silth struggled and freed himself. Whoever had possessed this unfortunate man was powerful indeed.

Silth's voice altered in an instant and became deeper, coarser, and more menacing. "Our Lord will not be beaten! He will return to this cesspit and claim his rights, he will enslave these puny people again, mark you I say!"

The bishop took a cross from his pocket and held it in Silth's face. "In the name of Jesus Christ, I command you to tell me who you are."

Silth recoiled and his body contorted in painful agony. The voice inside was tremulous now.

"We shall not pay heed, we shall not obey your words." The demons were striving to break free and the words came out of Silth's mouth broken and sharply separated. "We are legion!" they cried in alarm.

Unseen by the bishop and Richard, another figure was approaching in the darkness, using the dark shadows to remain hidden from sight. It was Stannard, and he carried the loaded pistol that Rimmon had given to him.

"Now is your opportunity," barked Zurvan, "do not fail us."

Stannard edged closer, his arm shaking, yard by yard he came until he was close enough to the bishop to take aim and be sure of hitting his target. He raised the gun and placed his finger on the trigger.

One of the angels with Samuel was ready to spring upon Stannard to upset his aim, but Samuel, remembering Bezalel's words, put his hand on his companion's arm and restrained him.

"This time, it is not our fight. Let us trust in God."

"In the name of the Father, the Son, and the Holy Spirit, I command thee, come out!" The sacred words were delivered with such holy ferocity and spiritual power that Silth broke away and threw himself to the ground, writhing in agony as if he was having a grand-mal fit; his teeth ground together noisily and his hands clutched desperately at his head as if trying to rid himself of something evil.

The bishop leaned over Silth and once more abjured the demons to depart. "Be gone from this man, I say!"

"Do not send us into the void!" Many voices now screamed from inside Silth. "Give us another soul to inhabit. Mercy—be merciful O Great One!"

"Be gone, I tell you!"

At that moment, the demonic spirits convulsed the poor man's body. It shook and quaked, and then his mouth opened impossibly wide and out from inside him came an evil stench and a blackish-gray vapor burst forth, which seemed to contain hideous forms in its very essence.

Stannard squeezed the trigger. The disembodied demons spied him immediately and flew past the bishop and entered him. The gun fired upwards as he was thrown back by the force of the demonic possession that hit his body. His head crashed down upon the hard concrete, killing him instantly, the gun still in his hand. Blood began to ooze slowly from the back of his scalp.

The demons had chosen ill, for now their only recourse was to take hold of Stannard's screaming soul and transport him straight to that netherworld inhabited by all things evil that exists between the Kingdom of Heaven and Earth. Zurvan crept away into the dark.

At the sound of the gunshot, several people came running from inside the church.

Silth lay still upon the ground. As his eyes slowly opened, he saw Richard kneeling over him. The bishop had rushed over to where Stannard lay in the hope that he could help the man, but it was too late. The bishop removed his coat and placed it over the corpse's head. One of the stewards was now standing beside him.

"John, telephone the emergency services for an ambulance, will you please? Tell them someone has been killed. After that, find someone to stay with the body until the emergency people arrive. I'll keep everyone inside the church."

The bishop walked back to where Richard and some others were raising Silth to his feet. He seemed confused and dazed by his awful experience, but probably knew nothing about it.

The bishop asked him, "What's your name, friend?"

Silth turned to see who was speaking to him. He stammered out a reply, "It's . . . er . . . Jonas, Jonas Silth. Am I under arrest? I swear I didn't mean to take the money. I put it all back!"

Samuel leaned over the tower parapet. "Well, I'll be! It's the little thief returned to the scene of his crime."

"Arrest? What on Earth for, my man? He's still in shock, I should think. Richard, here's your first duty as vicar of St. David's: Take this unfortunate fellow and give him a much needed hot mug of tea, and plenty of cake besides."

Richard took Silth's arm and led him away.

The bishop looked towards the heavens and said a silent prayer of thanks to God for saving his life.

By the end of the night, many more had decided to give their lives to Christ among some of the great and good. Finally, the church doors were closed and the equipment was safely stored away. It had been an eventful time for all concerned.

Richard and Sarah sat with Simon and Serena in the church hall, sipping mugs of hot chocolate.

"You know, in all the years Serena and I have been doing these evangelical outreaches, I think I can safely say that we have never experienced such an outpouring of the Holy Spirit."

Richard picked up his Bible and turned the pages of the Old Testament until he found what he was looking for.

He read the verses aloud. "And afterward, I will pour out my Spirit on all people. Your sons and daughters will prophesy, your old men will dream dreams, your young men shall see visions."

"That just about sums it up," said Simon reverentially.

"I heard some important people saying after the concert that this was the first time in many years that the gospel had been heard in this church, and that they were glad to hear it," remarked Sarah.

"And I heard quite a few people say that this reminded them of the last great Welsh revival in 1904," said Serena.

Sarah looked at Richard with love in her eyes. "Perhaps my wonderful husband will be another Evan Roberts."

Simon stood up and raised his mug of chocolate. "Let's all drink to that!"

Epilogue

Detective Inspector Stewart had already been to church and had arranged to take Sadie and her daughter to lunch at the Castle Hotel. He had an hour to spare, so he walked over to the church to consider the demise of Sydney Stannard, the late vicar of St. David's. He honestly admitted to himself he couldn't feel any sympathy for the man. From what the bishop and Richard had told him about Jonas and possession, and what had happened to Stannard, he wondered whether there was more to it. Looking down at the bloodstained concrete path, he convinced himself that Stannard must have slipped or tripped over just as he was about to assassinate the bishop. Was that God intervening at just the right moment, or was it simply an accident and quite coincidental? He strolled to the opposite side of the church and stopped at the place where Jones had met his end. He scratched his head and then became aware that someone was standing behind him. He turned quickly to see Samuel in human form, dressed as a smart young man.

"Can I help?" said Stewart.

"I think it's more to the point how I can help you, Inspector," said Samuel kindly.

"Wait a minute, I know you, don't I? You're the guy that handed me Emily on Friday night." Then Stewart's face clouded over. "Then that means you," he hesitated and then continued, "you are an angel!"

Samuel simply nodded. "I have been given permission to enlighten you. It seems God does not want you to live in darkness. Take my hand."

Stewart felt a bit foolish taking hold of the young man's hand but as soon as his flesh encountered Samuel's being, the whole world around him disappeared and day became night.

He was suspended several feet above the church tower and saw before him a desperate struggle in action. He recognized the curate Maynard Jones being roughly handled by a demon. Then he witnessed the moment of Samuel's intervention, vainly trying to rescue Jones from Gathan's clutches. Seeing the curate hurtling to his death, Stewart looked away to avoid seeing Jones hit the ground.

The vision before him disappeared from sight. Again it was night, and he spied Richard and the bishop trying desperately to overpower Jonas Silth. Then, to his left, he saw Stannard stealthily emerge from the shadows and point the gun at the bishop's exposed back. What he saw next troubled his own spirit. He watched in horror as the hideous creatures that had possessed Silth flew screeching out of his prone body and rushed straight into Stannard, causing him to jolt backwards in terror. The gun fired harmlessly into the air. Stewart turned to speak to Samuel, but the angel had gone, and he was alone again, standing once more on the church pathway in the midday sunshine. Incongruously he thought to himself, "Guess it's about time I was reinstated to my job and got back to work."

* * *

Bezalel and Samuel sat on the roof of the church, looking down at the Sunday afternoon shoppers.

Samuel was the first to speak, "What will happen to Jezebel for her part in the kidnap of the child?"

"You mean Grace! I suspect nothing. She has seen the error of her ways and how frightening it can be when you choose to get mixed up with the occult and the dark arts. She prayed on her knees with Sarah on Friday night and renounced all her evil ways. She said she would like to burn the spirit center to the ground, but will have to be content to close it down and take all the contents to the town dump. She then plans to accept Sarah's invitation and go to church at St. David's."

"That's wonderful, sir. And the inspector, what of him?"

"Thanks to your help, Samuel, he will sleep easy at night. All he has to do now is incorporate the world of angels and demons into his own skeptical consciousness. But I think he will get help with that from a certain godly female that he has taken a shine to and she to him."

Samuel smiled at this, knowing what the captain meant.

Bezalel turned to Samuel and said, "You are to continue guarding Richard and Sarah. Much responsibility will be placed on their young shoulders in the years to come. You can bet Rimmon and his hordes of demons will be planning their counter-attack. Satan will not let this town remain in our control without another fight. We'll be ready for him."

"And I will too, my captain."

"By the way, your little friend Jonas, after having such a traumatic experience, seems to have woken up at last as to what life is really about. Mark my words; we shall yet see good things from this man. He is one of the chosen," said Bezalel kindly.

"Really! Then I won't have to limit his activities again!" joked Samuel.

Neither spoke for awhile as they watched the townspeople go about their daily business.

"I don't know what we'd do without you Samuel, my friend, and by the way I have decided to give you a promotion, from henceforth you shall be known as Lieutenant Samuel, angel warrior first class."

Samuel whirled around and spun into the sky, singing at the top of his beautiful voice.

It snowed later that night, and a thick carpet of snow covered all. The light from the full moon sparkled and shone on the icy snow. It was as if God had given a sign that all the dark things of the town He had made good again, and now it is as white as the unblemished newly fallen snow.

END

Author's Notes

It may come as a surprise to readers to find out that some incidents and scenes in the story are not fiction, but are really based upon fact.

The incident involving Richard and Sarah watching the stars and asking God for a shooting star really happened to the author and his wife. The brightest, most beautiful shooting star crossed the heavens; we even heard it "whoosh" as it travelled across the night sky.

The scene with the crowd of people outside of the police station asking for the Christian policeman to come out and lead them to salvation actually occurred during the Scottish Revival (Western Isles) of 1949-1953. During this time, people were saved on their way to church. It takes the supernatural to break the bonds of the natural. For more information about this religious revival and the South Wales Revival of 1904, simply interrogate any good Internet search engine.

Also, the amazing incident where a group of pastors from different churches who had known each other for many years in the same town, but did not fellowship with each other because of their ingrained religious differences, and had their emotional and intellectual prejudices broken down by the Holy Spirit on the eve of a crusade did happen. It was in Connecticut in the USA in 1988, and this author was at that extraordinary event leading the crusade. The elder pastor of that town said privately afterwards, "It's just like God to bring a man from another country, an Englishman, to shine a light on our darkness. That was your mission, that's why you were brought here to bring us back to God. It wouldn't have happened without you."

What happened to the attaché case and the £50,000 and the valuable stamps? You'll find out in Book Two, entitled Light of the Holy, when it's published in the latter-half of 2010. Thank you for reading my book. I hope it leads you to the Living God.

Fred Hurr
Conwy, North Wales,
United Kingdom
December 2009

Lightning Source UK Ltd.
Milton Keynes UK
10 September 2010

159718UK00001B/78/P